Dr Steinm.

Thanks! For a great Job

Well Done!

Ron Harris

The Ruby Sea Glass

2015

A Novel
By
R. Juan Harris
December 13, 2013

ISBN: 1494770180
ISBN 13: 9781494770181
Library of Congress Control Number: 2013923501
CreateSpace Independent Publishing Platform
North Charleston, South Carolina

I

On a Sunday morning in mid-June of 1994, a flotilla of sail and power boats was anchored in a cove off the northern tip of Catalina Island. A dozen or so boats all flew the black burgee. Most had arrived the night before. Two sailboats were rafted with Sloan's sturdy 42-foot sloop, the *Akubra.* On her port was Jones' vintage 37-foot Endeavor and on her starboard was a regal Hinckley 52 skippered by Alex Bryson. Friends had gathered to reminisce and reflect on the loss of Sloan's best friend Jake. They came to reflect on better times and to drink good Scotch in honor of Jake's passing. But now, sober and sad, they would read eulogies and commit Jake's ashes to the sea where they had so often anchored to dive and party.

Some mourners cast flowers on the water. One dive-boat captain dropped a six pack of Jake's favorite German beer tied to a diver-down float. Sloan heard the splash and watched as the float was caught by the tide and drawn onto open water.

Others related anecdotes showing Jake's lighter side. Sloan was the last to speak. His hands shook as he unfolded his notes. The paper flickered in the morning breeze.

He began slowly, searching for the right tone.

"Thank you all for coming," he finally said. His words echoed off the cliffs. "We're gathered here today to bid farewell to our good friend Jake. As most of you know, me and Jake go back a long way, to our college days where we shared a room in the ROTC barracks."

Abigale stood close beside Sloan and forced a smile to encourage him. She put her hand in his to give him strength.

He stared down at his notes. "I must say, in those days Jake was damned untidy, but in spite of that, we became great friends. Looking back, I realize that he helped me see myself as others did—as I really was. He had that gift, he called a spade. In many ways, we were complete opposites. I was focused on the pursuit of prosperity, and Jake just took each day as it came."

"Our military careers took us to Europe. Jake did his time in Germany where he met Edie." Sloan nodded and waved to Edie.

"They married and had two lovely daughters. Edie and the girls are here on the *Akubra* with me." He pointed with the hand that held the now crumpled notes. The black burgee flickered as the wind howled through the rigging. Sloan suspected she had been holding back her tears all week. He smeared his eyes with the back of his hand. "His mom's here too, from Cleveland."

Sloan looked around at the faces that stared back at him. "Jake would want me to tell you all how much he loved every one of you."

"We finished our tours in Europe and ended up here in Southern California where we found jobs and a passion for sailing and diving."

"We all shared some great times with Jake. Some of you may remember that trip the dive club took down the Baja. We spent a week diving and snorkeling in that beautiful clear water along that peninsula. I recall that day we caught our weight in lobster. That night we served a feast to the dive club and langosta to the village. When it came to skin-diving for bugs, Jake had the best pair of hands ever."

Sloan lowered his head and took a deep breath. "Now it's time to send Jake to his final rest."

He picked up the urn and made his way to the bow of the *Akubra*. "Our final act of love and friendship will be to cast Jake's ashes on these waters."

Sloan imagined he could hear Jake telling him to get it over with and break out the booze. Sloan gripped the urn, unscrewed the lid. He kneeled on the fore deck and poured the contents onto the morning breeze. Ashes were caught in a whirlwind that blew between and around the flotilla. Dust fell on the calm blue waters, blew over the *Akubra* and permeated Sloan's nostrils. He was reminded of lilacs in spring. The aroma lingered long after the dust had settled on the sea or was carried out on the morning breeze.

Jimmy Bryson blew Taps from the bow of his father's sloop. He held the last note until he was joined by a long blast from fog horns on the other boats. The mournful sound echoed off the cliffs and lay on the calm blue water.

Ashes to ashes, dust to dust, Sloan thought.

Everyone took this to be the benediction, so they prepared their boats for the voyage back to the mainland.

Sloan's passengers and crew huddled in the cockpit of the *Akubra.* The mood of the wake hung heavy over them.

He spoke softly, "I've arranged for all of you to return to the mainland aboard Bryson's boat."

Abigale was surprised and puzzled. She turned and looked him squarely in the eyes. "Sloan, what in hell are you—what's this all about?"

"Listen, Abby, since Jake—me and you, we haven't had a minute alone to talk about us or the kids or any of that."

"What about us? Is there something we need to talk about?"

"Not really. Not just now anyhow. I've decided to stay on the island for a few days, that's all. I need some time to think. Me and Jake got some Scotch to drink. Bryson's gonna see you all get home safe. I trust him even though—well, he's a damn good sailor and you have a beautiful day to cross the channel. You'll be home before you know it."

Sparks flew in Abigale's hazel eyes.

"With no crew, just how 'n hell do you plan on getting back?"

"She's rigged for single handing."

"Rigged, sure but have you ever taken her across alone? And if a storm blows up, then what?"

"I'll pick my time. I can hole up here indefinitely if I have to. If I get hungry, I'll go ashore . . . into Avalon, always a good crowd at Monger's."

"What the hell? I'm staying too," Abigale said.

"No! I want you to—" He put a hand on her arm. "That is, someone needs to go back. You know the kids need help with their wedding and someone needs to see that Jake's mom gets home okay. Edie's not up to it. Besides, you have a job to go back to. Nobody's expecting me."

Wendy overheard the debate and butted in, "You *will* be back in time for the wedding, won't you Dad?"

"Giving the bride away, aren't I? But if I'm not back for some reason, promise me you'll go ahead just like you planned."

"Don't talk that crap," Abigale said. "You get your butt home Wednesday at the latest. I can't be expected to handle all this on my own." Just for an instant her anger had overcome her grief. He ran his hand down her arm. "For sure by Wednesday. . . promise, come hell or. . . just give me a few days. I need some— I got no more to. . . a few days, that's all." He took in a deep breath. . . I got no more to give."

Sloan looked on as Abigale turned to watch the excitement on board Bryson's Hinckley. Alex and his son Jimmy made the Hinckley ready for the cruise to the mainland. Father and son worked like an Olympic team as they raised the sails and winched them into place. They exhibited great care in making their new passengers comfortable. Jake's mother huddled in the cockpit with her granddaughters. Jimmy wrapped a blanket around her and tucked it in.

Sloan watched from the *Akubra* as Abigale found a place on deck, away from the others.

He waved and blew her a kiss. She braced against the lifeline and stuck up her finger at Sloan then motioned him to follow

Bryson as they motored out of the cove. Sloan was steadfast in his determination to stay behind and say his private farewell to Jake.

Arms crossed, he stood by as Bryson set his course for Marina Del Rey. Sloan pulled his windbreaker close around him to ward off the morning chill and somehow subdue the sadness and aloneness that clouded his thoughts.

He wondered if letting Abigale go without him had been a wise decision.

The Hinckley disappeared into the remnants of the morning fog and, with it, Sloan's connection to his family and loved ones.

The day was turning sunny with light breezes, ideal for sailing.

At last, he had the aloneness he craved. He needed time to grieve, to remember, to reminisce and, yes, to rejoice in the life and great times he and Jake had shared. He'd think about Abigale tomorrow or the next day. He had the rest of his life to be with her.

He went below and found a bottle of Jake's favorite Scotch and a stainless tankard. He returned topside where he filled the tankard with fine Scotch and poured it over the rail and into the cold Pacific. He held the tankard up to the masthead.

"Jake—you son of a bitch—I'm gonna miss you."

He refilled the tankard and took a long draw. The vintage malt burned in his gut. He threw cushions on the deck and made a pallet against the mast and there he settled in to relax.

All that remained of the fog were a few white clumps floating like giant cotton balls along the cliffs, in the cove, and out on the horizon. He drained the tankard of Scotch and poured another then gave in to dozing on his makeshift pallet.

II

Back on the Hinckley variable winds were proving an inefficient and unpredictable means of crossing the channel, so Bryson cranked his diesel and dropped his sails. That day of all days the safety and comfort of his passengers was more important than bucking rough seas for a few hours just to chalk up another channel crossing under sail.

Abigale stood on the bow of the Hinckley, holding fast to the forestay and watching other sailboats as they made their way home. More than three hours had passed since they'd set sail from Catalina Island, leaving Sloan to drink with Jake.

To Abigale, the very notion was absurd.

As they approached the outermost buoy that marked the Marina Del Rey breakwater, Abigale spotted a flashing red light. She shaded her eyes for a better look. "Hey, Bryson I can see a signal light coming from the marker buoy. What do you suppose it means?"

He grabbed his ship-to-shore and tuned in the Coast Guard. His devil-may-care smile faded and turned down the corners of his mouth. He went forward to the bow where Abigale, Wendy and Brad were studying the Morse code being transmitted from the buoy. Brad had already begun to decode some of the signal.

Bryson motioned Jimmy to join them on the bow where he spoke in a hushed voice to avoid being overheard by Edie and Jake's mother. "There's been an earthquake in a deep canyon about a thousand miles off the coast. That would put it half way between here and Hawaii. The quake has kicked up a tsunami that will most likely hit the coast of California sometime later today. An evacuation order's been issued for all low-lying coastal areas. Not sure what we can do except dock the Hinckley and run for high ground like everyone else in Los Angeles. One thing's for sure we better get out of this boat and the marina damn quick."

"My God, Sloan's still out there!" Abigale said. She covered her eyes to hide the terror she felt.

"I know," Bryson said. "Look, I'll try to raise him on the ship-to-shore. No need to worry. If he's still at anchor off Catalina, he'll be okay. I'd rather be with him in rough weather than any sailor I know—except maybe yours truly."

Abigale wrapped her windbreaker close around her and listened for any news that might come their way. The radio screeched and hummed as Bryson screamed into the mike. "Bryson to *Akubra.* Come in *Akubra* . . . Sloan, if you read me, come back." With each call, his voice became more shrill.

Abigale grabbed Bryson by the arm, "Listen, can you manage Edie and her bunch without our help?"

"I can fit everyone into the van, no problem. You guys should make a run for it in Sloan's coupe."

"Okay, that's our plan," Abigale said. She huddled with her son and Wendy. "Get your gear together. Soon as we touch the dock, I want you off this boat and in Sloan's car. Understand?"

"Where we headed?" Wendy asked.

"High ground," Abigale said. "Any ideas?"

Wendy looked out over the open water behind them. "What about Dad? He's out there somewhere. He could be in real trouble. He needs our help. We can't just leave him."

"Nothing more we can do for him now," Abigale said. "We can only hope he got word and found shelter in Avalon Harbor. My guess is, that just about now, he's ordering swordfish at Monger's."

"Yeah, if he remembered to turn on his radio," Brad Junior said.

"Why should he have to remember?" Wendy asked.

"Because, he turned it off before the ceremony so we wouldn't be interrupted during the service."

"Great!" Abigale said. Tension went up her back and tied knots in her neck. She hugged her duffle and looked into her son's eyes for guidance.

"We could go to Mom's house on Palos Verdes," Wendy said. "Highest place around and she'll want some company."

Abigale frowned. "Must be something closer."

"Come on, Abigale. My mother won't bite."

"You sure about that?" Abigale turned to Bryson. "We're high-tailing it as soon as you're moored, if that's okay."

"Where can I reach you if I hear from Sloan?" Bryson asked.

"Looks like we're headed for Regina's place on Palos Verdes. You can try us there or on my mobile."

"Regina's? Are you—man, this just keeps gettin' better."

"I'm pretty sure you know how to get in touch with Regina, huh, Bryson?"

"Hell, Abby. Ain't like I need Sloan's okay to put moves on his ex."

"Honor among men and all that crap, right Alex?"

Bryson skillfully steered his big sloop into the marina where they were met by a carnival of boats, all in a panic to secure their vessels and get the hell out of the marina before disaster struck. Some were sinking their big flat-bottomed boats in hopes the wave would wash over them, leaving behind a healthy insurance claim.

"What are you thinking, Bryson? You gonna sink this beauty and hope she stays put?" Brad Junior shouted over the roar of people and traffic in the marina.

"Thinkin' I'll tie her loose and let her float up. She'll get a little banged up, but she might just stay off the bottom."

"Jimmy, you and Brad can put them extra fenders along the toe rail. Use the life vests too, for extra padding."

Brad climbed in behind the wheel of Sloan's coupe and Wendy took the passenger seat. Abigale slithered into the jump seat. Brad pulled the regal machine into grid-locked traffic and fought his way toward Palos Verdes. They had about three hours to travel fifteen miles, and at the rate they were going, it looked doubtful they would make it in time.

Wendy tuned the radio to a local station:

".... coastal cities are in gridlock. Thousands are fleeing while others are trying to reach a vantage point along the shore where they can witness the impact the wave will have on the southern California coastline. Some are making their way to the beach with their surf boards with high hopes of riding the crest of the tallest wave in the history of surfing."

What a foolish notion, Abigale thought, almost as dumb as getting drunk with a dead friend.

"The wave is expected to make landfall around six o'clock. Forecasters are predicting the height to be in the range of fifteen to twenty feet. It will have the potential to flood the coast line for up to a mile inland."

Abigale stretched out on the jump seat and rode in silence. She closed her eyes and thought about Sloan. She could see him sitting on the deck of the *Akubra.* He seemed to be counting the minutes until everyone was out of sight, leaving him alone with his grief.

If he had heard the warnings about the wave he would be ordering dinner at Monger's and watching the action on TV. His tongue loose from the Scotch, he would be blabbering about his experience to anyone who would listen.

But, why had he not called to assure her that he was safe? He must've known she would be worried. When she first learned of the wave, she had tried to reach him, but his mobile phone was either out of order or turned off. If he was at Monger's with his cell turned off—there'd be hell to pay.

Brad jammed on the brakes to avoid a light truck that was trying to muscle his way into the line of stymied traffic. The sudden lurch threw Abigale to the floorboards and jerked her back to reality. She sat up and draped her arms over the back of the seat.

"Sorry, Mom. That idiot wasn't watching. You okay?"

"Sure, Son, I'm okay. Just be careful. We would never make it to a hospital in this mess."

"So, Wendy, tell me about your mom. What's she like?" She had seen Regina once, years ago, in another time, another life. And then only from a distance.

"Not a lot to tell. She lives alone with her Spanish maid in that big old house where we all lived before the divorce. She doesn't seem to have an interest in remarrying, but she does go out some. She likes to tie one on, go dancing, or to a tennis match. Being married to Dad must have been so boring."

"She has a live-in maid?"

"Arbela. She's been with us for years, but she won't be there today. Sundays she takes off to visit family in Long Beach."

"Sloan never talks about her," Abigale said. "He never says much about the divorce or any of that. Is there anything I should know before I meet her? Does she hate me? Will she try to scratch my eyes out?"

"There's always that possibility." Wendy smiled then laughed, as she turned to look at Abigale who was once again stretched out in the jump seat. "She may want to talk about your time with Dad. She knows you two were engaged before I came along. She knows you're involved now and may think you had a hand in the breakup."

"Great! Perhaps I should just get out here and take my chances as a hitchhiker," Abigale said. "So, the divorce thing didn't go well for her?"

"You kidding? Mom got everything: money, cars, houses, you name it. About all Dad had left was the *Akubra* and some worthless stock in his company, and you know all about that."

"Sloan hates to lose," Abigale said, with trepidation in her voice. "Explains why he doesn't like to talk about it."

Police officers pulled them over and signaled Brad to take the north road out of the city and away from Palos Verdes. Wendy rolled down her window and flashed her driver's license to the officer. "I live just up the road another mile," she screamed at the officer. "My mother's expecting us." The officer quickly confirmed her address and directed the officer guarding the roadblock to allow them to pass.

After two hours of fighting their way through gridlocked traffic, Brad turned into Regina's drive. Regina was in her yard talking with neighbors.

"Hi, Mom," Wendy called. "Want some company?"

"I'll be damned, look what el gato coughed up."

With Brad's help, Abigale climbed out of the coupe and stood next to her handsome son. Abigale looked on as Wendy embraced her mother,

"Sure! Join the crowd," Regina replied. "We're just watching the world come to an end."

Abigale shook her clothes free of wrinkles and ran her fingers through her thick brown hair. "Please, Wendy. Introduce me to your mother."

"So, Abigale," Regina said. "We finally meet. Nos encantó el mismo hombre."

"Si," Abigale said. "We *have* loved the same man, and you used the oldest trick in the book to win him."

"But I *did* win him." Regina replied. "And winning is all that matters, don't you agree?"

The two women turned to face one another. Brad put his arm around his mother.

Wendy and Regina stood arm in arm. Abigale folded her arms and stared into Regina's black eyes, but she did not respond.

"Speaking of this hombre we both love, where is he?"

"Dad's missing," Wendy blurted. "He stayed behind on the *Akubra* and now he doesn't answer his phone." She burst into tears and threw her arms around her mother's neck.

"What's this you say? Sloan's missing?" she pushed Wendy away and looked into Abigale's eyes. "How can this be?"

"We don't know for sure," Abigale said, hoping to neutralize the hysteria she saw growing with Wendy and her mother. "He stayed behind to drink with Jake and that's all we know for sure."

Regina tapped her forehead, "Maldito loco!"

"Crazy's right. Wouldn't listen to reason. To be fair, this morning when we left him on the island, no one knew this wave was coming. Rotten timing, that's for sure."

Regina lifted her chin, "As it always is."

Abigale thought Regina was incredibly beautiful, but distant and aloof.

"So, Mom, how is it you're back from Uncle Jake's memorial ahead of the rest of us?"

"I went with this guy from the dive club. He has a big, fast motor boat. Problem was, we got halfway there and the engine stopped. By the time he got it fixed the show was over."

"Damn it, Mom, you missed the whole thing."

"Was it nice? Did everyone have good things to say about Uncle Jake? He was a dear sweet man and a great friend."

"Mom, you should have come with us on the *Akubra.*"

"You know me and sailboats. Too slow and dangerous. Always tipping over."

"We had a smooth ride back on Mr. Bryson's sloop."

"I had my chance to go on that sailboat but turned him down. So, you've come to wait out the big wave, huh?"

"Yes," Abigale replied, "and as soon as it passes and we know Sloan's okay, we'll get out of your hair."

"In the meantime, we can drink wine and talk. We can have—how you say—hurricane party. Please everyone, follow me. We can go to the back of my yard where we can see the beach."

"I think it's about to happen," Brad said. He held his shortwave up to his ear.

Regina began at a brisk walk and then ran. Everyone followed her through manicured English gardens and past craggy pine trees to the cliffs that overlooked the Pacific Ocean and the beach below.

Regina waved her hands at what she saw on the horizon. "Who knows? Sloan and the *Akubra* might float by."

"I find that comment hurtful and thoughtless," Abigale said. "Don't want to seem ungrateful for your hospitality, but I'd appreciate it if you'd keep such remarks to yourself. I happen to love Sloan and I'm praying for his safety."

"Sorry. Didn't mean to sound like I don't care. Hell woman, he's been a big part of my life too. Just thought a joke would relieve some of the tension. We are all so uptight. Please forgive me."

Abigale nodded and turned to fix her gaze on the horizon.

"On a clear day like today, you can see the island," Regina said, "but now it's hidden behind the spray."

They were about to witness a colossal disaster yet the sky was almost cloudless and the wind calm.

The sun was low in the western sky soon to sink into the Pacific. Clatter from the city did not reach the pinnacle of the peninsula. Other than the crackling of Brad's shortwave and the honking from a frustrated motorist on the road below, there was no hint of the enormous destructive wall of water that was about to make landfall on one of the largest population centers in North America.

"Look!" Brad shouted, pointing at the wall of water that seemed to rise some thirty feet out of the ocean. Two surfers were poised to catch the wave.

Abigale wondered if they would know what hit them. Surfboard or no, they were destined to be slammed into the cliffs.

"Those guys are asking for it. I hope God takes care of fools and drunks," Abigale said. "Let's pray he's looking after our fool who is more than likely drunk."

Sloan's forlorn disciples stood in prayerful silence and disbelief of what they were about to witness.

"How fast do these things go? These waves, how fast can they go?" Abigale asked.

"Varies. They're saying on the shortwave that this one has been moving at over a hundred miles an hour. Maybe faster in open water. When it gets into shallow water it will slow down but increase in amplitude. That's how tall the wave is," he said. "If Dad got into deep water he might not have a problem. The wave could go right under him and he would scarcely notice it, but if he didn't see it coming, he might have been forced to ride it out. When it wraps around the island, it's anybody's guess as to what will happen."

Abigale threw her arms around a tall pine tree at the edge of the cliff. She hugged the giant tree with her eyes fixed on the horizon. He was out there, somewhere, on the *Akubra,* in grave danger. By now, his seaworthy sailboat would have been ravaged by tons of water. He might have escaped in his raft and be bobbing around in open water like a wine cork in a swimming pool. He might be trying to coax a radio signal from his ship-to-shore with wet batteries. She had to face facts.

Not till I know for sure, she thought.

Wendy pointed and screamed. The leading edge of the wave had formed a deep trough exposing the shallow bottom along the shore. On its heels, came a mountain of water capped by a crown of foam, kelp, and debris. A boat that was anchored and protected from the brunt of the wave should not end up as trash along the California coastline, Abigale tried to reason. Her heart pounded. Her imagination ran amuck.

The wave came onshore with all the fury of a Labor Day hurricane, and about as quickly as it had arrived, it beat a retreat back into open water.

The intrepid surfers who were poised to catch the wave of their life had vanished without a trace. Abigale scanned the shoreline, praying they'd resurface.

The ocean returned to an eerie calm, like a giant sea monster having devoured then regurgitated an entire village.

They stood frozen, silent, and unable to move or utter a sound, each with their own private and horrific thoughts. An hour passed or a minute, who could say? The raw power of the wave was more intense than they could ever have imagined.

Abigale had to remind herself to breathe, first in gasps, then a shrill scream. "Sloan! Oh my God," came out of nowhere." She ran into Brad's arms.

"Mom, what 'n hell just—"

"Sloan," she murmured as she looked out over the ocean expecting to see him walk off of the crest.

Regina's knees buckled. Wendy squatted next to her. "Do you think he—"

"He's safe? I know. . . just doesn't feel to me like he's—"

"What say we get drunk?" Regina said.

Abigale extended her hand to Regina and pulled her to her feet.

Abigale squeezed Regina's arm. "Count me in."

The two locked arms and made their way back to Regina's foreboding castle on the cliff.

"Listen, Regina, will it be okay if we stay here until we have some news? Brad Junior and I would appreciate your hospitality."

"You must stay. I don't want to be alone with my thoughts, the good ones or the not so good ones. Yes, please stay at least until tomorrow. She waved a hand toward the devastated coastline. "Give them time to clean all this up."

III

The *Akubra* rolled in the afternoon swells. A loose halyard slapped against the metal mast. The clanking made a musical racket. Wind whistled past the halyards like fingers across a banjo; she strained against her anchor. Seagulls and pelicans screeched as they soared on the wind, over the sloop, and along the shoreline.

Sloan shook the fog from his head. His mouth had grown dry. If he was to while away the afternoon toasting Jake, he would need shade and sustenance. He went below and found a sandwich, three boiled eggs and another bottle of single malt left over from yesterday's wake. He located a tarp, stretched it over the boom, and made the corners fast to the lifeline.

He moved his makeshift pallet under the tarp and poured another tankard of single malt. He settled back against the mast and fixed his gaze on the horizon where he saw what appeared to be the makings of a spring squall. While he'd dozed, the fog had lifted to reveal what appeared to be angry thunderheads out on the horizon. He leaned against the mast and watched the weather as it took shape. The Scotch had robbed him of all sense of urgency. A profound feeling of aloneness flooded his consciousness.

The sun had begun its journey down the western slope of the brilliant blue spring sky. The *Akubra* was sheltered from weather by the cliffs along the rugged, rocky island. The wind howled around her naked mast. The jib remained neatly folded on her deck.

He thought about the Hinckley as it had disappeared into the morning fog. Abigale had been displeased with his decision to stay behind. He would have fences to mend on Wednesday when he returned home for Brad and Wendy's wedding.

He marveled at the miracle that had brought together Abigale's son Brad and Wendy, and had brought Abigale back into his life. He pondered the irony of the two of them being reunited by their children after being separated more than twenty years.

Seven hours had passed since Bryson had departed the island on his return to Marina Del Rey. Abigale was probably in the car on her way home.

When it came to sailing, Bryson had an ego as big as all outdoors.

Sloan leaned forward and roped his arms around his knees.

When he had dozed off, there had been no threat of weather. The Coast Guard had not forecast anything beyond that early morning fog typical of the season, but now he was witness to what appeared to be a squall moved off the horizon and onto a direct path for Catalina Island and the *Akubra.*

He studied the threat through his binoculars. The Scotch had impaired his vision and his judgment. Through his stupor, he realized the storm was not weather related at all, but a large menacing wave that now spanned the horizon. It looked to be some thirty feet tall. At its crest, it was translucent and capped by a blondish yellow froth like the foam on a good German beer.

Sheer terror cleared his head.

What in—where 'n hell did this come from? he thought.

Sloan, by his very nature was risk averse. As a rule, he never ignored signs of danger, but today his judgment had been clouded by grief and an over-indulgence in single malt Scotch. Now he was face-to-face with this unmitigated phenomenon, the likes of which he could only guess. He had read of rogue waves but they were rare in the Pacific and usually occurred much farther from land.

Behind him were the cove and the cliffs that rendered the island beautiful, but now— foreboding. He may have missed reports that would have alerted him.

If he stayed at anchor, his sloop might be ripped from its mooring and dashed to splinters on the rocky shore behind him.

He cranked her engine, engaged it to full power and steered in the direction of her anchor. He raced forward, stumbling over the lines and rigging left from rafting. He drew his rigging knife and with one swift slash freed the *Akubra* from her tether to the ocean floor. Racing back to the cockpit, he grabbed the tiller and steered a course directly toward the huge wall of water. It was closing on the *Akubra* faster than the seven knots he was forcing on her.

Willing his hand to hold her steady, he studied the huge wave through his binoculars and estimated the distance to be four thousand meters. Two minutes passed. He took another sighting. He was closing on the wave. His estimate of the distance now measured three thousand meters. The island was a mile or more behind him. In less than three minutes, the *Akubra* would crash headlong into a wall of water.

He grabbed the Scotch and took a long drag.

"Jake, you son of a bitch, I'm in one hell of a jam. Could've picked a better time to get yourself . . . Like I didn't have enough to worry about with Wendy and Brad . . . Abby. Now this dammed wave." The *Akubra* rolled and he struck his knee on the gunwale. "You could've waited, picked a better—"

You gonna blame me for your trouble, or we gonna figure our way out of this mess?

"Like you're gonna be a great lot of help."

One thing I can say for sure . . . you got to come north ten degrees.

"What makes you so cocksure?"

Trust me. You want to hit this baby head on. Broaching will be the kiss of death.

"Okay, smart ass, I'm coming up. There . . . ten degrees," Sloan shouted over the roar of the wave, knowing full well that Jake was not there, but somehow he found comfort in the sound of his own voice.

Go below and get a safety harness.

Obedient as a retriever, Sloan went below to the forward locker and returned wearing a safety harness which he tethered to the lifeline.

If you stay with the sloop, at least you have a chance. If you're washed overboard, you could end up bobbing around in the ocean like so much shark bait. If she sinks fast, you can cut your tether and let her go.

"Sinks? What 'n hell makes you say she'll sink?"

Check that distance. Getting close.

Sloan stared through his high-tech binoculars. His hands shook. Knots grew in his gut.

"Three minutes, maybe two," he told his imaginary partner.

Remember—hold her straight at impact. If she broaches, we're toast. Better take another swig; it'll calm your nerves.

Sloan grabbed the bottle in his free hand, pulled the cork with his teeth and spit it out. He took a long drag then tucked the bottle behind a cushion where he could grab it easy.

If we come through to the other side, you best get that life raft in the water, and damn quick.

"Hope it inflates."

Fine time to think of—

"Life raft was your job."

Bring her south two degrees.

A deafening roar drowned his thoughts. The salt spray and foam blew off the crest and into his face like smoke off brimstone. He straddled the tiller and clutched it in a death grip.

The *Akubra* plowed head-on into the wall of water and was suspended in the churning, frothing sea. He levitated beneath his makeshift canopy. His head struck the boom and he slammed onto the deck like a side of beef in a slaughter house. As the wave passed over the *Akubra,* his lifeline went taut and jerked him back onboard. His shins took the brunt of the fall. It felt like being under tons of water, the way he remembered diving to sixty feet.

The stainless forestay snapped like a kite string. The mast buckled and fell across the deck in a snarl of lines and cables.

The *Akubra* bobbed to the surface behind the wave and slid off the backside into an eerie calm, spinning like a tea cup at a carnival ride.

Warm blood flowed into his eyes and down his neck. He tried to right himself but his eyes wouldn't focus. The automatic bilge pump kicked in.

He lay amidst the wreckage and tried to survey the damage. The island had disappeared. The wave moved away, leaving foam and froth and the *Akubra* in its wake.

His eyes rolled back into darkness. His body, buoyed by his life jacket, floated in the cockpit.

Hey man, wake up. Don't you feel that cold water? Get a move on or you're gonna end up at the bottom of this here trench. Remember what I told you. Get that life raft out and throw it in the water, pronto! You do remember where it is?

"Must be in the stern locker." He tried to stand. Terrific pain from his head reminded him that he had collided with the boom.

Come on Sloan—move!

"Who's the captain of the *Akubra* anyhow?" Sloan shouted back at thin air. The crippled sloop wallowed in the sloshing sea. Sloan tried again to stand. He struggled to maintain his balance. He pulled himself to the companion-way and fell into the aft salon where he landed in knee-deep frigid brine.

He waded to the starboard locker where he found the canister containing the raft. Struggling under the weight, he made his way back to the companion-way and shoved the container up and into the cockpit. His head throbbed under the load. Once back on top, he tethered it to a stern cleat. He pulled the inflation lever and pushed the container overboard. Gas hissed as it escaped from the CO_2 cylinder. The small grey bundle morphed into an eight-foot hexagonal orange raft. A canvas roof covered almost two thirds of the raft. The plastic container that had contained the small boat slowly filled with water and gently sank out of sight.

The automatic pump in the bilge of the *Akubra* groaned to a halt and the *Akubra* settled as the cockpit began to flood.

Get off her—now! Grab that bottle; it'll come in handy where you're going. And that flashlight too.

Sloan dragged his bruised and bleeding body over the toe rail and fell into the raft.

He unbuckled his safety harness, untied the raft from the stern cleat, and pushed it away from the sinking vessel. The *Akubra* hissed and moaned in a death rattle. Pockets of air escaped from her cabins as she slid beneath the surface.

He imagined he could see Jake sitting on her boom as their beloved yacht found her way down and out of sight in the blue-black ocean.

"You coming?" Sloan shouted to a figure that sat astraddle of the boom.

See you later. . . not ready to say goodbye just yet. He saluted Sloan with his left hand. Sloan returned it with a two-fingered civilian salute.

Sloan folded back the flap to expose almost half of the raft. With the last rays of the setting sun, he searched the boat for anything that would improve his odds for survival.

The lifeboat had not been deployed since Jake had donated it to the cause over five years ago. It came equipped with everything a marooned sailor would need. He found a shortwave radio and switched it on. No response. He removed the back cover and exposed batteries that were corroded beyond use.

Everything electronic was ruined, including three flashlights. Fortunately, he had brought one from the *Akubra.* The flare gun would probably fire, but he'd wait until he had a need. Why waste a shot to test it?

His head throbbed like a carpenter's thumb. Blood ran down his forehead and into his eyes. He had nothing to wipe it away except the sleeves of his jacket. His head hurt like the time he took a helmet to the head in that game against Midland.

The sun settled onto the horizon. A first quarter moon rose out of the east and lay on her back in a sea of stars.

The vision took his breath.

Spellbound, he watched the night unfold. He was in one hell of a jam.

Had Jake come to his aid in some inexplicable way? Someone or some-thing had guided him through a head-on collision with a wall of water.

Moon shadows grew long.

His psyche ran amuck.

He swore at the darkness that pervaded the lifeboat.

He thought it better to swim in a large empty ocean than to be held captive in the confines of this minuscule, ill-equipped, floating kiddy pool.

Struggling to his swollen knees, he hung his flashlight from a lanyard at the pinnacle of the tiny boat. The light gave a new dimension to his world and brought some relief to his now acute claustrophobia.

He searched his pockets for all his earthly possessions. He found forty dollars in cash, soaking wet, three credit cards, some loose change, and the lucky silver dollar his father had given him on his sixteenth birthday. He rubbed it on his sleeve, kissed it for luck, and returned it to his pocket for safekeeping.

A rigging knife in a scabbard was clipped to his belt next to a mobile phone which was waterlogged beyond use. The knife would be key to his survival. With it he could skin a fish, spear a bird or, when his plight became hopeless, he could slit his throat. The third item on his belt, thanks to his retentive nature, was his antique bronze compass. He'd bought it in a little shop in Madrid when Wendy was a baby.

He found three tins of war surplus K rations that might still be edible. He would wait until starvation was at hand before he opened them. There was fishing gear in a sealed container that appeared to be in working order.

When the sun comes up, I'll try my hand at catching sushi.

Through the floor of the thin rubber raft, the frigid Pacific sucked the heat out of his cold, wet body. Blood continued to leak from the gash in his head. Thanks to the cold floor of the raft, his shins were no longer bleeding, but had turned to ugly purple bruises. He found a first-aid kit with gauze and tape and managed to fashion a crude bandage for his head. He hoped to apply pressure to the gash and slow the bleeding. There was very little else he could do to improve his situation until morning.

He wondered if there would be enough blood left in his veins to keep him alive until his body could make more.

With his compass, he found magnetic north. A strong current was moving him from southeast to northwest. If he continued on this course, he might end up in Frisco Bay or further north, perhaps Seattle or west to Santa Barbara Island. His next port of call, some twenty-seven hundred miles north and west, give or take a couple hundred miles, might be the Hawaiian Islands.

At the speed the raft was drifting, he would starve to death long before he reached Hawaii and all those delicious pineapples. Even if he was still alive, the odds were good he would drift right past Hawaii without seeing even one palm tree.

He prayed that he would soon be picked up by a passing ship, but until then, he was just another dot in the huge Pacific expanse, one more piece of debris left behind by a rogue wave. On the bright side, he had achieved the ultimate in anonymity, but he found little comfort in that fact.

Sloan had no notion of the circumstances that existed along the coastline. For all he knew, the entire west coast could be in a state of disaster. Los Angeles might be under water or gridlocked from flooding. He imagined a glut of humanity, fleeing for their lives.

My God, what of Wendy and Abigale?

That Hinckley of Bryson's is probably as bad off as the *Akubra.* He did the math. Based on his calculations and knowledge of what time the wave hit the island, Bryson should have made it to the marina with Wendy and Abigale well ahead of the wave.

He naturally hoped he would be rescued quickly, but he realized it could take weeks, if ever. By the time they found him, he could have drifted halfway to Honolulu. He couldn't count on the Coast Guard or anyone else to come looking for him. They would have more than they could handle just draining the water out of one of the largest metropolitan centers in the world.

Abigale would be armed with a barrage of "I told you so's." He was sure she and the kids were on solid ground before the wave hit. Exactly where they took refuge he couldn't say. The safest place would be on the Palos Verdes Peninsula. A smile crossed his face when he thought about Abby and Regina weathering this flood together.

He turned off the flashlight, settled back against the bulkhead and tried to relax, but the darkness frightened him. He clicked it on again. Then off. Got to save the batteries. Bruised, bleeding, and shivering he tried to make a plan.

Tomorrow I'll open a tin of K rations. If it's spoiled, I'll use it for fish bait.

He rubbed his arms, trying to stay warm.

Abigale had looked radiant as she sailed away with Bryson, he thought. She was wearing the ruby sea glass necklace he had given her over twenty-three years ago. Its magic had brought them back together. If he died, she would make a life with someone else. As long as she did not take up with Bryson, almost anyone else might be acceptable. Rumors were flying around the yacht club that Bryson had an interest in Regina. Despite the way she had treated him, he hoped better for her too.

He groped for the Scotch bottle then held it out. "One swig left. Hope you don't mind."

No—go ahead; you need it more 'n me.

"Tomorrow I'll be picked up. . . for sure. Don't you think?"

If you say so.

Sloan downed the last mouthful of single malt.

Damn fool optimist.

IV

Morning came and Abigale pulled on her sweater and wandered down behind the Abernathy house where, last evening she had stood and stared out over the Pacific. The big island stood tall, skirted by plumes of white fog that rendered it distant and foreboding. Her heart cried out for Sloan. Try as she did, she could garner no sense of his whereabouts. He could be sitting on the *Akubra* looking at her just as she had last seen him.

She found her way back to the house where Regina was brewing coffee and toasting bagels.

They embraced warmly. "No sign of him?" Regina asked.

"If he's out there, I can't see him," Abigale said.

"He'll show, soon as we give up on him. You watch."

The aroma of coffee and the clatter of the kitchen soon drew the kids back to the kitchen and around the table to reconnoiter.

They passed a look, one to the other, but no one was ready to hear the answer to the pregnant question. "Guess we haven't heard from him," Regina finally volunteered.

"I tried calling the Guard around four this morning, but couldn't get through," Brad said.

"Those poor bastards must be going crazy."

"They answer at all?" Abigale asked, her eyes shiny and her arms crossed in defense of his answer.

"No, Mom. I let it ring for five minutes, maybe longer."

"Keep tryin', will you, Hon?" Regina said.

"Six days till the wedding. Any bright ideas as to what we should do?" Brad asked. "Is some supernatural power trying to prevent us from—"

"Nonsense Hon, you and Wendy are meant to be together. It's the most natural thing I can imagine. It's times like this we must have faith in God and in Sloan. We shouldn't write him off, not by a long shot. He can be damned resourceful when the chips are down."

"I'll give him till our first anniversary," Wendy said." If he's not home by then, I'll start to worry. This is my Daddykins we're talking about here and I want him home." She buried her face in her hands.

"Who wants a burned bagel?" Regina said.

"Haven't lost your touch, huh, Mom?" Wendy said, snuffing back her tears.

Regina opened the wine cabinet and counted the empty slots. "Looks like we went through a few family heirlooms last night...hope the bride and groom enjoyed the one they took upstairs."

Brad Junior shrank back into a corner. "Don't worry, Mrs. Abernathy. We put it to good use."

"That's what I'm afraid of," Regina replied as she gently closed the cabinet. "Where I come from, people spend their lives making good wine just so we can have it to drink on just such occasions. Thanks for bailing out early. You gave us time to catch up on what happened all those years ago, before the two of you came along."

"We haven't heard a word from Sloan since yesterday morning," Abigale said, "so we have to assume he ran into trouble; otherwise, he'd be in touch with one of us long before now. He's probably okay, just not able to reach us. If the *Akubra* got swamped, he would have launched the lifeboat or gotten to shore somehow." Abigale looked around the table in hopes of finding a consensus. There was none.

Regina stared back at her soulfully, "You don't think—"

Abigale looked down at her coffee. "I'm not ready to go there. As far as the wedding is concerned, you have two choices. You can go ahead with our plans and hope he arrives in time, or you can put it off till we know for sure, and that could take days or even months. We may never know. If you go ahead like we planned, you're married and that's that. If you postpone it and he shows up—well . . . I sure as hell don't want to be the one to tell him we called it on his account."

"I for one refuse to consider a scenario that doesn't include him arriving on time," Wendy said, "but if he isn't here on Saturday, he's MIA, and that's all we know for sure. Mom will just have to give me away."

"Look, before we go too far down any road," Brad broke in, "you should all hear what's on the news."

"So what's the latest?"

"As of this morning, LA County's been declared a disaster zone. No surprise there. Everything below fifteen feet above sea level was flooded, but within minutes most of the water drained back into the ocean. There may be thousands of fatalities. No one knows for sure. Bryson's boat is most likely scuttled in the marina, sunk right at her moorings."

"Doesn't seem right to be concerned about getting married when so many people have lost everything," Wendy said.

"On the other hand," Brad said, "life goes on. We all have to pick up where they left off. A marriage is the beginning of a new life. What could be better? The chapel at the school is probably okay—assuming we can get to it—but the marina, the yacht club, Sloan's townhouse? Well, that'll be a different story."

"See, there you have it," Abigale said. "Good thing he's on the *Akubra* or he might be in real trouble. We should all just stay put and let things get sorted out."

"What would Sloan want us to do?" Brad asked.

"Get married like you planned. He made that plain yesterday." Abigale said.

"I agree," Regina said, "and we know him better than anybody."

"I think we need an alternate plan," Abigale said, "just in case the chapel is closed and the yacht club is out of business."

"Heck, we could do the entire show right here." Brad said. "Regina has everything we need for a great garden wedding. Plenty of parking, a meadow where we could set up an altar—"

"And we could have the reception around the pool," Wendy chimed in. "It would be something special, especially if Daddykins makes it. . ." Her voice trailed off.

Renewed energy flowed into the group as they began to formulate a plan. The world had not come to an end. There was hope for a future and brick-by-brick they began to put it together.

V

The *Akubra II* bobbed around in an ocean of ink. Above was a sea of stars. Sloan switched on his flashlight to check the time: Mon 04:37a.m. In about two hours, the sun would peak over the eastern horizon.

Something large and solid bumped into the raft. It could have been a dolphin, a shark, or floating debris. Had to be plenty of that, he thought. He saw no need to show himself outside the raft just in case a stray shark was cruising by. At first light, he would try his hand at fishing.

Sushi might be my only means of survival.

Blood from his head wound had pooled in the bottom of his raft and begun to smell. The stench brought dry heaves to his empty stomach. Come morning, the first order of business would be some housekeeping.

He gave in to short fitful naps. At last, after a bone-chilling night, the sun shone above the horizon. He bowed to the east and gave thanks for the day he was about to receive. The warm rays of sunlight flooded his abode and melted his demons. At sundown, they were sure to return and he would have to suffer through another cold night . . . unless he was picked up, rescued by the Coast Guard or some big commercial vessel. Rescued was rescued. Didn't much matter to him as long as he was out of this little boat and headed for port… any port.

He scooted around the raft on his butt until he located the empty Scotch bottle. He used it to decant the bloody fluid from the raft and pour it into the ocean. Pouring blood into the water made him shark bait for sure. He had learned from his diving experience that a small amount of blood could attract sharks from a considerable distance. He had to chance it. He couldn't tolerate sitting in his own blood.

He located a tin of K rations and removed the lid. The stench was so repulsive he threw the container and its contents into the sea. The sight and smell of putrid roast beef sent him over the side to heave.

Before he opened the second carton, he would have to render his boat and himself free of the mess. He sloshed seawater into the raft and continued to fill the Scotch bottle and dump the contents overboard until the raft was dry and free of blood.

He squinted at his watch: 8:14 a.m. on the first day of his new life, lost at sea. Anonymous. He missed the simple pleasures: watching the news and reading the morning paper. He wondered how this wave had affected Abby and Wendy. At this moment, his family seemed so distant . . . like a small picture in a large frame. Wendy, Abigale, Brad. What a fine young man, the son he never had. If he'd married Abby all those years ago, Brad would not be in this picture. Or would he? Who could say for sure?

Sloan was adrift at sea, rudderless. The only navigation aid was his compass and the rising and setting of the sun. If he had had a sail, he could not be sure where to point his craft.

He stripped naked and rinsed his clothes in the frigid ocean then spread them on the roof of the raft. With the laces from his shoes, he secured his jacket, pants and shirt to the raft to allow them to dry.

He imagined being rescued—buck naked. The image caused him to laugh aloud. The laughter cracked his dry lips, but left him feeling better.

Blood continued to leak from the gash in his head. With his rigging knife, he ripped his boxer shorts apart and crafted a bandage, using the elastic waistband to hold it in place.

Sloan unwrapped the fishing gear in hopes of catching dinner. His gear consisted of a twenty-foot piece of heavy gauge nylon line with one large hook and one small one and a lead weight to make sure the bait sank. On the other end of the nylon line was a clasp suitable for tethering the leader to the boat.

Standing in the raft was like walking on a waterbed. His throbbing head felt light. He screamed with pain when he put weight on his bruised shins. He fainted, falling face down in the raft. He awoke with a groan and rolled over onto his back. The sun warmed his naked body. He was unsure how much time had passed. He held his arm between his face and the bright orb. The sun had jacked itself a few inches up the sky. It was Monday, 1:44 p.m., and his floating home was being jostled about like a backyard wading pool. Afternoon swells and a strong breeze were having their way with the circular flat-bottomed, rudderless raft.

He crawled to the pie-shaped opening and peered out. His laundry had blown off the roof and into the water and was serving as a rudder of sorts. He leaned out to recover his clothes and fell headlong into the frigid ocean. He felt himself sinking. He opened his eyes. Bubbles from his mouth floated in front of his face. If he provided no resistance, he might just sink, but the shock of the cold water revived him and cleared his head. He kicked his feet and popped to the surface. The raft was moving away from him at a rapid rate.

He did a sloppy crawl after it.

If I can only reach my shirt, he thought.

He flailed against the afternoon chop until he was close enough to his shirt to grab it and pull it to him.

He threw one arm over the side and held on until he could catch his breath. The cold brine found every scratch and tear in his skin.

Blood still leaked from his head wound and spread on the water. Trolling for sharks was not the way he wanted his life to end. He mustered his strength and pulled himself back aboard. The lifeboat was no longer claustrophobic, close or small, but rather it was warm, roomy and safe. Being doused in the ocean had revived him and his body was free of clotted blood and the putrid mess that had escaped from the K rations.

He re-hung his wet laundry then opened the second container of K Rations. It too was rancid, but he managed to hold his breath and bait the small hook with ten-year-old roast beef. He threw the baited hook overboard along with the remaining contents of the K rations. Sharing his space with this putrid mess was his worst nightmare. He watched as the baited hook and lead weight sank below the raft.

The afternoon sun dried his clothes and warmed his naked body. He watched the baited hook fifteen feet below him. There were no takers. "Come on ya damned fish!"

Does that damned fish have a name?

"Gibbs. I'll call him Gibbs." His choice of names brought a victorious smile to his sunburned, swollen face.

Still no takers. Maybe if he ignored his line, Gibbs would come.

He surveyed the flat plane of the ocean. He was drifting north, or was he going south? He squinted into the midday sun. He had not eaten since yesterday morning and the closest thing to drinking water was that swig of Scotch he'd had the night before.

His clothes were dry and stiff with salt. When he shoved his arm into the sleeve of his shirt, it felt like coarse sandpaper against his bare sunburned skin. At least his clothes were free of clotted blood and maggots. He missed his boxers, but thanks to them, his bleeding head had slowed to a trickle.

As evening settled over Sloan and his round boat, he braced himself for another cold night. The hook hung motionless in the water. He was not fond of fishing. Cleaning fish on the deck of the *Akubra* left a mess. He preferred having fish served to him at Monger's or grilled on the deck behind his townhouse with just a little salt and pepper.

Perhaps I'll open a nice Chardonnay or a smooth Pinot to accompany my sushi and steamed rice. No . . . forget the rice . . . too many carbs.

With the setting of the sun came the end of the second day, or was it the third?

Sloan hadn't eaten since Sunday. Boiled eggs, a sandwich and that jar of Scotch, good Scotch. The *Akubra* sank in that storm on Sunday, or was it a rogue wave? He was so thirsty he would drink his piss if he had any. Rain's the only hope for water.

He studied the darkening sky. Not a cloud. Water . . . water. How would it be if he drank just a little seawater? Who would know? Fish drink it and I eat fish...if I had any. Where in hell is Gibbs?

Glass of warm milk? "First you gotta catch the cow." That's what Daddy used to say.

The sun rose to a rich blue sky dotted with fluffy white clouds plopped around like Grandmother's biscuits. It was truly another Chamber of Commerce day. Sloan had benefited very little from his fitful night of sleep. He couldn't remember how many days he'd been floating around. Three? Four? More?

He peered at his arm, shook it. His watch had stopped. Must've taken on water. Too many dips in the pool.

"Am I already dead and don't remember dying? They say your life flashes before you. What's that they say about a tunnel with a bright light at the end? No tunnel, can't see no tunnel . . . remember that night I went fishing with Dad . . . caught in a storm. Thought I was gonna die. Life flashed before my eyes just like they . . . All fifteen years, short life. Still a virgin.

He collapsed back on the floor of the raft and stared at the sky.

Remember that night in Madrid? What a night. Never met anyone quite like Regina. Talk about hot—gentlemen don't.

He laughed. Wealth and anonymity had been his goals in life. What was more anonymous than being on my own sailboat, out of sight of land, tacking a stiff breeze to nowhere?

I'm bobbing around in the ocean like a cork, he thought. The *Akubra* is on the bottom of the Catalina ditch. I can always get another boat; another life might not be so—

He found a tin cup that had been part of the survival gear and used the shiny bottom to look at his reflection. He was sporting more beard than he had seen on his jaw since those days in Spain when he'd sailed for a week without a shave.

Could he have been floating in this raft for a week?

Panic shot through him.

The kids are getting married on Saturday. Could be Wednesday or Friday?

He hadn't eaten since Sunday, pretty sure, as sure as he could be about anything.

He decided to try the small hook again. Perhaps he could catch a school dolphin or a sun perch.

"Every hand's a winner Johnny boy." Daddy always called me Johnny, even after I started going by Sloan…may he rest in . . .

Least ways you listened to something I said.

"Listened to more than you ever knew," Sloan spoke to the clear blue sky overhead. "If it hadn't been for you I would've let Wendy go to the highest bidder so I could marry Abigale. Wendy would've grown up a bastard in some orphanage in Spain. Can't imagine my life without Wendy. Damn, she's gonna be plenty pissed if I miss her wedding."

Night fell. The half-moon was perched high over an endless expanse of water. Sloan gave in to dozing and dreaming.

A sudden irregular motion woke him. The fishing line had gone taut and jerked the raft onto a decidedly southern tack; the moon now lay to his left. The fishing line glistened in the moonlight. He sensed the leisurely motion of a large animal trying unhurriedly to swim away from him. It might be a dolphin, a marlin, or a sea turtle.

A large dorsal fin cut through the surface of the slick water and swayed side to side flickering in the moonlight. Gibbs had taken his bait. Sloan watched as the large critter continued on a southerly course, dragging the raft behind him.

Sloan prepared for battle.

His weaponry consisted of his rigging knife and a flare gun with three twelve-gage cartridges. He tried to steady his shaking hand. A misfire would decide the battle in Gibbs' favor. He had one chance. If he missed his target, the startled fish would sound and take Sloan and his flimsy raft with him. He could unhook the fishing line from the boat and let it all go with Gibbs, but the flesh of this fish was his only hope of survival, and without the fishing tackle, he would be left to a slow death by starvation. Gibbs would have won again.

I won't let that happen.

At point-blank range, the flare gun would have the killing power of a twelve-gauge shotgun. He put the grip of the pistol in his mouth to free his hands for battle. He would have to make sure he got his one shot to a vital area. The eye was the best target.

Sloan found his rigging knife, opened the marlin spike, and tucked it under his belt like Tarzan.

He unhooked the fishing line from the raft and slowly coiled it inside. He was careful not to become entangled in it. If this big fish didn't take kindly to being shot in the eye, he might beat a hasty retreat straight down a dozen fathoms.

Sloan coiled the line into the boat beside him.

He slowly pulled the raft closer to his prey. Sloan could count each breath as he pulled the raft near enough to reach out and touch the fish. Beads of sweat formed on his forehead. Trembling hands put a successful kill at risk. He hunkered on his bruised knees, took the pistol out of his mouth, gripped it in both hands and leaned out of the raft. He held the flare gun as close to Gibbs' head as he dared, and in one quick motion, he placed the muzzle to the saucer-sized eye of the beast and discharged his load. The pistol recoiled in his hands. Blood and pulverized flesh splattered over him and his boat. The startled eight-foot predator leapt into the air, spun a full turn, and fell straight down into the water.

The carefully coiled line sang as it unwound from inside the boat. Sloan was feeling thankful he had unhooked it.

A coil of the cable looped around his ankle and snapped tight.

The sheer power of the huge fish jerked Sloan out of the boat feet first and down into the ink black ocean. The moon and the raft disappeared above him. Perhaps now his life would begin to flash—but no—as quickly as Gibbs had sounded he stopped, dead still, and began to ascend.

Gibbs could be stunned or dead; Sloan could not say for sure. He could feel the sting of saltwater on the fresh cut around his ankle.

His head broke the surface.

The raft sat on the horizon some fifty feet away.

He found the end of the fishing line, untangled it from his ankle, tied it around his waist and began swimming toward the raft.

Gibbs became little more than dead weight. All the fight was out of him. With minimal effort Sloan towed the carcass toward the *Akubra* II.

It seemed as if he had been swimming for an hour, but in spite of his effort, he was no closer to the raft. A light wind or surface current seemed to be pushing it away. His only chance to survive was to let go of the fish and swim hard for the boat. He loosened the line from around his torso but could not bring himself to let it go.

"You're not going to win, damn you Gibbs, not this time."

Without provocation, the raft began to move in his direction. Encouraged, he swam a side stroke pulling Gibbs behind him. He approached the raft only to see more finned animals circling around it. Had all the excitement and commotion drawn more sharks? As the raft came closer, he could make out a pod of dolphins. Their silver bodies glistened in the moonlight as they circled the raft. Each dolphin took a turn nudging the boat in Sloan's direction.

He reached the raft and reattached the fishing line that held his big dead shark. He threw one leg over the side. Two of the dolphins swam close and nudged, then nuzzled him as if lifting him. With one concerted effort, he pulled his shivering body over the bulkhead. He leaned out of the raft and saluted his rescue team. The dolphins disappeared into the night without acknowledging Sloan's expression of gratitude.

He pulled the monster fish alongside the raft and tied it up short. Gibbs' huge jaws, full of pearly teeth, moved in a biting motion but his eye, the one remaining, was fixed and staring past Sloan into space.

"I won! Gibbs, you son of a bitch, I won!" He carved flesh from the carcass. Seawater and shark blood filled the bottom of the raft. He pried a few teeth free from Gibbs smile and stuffed them in his vest pocket. Without proof, Abigale would never believe his story.

He followed the fishing line into Gibbs' mouth and freed the hook then gave the remains a hard shove to set the carcass adrift. He worried that sharks would smell the blood and make him the subject of a feeding frenzy.

In an hour, the sun would be up. His hopes for survival were high. He had food, shark sushi, enough to last him a few days, or until it spoiled, in which case he would bait his hook with leftovers and fish again.

When the sun rose, Sloan would have breakfast, clean his quarters, and settle in for another day of anonymity on the high seas.

VI

In 1969 Sloan started at first-string offensive end on the high school football team, and for about three months during his senior year, he dated a foxy blond named Jackie who was captain of the drill squad. Then, without warning or proper notice, Jackie took up with the team quarterback, Buddy. The sudden change took Sloan by surprise. For several days, he moped around like he had been gored by a Brahma bull.

Late in the afternoon, Sloan arrived home from football practice and pulled his old pickup in behind his family's home. His dad was in the alley, hunkered over a welding project. Pete, Dad's old screw-tailed bulldog, lay stretched out on the cool sand in the shade of the backyard fence. If old Pete could talk, he would have told Dad to head back in the house and get out of this hundred-degree heat.

Sloan was in no mood for a protracted discussion with his father, so he tried to slip unnoticed into the house.

"Hey, Johnny!" His old man called him Johnny. "Why so down?"

"Ah, Daddy, you wouldn't understand." He looked away in hopes he could avoid his father's gaze.

"I wouldn't, eh." With one eye closed, his father squinted up into the hot west Texas sun, his strong face smeared with dirt and grease.

"You got girlfriend troubles, don't cha, Johnny?"

"Guess you could say that." Sloan stopped short and shoved his thumbs into the pockets of his jeans. "How's it you already know that?"

"Mom knows, don't she? You don't think me and her keep secrets? Ain't you never heard of piller talk?"

Beads of sweat poured off the old man's forehead, ran down his Romanesque nose, and dripped onto his sleeve.

"Damn it, Daddy, I didn't even know pillers *could* talk." Sloan scratched old Pete behind his floppy ear.

His dad ignored Sloan's attempt to be a wise ass.

"From what I can make of it, Jackie dumped you fer that cocky quarterback. Ain't that right son?"

"'bout the size of it."

His dad spat tobacco juice, making sure it went downwind.

Sloan didn't much like talking about his personal problems to anyone, especially his dad who thought of him as a macho high school jock. Besides, he never figured his dad to be the one to understand his complicated high school social life.

"Wanna tell me 'bout it?"

"No. . . But if you really want to hear, it came on kinda sudden."

Sloan dropped down to a crouch next to his old man. "One minute, we was tight as ticks and next thing I knew she was walkin' to class with Buddy."

Dad nodded then picked up a slag hammer and began chipping away at a piece of steel he had just been cutting on. "So, like we'd say in the oil patch, Buddy done skidded yore rig." Daddy wiped his brow with a soiled bandanna and went back to chipping at the slag.

Sloan frowned, "Rotten bitch. Hope she—"

"Now come on, Johnny, you can't blame 'er none. She's just caught up in all that hero worship crap, and when she can share the spotlight with the town stud, hell son, put yourself in her place."

"To her, Buddy's some kind a damn rock star."

Sloan dragged a finger, drawing a big zero in the sand. "She says that when he throws a pass on Friday night, the whole damn town's watching and cheering. You're right, Dad. She gets off on all that attention."

"Look, Johnny. You've got the rest of the year to put up with all this, so just hang in there. When you get to university, things 'll be different. More like the real world where folks get ahead on their smarts. In that world, it'll matter more what you got 'tween your ears than 'tween your legs."

Sloan snickered.

Daddy had attended a country school in Oklahoma and only made it to third grade, so for him to understand the dynamics of modern-day high school social life came as a surprise to Sloan. He sat cross-legged in the dirt and watched his old man work and listened to him talk. He soon found himself fully invested in this session of his father's cracker barrel wisdom.

"At the university, quarterbacks will be a dime a dozen." His dad dipped a hot piece of iron in a bucket of water to cool it. "Couple of the better ones will make the team and the rest'll set out the first year on the bench. Next year, Buddy's gonna be just another one uh them guys, not as smart or interesting as you so, just bide your time, Johnny. Things'll come around to your way."

He sat back on his haunches and wiped his face one more time. "Take my word fer it Johnny, this won't be the last time you'll get jilted, and it won't get no easier. Just remember what I tell ya. If you're man enough to put it in, you better, by God, be man enough to back it up."

Sloan looked away. "I know all about—you know—protection and all that crap."

"Sure you do. You know you can use a rubber, but how can you be sure that it weren't packed by some prankster with a hat pin. Says right on the package: For Prevention of Disease. How plain is that?" He rested a greasy hand on Sloan's shoulder. "Just remember, there's ways of havin' fun without getting young girls in trouble. Don't take the chance 'less you're gonna be responsible for what happens. Most important thing of all is to spend time with them that are right for you. If you don't, you may as well be farmin' a patch of weeds."

"Weeds?" Sloan laughed. "What 'n hell are you talking about Daddy?"

"As I recall, there ain't no market for weeds," his dad replied soberly and stared down his long nose at Sloan.

"Oh, I get it," Sloan said.

"Just take a page outta your big brother's book."

"Wayne? What in hell's he got to do with it?"

"He done it right. Graduated college, met a nice girl, settled down, and got busy raisin' kids. It ain't a bad way to go, Johnny."

"I'll get there, Daddy. Just give me time. There's no real rush to get saddled with all that responsibility."

His dad cocked his head toward the house. "Now get in there and give your Ma a hand with dinner and when you have some time out of yer busy life, let's get back there and finish off that game of Eight Ball."

"Anxious to get beat again, huh, Daddy?" Sloan shouted over his shoulder as he disappeared through the back door.

Sloan left that backyard talk with a whole new perspective on his old man. He counted himself lucky to have a dad who understood him and expected him to do the right thing. How'd he get so smart and never go to school? Sloan wondered. He didn't know long division or multiplication, but he managed to do some complicated engineering and construction jobs. He'd taught himself welding and all about metals. He could work fast to get a job done. And maybe he was right about weed farming, too.

VII

Sloan played football, ran track, and graduated with high honors. With the exception of dates to the proms, his only real love interest had been Jackie. Unfortunately, she had been unable to finish high school due to some family issues. Shortly after she dumped Sloan, she moved away for about six months. Soon after she returned, her parents adopted a baby girl from an agency back east. Sloan figured that the reason behind all those maneuvers had to do with Buddy being a weed farmer. Jackie finished high school a year later and took a job with a new hamburger chain that had started in California and was spreading across the country. Over the next ten years, she worked herself up from fry cook to store manager and then to regional manager before she resigned to raise a houseful of kids.

That summer, after his senior year, Sloan worked as a roughneck in the oil fields of west Texas. The physical nature of the work hardened him even more than playing football.

In the fall, he registered at Florida State University to study electrical engineering and take advantage of a football scholarship. The course work was difficult but, in keeping with his father's expectations, he studied with abandon.

Halfway through his spring semester, his brother Wayne called Sloan from Odessa.

"You better come home for a few days."

"Yeah, like I can just drop everything and race back to Texas. Why? What's up?"

"Normally, Mom wouldn't ask, but Daddy's not doing well and she thinks it best if you come home for a few days."

Sloan switched the dorm phone to his other ear. "There's nothing wrong with that old codger that a pint and a few racks of pool won't cure."

"If you say so," Wayne said. "Mom bought you a ticket on Southwest. Just go to the ticket counter and pick it up tomorrow at one o'clock. I'll meet you here when you land. Meet me out front."

Sloan blew out, exasperated. "Okay. I'll be there but it'll cause me to miss a test and maybe take a B in English Lit. And you know how Dad hates me making B's."

"You don't need English Lit to do engineering."

"Tell that to Dad."

"Just you be on that plane, damn you."

Wayne and Sloan arrived at home shortly after dark and were met at the door by his mother. Sloan threw his arms around her and began to cry. "Dang, Mom," he finally said, "this is terrible. What 'n heck are we gonna do?"

She hugged him without answering his question. She looked past him to Wayne. "What have you told him?"

"He knows all I know," Wayne said. "Has there been any change since we talked this morning?"

"No. He's been asking for Johnny all day."

They entered the foyer of the modest home and went down the long narrow hallway past a gallery of family pictures. The house had taken on the odor of a hospital. As they approached the spare bedroom, Sloan could see his father propped up on a rented hospital bed.

His dad was being attended by old Doc Wisner who had been their family doctor for as long as Sloan could remember.

Sloan put out his hand and his father took it and pulled him up close.

"Boy," he whispered. "What took you so damn long gettin' here?" His voice rattled hoarse and raspy.

"Sorry, Daddy. Don't know my way around airports. Got lost in the terminal. Wayne had to come find me."

His father's frail hand felt boney and weak. Bandages on the back of his hands were a testament to his being punctured for too many IV's. He was not an old man, Sloan thought. Forty-five, maybe fifty.

Doc Wisner adjusted the IV fluids that were being passed to him through a needle in his arm.

"So, what's this I hear?" Sloan said. "Got some kind of cancer? Thought you was tougher than to let a little thing like that get you down."

"Oh, they got it all wrong, Johnny. Me and you's gonna be back at that pool hall in a damn few days. But just in case it takes me a little longer than I figure, I need to tell you some more stuff—you know—'bout how to live right and that kind a crap. It'll come in handy when you finally get out in the world."

A sadness hung over the room like gnats in summer. "Sure, Dad. You know I need all the help I can get."

"So, tell me, Johnny, straight up. How's school. You makin' all A's?"

"Damn straight, Daddy." Sloan dragged his chair over close. His knees bumped the bed and he leaned over with his face close to his dad. "Every class, Daddy. I swear."

"That's great. Now promise me you'll make a perfect score all the way, all four years."

"Don't know about that, Dad. Damn university's tougher 'n high school."

"Don't give me that crap, boy. You promise me!" He coughed violently. Doc Wisner lifted him up by the shoulder and pounded him firmly on his back. His eyes closed and, for a minute, it looked as if he was gone. Sloan squeezed his hand. The old man struggled to open his eyes, first one and then the other. "I might not be there to see you get that sheepskin, so I want to know right now that you're gonna do it."

"Football's takin' lots of time. They want me working out late every day."

"Then ditch that damn football. They ain't payin' your way no how."

"You want me to quit? But what about my scholarship?"

"Find a nuther way to cover it. Rough neckin' in the summers should be just as good. Now promise me."

"Okay, Dad. Sure . . . I promise, but—"

"No buts, damn it, Johnny." He held up a frail hand. "You gotta get the damn job done. Do it fer me. Hear?"

"I will, Daddy. It's a promise."

With a long sigh, the old man settled back against the pillow, his face ashen gray.

"Got a girl?" he asked weakly.

"No time for women. Too much—"

"Probably best. Just don't get no girl in trouble less your gonna do right by her. And that ain't no way to go 'bout it. Now listen, Johnny. Don't be doin' no weed farmin', now hear? 'Member what I taught you."

"You got nothin' to worry 'bout on that count."

"It'll happen. You'll meet her when you're just walkin' down the—"

A fit of coughing overtook him. Doc Wisner looked past Sloan and into Wayne's tear-filled eyes. With a gentle nod, Wisner removed the needle and with it any hope that Sloan's father would be attending Sloan's graduation. Wayne prepared to administer the last rights.

VIII

Sloan quickly learned that partying and catering to his libido was incompatible with making the 4.0 that he had promised his father. His aim was to graduate with high honors, a goal he could scarcely achieve if he spent every waking hour trying to push some coed into the sack. His father had made the point that, in his view, college was serious business. Missing a question on an exam was proof that he just hadn't tried hard enough.

During his first year on campus, he had managed to score a few one-night stands that were purely physical. In some cases, he didn't remember their names or what they looked like. He did recognize full well that this behavior went against his father's guidance. He was weed farming, pure and simple, but he hedged his bet by always using a rubber which he blew full of air just to make sure some prankster with a hat pin hadn't handled it first. This practice often drew a jaundiced stare from his conquest of the evening.

Sloan fantasized that he would meet an attractive female engineering student who shared his goals of academic excellence *and* his biological need for a regular romp in the sack. In this imaginary world, they would study until they tired of the books and then climb in the sack for some relaxation.

Such an arrangement proved difficult to find. Girls who pursued engineering degrees were seldom interested in a steady diet of study *and* sex. They wanted to be taken out on a date and shown a good time. In Sloan's view, this was a time-consuming distraction.

Then in his sophomore year, he met Brenda in his American Literature class. She was a sexy Florida girl with long flowing auburn hair, hazel eyes and a great body. She was not strong academically, but great fun at a party, and she shared Sloan's enthusiasm for the physical side of a relationship. On their fourth date, they had great sex on the bench seat of his old truck. He realized immediately that she brought more to the union in the way of experience than he did. She knew to throw her leg over him and sit on his lap facing him. She brought this and much more to their partnership and he welcomed it.

There was no talk of who was a virgin and all that. It was what it was. Great sex. She seemed to get that he had to keep his hormones in check in order to put in a full measure of effort on his studies.

When he had a need, she was almost always available. He'd stop by her dorm with a quart of Coors and they'd sit in his old truck and drink it while making out on the bench seat. The entire evening would set him back a whopping three bucks.

Beyond the fact that she was damn good-looking and loved to make out, she was also on the pill, and for Sloan that completed the package. No accidental weed farming for him.

Halfway through her junior year, Brenda, under financial pressure from her folks, dropped out of school and took a job in town. She could have gone home to Melbourne and found work at a big aerospace outfit where her father had worked for more than twenty years, but in the spirit of keeping the arrangement intact, she rented a little efficiency close to campus and convenient to her work. The apartment gave the couple a place to go besides the front seat of his truck or under a blanket in the park. If he showed up with a pizza, or a bag of Krystal's and a six-pack of Coors, it bought him sleepover privileges. On days when he needed to get back for an early class, he left around midnight, after the national news. Other nights, he slept at the apartment and went straight to class the next morning.

Sloan and Brenda had an arrangement. He never thought of it as anything else. Each had needs the other met. He never led her to believe he intended to marry her. The words "I love you" were never uttered by either of them. He was in love all right, with the setup—a beautiful girl with the hots for him, a job, her own apartment, and a prescription.

One of the benefits of ROTC was free billets for which most cadets became eligible in their junior year, provided they were in good standing academically. The good news was that barracks accommodations were usually free to all who qualified. The downside was that every room came with a roommate who could be a square-shooter or a goofball. It was the luck of the draw.

Near the end of his junior year, Sloan moved into the ROTC barracks where he was assigned a semiprivate room. The crapshoot of being paired with a roommate went full in the face of Sloan's risk-averse nature.

He loaded his clothes, books, and personal affects in the back of his old truck and drove across campus. He parked in front of the ROTC dorm, grabbed an armload of stuff, and made his way inside to room 222.

The smallish room was furnished with bunk beds, two study desks, and two hardback chairs. His new roommate was sprawled on a rickety lawn chair, watching people go by outside the only window. On first impression, the roommate exhibited none of the qualities Sloan expected in a core-happy cadet. His shaggy hair hung over his ears. His tattered jeans were soiled beyond salvage and he was wearing a t-shirt on loan from the FSU athletic department.

Sloan stuck out a hand. "Hey, name's Sloan."

"Sloan? I'm Morgan, Jake Morgan." He pushed back on the window sill almost to the point of teetering on the rickety chair and shook Sloan's hand without actually exerting the effort to stand.

"Saw you drive up. Good lookin' truck. What's your first name?"

"Sloan *is* my first name, John Sloan Abernathy. I dropped the John and just go by Sloan."

"John's better. I like John better 'n Sloan any day. You just look like a John."

"Yeah, well, you may as well get used to Sloan. Ain't changing it, not for you or nobody."

"Hey, don't get surly." Jake crossed his arms over his skinny chest.

"Just call me Sloan and we'll get along fine."

"You are. You're gettin' surly. You can call *me* most anything, long as you smile." He raised an eyebrow. "But okay, Sloan it is."

Sloan went about stowing his gear in one of two closets in the room.

"So, Jake, what're you doing in ROTC anyhow?"

"What you're sayin' is, you don't think I fit the image?" Jake spread his arms and laughed.

Sloan leaned back out of the closet to look him over. "Not exactly, man."

Jake shrugged. "Needed a little help on the financials. My old man went off to Korea when I was just a lad and ain't made it back yet. Left Mom without any visible means. Much as she would like to, she ain't much help when it comes to payin' tuition, so I'm in ROTC for what it can do for me: three hots and a cot, books and tuition, and this great view of the field of torture. We'll likely spend half our lives right out there on that parade field. Left . . . left . . . yur left, right, left. Sound off . . . Your pants are lose, your leggins are—"

Sloan finished the verse. "left. . . yur left, right, left," They both laughed.

Jake gathered himself up off of his lawn chair, moseyed across the room and stretched his gangly six-foot frame on the lower bunk. He laced his fingers and put his hands behind his head. His feet dangled over the end of the war surplus bed. He stared up into the mesh that supported the mattress for the upper bunk. "You can have that one." He casually pointed to the upper bunk. "I'm takin' this here one. By trade, I'm a sculler," he added.

"One of them narrow, one-man rowing boats?" Sloan said.

"That's right. It's called a single rowing shell to those of us who know the sport."

"I'll keep that in mind," Sloan replied. "By the way, I want that bunk you're on."

Jake rolled on his side and pushed up on one elbow. "No deal, Johnny. This here's my bunk. I got here first, I get first pick. So . . . tough shit."

"*Rowing*?" Sloan said, giving Jake the impression he had lost sight of what the argument was all about. "Why didn't you say so? Who ever heard it called sculling anyhow? You any good?"

Jake shrugged. "I'm in Rotcie, ain't I?"

"Couldn't make the cut, huh?"

"You're smarter 'n I thought," Jake said. "Can't decide if I like you or not. But let's talk about what really matters on this campus."

"And . . . what's that?" Sloan asked.

"You gettin' any? You know. . .got a girlfriend?"

"Sure. Guess you could call her that. We've been spending time together for almost a year."

"So, you're serious?" Jake said, "You gettin' married?"

"Hell, no! We have an arrangement, if you get my drift. By no means are we engaged or anything of the kind. I haven't met that woman yet. You know, the one I'd take home to Mom."

"Well, ain't you one lucky son of a bitch? But I don't get it. Why're you hanging with one hen when the barnyard's full of 'em." Jake was clearly rankled over Sloan's setup with Brenda.

"Time, man. It's all about time. If I meet a girl, take her out a few times, and get her in the sack, all that could take weeks.

Not to mention the dough it costs. I just don't have it to spare and what if you knock one of 'em up? Then you're really in deep shit. I might not even like her, now I'm stuck with her."

"Hell, man, there's ways around all that."

"Like what . . . abortion? You can forget that crap. My old man said I shouldn't be no weed farmer."

Jake threw his head back and laughed. "Weed farmer. Never heard it called that. Trust me on this, man. When it comes to women and sex, I'll take quantity over quality any day. You won't catch me spending that kinda time and money just to get laid."

Sloan crammed his hand in his pocket and produced a silver dollar.

"Flip you for the bunk."

"Flip me?" Jake took a minute to ponder the proposal. "Sure, why not? I'm feelin' lucky." He spat in both hands and rubbed them together.

"Call it," Sloan demanded as he tossed his lucky dollar in the air. They watched as it tumbled end over end back to earth.

"Tails," Jake shouted, cocksure as a riverboat gambler betting on a rigged shell game. Sloan's lucky dollar landed and came to rest on the floor in front of them.

"Heads. Its heads." Sloan announced with all the verve of a carnival barker in a sideshow.

"You lucky son of a bitch," Jake moaned. "How 'bout two outta three?"

"Get out of here with that crap. You're on my bunk."

Sloan unloaded boxes of books and stacked them on one of the small study desks. "Okay if I take this one? Or did you want to flip me for it?"

"Take it," Jake waved a hand. "Night before a test, I kick back with Hefner and study some of his babes."

"Hefner? Hefner who?"

"Don't tell me you're one of them guys who all the time has his nose in a book."

"Hope it don't mean we can't be friends 'cause I do put in lots of time on the books. Promised my Daddy I would do my best."

"What do you do with your free time? Besides hang out with that babe of yours?"

"If I have any, I spend it figuring out how I can accumulate great wealth while remaining anonymous."

"Anonymous?" Jake screwed his face into a question mark. "You mean famous, right?"

"No man. Rich and unknown is the best of all worlds." As he explained his plan to Jake, he knew he sounded like the complete nerd that he was. "You might say I'm something of an Existentialist." Sloan didn't have a clue what he was saying, but talking about Nietzsche made him sound cool and intellectual.

"Not sure what an Existentialist does," Jake said. "Never could figure out what'n hell Nietzsche was getting at. Reckon you'll want me to cover for you on those nights when you're at the apartment?"

"That would be great. You know, some of those junior officers can be less than understanding when it comes to cadets spending too much time off campus. How do you think we could work it?" Sloan was ready to yield to Jake's street smarts.

"Easy. I'll just tell the duty officer that you're in the head studying. I'll put a pair of combat boots in a stall and hang a towel over the door. That should keep them guessing till you graduate." Jake sat on the windowsill and crossed his ankles. "Listen, man. One of these Thursday nights when you're not busy with your "arrangement," I'd be glad to show you what you're missing on campus."

"And just what would that be?"

"One of my favorite games is crashing cocktail socials at the sorority houses. All you need to gain entry is a blazer and a striped tie. I call it my Frat Rat Uniform."

"I'm no Frat Rat. Who in hell can afford the dues?"

"Don't matter. By the time we're inside and showing the girls a good time, no one will dare ask us to leave. If nothing works out for us, we can always go to Joe's and hang out."

"Joe's? Where's that?"

"Don't tell me you never been to Joe's? A slum of a joint, just a few blocks off campus, You know, man, you're wasting the best years of your life with your nose in a freaking book!"

IX

That summer, Jake hopped a bus to Cleveland and found work in construction. He spent the summer nailing up drywall during the day and nailing a different barmaid every night. Or so he claimed in his infrequent postcards to "John." His mother was thrilled to have him home for the summer and she appreciated his help with the monthly expenses, even though she seldom saw him.

As soon as Sloan's last exam was finished, he loaded his truck and drove to West Texas where he found work as a roughneck on a drilling rig. The money was good and the rent at his mother's house was hard to beat.

In late August, the men returned to room 222 to pick up where they had left off.

"Sure you don't want to swap bunks?" Jake asked.

"Nope."

Sloan was fully charged and ready to wrap up his four-year college career. Brenda welcomed him back to the apartment with a home-cooked meal and an all-night romp. He casually checked the bed stand to make sure that the ever-present packet of pills was still in use. If Brenda had taken up with someone in Sloan's absence, there was no trace of him. He saw no evidence that another suitor had "skidded his rig" during his absence. But if they had, so be it. It wasn't like she was his true love.

Jake returned to campus claiming to have a good many new notches on his gun from his summer of hard labor and bar-hopping. Late summer was the hot season for shopping the freshman sorority girls and Jake approached the endeavor with renewed enthusiasm.

Each man pursued his dreams in his own way. Sloan continued to maintain his vigil on Brenda's apartment just as he had for over a year. Except for an occasional foray to a sorority house for Thursday evening cocktails, his only diversion from his "nose to the grindstone" college life was his domination of the pool tables at Joe's. Nothing came between Sloan and his pursuit of a four point. A promise was a promise and he had made one to Daddy—all aces.

Jake, on the other hand, took life as it came. If his GPA got much above a two-point he slacked off and found new ways to fill his time. When it came to women, he considered three dates to be a long relationship. More than five and he became commitment-phobic. He never departed from his golden rule:

Sex is all about quantity not quality.

X

Sloan was well into his last semester and had begun to contemplate life after graduation. He thought of pursuing a career with an electronics company or a large aerospace firm. Thanks to his perfect academic record, job opportunities were plentiful. Interviews with campus recruiters were easily arranged and went well until they learned of his two-year commitment to active duty.

He had finished his preparation for Thursday's lectures and decided to swing by Joe's for a burger and to check out the game in the back room.

He was having one of those nights when the pockets looked as big as gallon buckets. His burger and three beers were gone before he realized it was approaching midnight. He racked his cue and headed over to the apartment. He turned his key in the latch and swung open the door to the darkened apartment. He shed his clothes in a pile, crawled into bed behind her and ran his hand under her night shirt to fondle her ample breasts.

"That you Sloan?" Brenda snorted. She seemed unwilling to stir regardless of the temptation.

"Who were you expecting? The super? Or that guy in 3-B?" He pulled her close and kissed the back of her neck.

She pushed his hand away. "Why'n hell are you so damned late?" she growled.

"Pool. On a streak." He snuggled close and ran his arm around her waist.

"I should kick your ass out of bed right now. You know us workin' girls gotta get our rest. Not like I can cut class and sleep in just cause you had a hot stick goin' at Joe's."

She rolled over to face him. "You do have some *hot* stick." She giggled. "But still—"

"Want I should leave?"

"Yeah, but not just yet."

She threw her leg over him and pressed her moist full mouth on his. He rolled over on his back and pulled her nightshirt off over her head. She liked being on top, left over from their days on the front seat of his truck. It still worked.

Sunlight flooded the apartment. Sloan squinted at his watch and playfully slapped Brenda on the butt.

"Know what time it is?"

"No, but I'm sure you're 'bout to tell me."

She swung her pillow at him then buried her face to hide from the brilliant morning sun. Her long auburn hair lay strewn over her shoulders and down her naked back.

"Eight-fifteen. Got a class at nine. Gotta get goin'. High time us school boys was having breakfast and heading out so, "get in dat kitchen 'n rattle 'em pots 'n' pans'." He jumped out of bed, did a little dance and clapped his hands to the tune.

She sat up in bed and ran her fingers through her hair. "If it ain't sex, it's food. What's a girl to do?"

"We had some great sex, so how about some great eggs 'n coffee." Sloan could barely contain his enthusiasm for the day.

"All right, I'm gettin'." She slipped her well-worn terry robe on over her supple shoulders and made her way to the kitchen. "I swear, Sloan. What I don't do for a little ass."

He found his jeans and pulled them on. Green chalk dust on his fly was the only proof of last night's hot streak on the pool table. That and a wad of bills in his pocket.

He found his sweat-stained t-shirt, took a whiff, shrugged and pulled it over his head.

"Still takin' that pill, huh, kid?"

"What pill's that, Sugar ?"

"Don't be cute. You know damn well what pill."

"Come on, Sloan. You don't think I want little Sloan's runnin' round here, now do you? Damn place's too small for me and you. Let alone a curtain climber."

"Last thing I need," Sloan said. "Besides, Daddy wouldn't have liked it."

"Your Daddy's gone and you're still here, so what's he got to say about it?"

"Made me promise."

"What? That you'd marry me?" She batted her eyelashes, pulled her robe up around her neck and grinned wickedly.

"Not exactly, kiddo. Nice try."

"What, then?"

"He told me not to knock 'em up unless I was gonna take care of 'em, and abortion is sure as hell not something I would want to do. Might be killing my kid, Sloan Junior."

Brenda rinsed and filled the coffee pot and turned the burner on under the skillet.

Sloan flicked on the TV and tuned it to the early news.

"You got nothing to worry about. I'm not about to get pregnant. Not if I can help it."

"Just keep thinkin' like that, kiddo." He gave her a quick kiss on the forehead and patted her on the butt.

"What you got on for tonight? Gonna study at the dorm or might you be droppin' by after your pool game?"

A visit from Sloan on consecutive nights was rare, but it did happen.

"Jake wants to check out one of them sorority parties and I was thinkin' I'd tag along, just for the hell of it. Free food and spiked punch. Besides, if I show up here too often, you might get tired of me."

"Who says I'm not already?"

Sloan found two clean plates and forks and placed them neatly on the chrome dinette. He carefully folded two paper napkins and placed one by each plate. Brenda broke eggs in a skillet and stirred them with a fork. She hunched her shoulders to hold up her robe.

"Still looking for Miss Right, huh, Sloan?"

He held his palms open to her and waxed coy. "Hey, give me some credit."

"So, what's all that make me?"

"You? Why you're a good buddy who is great in bed and you let me sleep over now and again. You take care of me. Hell, Brenda, if it weren't for you, I'd probably have flunked out long before now."

He located his denim jacket and hung it on the doorknob. His plaid shirt was still draped across the chrome dinette chair where he had flung last night in his haste to join Brenda in bed.

"Need to clean this place up," he said, hoping to change the subject.

"Next time you're over, you can give me a hand," She scooped the scrambled eggs onto the plates and tossed a slice of toast on each one.

He needed to say something to relieve the tension and keep Brenda in the game. "Look Brenda, we're the best of friends. It's just that I'm not ready to settle down. I have to get through school and then there's that active duty thing hanging over my head. When I'm ready, you'll be the first to know."

"Oh, just what every girl wants to hear."

His arms dropped to his sides. "Listen, it goes both ways. You could meet someone you fall hard for and you'll dump me quick as anything."

She turned away quick, but he saw her eyes shine. "Truth is Sloan, I'll never be anything more'n a stopover, a placeholder till you meet this certain someone and fall in love. It's my lot to be here when you feel the need for a piece of ass. That's it in a nutshell. Ain't that right, Hot Stick?"

He'd never led her on. His feelings had not changed in almost two years he had been seeing her. Convenience and safe sex made it work for him. Her too, he'd thought. But now she was making noises like she wanted more. "How would it be if I come by on Saturday like I usually do? We can go for a pizza and take in a movie. How's that sound?"

"Sure, Hon. Sounds great. I'll be ready 'round seven."

"Okay, it's a date." He acted like he didn't hear the defeat in her voice.

"You'll call if you're gonna be late or you got another one of them hot sticks going at Joe's?"

"Don't I always? Trust me."

Sloan gobbled the scrambled eggs and toast, washed them down with black coffee, and headed for the door. He felt driven by an inexplicable need to vacate the premises and be quick about it.

As he unlocked his old truck, he glanced at the upstairs window. Brenda was watching, palms pressed to the glass. With a quick wave, he climbed in and sped away. Gripping the wheel, he remembered the time she had skipped a dose of the pill, but lost her nerve and started taking them again. It wasn't until a few weeks later that she owned up to it. The news had given him the shakes. He'd never imagined her having a treacherous side.

She was in one of her moods, but maybe the whole thing would blow over by Saturday. He knew he wouldn't visit her on Thursday unless the evening at the sorority bash failed to produce a prospective date *and* he was sober enough to find his way to the apartment. He never risked driving after having too many beers.

Sloan made his way back to campus for his nine o'clock class. He soon forgot about Brenda.

XI

Sloan and Jake freshened up in the ROTC shower room, donned their Frat uniforms and headed for the sorority house. They entered through the front door and were motioned past the reception desk, signaling they'd passed muster.

A bowl of punch, cups, and finger foods decorated a large table in the center of the room. Coeds in cocktail dresses lined the walls. Men in obligatory sports jackets and preppy ties mingled with the girls or stood in small groups sizing up the talent. A small dance band played "get acquainted" music.

When it suited them, the men would invite a girl to join them on the dance floor. Early in the evening, it was a crowd of individuals, but before the evening was over, couples would form. Sloan passed the time making small talk with Jake and several of the other men.

"Got your eye on anyone in particular?" Jake asked.

Sloan shoved his hands in his pockets. His tie was slightly askew. "Nope. So far nothing looks promising."

"Joanie likes you. Thinks you're *cute.*"

"Cute, huh? Which one's she?"

Jake pointed her out and Sloan sized her up.

"More your type. She's too . . . you know—"

"Plump?" Jake said. "You think she's fat, right?"

"And it's too early to settle, we got all night. Something good could show. Never pays to rush these things."

Sloan spotted an attractive brunette. Her short wavy hair bounced as she skipped around the room, greeting her sorority sisters and flirting with the fraternity men.

"Like her." Sloan said as he broke away from the stag line and made his way to where he had last seen her.

He approached her, all the while formulating his battle plan. He would try a Rhett Butler imitation. It often worked well with his southern accent. He made his move.

"Evenin' ma'am. Name's Sloan." He spoke with an exaggerated southern drawl. "May I fetch you a sarsaparilla?"

She smiled in amusement and went along with his second-rate Rhett Butler imitation. "No thanks, honeybunch. Just put one out," she said.

"Bogart movie, right?" Sloan said.

He feared he was no match for her knowledge of classic movie trivia so he changed his approach on the fly. "Haven't seen you here before." It sounded corny but often worked. It was his and every other guy's last ditch standby pickup line.

She rolled her eyes, but when he put his hand out to offer a dance, she followed him onto the dance floor. She could not resist his boyish smile.

"Lovely paaty. Don't you agree?"

Who was this lovely lady with the crisp New England accent? Sloan felt awkward as they moved around the floor. First, he attempted a foxtrot.

"Thanks for sparing my toes," she said. She did her best to follow his erratic moves.

"Ballroom dancing's not my thing," he confessed. "I'm more at home with country."

In spite of his awkwardness, she didn't seem to mind being in his arms. She smiled privately as he attempted a Cuban run.

He gazed into her laughing hazel eyes. She might be just about the most beautiful woman he had ever seen. Not like Lauren or Marilyn. Not that kind of beauty, even though she had set a caldron to boil in his loins. He could see beyond the sparse application of eye shadow and mascara. He imagined a connection, like he was tuning his FM receiver to a station on another planet. At first, static. Then a clear transmission. She was unlike anyone he had ever met.

They moved around the floor. Her words seemed to come through the fog that surrounded them.

"Transferred in from Boston College. Travel under the name of Abigale. That's Abby G-A-L-E."

Even as they moved around the floor, he realized that he did not have her full attention. Her eyes remained fixed on the front door. Could she be expecting someone?

"So, Gale—why FSU?" He did his best to steer her away from the door or put someone else between them and the door, but his attempts were futile.

"Simple, really. I want to finish my undergraduate here in Florida near my parents. They winter in Vero Beach, *and* FSU has a better Marketing Communications program than BC."

"More prestige for your field. Or does Gale just fit better with a state known for—well—gales?" Sloan blushed, embarrassed. How could he make such a lame observation?

She smiled politely. She seemed to take his comment in stride. As they moved to the music, she continued her vigil on the front door. Each time he diverted her attention, she managed to take the lead just long enough to regain her focus.

"So, tell me, Sloan. What kind of higher learning are *you* in pursuit of?" She looked over her shoulder. "No, let me guess. You're a jock, right?" She turned back to face him.

"Darn, what gave me away? Was it walking across the room without spilling my drink?"

She held him at arm's length and looked him up and down. "Baseball?"

Lying might have scored him points, but he feared the consequences once the truth came to light. Any answer was a crapshoot, so he went with the truth.

"Electrical Engineering," he admitted.

"Oh, so you're *not* a jock? You have more brains than I gave you credit for."

"I warmed the offensive bench in my freshmen year, but now I'm a Rotcie lieutenant."

"Army man, eh?"

"No, but I have a couple of years on active duty when I graduate, which is nothin' compared to the price of an education."

"Hot damn! I had you all wrong." She leaned back in his arms for another long look. "That explains the haircut."

He ignored her catty remark and went for a quick close.

"How 'bout dinner? Would you have dinner with me?"

"Dinner? You and me? Maybe. When?"

He suppressed a grin. He'd cleared the first hurdle.

"Saturday. Say, seven?"

"Would that be at the ROTC mess? Or the Golden Arches?"

"I can manage burgers and a beer at Joe's, if you're not too thirsty."

"Don't know about that. Me and the girls at the house usually do the bars on Saturday night. You know, crawl all the pubs, but manage to drag our butts home just before dawn."

She found a napkin and pulled a pencil from Sloan's vest pocket.

She looked at the mechanical pencil and the pocket protector. "Should have known you were an engineer." She scratched her number and stuck the pencil back where it came from.

"Here, give me a call. If I think I can get by on one beer, I just might join you."

"I'll call you tomorrow," he said.

"Let it ring a long time. After this shindig, I'll most likely be hung over." Before she had time to stuff the note in his pocket, a tall athletic man came through the front door and surveyed the room like Captain Ahab looking for the great white. He spotted Abigale on the dance floor and strutted in her direction.

With some urgency, she extricated herself from Sloan's embrace. "Give me that. Can't trust you to call." She crumpled the napkin in her hand. "You'll forget. Look, I'll meet you at Joe's on Saturday around seven. Now, if you'll excuse me, my real date is here and he thinks he's the only man in my life." She smiled. "You know how it is."

She left Sloan stranded in the middle of the dance floor and rushed to meet this handsome man who was recognized by anyone who had seen an FSU football game in the last three years.

Brad Hager, the star quarterback and Heisman hopeful, was there to fetch Abigale for dinner. As he strutted toward Abigale, men put up a high five. He returned a few then continued in Abigale's direction, never taking his eyes off her.

"Don't be late," Sloan said. Hate it when women are late, he thought.

She and Brad turned and made their way to the door. Sloan watched in hopes of making eye contact once more, but she was too preoccupied with this bigger-than-life footballer to even glance in his direction.

Sloan rejoined Jake and the gang of stags on the sidelines.

"Talk about outclassed, huh, Sloan?" Jake laughed and slapped Sloan on the back.

"We're having dinner Saturday."

"In your dreams," Jake said, hanging an arm around Sloan's neck and snickering in his ear. "Once she gets a taste of that stud, she'll forget she ever met you. So, come on, let's head for Joe's. We need to stuff some burgers down our throats and swill a few beers. Who knows, we might get lucky. By the way, old sport, can you spot me a few bucks? Running a little short this month."

Sloan stared at the empty doorway. Jake was probably right. Jocks have ways of turning a lady's head, especially all-conference quarterbacks. He had already lost one girl to a football hero. She'd probably be overwhelmed by that big-dog quarterback and forget she'd ever met him.

XII

Abigale retrieved her shawl from the coat rack and made her way to the door. Brad pushed it open and led her to the street.

"Who's he?" Brad asked.

"Who's who?"

"That guy you were dancing with."

"Oh, him," she waved a hand dismissively. "Some frat rat I know. We have a class together."

"Don't be late—to what?" Brad pressed.

"To class . . . always late to that class."

"So, big shot. What have you been up to since our coke date last week?"

"Same old boring classes and super hard workouts."

With a broad smile, he slid his hand around her waist and pulled her up close.

"Watch yourself, handsome, I don't know you that well yet."

It was a balmy night and the sounds and smells of spring were everywhere. Azaleas were in full bloom in the hedges along the walk leading from the sorority house to the street.

"Where did you paak?" she asked.

"Over there." He pointed to a shiny red Corvette under the streetlamp in front of the sorority house.

"You paaked your car in Handicapped Parking?"

He seemed pleased that he had managed to park so close to the door. "Handicapped? Damn it. I thought that said

Star Quarterback." He pointed to the vanity plate on the red Corvette convertible that read: BRAD. "Trust me cutie, they wouldn't dare tow a car in this town with that plate."

"Good to know I'm in the company of the Big Man on Campus. I, too, have a sports car."

"Yeah? What kind?"

"Austin Healey 3000. You know it?"

"Nope. Never heard of it. Must be one a them foreign ones." He popped the passenger door.

"Yes, it must be."

"Hop in. We got dinner at Ricardo's in fifteen minutes." He rushed to the driver's side.

"Ricardo's? Are you trying to impress me?"

"Figured I'd already done that." A wide grin crossed his handsome boyish face. "You know how it is. I get all these gift cards from places in town. If you ever need any dry cleaning done, all you have to do is ask."

"I'll bear that in mind."

She hiked her skirt and climbed in the passenger seat. Brad, already behind the wheel, cranked the engine. She closed her door as he wheeled the regal machine into the street and expertly negotiated traffic into downtown Tallahassee. They could not converse over the blaring radio tuned to a local rock and roll station. He turned into the valet parking zone at Ricardo's and slid to a stop.

Abigale immediately began to repair the damage done to her hair in the open air ride to Ricardo's.

Two parking attendants jogged out to meet them. "Evenin', Brad," the first attendant said.

Brad hopped out and tossed the keys to the attendant as if he was on the playing field. The attendant bobbled the toss, but managed to catch it before it hit the asphalt. The second attendant opened Abigale's door and offered his hand.

The first attendant climbed in behind the wheel and pulled Brad's Vette right up front in plain view of most anyone fortunate enough to have a view of the parking lot.

"And don't worry Brad. There won't be a wait when you're ready to leave," the attendant said, as he tossed the keys to his assistant to be properly racked at the valet station. "Ricardo likes it when the Voodoo Vette is out front. Figures it's good for business."

The maître d' seated the couple at the best table in the house, also in plain view of the other patrons.

When it came to ordering dinner, Brad followed the customary format, ordering exactly what she would have predicted. He had the filet mignon, rare. She chose the lobster tails with drawn butter. Brad made full use of his limited knowledge of wine by ordering a glass of the house white for her and a glass of red for himself.

Football rhetoric flowed non-stop from the moment they sat down until they got up to leave. When the last bite of dessert disappeared from the dish in front of Brad, he put his elbows on the table and leaned toward her. "What say we blow this joint and head back to my place for a night cap? We can listen to some music and kick back, just hang out for a while? How does that sound?"

She put her elbows on the table and leaned in too. "Gee Brad, I'd love to, but I'm feeling a cold coming on and it's a weeknight. You know how we serious students need to be on the ball for our eight o'clock classes. Oh, but you wouldn't know much about that now, would you? Being a big-time jock and all."

She gave him the smirk-smile she had perfected for just such an occasion.

Unfazed, he leaned back in his chair. "We could look at my scrapbook. Goes all the way back to when I was in grade school. Or better still, we could watch the highlight reel from this year's regionals. Bet you were there, huh?"

"Damn it, Brad. I missed that one, too."

"I won: 46 to 13."

"You? All by yourself? My, my."

Brad settled the bill and the pair headed for the door. The parking attendants were waiting at the curb with Brad's Vette all revved up and both doors gaping.

He offered the attendants two bucks but they refused it.

"Hey, man. It's an honor just moving the Voodoo Vette around on the lot. *We* should pay *you*."

Brad shook hands with the first attendant and slapped him on the back.

"Thanks, man. See you 'round."

"Go Noles!" the second attendant shouted from the lot where he was retrieving another diner's car.

Knees together, Abigale turned toward Brad.

"Voodoo Vette? Why'd the attendant call your car—"

"Oh, nothing. Just some joke going around campus."

By Abigale's reckoning, they had already covered all the common ground between them, so the drive to her dorm was devoid of casual chitchat.

The big red Voodoo Vette roared through the city streets. Brad seemed to welcome the occasional traffic stop as an opportunity to put his machine through its paces. When they arrived at her dorm, he sprang from behind the wheel with all the zeal he would exude if he were going back for a Hail Mary which, in some respects, he was.

He jerked the passenger door open.

She swung out of the vehicle and made it to her feet without giving him as much as a peek.

They walked the short distance to the front door where Brad put his arm around her waist, pulled her up close, and maneuvered for a goodnight kiss.

She covered her mouth with her hand. "Cold coming on, remember? You could miss a week of spring training."

Before he could think of a retort she disappeared behind the big wooden doors.

Abigale may have met her intended that evening, but if she had, she was not fully aware of who he was.

The crowd at the mixer began to thin out, so Sloan drove the old truck over to Joe's where he and Jake wasted the rest of the evening flirting with some of the regulars and the also-ran's from the mixer. Among them was Joanie, the one who, according to Jake, thought Sloan was *cute.* He was not quite sure what that meant, but he knew he had the green light to put some moves on her.

On another night, he might have followed through, but after meeting Abigale, Joanie held no interest for him even though Jake's hot, beer-soaked breath in his ear assured him she was a sure thing. "Don't forget what I told you man, it's all about quantity not quality. Wouldn't want you waking up tomorrow and wishing you had. Me, I'd do her in a New York minute."

Sloan had another beer and headed for the dorm. Joanie saw him on his way out and hitched a ride back to her dorm.

Sloan arrived at the barracks, stripped down to his skivvies, stretched out on his bunk and stared at the bottom of Jake's bunk.

Sometime after midnight Jake, drunk and disheveled, stumbled into room 222.

"Didn't have ta wait up. How'd it go with Joanie?"

"Dropped her off at her dorm and came here."

"You let 'er go?" Jake blinked in disbelief.

"Yep. Like freeing a trout back into a mountain stream. She's just not my type."

"Fat?" Jake slurred.

"That too. Besides, I couldn't get that other babe out of my head."

The bed shook as Jake climbed onto his bunk in all his clothes and fell back in the top berth. "Hey Jake, do you believe in love at first sight?"

"Mean lust?" Jake laughed at his joke. "Never thought much 'bout it."

"Why'm I having this conversation with a drunk?" Sloan said. "Go to sleep. Tomorrow you can clean your half of our pigsty."

"Nag, nag, na—" Jake fell into a deep slumber and began to snore contentedly.

Sloan thought about holding Abigale and dancing around the room. He thought about the way she'd felt in his arms, the fragrance of her hair, her cutting wit. An hour passed before he drifted off to sleep.

XIII

The aroma of fried shrimp, grilled burgers, and spilled beer overpowered the hayseed stench of the sawdust on the postage-stamp dance floor. A three-piece country band moaned away on the small stage at the rear of the bar. Two couples were rearranging the sawdust as they rubbed bellies to an old Hank Williams tune.

Sloan sat alone in a booth and watched the action. Pool balls rattled on the tables in the back room, the song of the sirens that might well draw him in should Abigale fail to show. He would give her a few more minutes. She seemed positive about meeting him, but that was early in the evening before Brad had influenced her thinking.

He checked his watch. Abigale was late. He had his doubts she would show. The big-dog quarterback may have won again.

Moving on back to the billiards room was beginning to look like the best idea when, out of nowhere, the aroma of fine perfume pervaded his booth. He raised his eyes to hers. She had ditched her sorority garb in lieu of jeans and a blue-checkered blouse. Her short, wavy, brown hair was pulled close and held with ribbons to match the school colors. Hope that doesn't mean she's carrying his torch, he thought.

He attempted to stand and greet her, but before he could get to his feet, she plopped into the booth opposite him.

"Preppy?" she said. "You're still here? Guess that proves you wanted to see me, or you're desperate for a date. Which is it?"

"Little of both." He leaned back in the booth. "I would've waited all night just for bragging rights."

"Bragging rights? You'll have nothing to brag about tonight. Of that I can assure you."

"Burger and a beer with Brad Hager's main squeeze? What more could a guy ask for?"

"Yeah. He's cute, ain't he?"

"But can he eat in the ROTC mess?" Sloan said.

"Can't say as he'd ever want to. And I'm not so sure about being his main squeeze. That was our first real date and it was courtesy of the town fathers."

"Huh?"

"Everyone in town wants to incur his favor. You know, free dinners, you name it."

"Tonight dinner's on me." Sloan said.

Her warm smile gave him a queasy feeling in the pit of his stomach. He wanted to get on with the evening and move beyond Brad and his big red Vette.

"Want a beer?"

"Sure, Preppy." She pointed to a hamburger being served at the next table. "And one of those burgers with a mess of fries would be great, too."

"How do you like 'em done?"

"Burnt, all the way through," she said. Her smile and dancing eyes warmed him through.

He signaled the waitress and placed an order.

"What's with this Preppy stuff?" he said.

"Surely you've seen the movie." She hummed the theme song.

"Love Story? Sure, several times. Six Academy Award nominations."

"Seven," she corrected him.

"Besides," he said, "you're the Yankee at this party. Did you 'paak' your 'caah' in the 'paaking' lot?"

"Wise, Preppy. I love my Boston brogue. It's kind of cute, don't you think?"

"You're cute as a bug's ear, all around. But I'm afraid you have me in the wrong pew when it comes to prep schools. Fraternities, too. Growing up, I never heard of such a place."

"You're telling me you were a gate-crasher at our little social the other night? Why, I'm plum shocked, Honeybunch."

She turned her head and shot him a coy smile batted her lashes to fake astonishment. "Hell, Sloan. Prep schools are common as dirt in Boston. One on every corner. I didn't attend one either, but I could have. My father would have gone along with anything I wanted. I attended Ecole Bilingue. That's a high school in Cambridge and I loved it. French, you know. All the classes were taught in French. I bet you never heard of it, have you?"

"A French high school, huh? So, you're bilingual?"

The waitress slammed down two mugs of Coors. The frothy, foamy brew sloshed out and soaked the table. She tossed down a towel. "Sorry 'bout that." She kept on moving to her next delivery.

"How about you, Sloan? You speak another language besides the one you're murdering here tonight?"

He leaned back and looked at the ceiling. "Well, let me see…Mexican. I know some Mexican. Mostly the guttural stuff. And Texan. I grew up in West Texas. Some folks would say we speak a language all our own."

"I got into Boston College without any trouble, so I don't think my attending a French high school did me any harm."

He wiped the spilled beer off the table and tossed the towel to a waiter who was making his way through the now crowded restaurant. "Closest anyone ever came to a prep school in my hometown was when the Williams brothers went to a military academy to stay out of reform school."

She cocked her head. "Oh, so you were deprived as a child."

"No, not really. I had a fine childhood. The Williams boys had it rough though."

"What were they to you?" she asked.

"Friends. Stole their daddy's car and wrecked it."

"Nice crowd."

"But, for sure, I'm the last one to answer to Preppy. That guy in the movie? He was a third generation Frat Rat from Harvard. Excuse me, Havvad. I'm first generation FSU and *not* in a fraternity. My folks didn't finish high school, let alone attend college."

"You've had a rough life, huh, Sloan?"

"No complaints. If you don't know what you're missing—"

"Who gets the well done?" The waitress shouted over the roaring crowd of rowdy college students. Before Sloan could answer, she dropped both plates as if they were burning her fingers. "Fries'll be out in a jiffy," she announced, moving on to the next table to deliver a fistful of brews.

"So, what is it about you, tall dark and lonesome? No steady string of babes?"

"Are you kidding?" He looked at his watch. "Got a late date tonight and don't want to keep her waiting, so hurry up and finish your burger."

"Hell, Sloan. I don't even have my fries yet."

"She'll eventually get around to them."

Sloan's wise talk reminded him that he had forgotten to tell Brenda he wouldn't be seeing her. He wondered if he should excuse himself and call her or wait until morning. Morning would be soon enough. The damage was already done.

"I don't know about you, Cowboy." She leaned back against the bench seat. "Guys who have lots of options don't usually hang around for an hour waiting on a long shot."

Her response turned his mood serious. "I think you have me figured. At least in one way, I'm a little like Preppy."

She looked down her nose at him through half-closed eyes. "How so, big guy?"

"I believe people fall in love the first time they meet and they stay together for life."

She leaned forward and put her elbows on the table. Eyes wide, she stared into Sloan's.

"So, Preppy, are you thinking I might be your one and only?"

"Too soon to say." He studied her intently. "Beer and burger's a good start."

"And, eventually, I'll have fries."

"Let's dance...give 'em time to get the kitchen back in order. They don't have many calls for Frenchie fries."

The country ensemble was droning out an old Willie Nelson tune.

Hello walls (hello hello) how'd things go for you today.

Don't you miss her, since she up and walked away?

And I'll bet you dread to spend another lonely night . . ."

"To this?" She held up both hands.

She had been comfortable on the sorority dance floor, but this so-called music was different. It was not what she was accustomed to at BC or the Cambridge neighborhood where she grew up. This was rough and tumbles, earthy.

Sloan stood and offered his hand, but she pulled back to reconsider a close dance in this smoky bar with a Texas roughneck.

"Oh, why the hell not?" She took his hand and trailed him to the dusty dance floor. "Guess I can chance it. Tell me what to do."

"Here at Joe's, we call this belly rubbin' music. It's a kind of two-step. Just follow my lead. If I'm not mashing your toes, consider yourself lucky. When I start something fancy, I'll signal you with my left hand. It's really no different than ballroom. We just scoot around in the sawdust a bit more."

"The best part of dancing is holding the girl," he said as he put his arm around her waist and gently guided her to the center of the floor.

The close dance to that old western tune broke the ice. Holding her felt good, so natural. He was overpowered by the fragrance of her hair, her perfume.

"Man, do you smell nice." He was embarrassed that he sounded so dumb.

"Jessica McLint—something or other. Mom gets it for me in Boston. She says it's guaranteed to drive 'em wild."

"It's workin'. Let's head back to the table and try to locate another beer and your fries." Sloan waved at the waitress and by the time they arrived at their booth she was there with two frosty mugs of foamy beer.

"Still want them fries?" she chirped.

Abigale shook her head.

"After this one, we should call it a night," Sloan said.

"Why so soon, Cowboy? I'm just now gettin' the hang of this barnyard shuffle. Oh, I get it. You're afraid I can't hold my liquor, right?"

"More worried about me. One more Coors and the beer might take charge of our evening."

"You wouldn't take advantage of this sweet little Boston lass, now would you, Honeybunch?"

"Just don't want to give Adolph all the credit or the blame for this great evening."

Hand-in-hand they strolled to her dorm. She stood on the first step of the stairs leading to the front door, fully expecting that he would want to kiss her goodnight. Instead he took both her hands in his.

"Had a great time. Wanna do it again?" Sloan asked. ". . . go out?"

"Sure. Love to. You've got my number."

"No, actually, I don't. You decided not to give it out, remember?"

She turned and scampered up the stairs. "Guess I'll call *you.* If I get around to it and can remember your name. Okay . . . goodnight, Sloan. Name's Sloan, right?"

She must have thought him nervy, making her call him for their next date, but he figured if she had an interest she would, and if not, she wasn't his true love after all.

Sloan waved goodnight and sauntered off in the direction of the ROTC barracks.

XIV

Sunday mornings were quiet in the ROTC dorm. Most of the men were on extended dates or sleeping off hangovers. Sloan was awakened by the ringing of the phone in the hall. After eight rings, he dragged himself off his bunk and pulled on his jeans. Jake's undisturbed bunk was evidence that he'd had a successful night. Sloan staggered to the ringing phone and grabbed it off the hook. He rubbed his fingers in his eyes.

"Hullo."

"At you, Sloan?"

"Oh, hello, Brenda."

"We had a date last night or did you skip town and forget to let me know?"

"Geez . . . completely. Sorry. I made other plans at the last minute and forgot to clear them with—"

"Forgot?" In the long pause that followed, he knew she was twisting the phone cord around her hand and stretching it taut. He hoped she would pull it out of the wall. "How could you forget? Like we have a standing date every Saturday night come hell or—all you had to do was call. Not like I'm gonna get pissed 'cause you break a date. The least you owed me was a call."

Exasperated, he dragged a hand down his face. "Hey, I don't blame you for being steamed. You have every—got busy and forgot, that's all. Look, can I make it up to—"

"Like how?"

"I'll come over. We can go out for some breakfast."

"Is it breakfast you're wanting or is this your way of gettin' a Sunday morning quickie?"

"Quickie? No, I'm talking breakfast. The whole nine yards, honest. First class. We can do brunch at the Marriott. I know how you love it there."

"Okay. I guess . . . sure. I'm not doin' nuthin'. What time were you thinkin'?"

"How about I pick you up around eleven?"

"A quickie might be okay, too," she said.

"Maybe," he said. "But after breakfast, if we're in the mood." He needed to stay the course, get through this meeting without a scene. Sex just minutes before his breakup speech might blunt the point.

Heavy morning dew had coated the windshields and rooftops of the cars parked in front of Brenda's apartment building. A light rain had snuck in during the early morning hours and had added to the already oppressive humidity. As his old truck rolled to a stop in front of her building, he saw her watching from the third-story window. He touched the horn and waved. A moment later, she appeared in the door. Her beautiful, auburn hair flowed over her shoulders and glistened in the midmorning sun. She had paid a visit to the beauty shop, and by the look of it, she had extended her credit in the dress department at Dillard's.

She did a little turn, her heels clicking against the sidewalk. "Like my new dress?" She smiled.

"Sure do. Looks great with your hair."

She slid in beside him on the bench seat of the old Ford and greeted him with an affectionate peck on the cheek.

He pulled away from the apartment building and made his way to the Marriott. He felt that she deserved the best and the best was going to set him back a few bucks, but it would be worth it to end their time together on good terms. It wasn't that he didn't like her and she sure as hell turned him on. Even after two years, he had not grown tired of the sex. He just had no strong feelings for her one way or the other. He had never once considered taking her home to meet his mother. The thought of spending his life with her left him cold. He put his hand in her lap and fondled her thigh. He thought about the quickie and found himself regretting that he had not taken her up on it.

He pulled into the parking lot at the Marriott.

"This okay?"

"Sure, Honey. It's great. You know I love coming here, but you don't have to go all out just 'cause I got a new dress and had my hair done."

"And you do look great."

"Thanks. Got it on sale."

"We can have some quiet time to talk. And the food's good too." He read concern in her face and remembered how he'd felt when Jackie dumped him. He had not seen it coming. What he was about to do to Brenda made him no better than Jackie. But hell, he had always been honest with her. He had never lied about his intentions or his feelings. He had not misled her. If their deal had not been to her liking, she could have broken it off any time.

If only she wouldn't cry. He couldn't cope with a woman who cried. A face full of tears might buy her a few more days or weeks but nothing like a complete reassessment. No amount of crying would bring about a reversal of his decision to move on. It might prolong the agony, but it would not change the outcome. From now on, he hoped to spend all his free time with Abby. Brenda didn't deserve to be hurt, but his conscience was clear. She'd known the score.

Sloan chose a booth near the rear of the large dining room. The waiter returned with two frosty drinks. "Both twenty-one, right?"

They looked at one another and back at the waiter. She nodded timidly. The waiter winked and smiled.

"The buffet looks great today. I'm sure you'll enjoy it."

"We'll try it. Yes, we'll do the buffet," Sloan said decisively. He glanced her way. Brenda already had the straw between her lips, but he thought he could see apprehension in her hazel eyes. She wore a look of concern.

"Love the smell of lime and the tangy Tabasco," she said. She drew another long sip and forced a smile without removing the straw from between her teeth.

"What say we check out the spread?" Sloan said.

They found a place in the queue leading to the well-stocked buffet. They took plates and filed past the warming trays like mourners at a funeral. Sloan opened a tray and found sausage, bacon, hash brown potatoes, and eggs done three ways. They sampled everything, piling their plates high then returned to their booth and scooted in behind their drinks. Sloan was more intent on getting through the morning without a breakdown than enjoying the feast.

Brenda had no more than a passing interest in eggs Benedict or pigs in a blanket with real maple syrup. He hoped she would make the first move, but the longer he waited to spring his agenda, the more nervous they both became. He feared he might lose his nerve and change his mind. After all, she *was* great in the sack. That had to count for something. Abigale might be a prude and not go along with some of the kinky stuff he and Brenda did on occasion. And what made him so sure Abigale was "the one?" When it was all said and done, he might regret he ever let go of Brenda.

Brenda pushed her eggs around on her plate and glanced up at Sloan. "Any news from the Army, you know, on where you'll be going?"

"No, none. They'll wait till the last minute. It could be June before I know for sure." He looked at the ceiling and sighed deeply.

"Thought maybe you'd heard something." She focused on a link sausage that was floating in syrup. She carved it into small bites and chewed one without swallowing.

"Won't be surprised if they make me wait till graduation and expect me to be someplace the very next day." He glanced around the room to see if there was anyone there he knew.

"So, Sweetie, how're things at home? Your mom doin' okay? She get over that flu bug?"

"Yeah, she's fine. Working at her church a lot. Not much going on with her these days."

"And what about that brother of yours. Think he'll ever amount to anything?"

"He's happy doing what he loves so, hey, what do I care? We stay in touch. That's about all."

"Things going good for you at school? Not flunkin' out are you?"

"Nope, still making A's where it counts."

"That's good. Your daddy would be proud."

"Hey, what is this? The third degree?"

"No, Honey. Just trying to make conversation. We hardly ever talk, you and me." She folded her hands on the edge of the table and squeezed them tight. "Don't you think I care what's goin' on with you?"

Sloan parked his fork beside his plate. He had given up waiting for the right moment.

"Look Brenda, being with you these past two years has been great, and you know I care a lot about you. It's just that—well—I met someone at school and I want to spend more time with her. In a couple of months, I'll be leaving so we would be parting company then anyway. We always knew it would work that way, right?" He had gotten through the hard part without stumbling, losing his nerve, or changing his mind. It was short and sweet and to the point.

Brenda sat in silence and stared down at her plate. She carved and forked her eggs Benedict then shrugged. She glanced up at him. "You could still come over a few nights a week. She wouldn't have to know."

At first blush, it sounded like the best of both worlds. He imagined how it would work then thought better of the idea. He found it so difficult to let go of such a fine sack mate.

"That just wouldn't work. I'll have less time these next few months, you know, finishing my senior level course work. You know how hard that will be."

She studied his face in hopes of finding some way to break him down.

"She on the pill?"

"Come on Brenda, I barely know this chick. We sure as hell haven't gotten around to that. Least ways, not yet."

"I'll keep the apartment cleaner," she said looking at him with shiny eyes. "I know how you like everything neat all the time."

"That wouldn't change things."

She stared into her drink and stirred it with her straw. Tears formed in the corners of her eyes. Sloan knew he had better get it done before those tears got the best of him.

"It's over Brenda. Just accept it . . . let's be friends."

"Friends?" She stood and threw her napkin on her plate. "I want to leave," she demanded. "Take me home." She marched to the door and out into the covered parking area without looking back to see if he was following her.

He paid the check and found her waiting next to his truck. He drove back to her apartment and parked at the curb.

She stared at the dashboard and spoke in a monotone. "Tomorrow I'll put all your crap on the front porch. If you don't get it, the trash man will."

"Sounds fair."

"I hope you flunk your sorry ass out of school and have to take work baggin' groceries."

So much for a quickie, he thought.

XV

Thursday afternoon Sloan was at his study desk with a steaming cup of tea. Open books and papers were strewn over the desktop and onto the floor. It had been a tough week. With midterms looming, he'd had no time to think about Abigale. The specter of a sliding GPA was omnipresent. He had maintained a four point for three and a half years. He had worked hard for every grade, and if he could keep it together for a few more months it would all pay off.

Jake was lounging on his lawn chair and thumbing through a dog-eared issue of Playboy.

"Something's going on here, Sloan. You ain't been to the apartment all week. What gives here, professor? She's never been closed to the public for this long before."

"We kinda broke it off."

"Hot damn—my turn." Jake came right up on the edge of his seat.

"You'd do that? Move in on your roommate's stuff before he's sure he's done with it?"

"What? You thinkin' you'll double back?"

"If this new thing don't work out, sure. Why not?"

"So, this new thing—let me guess—is the Boston babe, right?"

"Nothing's for sure. It's been damn near a week since our date and zilch, not a peep."

"What do you figure? One date with you and she's back in the Voodoo Vette? Could be she wants to make old number seven a little jealous."

The phone rang and Jake grabbed it off the hook.

"Jake here. Yeah, you got the right number. If I can get him to come out from under a pile of study notes. . . cramming, midterms . . . I know… I told him the—Let me see if I can revive him. Don't mean you and me can't take in a movie until he gets freed up . . . okay . . . think he's coming around." Jake cupped his hand over the receiver and shot a leering smile in Sloan's direction.

"Are you *in* for some babe with a Yankee accent? Sounds nice. Think it just might be the Boston babe."

Sloan grabbed the receiver out of Jake's hands and took a deep breath. "Hey Abigale. What's happening?" He feigned indifference.

"What're you doing on this gorgeous afternoon?" she asked.

"Putting some time in on the books, what else?"

"Don't tell me you're cramming for midterms! If you don't know it by now—"

"You could be right. Not exactly cramming, more like brushing up. I'm a slave to the old GPA."

"What say you throw all that crap in the corner and buy me a basket of fried shrimp?"

"Sounds like a great idea. I could do with some of Joe's shrimp—not always fresh though."

"To hell with Joe's. I'm talkin' Apalachicola."

He glanced down at his stack of study notes. "Apalach? Why didn't you say so? Give me a minute and I'll check the bus schedules."

"I've got wheels if your ego will allow a woman to drive you."

"I'm over that chauvinistic stuff. Got no pride. When?"

"I'll pick you up at two."

"Two? It's a quarter till now."

"Be out front in twenty minutes. We can be on the beach in an hour." Without waiting for a reply, she hung up.

"Where we headed?" Jake asked.

"We? Not this time, old buddy."

"What happened to sharing with your roomie?"

"Out the window. Get your own date. I hear Joanie's still in the market and she likes cute guys. Look, man, don't wait up. This could take a while. Here's an idea. While I'm out of your way, why don't you clean your half of our pigsty? As I recollect, the last time you made a move toward housekeeping was when you flunked inspection and pulled weekend duty. And that was with the OD standing over you."

"Least you could do is toss me Brenda's number, seeing as how you're done with her."

"Man, you got no shame."

"Look who's talkin'."

Sloan threw some beach gear in a duffle bag along with a bottle of cheap chardonnay. He squirted his underarms with a shot of Mennen and ran for the door. In no time flat, he was waiting on the curb for his ride. Before he had time to contemplate and analyze what was happening, a red roadster rounded the corner and screeched to a stop at the curb in front of the ROTC dorm. Dust bellowed up from beneath the low-slung carriage.

"Hey, good looking. Want a ride?" Abigale shouted over the roar of the tightly wound little engine.

"Where'd you—" Sloan stammered.

"Throw your crap in the back."

"You didn't tell me you had a sports car."

"Daddy bought it new in '67 and gave it to me when I turned twenty."

Sloan ran his hand along the sleek fender.

"If I'm not mistaken, this here's an Austin Healey 3000. Am I right? I've never seen one except in magazines and sure as hell never been in one. Man, she's a beauty."

"Get in," she screamed with excitement in her voice.

Sloan grabbed the windscreen and dropped into the leather bucket on the passenger side.

With no loss of motion, she rammed the little sports car into gear and popped the clutch, leaving tire marks on the pavement and smoke from burning rubber.

She steered her red Healey west and south out of town, giving the British six-banger all it would take.

"I know a place where we can get some great shrimp," he shouted over the roar of the engine and the five-speed gear box.

"Perfect."

"You like oysters?"

She made a face and stuck out her tongue. "Yuck. Too slimy for my delicate palate."

"Not supposed to chew them, you know. You just swallow 'em whole. They slide right down."

"You can have my share," she shouted back at him. Her scarf flowed behind the little red roadster.

The engine, the screaming gear box, and the wind howling through the open cockpit made conversation next to impossible. After eighty of the fastest miles the little Healey could muster and stay on the right side of the law, they topped the causeway and rolled onto St. George Island.

"Pull in over there," he shouted. "This is the place. They have good shrimp baskets and a great stretch of beach."

"You can stop shouting. I can hear you fine now." She steered the 3000 into the parking lot and skidded to a stop in front of a rundown seafood restaurant.

She brushed her hair off her face with the back of her hand. "Are you sure about this place, Preppy?"

"Yeah, don't let the looks fool you. It's the Ritz."

They pulled up the canvas top, fastened it to the windscreen, and went inside.

A square Tiki Bar with tall stools on all four sides provided a centerpiece for the beachfront diner. Tables with umbrellas were available on the deck. Sloan chose one with a view of the beach and the Gulf of Mexico.

"Hey Carol," he shouted to the waitress. "Bring us two shrimp baskets and a couple of beers."

"Sure, Sloan. Comin' up," Carol said. "So tell me, big guy, how's school treatin' ya?"

"Crazy. If I can only hold it together for a couple more months."

Abigale was astonished. "So, you know the wait staff too?"

"Her? Yeah, we're old buds. How about that beach?"

"Beautiful," she said. "Will we be able to see the sunset?"

"So, you like sunsets?"

"Yeah, love. My favorite time of day."

"No, we can't see it from here, but we can walk up the beach a ways and get the full show, if you want to."

"What? You don't like sunsets?"

"They're okay, but I'm a sunrise man myself."

Abigale shed her beach jacket.

"Nice suit."

She shrugged. "It's comfortable." She dug through her beach bag and came up with a well-squeezed tube of sun lotion and proceeded to liberally apply it to all that was not covered. Sloan was dying to offer his help, but thought better of it. He didn't know her well enough to be placing his hands on her. There would be time enough for that.

She pursed her lips into a "please," handed the tube to Sloan, and pointed to her back. How could he refuse? He squirted a handful of lotion in one palm and rubbed his hands together then liberally applied the lotion to her back.

A cool spring breeze moved across the veranda, bringing with it the scent of salt air.

"So Sloan, tell me something about yourself that I haven't already figured out."

"Let me see." He parked his sunglasses on top of his head like James Dean. "Where should I begin. So much to tell."

"Start with that name. Don't think I ever met a Sloan before."

"Mother's maiden name. Full name's John Sloan Abernathy. As a boy, I went by John, Johnny. In high school, there were lots of Johns but no Sloans—so I started going by Sloan. My old man still called me Johnny."

"Come on, Sloan. You missed a big spot right there, above my waist."

"Where?"

"There."

"Got that already."

"Put more. Don't you love the smell of cocoa butter and the Jessica McLint—

"Yeah, your perfume is driving me wild but you're about out of lotion."

"Now you know what to get me for my birthday."

"When?"

"Oh, sometime next year. Abernathy, is that Irish?"

"My great grandfather came over from Dublin. Mother's part Cherokee, from Oklahoma. Sloan is Celtic. Goes back to early medieval times, means warrior. Kinda fits, don't you think?"

"Why? Because you march around the quad in formation?"

"Who's ready for shrimp?" Carol asked as she parked baskets of golden fried shrimp in front of each of them.

"How about you? Tell me about . . . LaHolm is French, right?"

"You are so good at guessing games." She cut her eyes sideways. "French Canadian. My parents worked in fishing in Canada and then Boston, where I joined the clan. My father owned a fleet of lobster boats, but sold them. Now they live large in Boston and summers in Vero Beach."

"Explains the Healey," Sloan said.

"My father can afford a few toys, and he *loves* cars."

"He had his nerve naming you Abigale."

"Why so?"

"Abby g-a-i-l is the name of the girl in the *Witches of Salem* scandal that took place back in the sixteen hundreds, just north of Boston."

"Could be why they changed the spelling to g-a-l-e."

"You like surprises?" Sloan said.

"Oh, Sloan, I love surprises. Tell me, what is it?"

"Hope you're ready for this. I brought along a vintage chardonnay to enjoy on our beach walk."

"Mmm, sounds great. Let's see." He pulled the bottle of wine from his duffle bag making sure to cover the label with his hand to prolong the suspense. He slowly moved his hand down the bottle like he had seen David Niven do in an old black and white movie.

"Mogen David! What makes you think I'd drink from the bottom shelf? Just what kind of wino do you think I am?"

"Everything's relative, my dear. You haven't lived 'til you've toasted the setting sun with a good bottle of MD from fine crystal."

"Oh! You brought the good crystal too?"

Sloan retrieved two plastic cups from his duffel.

"Preppy, you're *full* of surprises. So, where's the corkscrew? Bet you forgot to bring it."

"This works fine." He took a knife from the table, pushed the cork into the bottle and filled both cups with the cheap, warm white wine. He held up his cup to offer a toast.

"Here's looking at you, kid. Let's walk. Toss me your shoes. I have room for them in the duffel."

"Don't you need to pay our bill?"

"They trust me."

They sipped their wine and walked west into the setting sun. He reached for her hand only to find her reaching for his.

"Tell me, Abby. Have you ever been in love?" He was embarrassed at having asked such a question, but he had to know more about her.

"No, don't think I have. But, let me see. In high school, I had a steady guy and in my freshman year at BC, I dated several men. But no one special. As soon as the new wore off, I lost interest. College men are mostly after one thing. I suppose I just haven't met that special someone."

Sloan could not help but wonder if she had slept with any of them.

They finished their wine and Sloan stuffed the plastic glasses back into the duffel for later.

She stepped out in front of him and walked backwards on the warm sand still holding his hand. The setting sun illuminated his face. She cocked her head, eying him with interest.

Sloan hoped she saw kindness, caring and sincerity in his face. He knew she would not be one he could push into the sack at the first opportunity, nor did he want that kind of relationship with her. "You a virgin?"

She feigned shock. "Hey, you're getting a little—"

"Sorry, didn't mean to—"

"Thought it went without saying. You?" she asked, still walking backwards and looking into his face. "Were you ever stuck on any one girl?"

Sloan kicked at a sand crab running for its hole. "Oh, sure. Lots of times. I had it bad for a girl in high school, but she dumped me for the quarterback." A long wave caught them by surprise and soaked them to their knees. They ran from the wave like two plovers.

"Not worried are you . . . that it could happen again?"

Sloan put his head down then looked out to sea and slung a seashell he had been carrying. "It has crossed my mind. High profile jocks can make an awesome impression on a delicate lady."

"Well, you needn't worry. He doesn't have a chance, and I'm no delicate lady, thank you."

"Second time you've told me that."

He stopped and reached for her other hand. "Listen, do you think we can have a relationship without playing games? Is it possible that we would always tell the truth, never lie to one another?"

A curious seagull swooped down for a closer look. "Walking barefoot in the sand feels wonderful," she said, leading him with one hand. "No games?" She looked back at him over her shoulder. "It's a deal. I'll always speak the truth where you're concerned. Now, back to your high school sweetie. What happened after she dumped you?"

"Pretty much what you would expect. She and this football hero started going steady. The usual story of high school love affairs. He knocked her up and left her high and dry. She had his baby and gave it up for adoption."

"He didn't marry her? The heel."

"Being a husband and father didn't fit with his plans, him being slated for a college team and all."

"You could've helped her. Why didn't you step in? You could've beat the guy up and been her knight in shining armor, her hero. She might have taken you back."

"Suppose so, but my old man would not have approved. If it had been my baby, my dad would've made sure I owned up and, between the two of us, we'd have taken care of her and the baby."

"Tell me more about him."

"Who, the quarterback?"

"No, Preppy. Your father. I want to know all about your dad."

"Dad? He was great. I always thought of him as a sagebrush kind of man."

"Not sure what that means . . . sagebrush man?"

"You know. Honest, tough, smart, and fiercely independent, but above all he cared about his family. He was all about tough love but he had a good heart. He was just about the best father a guy could have. Always there when I needed him. He didn't have much in the way of formal education, but he was plenty smart when it came to making things out of wood or metal. He worked hard all his life."

"Doing what? What kind of work did he do?"

"Mostly, he worked with his hands. He taught himself welding and made a damn good living in the oil field. He was faithful to Mom, at least as far as I know. I think they fell in love the first time they met at the barn dance on Saturday night. Dad played the fiddle and was locally famous as a musician and a poet. He learned all that on his own, too."

"You mean he never had lessons?"

"Nope. It just came natural to him. Mom and Dad used to tell the story of how they were living on neighboring farms in Oklahoma. Mom told us how the other girls were talking about Dad. She told them to keep their hands off him because she was going to marry him—and she did. Dad always carried her picture in his wallet. He had one that was taken about the time they were married. She was a beautiful woman and still is."

"So, your old man is your moral compass?"

"You bet. What he taught me about life keeps me on track—at least most of the time."

She swung his arm playfully. "Do tell. And what is it you learned from him that keeps you on the old straight and narrow?"

"First and foremost, he taught me a sense of duty and obligation to my family and loved ones. He taught me that I had to be responsible for my actions. If I got a girl in trouble, it was up to me to see her through it. And he taught me how to shoot a decent game of pool."

"It's good you have that to fall back on, you know, if you can't cut it as an engineer."

"He put my brother through college, but when it came my turn, the economy had tanked and he was out of work."

"So, ROTC," she said.

"My best hope for getting an education. That and working summers on a shrimp boat or roughnecking in the oil patch."

"That explains why you know the waitress."

"I spent a few nights on this beach. Shrimp, oysters, and plenty of beer to wash 'em down. Lots of good hell-raising takes place right here."

"Where's he now, your father? What happened to him?"

Sloan stared over her head at the horizon. "He died, over two years ago now. Lung cancer."

"Now, it's all coming clear," she said. "The real reason you're in Rotcie is that your Dad was sick and couldn't help you."

"Something like that. He left a little money behind, but Mom needed it."

"Any of your stories have happy endings?"

"Some. Mother still lives in the family home in west Texas."

"She remarried?"

"No, and I doubt she ever will. They were so close. She could never make it work with another man."

"She must get lonely though."

"My brother lives close by. He's an Episcopal priest with a small parish in south Texas. I get back home when I can, Christmas and summer breaks."

"Sloan, are you religious? Do you attend church like your brother?"

"Not often. I believe I have a soul. Don't need to go to church to prove that. My brother was always into the ceremonial side of religion, you know, the robe and all the rituals."

"So, in all these years at FSU you haven't grown any attachments?"

"There was one."

"Come on, tell. I came clean with you. No games, remember."

"It was nothing serious. A relationship of convenience. And anyway, it's over."

"And when did it end?"

"Sunday. I broke it off with her last Sunday."

She dropped his hand. "Sunday!" She propped her knuckles on her hips. "Sloan, today is Thursday. You're telling me you broke up with your girlfriend of two years just five days ago—after our first date?"

She crossed her arms, looked at her feet and walked on in silence making no effort to keep pace with Sloan.

"Hey, we agreed. No games, remember? Look, Abigale. I spent time with her to relieve the tensions of pounding the books night and day. She knew our friendship would end when I graduated and took a Rotcie assignment.

Sloan searched Abigale's face for signs of acceptance, understanding, or forgiveness. She returned a blank stare. He could feel her slipping away. It was time to play his trump card. "After our date last Saturday, I felt good about us. I felt a connectedness that I had never felt before in my life—with anyone." Her eyes were fixed on the sandy beach in front of her.

"Well, say someth—"

"You're one cocksure son of a bitch. Are you going to continue seeing her?"

"No. I promise you. It's over. That won't happen. I ended it."

"Look, Sloan. At this moment, we're just friends with no commitments, but if I hear of you going back over to your little love nest, you and me are done. Over. History. Can you dig it?" She shook her fist at him to make her point.

"Plain enough for me. No games there."

She kicked the sand hard, showering the edge of the surf. "Okay, let that be the end of it. We need say no more." She put out her hand. He took it and they continued up the beach. "Now, where was I?"

Gratefully, he squeezed her hand. "Your fisherman dad and his sports cars."

"Right. My dad, who loves sports cars, and his only daughter. Unfortunately for me, in that order. The two of you would have lots to talk about.

"Sounds to me like you've got it made, so why 're you knocking yourself out to get through school?"

"Suppose I *could* live off Mom and Dad, but what would that make me? Not a very interesting person, that's for sure. I want to be more than a housewife, not that there's anything wrong with raising kids. I just don't see myself as a mother and homemaker and nothing more."

"So, you don't want a family?"

"Not a baseball team, that's for damn sure. One or two would be manageable."

"Me, I want a basketball team."

She ignored his ridiculous family plan. "So Sloan, what're you going to do to make your millions?"

"After my two years are up, I hope to do something technical. You know, state-of-the-art engineering or research and development. And down the road, I'll go into marketing, or sales in a startup company."

"I could see you doing sales or even running your own company, once you grow up."

Sloan stopped short and stared out at the Gulf. "I have three goals. First, I want to accumulate enough wealth to be anonymous. Second, I want to sail away on my own yacht and never have to ask anyone for anything. Not saying I would, but I want to be able to if it suits me."

"Everybody wants the wealth part, but that anonymous thing is going right over my head."

"If you're truly anonymous, you can have all the money in the world and walk down the street without being recognized. It's that simple."

"I see. And the third? What's your third goal, Preppy?" He pulled the half-full bottle from his duffel along with the plastic cups and poured the last of the wine.

"Enjoying the MD? Good month, don't you agree?"

"The third, Sloan. What's your third goal?" She squeezed his hand and stopped dead.

"Soul mate, he said. "I want to find my soul mate."

"Oh? So what in hell's a soul mate anyhow?"

"Comes from Greek mythology. Plato talks about humans as having four arms, four legs, and a single head with two faces, but the great God Zeus split them in half so everyone would spend their lives in search of their other half."

"Where do you come up with this crap? You don't think for a minute you and I are—"

"It's just a concept, a way of explaining how people meet and fall in love. Dad said it was love at first sight when he met Mom."

Sloan spotted a dead tree that had washed ashore in a storm. "That should be a perfect place to sit and watch old Sol take his last bow before he disappears into the sea." As they were walking toward the tree, he saw something on the sand and stopped to pick it up. He wiped it clean with his shirt tail and handed it to Abigale.

"Know what this is?"

She took the small irregular object in the palm of her hand and rolled it around to inspect it. "Not sure Sherlock, but I would say that this here's a piece of broken glass."

"Ah, true but this is no ordinary piece of glass. This just happens to be a fine specimen of ruby sea glass."

"Yeah, but still just a piece of an old bottle, right?"

"These beaches are strewn with glass that was cast off from ships at sea. It gets broken into small pieces and buffed by the sand. Brown and clear are common, but red is quite rare. This small piece of glass could be over five hundred years old."

"And you're giving it to me? How nice."

"A token of our—uh—friendship. The ruby glass most likely came from an old ship's lantern made in Europe. They used red lenses on the port side of the ship. Sometimes the ship's compass would have lanterns built into it to help them navigate at sea. More interesting than a bottle for rum or arthritis medicine, don't you think?"

Sloan climbed onto the dead tree and sat down. She backed into his arms so they were both facing the setting sun.

He put his arms around her waist, brushed her hair aside and kissed her neck.

She turned to face him.

He pulled her close and kissed her hard on the lips.

She put her arms around his neck. All the while she clutched the shard of ruby sea glass.

"We need to head back," he said quietly.

"Hell with that. I'm not going anywhere." She hugged Sloan around the waist and put her nose to his.

They kissed again.

"Midterms, remember?"

She pushed him away and looked into his eyes.

"Are you always going to be so dammed responsible?"

"Uh huh. It's the engineer in me." Sloan pulled her close and kissed her again.

They made their way back down the beach. Sloan found Carol and paid their tab. Abigale fired up the little red Healey, rammed it into gear and roared back over the causeway.

While Abigale was busy driving, Sloan had time to reflect. He tried to think of some way to commemorate the day. Something they would both easily remember.

"What day is it?" he asked.

"Second April," she said.

"You mean Millay's Second April from our American Lit?"

"Actually, it's April the second, Preppy."

"We must remember this day."

"The day we started our sea glass collection," she said. She handed the shard of red glass to Sloan. "Here, you'd better keep it. I don't seem to have any pockets in this bikini and besides, I'm prone to losing things. Remember that, if you ever decide to buy me a big diamond ring."

The hour was late and the sun had long since given way to a sky adorned with stars. Sloan knew she didn't see his smile. At least in his roughneck West Texas world, there was only one reason to give a girl a big diamond ring.

Abigale skidded the roadster to a stop at the curb in front of the ROTC dorm.

"When can I see you again?" he said.

"Most any time."

"How 'bout Saturday?"

"Hmm. Saturday might not be good. Can I let you know?"

Sloan's heart fell.

"Don't tell me. You have a date with Brad?"

"How could I have known you'd want to see me again?"

"Can you get out of it?"

"I think I feel a cold coming on and he's deathly afraid of catching cold. It might cause him to miss a workout with the team."

"So, we're set for Saturday? You can give *me* your cold. I won't mind."

"What time? And what are we doing?"

"Do you have a bicycle?"

"Sure, but—"

"I'll be at your dorm at one o'clock on Saturday."

XVI

Sloan arrived at Abigale's sorority house at one o'clock sharp. She was waiting on the front stoop with her bicycle. Everything she was wearing matched, from her helmet to her biking shoes.

"What is it with you?" Sloan asked. "You must have a subscription to the Neiman Marcus catalogue."

He placed his bike in the parking rack and put his hands out to greet her. He didn't attempt to kiss her. Even a West Texas roughneck knew better than to kiss a lady on the mouth in public.

She spread her arms and turned. "Like my biking duds? From the looks of it, you could use a little help in the fashion department."

Sloan was wearing a blue t-shirt and jeans with an elastic band around his right calf to keep his pant leg from getting caught in his chain. His bike was an old ten-speed Schwinn with saddlebags over the rear tire.

"What's in the bags?"

"Lunch and everything else we might need for a biking safari across campus."

"So, what's for lunch, Bawana?"

"Snacks, sandwiches, and the now traditional bottle of MD with fine crystal."

"And just what else do you have in there?"

"Usual stuff: bug spray, hand soap, compass, ground cloth, and blanket." He grinned devilishly. "You know. . . just in case."

"Usual stuff? A compass? I'm taking a bike ride with a dude who brings survival gear on a Saturday afternoon bike ride."

"Grab your bike. I'm hungry."

They meandered along roads and paths that led through the campus. After an hour, they arrived at a small lake, a vacant picnic table, and an inviting patch of freshly mowed grass. Sloan leaned his bike against a tree and spread the blanket on the grass. He retrieved sandwiches and snacks and laid them out on the blanket along with the wine, which he had decanted into a Listerine bottle to disguise it from a campus cop who might be itching to enforce some ancient campus liquor law.

"Not sure they'll believe we're so concerned about fresh breath, but if we *are* hassled, I'll fake a gargle."

"Please," she said. "I'd rather be arrested."

They spent an hour making small talk, sharing sandwiches, and sipping Listerine from plastic cups.

"The music department is doing a rendition of The Fantastic's. What say we check it out?"

"I've always wanted to see it." She roped her arms around her bent knees. "I love the music." He had never heard note one, but the show meant more time with her.

"If we have any hope of making the opening scene, we should start back. I presume your calendar's open for the evening?"

She faked a cough and a sneeze.

"I'll pick you up at seven," Sloan said.

"Are we riding our bikes?"

"I have wheels. Think you're the only one who inherited a vintage machine?"

"You have a car? I didn't know you had a car."

"Wheels," he corrected her. "Don't worry. If it rains, you'll stay dry."

At seven sharp, Sloan slid to a stop in the loading zone in front of Abigale's sorority house. In the crowd of people and traffic, she did not see him until he was halfway up the steps. She was waiting on the top step and looked past the old pickup truck. "Where did you paak?" she asked.

"Right there. In front."

"Not that jalopy?"

"Ain't she a beauty? My father bought it new and gave it to me when I turned sixteen."

He opened the passenger door and extended his hand as if he were ushering her into a horse-drawn carriage for a ride through Central Park.

She hesitated, then climbed in. "Let's get out of here before anyone sees us."

"Yeah, they'll want to ride in back. Happens all the time."

They arrived at the campus theater just as the first act was getting underway. She chose perfect seats, halfway down and on the aisle.

As the performers were singing the last chorus of *Deep in December,* Abigale and Sloan made a dash for the exit. Sloan always thought it best to beat the rush and avoid being caught up in a crowd of people who might waste his time.

"Must be a miracle cure," came a boisterous male voice from behind them.

"Yes," Abigale said, without turning to face the rude young man. She gestured toward Sloan, "Thanks to this genius, he knows an old home remedy for the common cold. Brad, say howdy to Sloan."

Sloan turned to face his nemesis. They shook hands like two prizefighters about to retreat to their neutral corners.

"That's right," Sloan said. "Old family recipe. You should try it."

"Tell me more," Brad said, moving close to Sloan almost to the point of being nose-to-nose. "Nothing I hate more'n a cold," he added, with a grin that broke the tension between them. Sloan took a step back. "Chew two aspirin and gargle some warm whiskey. Works every time. Guaranteed."

"And don't forget the Listerine," Abigale chimed in.

"Listerine, huh?" Brad seemed skeptical.

"So Brad, I didn't know you were keen on theater?" Abigale said as she looked up into his face.

"Class assignment. I'll get extra credit for my ticket stub and, thanks to your cold, I had a free evening, so I decided to check it out. I thought it was pretty damn good for a bunch of sissies dancing around on stage. What about you?" He directed his question to her, turning his body in a way that shut Sloan out of the discussion.

"I wouldn't have even known about it if Sloan here hadn't told me." She threaded her arm through Sloan's. "He's all into this cultural stuff, but he knows football too."

"Yeah? That's great." Brad chuckled, taking a couple of steps backwards and out of Sloan's space. Sloan figured Brad was cutting his losses and moving on until the odds were in his favor. "Good meeting you, Slag."

"That would be Sloan," Abigale corrected him. "Name's Sloan, J. Sloan Abernathy." She said it as though he might someday run for president.

"Beg your pardon. Sloan. Call you soon, Abby. Catch ya later, J. Sloan." With that farewell, Brad jogged up the walk to rejoin his teammates.

"Nice guy," Sloan said. He hoped this would be the last time he would have to deal with this smart aleck footballer.

They found the old truck and drove in the direction of the sorority house.

Abigale laughed quietly.

"What's so damn funny?" Sloan asked, still somewhat rattled over his nose-to-nose confrontation with Brad.

"Just wishing he had seen your ride, that's all."

"And what's wrong with my ride? I don't see anything funny about a vintage, American-made, not to mention classic, pickup truck."

"No, nothing. Really. To get the joke, you'd have to see what he drove on our date last week."

"Oh, no!" Sloan exclaimed. "You didn't ride in the dreaded Voodoo Vette?"

She turned toward to him in her seat. "How'd you know Brad has a Vette? And what is this crap about Voodoo?"

"It's all the talk on campus. Legend has it that once a girl rides in the quarterback's red Vette, they're spoiled, hexed, ruined for any other man."

"Sounds like campus voodoo crapola to me. No man's gonna ruin me with a ride in his car, and that includes you with this beat-up old wreck."

XVII

In the weeks that followed, Sloan and Abigale became inseparable. They rode their bikes through campus and stopped at quaint shops for coffee and sandwiches or pedaled to Joe's for burgers and beer. They often met Jake and his squeeze du jour for a few rounds at Joe's or some other local hangout. Jake never kept a girlfriend for long, but was never without at least one potential conquest. Abigale arranged dates for him with her sorority sisters, but the relationships never lasted for more than a few outings. When it came to female company, Jake had his own agenda. For him it was all about being there, not about having fun along the way.

On weekends, they drove the Healey to St. George Island where they splashed in the surf, ate fried shrimp, and took long walks on the beach. They talked about what each of them would do after graduation. Sloan anticipated being assigned to a military base in Florida, Georgia, or Texas, and Abby had another year before she finished her degree.

Sometime during the course of this whirlwind romance, it became evident to both of them that they wanted to spend their lives together. There was no one time or event that established the fact. Sloan did not propose marriage or suggest a lifetime commitment, nor did she broach the subject with him. It just became evident, as time passed, that they had bonded for life. Their conversation became more "we" than "I" or "you and me." The plan for building a life together happened almost without discussion. It was as if they awoke one morning and found themselves of one mind. She would graduate in a year and join him on some military base for the duration of his active duty. What could be simpler?

Late on a Saturday after a long walk on the beach, they sat down to watch the sunset. Abigale was cold, so Sloan gathered driftwood from the dunes and stacked it teepee fashion on the sand. He stuffed scraps of paper and dry leaves under the pile and lit it with a lighter that had belonged to his dad. The flames licked the driftwood and the pungent smoke followed them regardless of where they sat around the fire.

"A good omen," Sloan said. "The great chiefs in the sky send us message." He mocked an Indian dance around the fire then grabbed her hand and pulled her to her feet. They did a sort of jitterbug in the sand then both sat cross-legged looking at the fire. He put his arms around her. She leaned back in them.

"Graduation's next week. Think you'll pass?" she asked.

"No, thanks to you. It's a good thing we didn't meet last year or I'd be squeaking by with C's."

"I wouldn't consider myself much of a distraction if I couldn't knock you down at least one grade point."

The sun sank to the horizon and hid from view behind thunderclouds that lingered on the western horizon.

"Just look at those storm clouds," Sloan said. "Reminds me of when I was working on fishing boats. Weather like that can make it tough on fishermen who are out there trying to pull their living from the sea. All a fisherman wants out of life is to fill his boat and get home in time for mass on Sunday. They live simple, straightforward, honest lives."

"Hard work made a man out of you, huh, Sloan?"

"It helped. Not sure I've made the grade yet. Want some coffee? I spiked it with some of that brandy you like."

"Sure."

"Wonder if Daddy would think I've become a man?"

She studied his strong face in the flickering light. "I think he would."

The cups warmed their hands and the hot spiked coffee fortified them against the evening chill. They watched the cold front as it moved across the Gulf.

Sloan stretched out on the sand and propped his head on his elbow. Abigale snuggled between him and the fire. The cheerful flames warmed their shadows as they drifted into a meditative silence, mesmerized by the crackling fire, the setting sun, and the stars that began to show. First there was one, then ten and, in another instant, a thousand.

Abigale broke the silence. "Something I've been meaning to ask."

"Ask." He thoughtfully poured a handful of sand out of his closed fist and watched the grains fall as he studied the angle of repose.

"Children. You don't seriously want a large family, do you?"

"Not real big. I'm thinking four boys and three girls, but I'll leave the final count up to you. After all, it'll be you who has to do all the work. Carrying them around for nine months."

"Two," Abigale said.

"Pretty sure it's nine months," he said.

"No silly, a girl for you and a boy for me, and that's my best offer. Sloan Junior and Wendy."

"If you already knew what you wanted, why'd you ask? And Wendy? Where'd you come up with that?"

"Just seems like the right name for our daughter. I can see her now." Abigale laced her fingers and put her hands behind her head as she stretched out on the cool sand. "Our daughter will be so full of fun and mischief."

"Wendy. I can see her too, running through the house or riding her pony in a field. Always dreamed of having a pony when I was a kid growing up."

"Wouldn't Daddy buy you a pony?"

"No place in town for a pony," he said, ". . . and she would call me Daddy."

"Daddykins." Abigale assured him.

"No. Pretty sure I wouldn't put up with that." He pulled her close and kissed her.

"What say we get started on the first one right now?" he said. "All this talk of having babies is making me crazy."

She pushed him away and propped herself up on one elbow. "What gives here, Sloan? You going soft on our vow of chastity?"

"Maybe. Aren't you? I can't wait."

"I can and so can you. I want our lives to be perfect and if I got pregnant now, you'd feel trapped. I'm not on the pill you know. Never have been."

"So, trap me. It would be cool to think our Wendy was conceived here on our favorite beach under this spring sky with those pesky plovers pecking at our toes."

"Sloan, you are such a romantic. Okay–let's do it!"

Sloan was surprised by her sudden change of heart.

He unbuckled his belt, rolled over on top of her, maneuvered his knee between her legs and put his hand where he had never dared before. Her eyes closed. He saw excitement and passion reflected in the flickering fire. She shivered from his touch.

"Wait, no. Enough of this nonsense." With one hard shove, she pushed him off.

He rolled into the edge of the fire. His nylon jacket ignited like gasoline.

She dragged him free of the fire and smothered the flames with a handful of sand.

"So, that's what they mean by hot in the sack," she laughed hysterically and grabbed another handful of sand and playfully rubbed it in his hair. He lay back on the sand and she snuggled into the crook of his arm. Breathing hard, they stared at the now moonlit, star-studded sky. The mood passed. Sloan re-buckled his Texas-shaped belt buckle, the primeval mood thwarted.

"So much for the physical side of our love," she said, "but just for now."

These last few weeks had brought Sloan great joy and he rejoiced in his good fortune. In his wildest dreams, he would not have imagined he would meet his true love under such circumstances. So many stars had to be aligned. . . Had he not accompanied Jake to that sorority social . . . had Abigale not arranged to meet Brad for dinner.

If dog rabbit, Daddy used to say. If the dog hadn't stopped to scratch fleas, he'd a caught the rabbit.

For two years now, the Army had met Sloan's needs for tuition, books, and a roof. Soon it would be time for him to live up to his side of the bargain. He had to render his pound of flesh. He worried that he might lose his edge on the job market and his place with Abigale, but like it or not, Uncle Sam was calling the shots. His only hope was to get a good assignment where he could gain experience that would make him more valuable in industry and close enough to Abigale to see her on a regular basis. After all his work and sweat, he still had to rely on luck, which went against his grain as he did not believe in luck except for the kind he made for himself.

Sloan sat slumped over a beer. Abigale hopped onto the bar stool next to him. "So, what's up, Cowboy? What gives?"

He fumbled with an envelope and withdrew some official-looking papers. "Got my orders."

"Great! Where we headed? DC, the Pentagon, White House?"

He unfolded the documents and pushed them across the bar to her. He held his head in his hands while she waded through the military jargon. She looked up in total disbelief.

"Spain? Are there Army bases in Spain?"

"Several. This here's a small high-tech base located on the outskirts of Madrid. There's no more 'n a hundred people stationed there."

"We were thinking Kansas or Georgia, never thought we would be separated by an ocean. What the hell? . . . No big deal. When do we leave?"

"I have to be there by June the fifth."

"First week in June? That's not even two weeks. I can't be ready to move to Spain in two weeks. I'll need to renew my passport, get some new clothes. Nothing in my closet is right for summer in Spain. . . gets hot there in the summer."

"Look, Abby. I've been thinking. Might be best if you wait and come over once I get settled and know the drill. You have another year to go on your degree. Maybe you should stay and finish, then join me in nine months or so."

"Nine months? That sounds like such a long—I could have a baby in nine months."

"Well, we can talk about that later."

"I'm just about there," she smiled.

"I'll come back on leave and we can get married in Boston or Vero, or anywhere you want."

"If I don't go now, I'm afraid—"

"Of what?"

"Losing you."

He put his arm around her. A tear rolled down her cheek. He caught it on his sleeve. It is so unlike her to cry, he thought.

He took her by the shoulders. "Look, Abby. We're soul mates, you and me. You're the one true love of my life and I'll never let you go. Our time apart will make our love stronger. You can come to Spain and visit anytime you want or I'll come back on leave when I save some money."

"Promise?" She draped her arms around his neck.

"On Daddy's grave."

He meant what he said, but there was little doubt that Sloan was hearing traveling music. The idea of living in Madrid was exciting. He would meet new people, learn a new culture. He had not sacrificed for four years to be an also-ran and Spain—now that he thought about it—was a better reward for his efforts than Kansas or Georgia.

XVIII

The days leading up to commencement were fraught with anxiety. Sloan needed to arrange a flight to transport his mother to Tallahassee and air travel had not been on his college curriculum so Abigale took charge. She arranged the flight and garnered a commitment from Jake that he would drive Sloan's truck to the airport, collect Mrs. Abernathy, and tuck her safely into her room at a local motel.

On Graduation Day, Sloan occupied a chair in the auditorium along with hundreds of other students who had earned degrees or honors during the last semester. Abernathy would be among the first called, but about the last to exit the auditorium.

Before the first candidate received his sheepskin, the audience had to endure the obligatory commencement address. The school could not afford an important politician or a famous writer, so Dean Marshall did the honors. As the dean droned on about doing old FSU proud, Sloan wondered if these people ever had anything original to say.

The time had come to receive the long-awaited acknowledgment of his achievements.

Doctor Marshall stood behind the podium which was draped in the school seal and colors. As the candidates' names were called, Marshall surrendered the diplomas. When it was Sloan's turn, Dr. Marshall announced, with a full measure of school pride, "Mr. John Sloan Abernathy is graduating with high honors from the School of Electrical Engineering, having maintained a four-year grade point average of 3.95. One interesting note about Mr. Abernathy," Marshall said. "Up until his last semester, Mr. Abernathy carried a four point GPA, but something must have happened in his last semester that caused him to log a B in advanced differential solutions. Something tells me there's a story behind that B, huh, Mr. Abernathy?"

The audience cheered and applauded. Sloan levitated across the stage, took his sheepskin in his left hand, and held up his right for a high five with the dean.

Graduation signaled an end to four years of grinding out grades, meeting degree requirements, and balancing his libido with his determination to conquer the academic world. He had done it and he was damned proud. He owed a debt of thanks to so many—even Brenda. After all, she had kept him out of bars, off the streets, and focused on his goal. An enormous sense of pride welled up in him. He had done it. Dad told him he could and Dad had been right about so many things.

Sloan was omnipotent. He could do anything he set his mind to. He would be successful. He would marry Abigale and have children. He would land a great job and achieve great wealth and anonymity. Dad said it would be so and he was seldom wrong.

Once the mortar boards floated back to earth, numerous alumnae gathered on the front steps of the auditorium for pictures.

Sloan grabbed Abigale in a bear hug and kissed her in front of God and the entire student body. She didn't seem to mind.

"Come on, Mom. Pose with your son," Abigale said. "If it weren't for you, he'd most likely be in jail."

Sloan's Mom scooted up next to him and folded her arms in front of her. He hugged her and kissed her forehead. She looked so lovely in her spring polka dot dress and the corsage Sloan had given her.

"Wasn't anything I did," she said. "He did all the hard work. My part was easy. Johnny loved his daddy and Tom gave him lots of good guidance. I just wish he was—" She drifted into silence.

"Smile, Mom. Abby's taking our picture." Sloan put his arm around his mother, who seemed to have gotten much thinner since the last time he'd hugged her.

"I miss him too, Mom," he whispered. But the smile he turned toward the camera was the real deal. Sloan was on top of the world. He had his orders, his diploma, and his true love.

Sloan loaded his old truck with everything Abigale would need for a summer on the beach and everything he would need for two years in Spain. He then drove to Vero Beach to spend two days with Abigale's parents before he caught his flight to Spain.

The couple lay on the beach, soaked up some sun, and dreamt about their future.

Sloan and Mr. LaHolm lounged on the veranda with a few beers and relived the days when they'd worked fishing or lobster boats.

Mr. LaHolm reflected with some fondness on his own military service. "Did my time in the Army back in fifty-three. They trained me night and day for eight weeks, flew me into Seoul, where I joined a unit that had been dug in the jungle for almost a year. Next thing I knew, they signed a treaty of some sort and loaded us all on a boat bound for the States. Hell, Sloan. I learned more about the war from watching MASH than I did fighting in it. The only time I fired my weapon was to make sure it worked. Shot a tree or some damn thing."

"You mean they'd give you a weapon and you didn't know if it would even work?"

"Take my word, son. If they give you a weapon, you don't take anyone's say-so. You make damned sure it works. Your life could depend on it."

"I'll remember that, Sir."

"You know, Son. While you're in Spain, you won't have much use for that old truck. I might be willing to take it off your hands if your price was right."

"Sorry, Mr. LaHolm. Promised it to Jake. But if the deal falls through, Abby can get it to you."

Abigale and Sloan had just enough time to adjust to life without school when he had to board his flight to Madrid. Mr. and Mrs. LaHolm stood in the drive behind the condo and waved as Sloan and Abigale drove away in Sloan's truck.

"That boy's got it all," Mr. LaHolm said to his wife. "He's got a good head on him and the determination of a python. Anybody who can grind through four years at that institution and manage to come away with straight A's has my respect. And he really seems to love Abby. She could have done a lot worse."

"I'm not sure I can take him seriously," Mrs. LaHolm said. "All that nonsense about soul mates. It could be a lot of hogwash just to get in her skivvies. And I'm not sure he can be trusted alone in Spain with all those gorgeous women."

XIX

Sloan had flown his mom to Tallahassee for his graduation using most of what he had left in the bank. He would need a cushion to get settled at a military base, so there was not enough left over to pop for a diamond engagement ring. They had often talked of how they would spend their lives together, but Sloan had never fashioned any sort of formal or official marriage proposal. In his view, they had an understanding, but now that he was shipping out, he wanted to do something to cement the deal.

He still had the shard of ruby sea glass he had found on their first date. It struck him that he could take the crude piece of glass to a jeweler, have it put into a silver setting and hung from a silver chain. With an investment of a hundred dollars, he was all set with an engagement present.

They arrived at the Miami International Airport, checked in at the ticket counter, and found his departure gate. The only time he had flown on a commercial airliner was that trip home when his father was sick.

"Nothing to it," Abigale said. "You're flying first class, right?"

"I'm in the Army, or had you forgotten? My comfort is not their concern. It only matters that I arrive in one piece and can still recite my name, rank, and serial number."

"Then your best bet is to find a row of empty seats so you can stretch out and get some sleep. It'll be a long night. You won't forget me will you?"

"I promise I'll write every day. Even if I don't have any news."

"Not likely you'll ever be at a loss for words, even if some are pure bullshit." She kissed him again before he turned and ran down the ramp and into the belly of the 747. The anticipation of the unknown had him in its clutches, and in his excitement he had forgotten to give her the engagement present.

"Shit." He ran back up the ramp against the other passengers who *knew* where they were going.

"Abigale!"

She had turned to walk away from the gate.

"Almost forgot." He grabbed her shoulder and spun her around. "Had this made up for you. It's not a diamond, but it says it all for me."

"Nice gift box," she said as he unwadded the ball of tissue Sloan had used to secure the gift. She drew a quick breath when the pendant swung from the chain over her finger.

"The ruby sea glass!"

He put the chain around her neck and fastened the clasp.

She held the medallion in her hand to examine it.

"One man's garbage is another man's farewell gift, right, Sloan?" But she was smiling. "It's lovely. I'll keep it always."

"Remember the time we found it on the beach? Our first date. It's a five-hundred-year-old relic . . . of sorts."

He kissed her hard on the mouth, turned, and ran back down the ramp looking over his shoulder. He shouted back to her, "Means we're engaged."

"What?" she screamed, barely able to hear him over the roar of the engines and the hoard of travelers boarding the flight.

He cupped his hands around his mouth. "Engaged! We're getting married, right?"

"Right! I mean, yes! Yes, I will!" she shouted. For a moment they were the center of attention in a crowd of strangers, all witnesses to her acceptance of Sloan's proposal. After a quick thumbs-up he disappeared, and the crowd moved on like lava rock flowing down the loading platform.

She stood at the plate glass window clutching the medallion until the wheels on Sloan's airplane left the tarmac. She made her way back to the truck, climbed up on the running board, and settled behind the wheel. The sea glass glowed in the soft light of the street lamp. Did they have some connection to the five-hundred-year-old shard of glass? She tucked it inside her blouse where it lay cool against her breast.

She followed the signs out of the airport to I-95 and north to Vero Beach where she pulled into the guest parking area of the large condo complex. She locked Sloan's truck and made her way into the compound. The full placid moon floated out over the Atlantic. Sloan might be peering out of a portal at the same moon. He was on the threshold of a life-changing adventure, but she was not going with him. At least they had the moon to share.

She always took summers off to enjoy the beach with her parents and friends. Now, with Sloan in Spain, and an engagement in place, collateralized by a five-hundred-year-old shard of glass, she felt a sense of urgency to get on with her life. The sooner she could join Sloan in Spain, the sooner they could begin their own adventure.

XX

Sloan's flight landed in Madrid and he found his way to the base, checked in with the clerk on duty and was assigned a room in the Bachelor's Officers' Quarters, or BOQ as it was called in Army jargon. He showered, donned his dress uniform, reported to the command center and stood in front of the sergeant in charge.

"Lieutenant Abernathy, reporting." He snapped to attention and saluted the sergeant. The clerk glanced up at Sloan and saw the epitome of a spit-and-polish, rookie lieutenant.

The clerk, Sergeant Tobin, a senior ranking noncommissioned officer, nodded at the gung-ho green kid standing stiffly in front of him. "Good morning, Sir. Have a seat. Captain Gibbs will be with you shortly. Want some coffee?"

Sloan relaxed. "Sure, great. I take it black."

Tobin gestured nonchalantly toward the coffee bar. "Help yourself, Lieutenant. It's on the table over there."

Sloan had just scalded his tongue with burnt coffee when Captain Gibbs entered his office from the side door. Gibbs, a fit-looking man of forty, greeted Sloan with an outstretched hand. He wore a thick mustache that set him apart from the milquetoast officers Sloan had come to know in ROTC.

Unsure if he should salute or shake his hand, Sloan took the Captain's lead and shook his hand. Then, for good measure, he saluted him.

Awkwardly, Gibbs returned the salute and flopped down behind a vintage mahogany desk that might well have been the spoils of war. "Welcome to Madrid, Lieutenant Abernathy. I trust you had a good flight."

"Yes, Sir. Plenty of vacant seats to stretch out on."

Gibbs seemed mildly amused by Sloan's naive view of air travel and military protocol.

"In my estimation," Gibbs said. "A good flight is one you can walk away from. Anyway, that'll likely be your last commercial flight unless you pay for it. We fly military air transports or MATS as we call 'em. They come and go out of the Air Force hangars at Madrid International. They're not as comfortable as commercials, but a damn sight cheaper. I know you're surprised that we care about your tax dollars, but cost is one of the things we get measured on. It could make or break my next promotion, so if you want to stay on my good side, keep your expenses down. When it comes to protocol, we're laid back here." Gibbs swiveled his overstuffed chair and plopped his feet on the desk showing Sloan the soles of his shoes.

"Address me as Gibbs or John. That is, unless we have visiting brass, in which case, I'm *Captain Gibbs, Sir.* That clear?"

"Yes, Sir. Clear."

Gibbs stuck an unlit cigar under his bushy mustache and pushed it back to the corner of his mouth.

"Been lookin' at your file. You got some impressive academics, but on the soldiering side? Not so good. Your Rotcie commander calls it down-right slovenly. Your grades are a big part of why you're here instead of back in Oklahoma or Texas with the also-rans. I like people in my unit to think. Did I say like? Put it this way, I expect people to think."

"Think, Sir?"

"That's right. Use their heads for something other than . . . tell me, Sloan. Is it true you paid another cadet to stand in for you at an inspection?"

"Yes Sir, back when I was green, new to the corps. I needed to be at a chem lab and thought this guy could pull it off. I learned that lesson the hard way, but I still put academics ahead of everything else. If an inspection conflicted with a test, I favored the test and flunked the inspection."

"Pulling a stunt like that took guts." Sloan saw a glint of admiration in Gibbs' otherwise stoic expression. "We're big into the Cold War here. Electronic surveillance, lot of stuff you'll be good at. Protocol is important, but in my outfit, thinking and applying what you know is what counts. You'll spend weeks at a time in the field. I can't tell you any more about that till your clearances come through, so until then, just take it easy. Get to know the town and the men and women in your unit."

"But, Sir, what *are* my duties? What'll I be doing?"

"Not much now, but don't worry. The Army'll get its pound of flesh. By the time you finish your tour, you'll have earned every minute of downtime and then some."

"Not afraid of work, Sir. The more I do the more I learn."

"We're gonna get along fine," Gibbs said. "Sergeant Tobin will help you find an office and anything else you need, long as it don't cost me money."

Gibbs glanced at his watch and stood up, bringing the meeting to an abrupt end. "Got a meeting."

Sloan showed himself out of Gibbs' office.

Sloan and Sergeant Tobin prowled the vacant office bays until they located one with a view of the main gate and several wartime framed photographs left behind by a veteran of an earlier tour.

Sloan was assigned to an electronic espionage unit led by another young lieutenant by the name of Jameson, a West Point man with none of the corps-happy ideas one normally associated with the pedigree. The mission of Sloan's group, Jameson explained, was to use geo-positioning technology and other state-of-the-art electronics to track and observe Cold War threats to the U.S. and her allies. Sloan's access to sophisticated communications gear also made it easy to maintain contact with Abigale. He could place a call to her via military satellite or use commercial connections.

He found that the best times to reach her, considering the seven or so hour difference in time, was two in the afternoon. They often talked late into Abigale's night, provided there was sufficient fodder for conversation. Topics ranged from Sloan's work, which was at the moment mundane and routine, to planning their life. In the short time he had been in Spain, she had completely re-planned their wedding three times. Every time the topic came up, Abigale had a different idea about the venue, color scheme, or format. Sloan was fine with most any scheme she chose.

He reported daily to his new office where he awaited word that his clearances had been approved, and almost daily someone would call or stop by his office to ask questions regarding the minute details of his twenty-two years on planet Earth.

For Sloan, the days were long. At times, he felt the Army had forgotten he was there and available to do their bidding.

Gibbs often saddled him with menial tasks that did not require any skill on his part. On one occasion, he asked Sloan to drive to his home, fetch his wife, and drive her to the Base commissary for shopping. On another occasion, Sloan was instructed to collect Gibbs' daughters from school and drive them home.

Sloan became restless, discontent, and intolerant of the tasks to which he was being relegated, but he had little choice in the matter.

XXI

Abigale and her parents were dining alfresco at a small café on the beach. They had chosen a table overlooking the Atlantic. The sun was firing up the clouds that lined the shore to the east. They ordered dinner and a bottle of fine French wine. Abigale ordered a lobster tail which she scooted around on her plate and sent back to the kitchen.

The last of the wine was in the glasses and Mr. LaHolm was perusing the dessert menu when Mrs. LaHolm decided to find out what was behind her daughter's somber mood.

"So tell us, what's going on in that pretty head of yours? We get that you're missing Sloan but come up for air. He's only been gone a few days."

"I'm sorry to be so moody, not really unhappy, just giving some serious thought to my future. So if I'm less than great company, it's because I'm trying to understand where my life is taking me."

"So, let us in on it," Mr. LaHolm said. "What're you cooking up?"

"Sure, Honey. We understand that you're madly in love, but finishing your course work before you run off to Spain is the best plan. Don't you agree? Hell, he may be back in a year, or sooner. Besides, a year's not such a long time. When your father went off to Korea, I thought I'd die, but he was back almost before I knew it. I hardly had time to play the field." She smiled and lovingly patted her husband's strong weathered hand as he scooped up the last bite of key lime pie.

"The way I see it, another year in college is more of an obstruction than an accomplishment. Getting it done is what matters now. I've been thinking about the course work that stands between me and my degree."

"For sure, Hon, there's no way in heck you can finish all that in less than a year."

The waiter cleared their table and placed the tip tray in easy reach of Mr. LaHolm.

"Not if I lie around here and work on my tan all summer, but if I go back right away and enroll in both summer sessions, I could cut almost six months off my degree plan. That and a heavy load in the fall and I could finish in February and join Sloan several months ahead of schedule."

"Sure Kid, you could. But to me, it just sounds like too much work. I think you need your summer break." Her father peeled another five dollar bill off the wad he always carried and placed it on the tip tray. "It was exceptionally good service, didn't you think? I thought he did a nice job."

"Yes, Dad. The service was exceptional, but you always over-tip." She leaned toward her parents. "I feel a sense of urgency that I just can't explain. My life is with Sloan, and he's in Spain and I'm stuck here . . . in college limbo."

Mrs. LaHolm refolded her napkin and placed it on the table. "I'm surprised to hear you say you're willing to forgo your best year of college to be with that Texas roughneck."

"Not forgo, Mom. Shorten."

"If I was you," her father said, "I'd hop a flight to Madrid and close the deal right now before he gets a taste of freedom. Who knows what might happen next. Those Spanish women are hot-blooded." He glanced at his wife. "Or so I'm told. Not speaking from experience, mind you. The men down at the docks are always talking."

"I'm not the least bit worried." Abigale hooked the chain around her neck and held out the shard of glass. "After all, he did give me this necklace as an engagement present."

"Some engagement present," Mrs. LaHolm said, "a piece of broken glass. You deserve better. You deserve diamonds."

"Mom, he's a second Louie. Diamonds are out of reach. Besides, this piece of broken glass has special meaning for us. He found it on the beach on our first date." Abigale held the medallion in both hands and touched it to her lips.

Her father reached across the table and put his hand on her arm. "Look, Sweetie. You have our support whatever you decide to do."

Her mom nodded.

Early the next morning, Abigale loaded Sloan's old pickup with everything she would need to see her through the next three months and departed Vero Beach for Tallahassee.

She arrived at her sorority house early in the afternoon and struggled up the stairs with her luggage. She stretched out on her bed to catch her breath.

She smiled to herself. Sloan would be pleased to hear she had decided to make short work of her senior year so they could be together. She might not fully comprehend the magnitude of the move she had made, but making a big decision in her life felt good. She was learning to be her own person.

The phone in her dorm room rang. She instinctively grabbed it and answered, "Hey!"

"Abigale, is that you?" Sloan's voice did not carry well over six thousand miles of phone lines. "What's this I hear about you going back to school?"

"How'd you find out?"

"Called the beach house and got your dad, how else? He thinks you've lost your freaking mind."

"So does Mom. What do you think?"

"Gutsy. Real gutsy."

The summer session at FSU was intense. Classes met six days a week and assignments were due daily.

On her way to her eight o'clock, she heard heavy footsteps behind her. She did not turn around as eye contact might be interpreted as encouragement.

"Well, if it ain't Miss Abby Gale. Fancy meeting you on such a fine morning."

She stopped short and turned to face her former suitor standing in the middle of the path, clad in sandals, shorts and a t-shirt. His devil-may-care demeanor reminded her of the behavior that had drawn her to him.

"Brad Hager. You scared the crap out of me." She put her knuckles on her hips. "Don't you know women get jumped on this campus every day?"

"Jumped, eh?" He grinned.

"You know what I mean. Anyway, what're you doing on campus this time of year?"

"Making up for lost time. You know. Trying to catch up on my degree plan while the team is out for the summer. Speaking of lost time . . . how about dinner?"

"Don't recall losing any time over you, but you *do* know I'm in a committed—"

"What, with that sod buster? What's his name? Slag? Yeah, I remember him. Nice enough boy, but a loser just the same."

"Careful what you say, Mr. BMOC. You're talking about the man I love, and his name's Sloan, thank you."

"So, where *is* this dude?"

"Spain. He's on active duty in Madrid, and he's no dude."

"Spain, eh. So what's keeping us from stealing a night or two?"

"Me. I am."

She turned and walked away, but Brad followed her.

"I had you first. Don't that count for something?"

"Who says you ever *had* me? I don't call one dinner date at Ricardo's as being had, especially when you paid the check with funny money."

They arrived at the main annex of the Fine Arts Building. "This is where I get off," she said, dashing up the steps. "See you around, big shot."

XXII

Early on a Friday morning, Captain Jameson stuck his head in Sloan's office. "Hey man, when are you coming up for air?"

"You know how it is. Got to stay on top of the boss's busy work."

"One thing you'll learn about the captain. He hates to see time go to waste."

"And I got plenty of that," Sloan said, looking at a pile of folders on his desk.

"So, what's on your social calendar for Saturday night?"

Sloan faked a look at his desk calendar, "I'm clear. Know where we can find a good game of pool?"

"Yeah, in the dayroom, but I was thinking of getting away from work, not moving in with it."

"I shoot a decent game." Sloan made a bridge for an imaginary cue, hoping to interest the captain in a stag night.

"Dust off some class A's and we'll do dinner on the town. I know this place—you'll like it. Genuine Spanish grub and a chance to hobnob with some locals. Hell man, can't sit behind your desk and stare at that picture all the time. Got to get out and meet some people."

Sloan leaned back in his chair and gazed longingly at the picture of Abby. "Yeah sure, a night on the town sounds like fun."

Their evening began around nine with drinks and hors d'oeuvres at an authentic Spanish restaurant crowded with military personnel and Europeans. At around ten o'clock, they began to serve dinner. The first course was pasta then a salad, followed by the main course which consisted of baked chicken and rare roast beef. Around midnight, they served brandy and dessert. For some, the evening was broken up by frequent trips to the dance floor with whoever would consent to being hugged around the room to the rhythm of Spanish guitars.

Along with the first course, Captain Jameson introduced Sloan to a lovely senorita who was one of a large group of Spanish women, none of whom appeared to be paired up. To say that Sloan's introduction was prearranged would be a stretch, but there was an empty chair beside her and she did not resist when he sat down. The introduction was accompanied by a kiss on each cheek. The scene reminded him of one of those western movies where the dude from the east was put on a horse named Cyclone. Knowing Sloan was lonely, Jameson may have set it up and Sloan played along. Female companionship over dinner would get him through the evening without thinking constantly of Abigale.

Regina wore her raven hair pulled back and held in place by an array of colorful silk scarves. Her hair and the scarves fell neatly down her back, between her shoulders. Her black eyes were set in a sea of castellan, café con leche with a hint of rouge to decorate her voluptuous mouth. She was easy to look at, but her English seemed limited so if he could not reach her on some level, it promised to be a long evening. He began with simple questions in English at a pace he was sure she could follow.

"Tell me about you," he began. "Have you lived in Madrid for long? Did you grow up around here?"

For some reason, he felt the need to speak loudly to overcome the language barrier. She must have thought he was dim-witted.

Regina shrugged a bare shoulder. "I am not deaf you know. I come from a small pueblo south of Madrid. Mis padres make vino. Yo trabajor in the city as secretaria." She shrugged again, this time to convey boredom with her job. "Not too exciting, but yo amor a la ciudad."

Sloan didn't fully comprehend her broken English, but he got that she worked and lived in the city.

He caught a whiff of her perfume. He knew it shouldn't get to him, but he was coming off a long dry spell that went all the way back to that last night he spent with Brenda.

"So, swell." He leaned over to her. She smelled like the roses by the fence in his yard back home. "That's great. Mas vino por favor?"

She smiled revealing cute dimples. "Sí, gracias."

When she smiled or laughed, sparks flashed in her black opal eyes. "Tell me Senior, where is *your* home? Have you been in Spain for long?"

Sloan gave her the quick version of his life's story. How he grew up in Texas, the biggest state in America. "I went to college in Florida, another state. There are fifty in all."

She rolled her eyes; he hurried on.

"I studied engineering and graduated with honors and here I am, assigned to an Army base in Madrid."

At times, she gave Sloan the impression that she understood, but the next instant, a puzzled look would overshadow her beautiful face.

"So, welcome." She moved closer and placed her hand on his.

The evening progressed and the waiter continued to supply them with glass after glass of warm red wine. They began to lose interest in what was going on around them.

A trio of stringed instruments played soft Spanish music. He took her by the hand, pulled her to her feet, and steered her to the dance floor. When they reached the center of the room, she turned to face him, put her arms around his neck and pressed her supple body into his. He could feel her firm breasts through his starched shirt.

She clung ever closer as they moved to the melodious tones of the Spanish guitars. He knew she was leading, but as they moved together, he had the impression he wasn't such a bad dancer. She seemed to swoon in his arms.

As the empty bottles disappeared back into the kitchen, Sloan was vaguely aware that the wine had taken charge of the evening.

"Quiere ir a mi casa?" she breathed in his ear.

Sloan was not sure what she was suggesting "Vamos a ir a mi apartamento." Did he understand her correctly? Their situation was getting out of hand. It was best to return to the table and the safety of the other dinner guests. He turned to leave the dance floor, but she did not follow him, nor did she let go of his hand. When he turned to face her, she once again put her arm around him and playfully nibbled at his neck. "Vamos a ir a mi apartamento."

She's getting some serious drunk, he thought. Maybe we should get the hell out of this public place while we still can.

He saw Jameson across the room engrossed in conversation with another beautiful Spanish lady. He looked up and Sloan rendered a two-fingered salute. Jameson returned it and smiled knowingly.

Sloan and Regina quietly left the overheated restaurant. They went to the curb. He stumbled, but managed to recover his balance. He hailed a taxi.

It was clear that Regina had had a bit too much to drink. He would see her home safely. It was his duty as an officer and a gentleman. It was the right thing to do, he thought. Regina hadn't been drinking alone.

Once inside the cab, she instructed the driver who nodded and sped away.

She fell back against Sloan and snuggled into his arms. The aroma of her perfume overwhelmed him.

The driver brought the cab to a stop and the couple climbed out in front of a street-level apartment in an older section of Madrid.

Sloan stabbed a wad of bills at the driver. "Wait for me. I'll only be a minute."

She fumbled with the key, but finally turned the lock and they went inside Regina's cozy apartment. She dropped her sweater and purse on the floor and pulled at Sloan's lapels, "Come on, soldier boy. Let's get comfy."

"I should be getting back."

"No, please stay." She held up her index finger. "We will have one small glass only. How you say . . . nightcap." She retrieved a bottle of red wine from her antique fridge, pulled two ceramic vessels from the cupboard and poured two generous servings of rich Spanish vino. "From mis padre's uvas."

Sloan heard the taxi pull away. He thought about running to the street and waving the guy down, but his legs were too heavy move. It'll be okay, he thought. He could call another cab as soon as they finished their "nightcap." He struggled to keep his words and thoughts coming out in single file, but Regina was managing to articulate her thoughts with very little effort. The two glasses of wine sat untouched on the kitchen table.

They embraced and then kissed, first lightly, then passionately. He fumbled with the clasps, buttons, ribbons and belts that held her clothes in place. She stepped out of her dress. It dropped to the floor.

Man, is she beautiful, voluptuous, hot, he thought, as her fingers unbuttoned his uniform shirt.

He followed her to her bed.

They were enraptured, inflamed. He could not remember her name. She was Brenda and all the other girls who had helped him get through at FSU. She was what he yearned for with Abby. He didn't know or care who he was to her. He doubted she knew his name either.

He rediscovered the two glasses of now warm red wine. He took a gulp and handed one to her. They clinked them in a toast and sipped the nectar that had been years in the making.

"The vino is good, no?"

"Es good, si`." He drained his cup. Abby doesn't need to know.

Morning sunlight burst through the windows of the now cluttered apartment. Sloan woke from a sound sleep or was it a drunken stupor? His head was splitting and his mouth dry.

Regina was in the kitchen, clad only in what nature had given her. She danced as she went about making coffee.

She saw Sloan stirring on the bed. Giggling she ran for her robe.

"Hey, soldier man. Thought you would sleep all day." She spoke in almost perfect English with a slight, but charming accent.

"A pounding in my head woke me."

His trousers were draped over a chair on the other side of the room. He hid behind a sheet to retrieve them.

She laughed.

"How did we get here and what happened once we—"

"Lots of buen vino español," she said.

"Yeah, I lost count," he said.

"Who was counting and for Que pasó? Just look at the bed. Surely, you can remember what happened." She smiled demurely.

His tongue was thick and the brick that was his brain lay inert and useless between his ears. The brick could barely communicate in English, let alone Spanish. She seemed to have little trouble with either.

His clothes reeked of wine, smoke, and day-old cologne. The wrinkled state of his uniform would not pass muster. His feet were swollen two sizes larger than his shoes.

"What say we go for some breakfast?" he said.

"Desayuno? es, bueno."

She found a blouse and a skirt and put them on. She met him at the door and dragged her fingertips down his cheek.

"Cheer up, soldier man. It wasn't all that bad."

Bad, he thought. It was incredible.

They left the small apartment and walked, arm-in-arm down a narrow cobblestone street to a cheerful sidewalk café where they shared a pot of coffee and a bowl of fresh pastries. The strong coffee thawed his brain. Recollections of the evening brought a blush to his face as the rays of sunlight invaded her loosely tailored blouse. He thought of the lines in a poem he once read.

"Twist the opal on your hand
Cast your dark eyes
For I delight in irony.
Stop if you can,
The invasion of light beneath and all below"

He could not recall the rest, but it seemed to fit the occasion.

He sat guilt-ridden while gazing at her. He wanted to pretend the night had never happened. He had promised. No lies, no secrets. He had put his life with Abigale in jeopardy. If she knew, she'd drop him like a hot rock. She'd already warned him about Brenda. It was the wine. The wine and how much he missed her.

"Look Renhea—"

"Ra-gi-na," she corrected him.

"Ra-gi-na . . . this sort of thing—you see, I'm engaged, you know, to get married. My future wife, her name is—" he rubbed his eyes. "Never mind her name. She's coming to Spain. We plan to be, you know . . . in a few months we plan to marry."

First night out on the town and he'd fallen into bed with a perfect stranger. Yes, she *was* damn near perfect. Part of him wanted to turn around and go back to Regina's place and spend the day in her cozy boudoir.

"Si usted we will speak no more of this." She waved a hand in dismissal. "We can go our separate ways. Si, es bueno por me." He wasn't sure what she'd said but he liked the sound of "separate ways."

"Then, no hard feelings?" he said.

She looked surprised and then bewildered. "You have more hard feelings?"

"No, not like that."

"Too bad. I want to go now." She kissed his cheek, excused herself and sauntered out of the little café in the direction of her apartment. Now, she was truly perfect.

Sloan left the café and walked in the direction of the Base. It was only a few miles and the fresh air and exercise would do him good. He had abused himself unmercifully the night before.

After walking for an hour, he came to a small neighborhood church. He went in and sat for a while. He found the dark and the solitude inviting. The crucifix was illuminated through stained-glass windows along both sides of the nineteenth century chapel. He found a place on the rearmost pew where he sat with his elbows on his knees and his face in his hands. He thought about Abigale. He knew her so well. They could talk about anything, but he knew Regina in a different way, a carnal way. He knew her better from one night together than he knew Abigale in two months.

He wondered how it would be the next time he talked with Abigale. Would she hear shame or guilt in his voice? Would his betrayal be heard in the tone of his voice? He thought about the guidance his father had given him. "Don't be no weed farmer." If the old man was here now he would have plenty to say about my behavior, Sloan thought. Plenty . . . and he'd be right, as usual.

XXIII

Several weeks passed and Sloan's recollection of the night with Regina had begun to fade. She had not left him with a disease requiring medical attention. For that he was grateful, and his weed farming hadn't born any unwanted fruit.

His long distance love affair with Abigale continued as if nothing had happened. In his daily correspondence, he reassured her that he loved her more each day and he did. He assured her that the local Latin lovelies were no match for the French, Bostonian love of his life.

Their latest plan was to be married at her parent's summer home in Vero Beach. Sloan's mom would be there. His brother would perform the ceremony. His father's guidance hadn't been followed to the letter. Sure he had done some weed farming with Brenda and that one night with the Spanish babe, Regina, but he had done so without consequence. He had visited the wicked weed patch and escaped unscathed.

Early on a Tuesday, Sloan was busy at his desk when his phone rang. It could be the call from security informing him that his clearances had come through. He grabbed the receiver. "Good morning, Lieutenant Abernathy here." He spoke in his most authoritative military voice.

"Good morning, Lieutenant." The voice he heard on the line was not the officer in charge of base security, but a delicate feminine voice with a charming Spanish accent. "Mi nombre es Regina Gonzales. We met a few weeks ago. You came back to my apartment for the evening. Remember?"

"Of course. How could I forg—why? What's up?" He shifted the phone to his other ear. I thought we—"

"Can I see you? Can we meet someplace? I need to, that is, *we* need to talk."

Had he left something behind in her apartment? Did she want them to become lovers? Was her father out to kill him? He rubbed the back of his neck to relieve some of the anxiety he felt building. "Well sure, I guess so. Don't see why—what is it you want to—"

"Can we meet at that little café? You know the one where we had breakfast that morning, por favor?"

Sloan arrived early and chose a table under an umbrella in the warm fall sunshine. He ordered a beer and told the waiter that someone would join him. He passed the time sipping his beer and trying to read the Spanish menu.

He smelled her perfume and looked up. Regina was standing next to him at his table.

He stood and extended his hand. She looked at him for a moment then placed her hand in his and slowly raised her dark eyes to meet his. A shiver went through him. She wore a soft beige silk frock. Her supple body bulged beneath the sheer fabric. His face flushed as recollections of their night together flooded back.

Her chin still down, her black eyes looking up into his, she said with a half-smile, "You blush."

He leaned back in his chair and stuffed his left hand in his pocket, wanting to appear relaxed. "So, why are we—what did you want to—" He stammered like a moron.

"First, you order me drink. Deseo una margarita, por favor."

The waiter brought her drink. She sipped it. He swigged his beer. They exchanged pleasantries. During the intervening weeks, Sloan had learned more Spanish, so the communications barrier between them had been lowered to a ten-rail fence.

Their glasses empty, she folded her hands on the table. "Well," she began, "two days ago I saw mi médico."

"What's the matter, aren't you feeling well?"

Oh my God, he thought, she's given me a VD.

"Oh no Señor I am fine—por favor."

He raised his eyebrows. "Then, que pasó?"

"Mie periodo— it did not come."

"Oh?"

"Yo soy con niño."

"You're what?" He refused to understand her.

She cast her dark eyes down dreading to see his reaction. "I am sorry if I have taken you by surprise, Lieutenant."

"For how long?" he finally asked. He already knew the answer.

"How long since that night we met? Three, maybe four weeks." She spoke in the abstract as though it was someone else they were discussing, some unlucky third party neither one knew very well.

"How can your medico be so damn sure?"

"That's why he is a medico and you are not."

"And I'm sure he's a fine doctor. Please accept my apology if I suggested otherwise."

"Damn," she whimpered and covered her mouth and blushed, embarrassed that she had lost her temper.

With no apparent reason or provocation, she grabbed her purse and fled the restaurant.

"What the—" Sloan shoved his chair back and followed her through the door and into the street. "Vuelvo enseguida!" He assured the waiter over his shoulder.

She ran to a secluded corner of a small park next to the restaurant, threw herself down on a bench and began to weep.

"What are you running away from?"

"I see my uncle. If he sees me with an Army guy, he might tell Papa and then habrá mucho que pagar."

"Okay, look, I understand."

"Do you?" She looked up at him, her eyes shiny. "You will help me then?"

"Look, Regina, you must understand. I'm engaged . . . to be married."

She reached up and grabbed his hand and whispered, "We must be married and soon or mi Padre will kill us both, con sus propias manos."

"With his bare—" Sloan pondered. He clenched his hands into fists and shook them at her. "There has to be another—don't you get it? I'm already engaged, to my college—"

How can I explain all this to her?" We'll have to postpone our wedding plans at least for a couple of decades. And that promise I made to Dad?

Sloan spoke softly, "My father taught me that if I was man enough to put it in, I had to be man enough to back it up."

"Back it up?" she flared. "What means back it up?"

"Never mind. I'll explain later."

"How you say, aborto? You want I should do abortion?"

"Never! My soul would burn in infierno. Besides, I couldn't do that to my kid. She *is* my kid, right?"

Chin lifted high, she turned her now cold black eyes on him. "What you think, I'm puta?"

"No, of course not. I know you're no whore. I just thought maybe there had been, you know, one of your Spanish friends from school or work."

"I'm not like that, except when you are concerned. And what you mean, *she*? It could be boy baby for all you know."

"Don't know why I said—Freudian slip, I guess."

"Que es Freudian?"

"Hard to explain." He sat down on the bench beside her and put his elbows on his knees and his head in his hands. "Ask me again later."

He felt her hand on his knee. "What else can we do?" she asked softly. "Mis Madre will no help. Mis Padre would kill us and leave us in a ditch. Mis amigos would no comprende or cuidar. You are the only one I can turn to. Besides, it is your problem too. We were both there in the same bed that night."

"Okay, look. I won't leave you in a lurch."

"Lurch? que es lurch? You have so many funny words I never hear before, so talk straight. Tell me what you will do to help our mess we are in."

"I'll help you." His palms were no longer sweating. He wished he had the beer he left behind in the restaurant.

"You will marry me then. You will—back it up?"

"Is that the only—"

"What? You would have me go in the woods and have your baby?"

"No, not the woods."

She bumped his shoulder with hers. "For all you know, soldier boy, this baby, she might be the best thing that ever happens to us."

"Now, there *you* go with *she*," he said.

"It, I mean."

"Guess we need to make plans de boda," Sloan said. He hailed a taxi and the two rode together back to Regina's apartment.

They stood outside the door, Sloan jangling the change in his pockets. "Listen, I'll be here tomorrow at two."

"Can I trust you?"

"I'll be here. Two o'clock sharp. If something comes up and I can't make it, I'll call."

She kissed him on the lips and disappeared into her apartment.

He returned to the base and retreated to his room in the BOQ where he stretched out on his bunk and stared at the ceiling.

He tried to make sense of the mess his life was in. A few weeks ago he was living a charmed life. It was his dream come true. Now it was out of reach. He imagined the dilemma had he slept with Abby and *she* was pregnant.

How could he be sure Regina was telling the truth? All he knew for sure was that she *said* she was late. What in hell do I owe some bitch who invited me to her apartment under the pretense of having one glass of wine and now claims I knocked her up? Hell, maybe she's conning me. Why did she think it was my problem that she managed to get herself pregnant? She could've had someone else over the very next night—the same night even. She sure as hell was drunk enough. How 'n hell did she drink so much and not have a hangover. I was damn well sick for three days.

Was she drinking it or pouring it in the flower pots? She could be a world class liar, a whore, or a con artist working a scam and I'm her mark. She'll most likely come to me tomorrow with a proposition.

"Pay me ten thousand and I'll forget this ever happened."

I'd be a fool to marry this bitch and dump Abby. No way in hell am I gonna dump my Abby for some tramp con artist.

Morning came. Sloan stood under the shower until his thoughts began to congeal. He pulled on a fresh set of fatigues and sauntered in the direction of the mess hall. He ordered eggs over easy with sausage and found a vacant table where he could stare out of a window onto the compound. He shoved his food around on his plate.

What would Daddy do?

If you're man enough to put it in, you better, by God, be man enough to—what in hell did he know about backin' it up?

Jameson came through the front door and gathered some basics of the breakfast buffet. Sloan motioned him over to his table. They exchanged idle chit chat until Sloan could no longer hold his tongue.

"Remember that Spanish broad you introduced me to last month at the dinner party?"

"Yeah, sure. Regina, I think her name was Regina."

"That's her. What do you know about her?"

"Not much, actually. She shows up from time to time, usually with a girlfriend and they always leave together. Never knew her to take up with a Yank until you came along."

"So, you think she's legit?"

"I think she's a lovely Spanish girl, probably in her early twenties, who hopes someday to meet an American and live the good life in America."

"Why'd you set me up with her?"

"Figured you'd talk her ear off about your American sweetie and go home feeling good. Never expected you'd disappear for two days. So, what's up with her? She give you a dose of the clap?"

"Oh, hell no. Just been wondering about her."

"She ain't been back to the supper club since."

Sloan found a soundproof room where he could rehearse his talk and call Abby without being heard or interrupted.

"Abby, listen up, there's something I need to tell you. I have decided to get married . . . to a woman I met here in Madrid. She's lovely and ever so slightly pregnant with my child, or so she said, or so I think she said. Her English is not so good, but she's bright and can learn our American ways. Yes, I know what we were planning and all that but, what the heck, it might never have worked out, what with you there and me over here. Something was bound to come unbolted."

A young private banged on the door to the soundproof room. "Hey, Lieutenant, you got a call on line six. Want I should take a message?"

"Yeah, I'll be a while getting this job done." He leaned back against the rubber-coated soundproof wall and continued. "Look Abby, go on with your life. Marry someone who is not such a big jerk. I'm sure you will be happy, not as happy as we would've been but look at it this way, if we are truly soul mates we will most likely meet again in this life or the next. Who can say."

He stared at the phone. He would explain it all to her in a way that she would understand.

Who was he kidding? This news was going to break her heart, just like it was breaking his.

He placed the call.

It rang through.

"Hello!" she said.

"It's me." His heart jumped into his throat and began to pound.

"Oh, Preppy. I've been so worried when you didn't call yesterday." The connection was so good, it was as if she was with him in the soundproof room.

"Kind of busy these last few days."

"Why, what's up?"

"Clearances, my clearances came through," he lied.

"That's good, Honey. Now maybe you can do some real work, right? No more chauffeuring the boss's wife to the commissary, unless of course it's me."

"Yeah, well, there's something I have to tell you, so listen carefully. I don't want to repeat any of this." His throat seized up. He choked on the first word of his prepared speech and then went with a lie that came out of nowhere.

"I'm goin' on a top secret assignment and won't be back for weeks. I can't tell you any more than that. I'll call you when I get back to Madrid."

The lie left him breathless and he listened to the silence on the other end. She knew it was a crock.

"Wow, Mister Big Shot. Is that it? Your clearances come through and you're off on a secret assignment. I'll be here waiting for you. Stay safe. Call or write me when you can."

"Waiting. That's good. Yes, you wait. I'll be back in touch with the whole story. Got to go, can't talk, have to pack my gear."

There was silence on the line. She thought the connection had been lost. "Okay, Hon. I understand. I love you and can't wait until we're together."

"Goodbye." He listened to the dial tone then went back to his office, closed the door and wrote her a letter:

My Dearest Abigale,

I hope this finds you doing well and enjoying your fall session at FSU.

There is something I have to convey in this letter that will be difficult for you to accept or even understand. Several weeks ago, I attended a dinner party at a restaurant near the base. I met a woman there and the evening got out of hand. We went to her apartment. I don't know what came over me. I was pretty drunk. I know that's no excuse.

I was missing you so much and wishing you were here. She was merely a substitute for you, the real true love of my life. Luck was not on our side because a couple days ago she called me to say she was pregnant. You know how I feel about children and pregnant women, especially when it is my doing. I hope you understand that I have no choice. I have to marry her. By the time you read this, I will be married.

I know how hurtful this is for you. It does not bring an end to my feelings for you, but it does raise the question as to whether or not we will ever be together, a prospect for which, at this juncture, I hold out little hope.

Finally, what I told you about leaving on a long assignment was a lie. I had called to tell you the truth, but lost my nerve.

All my love, may it endure the test of time,

Sloan

He posted the letter in the outgoing military mail. It would travel to New York via military transport and be transferred to the U.S. mail. By the time Abigale received the news, he would be married to Regina.

XXIV

Abigale was in a queue at the library waiting to check out a book when she heard a familiar voice.

"Well, if it ain't that cute little Boston lass. Been thinkin' about you."

She turned to find Brad breathing down her neck. "Brad, you monster! With a bazillion students on this campus, how is it . . . are you stalking me?"

"Stalking? No, you're just lucky. Maybe we're—you know—soul mates." He flashed her an irresistible smile.

"I can assure you, Mr. Big Shot, our paths never crossed in another life." She put her free hand on her hip. "I come from aristocracy and you? You're definitely from common working stock . . . yep, common as dirt, that's for sure. What're you doing hanging around the library anyhow? Football season over? Or are you trying to learn to read something besides your playbook?" She cocked her head to read the title on the book in his hand. "Supply Side Economics?"

"Hey, those playbooks can get pretty complicated. But you're wrong as usual. I've got to get busy and finish my degree. One day it dawned on me that football wouldn't get me through life."

"Why not?" she said. "It sure has so far."

He rested his palm on the circulation desk and looked down at her. "Turns out my once charmed life is ever so slightly tarnished."

Abigale was shocked to hear Brad wax so honestly. "Surely you have some pro deal in the works."

"You're kidding, right? The NFL grinds up guys like me and feeds 'em to the linemen for lunch. Speaking of which, let's do dinner."

"Come on, Brad. You know I'm as good as a married woman."

"Better, I'd hope. I'll pick you up at seven?"

"Yeah, sure, why not? I could use a night out. We can grab some dinner then straight home, right?"

"Sure, whatever you say."

She had given him an opening for the classic response and to her astonishment he passed it up. The Brad she used to know would not have missed such an easy opening.

When Abigale appeared at the top of the stairs at seven on the dot, Brad was waiting at the bottom. She was wearing a carefully chosen Italian knit skirt and matching sweater. Not too short, and not too tight. She waved in her usual manner.

"Thanks for being on time," he said. "I'm always a little uncomfortable hanging around sorority house lobbies."

She raised an eyebrow. "Could it be because you're illegally parked?"

He held out his arm with a slight bow. She hesitated and then took it. He wrapped her hand around his arm and led her out the door and down the street past the empty reserved parking spaces.

"Did you mean in one of those handicapped slots?" he said. "You know they're reserved for people who can't get around as well as you and me." He smiled proudly and winked.

"Yes, *I know* what they're for."

After a short walk down a side street, he stopped at the dreaded Voodoo Vette, opened the door and offered his hand in assistance.

He gently closed the door behind her, climbed in behind the wheel, cranked the big V eight and eased it into gear.

"Joe's okay with you? I'm on a tight budget these days."

"Sure, Joe's is fine. Want me to pay?"

"Things aren't that bad . . . not yet anyhow."

She studied his profile as he drove. She sensed a vulnerability that allowed a kinder, gentler man to show through. He was a far cry from the boy who paaked in handicap parking, and took free meals and dry cleaning from the local merchants. He hung a wrist over the steering wheel and stared straight ahead. "It's just that life's not so great on campus for the big dog quarterback when he isn't winning."

"Doesn't matter to me," she said. If Brad had not been so cocksure the first time they'd met, things might've been different, she thought. Now there seemed to be room for someone in Brad's life in addition to Brad. Too bad she didn't have any room in hers.

He chose a table next to the plate glass window that looked out onto the street. They could watch traffic and observe strollers who stopped to investigate the action at the bar.

They indulged in Joe's standard fare: burgers, fries, and beer. Their table was far enough from the kitchen that the smell of sizzling grease did not overpower them. A three-piece band drowned away on an old country tune she did not recognize, but felt sure that Sloan would have. It was what he called belly rubbin' music. She bit her lower lip. It had been weeks since she had heard from him. Brad did not ask her to dance and for that she was thankful. A close dance to country music would have put her awash in déjà vu and over the top emotionally.

When they drained the last drop of beer from their frosted mugs, Brad leaned toward her.

"What say we go to my place? We can kick back and listen to some music. I got Mozart, Glenn Miller, and Lawrence Welk. Whatever suits you."

"Got any Carl Perkins?"

He pushed his legs out straight and leaned back in the booth. "I swear, girl. You sure as hell don't strike me as a Rockabilly."

"Just because I speak with a Bostonian twang? Forget it. Not going to your apartment. . . but if I did . . . would you behave? No funny business?" She raised an eyebrow and stared down her nose at him.

He held up his right hand. "Scout's honor. You're in charge."

"Then I'll go, but just for a little while. We can listen to some music, and when I say so, you'll take me home. Okay?"

She felt pangs of guilt for agreeing to be alone with another man. What would Sloan think? Him and his damned "secret mission."

"You can help me celebrate. Next month, I'm moving out of the apartment back to the dorm."

He parked the Vette next to the curb outside his upscale apartment complex. She felt excitement mixed with guilt. This is not where she wanted her life to go. She had promised to be with Sloan for a lifetime. They were engaged and that had not changed. She rested a hand on her chest, feeling the small hard knot of ruby sea glass against her breast. Brad was just a friend and right about now, she needed a friend.

She followed him down the carpeted hall to the entrance to his apartment. He unlatched the door and turned on lights that revealed a nicely furnished, but somewhat cluttered, bachelor pad. The same gaudy athletic posters were tacked to every wall. A sliding glass door opened onto a small patio where he had most likely been grilling steaks for another house guest. Female? She wondered. The lid to the grill stood open. An unmade bed was visible through an open door off the living room. From the hallway, she could see a yawning toilet in the powder room.

"Maid's month off." He quickly pulled the bedroom door closed. "Make yourself at home." He gestured toward the couch. He leaned over the stereo, touching the on button and adjusted the volume so as not to overpower their conversation. "Jimi Hendrix good for you?"

"Man, you really can't take a joke can you? Just put on some Mozart. Any movement will be fine."

In another smooth move, he grabbed an open bottle of wine from the fridge and two glasses off the drain board on the kitchen counter. On another night, it might have been the pigskin he was about to deliver downfield.

"Chablis?"

"Sure," she said. "One glass on top of two beers will be okay . . . won't it?" Who was she kidding? That was a big night's consumption for her. "If you get me drunk, I'll just go to sleep."

"Thanks for the warning."

She took her glass and settled back on the sofa, leaving room for Brad to join her, but he chose to sprawl on an overstuffed leather reclining chair and hung one leg over the arm. Once they were comfortable, he held up his glass to clink a toast.

She could not believe the changes a few months had made. She felt vulnerable, uneasy in his presence.

"So, what's the news from Spain and that guy you were dating. What's his name—Slag?"

"Oh, him? He's on a secret mission. Incommunicado. And his name's Sloan."

"So," he swirled the wine in his glass. "I take it you haven't heard from him in a while?"

"It's been a few weeks." She looked away. "Say, that's a great looking poster." She pointed to a large watercolor print that occupied half the main wall. "Is it by that famous—what's his name? The guy who does all those athletic scenes?"

"Neiman. That's right, Leroy Neiman. Me and him are big buds . . . Not really." Brad raised an inquisitive eyebrow. "So, what gives? What's the deal on Slag?"

"I think he's into something nefarious. You know, international intrigue and all that. He's patriotic and proud to serve his country. An admirable quality in a man, don't you think?"

"If you say so." Brad leaned against the back of the chair and stared at the ceiling. "But my take on his situation is a bit different."

"And just what would that be Mr. Know-it-all."

"Sure you wanna hear it?"

"Lay it on me. I can take all *you* have to dish out."

"As I see it, your man Slag has met a local woman. Beautiful, sexy, and available. She speaks little or no English beyond yes, thank you, and more, por favor. His lieutenant's bars make him as attractive to her as the QB number 7 did to the coeds here on campus, but in Madrid *he's* the BMOC."

"You're so full of crap," she said.

Brad took a long sip of wine and put his glass on the coffee table then stood and extended his hand. "How about a dance for old time's sake?"

"Old time's?" she echoed, but when he leaned toward her, she went into his arms. They moved around the room to a Mozart concerto. Neither the beat nor the melody was right for dancing. She found comfort in his arms. She was drawn to his gentleness, his strength. She craved closeness and didn't expect to feel the way she did.

She wondered if Brad could be right about Sloan. She still loved the roughneck, but four weeks of silence was too damned long. Something had gone wrong.

Brad touched the light switch and the room went to semi-dark.

She had to put a stop to this, but instead she buried her face in his strong chest. He pulled her close. She was immersed in the aroma of Old Spice, Sloan's favorite lotion. She raised her head to look into his eyes. "Brad, I—"

Her words were cut short by his strong mouth demanding that she kiss him. She complied then pushed him away. "Did you think I was joking about being engaged? I take this shit damned serious. I am pledged to Sloan until he says different. Now, take me home." She turned away and ran for the door.

XXV

Regina had spent her childhood on a bodega in the hill country south of Madrid where she worked alongside her parents and siblings to grow and process grapes. She professed that the work was hard and physical, but gratifying. Her father was considered by many to be an expert in the art and craft of grooming vines, growing grapes and turning them into fine wine.

With the help of Sergeant Tobin, Sloan managed to sign out a jeep for the day. With Regina's help, they found their way along country roads, among acres upon acres of vineyards, to the Gonzales family vineyard. Regina, over the roar of the military-issue Jeep, provided a running commentary about the families and the products they grew and processed on their farm.

After a two-hour drive through the country, they arrived at the Gonzales family home. The main house was a charming two-story stucco structure surrounded by a tall whitewashed fence. The front yard was accented by beautiful flower and vegetable gardens. Regina had explained that the farm was some three hundred acres, but little was wasted as the vineyard encroached on the house from all sides.

Señora Gonzales met them at the door and ushered them into the main drawing room. A buffet had been set up along one wall of the Victorian parlor.

Regina introduced him to her mother, two sisters, and a brother. Regina's family must have wondered why she and this stranger from America were in such a hurry to marry. Sloan assumed they knew the whole story but were too polite to ask the questions that would have revealed the truth about Regina's dilemma.

A selection of cheeses, olives, and a wonderful choice of wines, all from the local region, was attractively arranged on the sideboard. Sloan learned that the family grew the grapes for a wide array of wines, all of which were offered as refreshment to the soon to be married couple.

"Señor Sloan," dijo la señorita Gonzales, "Disfrute de la comida y servirte el vino. Papa de Regina estará con nosotros pronto. Él está trabajando en la viña. Hemos enviado a alguien a buscarlo."

Sloan nodded politely but Regina saw that he had no clue what her mother was telling him.

"My mother wishes that you will enjoy her buffet and please be patient as her husband, my padre, will be here soon. They have sent a workman to the fields to inform him of your arrival." Sloan nodded. Regina's mother smiled cheerfully and bowed politely.

Sloan and Regina selected cheese and fruit from the bountiful table. Regina chose a white wine and Sloan followed her lead.

No sooner had they returned to their seats than a sturdy frame of a man filled the parlor door. Sloan felt a nervous panic. This man had, on many occasions, forced his will on others. Regina embraced her father warmly then grabbed Sloan's hand and led him over to him. "This is Señor Abernathy who is a lieutenant in the American Army."

Arms crossed, the winemaker looked Sloan over as if he were a trader choosing a slave for the field. Convinced he was a good value, he thrust a burley hand out to Sloan. "Welcome," he said as he poured a glass of the red and handed it to Sloan

"Here. Try this rojo. Es one of my best. That one you have is sissy blanco por Regina and her Mama.

"This is hearty roho por hombres. You like, huh?" He gave Sloan a slap on the back, spilling the wine which Sloan managed to catch on his plate.

Sloan raised his glass. "Si gusta."

"So que los niños been up to?" He laughed nervously and struck himself in his barrel chest with a closed fist.

Sloan understood why Regina feared what this man might do when provoked.

It was time to explain the purpose of their visit and Regina took the lead. "We have been dating for several months now." She took Sloan's hand, lacing her fingers with his. "We met at a party and fell in love almost at once." He could see the fear in her eyes as she looked at him for confirmation. He nodded. For the moment he felt safe hiding behind his inability to add anything to her lie.

"This is true," Sloan said. "We enjoy many of the same things." He did not attempt to use his roughhewn Spanish in support of their alibi, but gave in to English and trusted Regina to translate when it was required.

"Si te gusta." Papa said with a bit of a leer across his broad face.

Regina squeezed Sloan's hand between hers. "It's true Mama. Señor Sloan loves it that I cook for him and we take long walks in the park. He loves children. Don't you, my love? We stop to play when we see niños in the park."

Sloan swallowed hard and hoped his expression did not betray him. All they had enjoyed together was one fine dinner, numerous glasses of wine, and a night of unbridled passion.

"Tell me, Mister Sloan," her mother asked, using her limited English to interrogate her prospective son-in-law, "where is your home? Do your parents grow?"

Sloan was puzzled by her question so Regina finished the translation. "She is asking if they farm. You know, do they grow food or grapes. Are they farmers?"

Weed Farmers, he thought.

"When I was a boy in Texas, we grew vegetables and flowers in our yard. My father was a welder."

"Que es welder?" Regina's mother asked. Regina could not explain the skill of welding.

"Do you have sisters and brothers in America?" she asked.

"I have a brother. He is a priest."

"Muy bueno." Regina's mother clasped her hands. "Usted es Católic."

Sloan felt embarrassment overtake his expression. "Episcopal. He's a priest in the Episcopal Church."

"Oh," her mother said, unable to disguise her disappointment. "You know if you marry my daughter you must raise your children to be Catholic."

Sloan pondered the edict. It seemed so unfair to his children to make that choice for them before they were even born. "I'm sure Regina and I will come to an agreement on religion when the time comes."

Senior Gonzales remained stoic throughout Sloan's interrogation. He was not eager to have his lovely daughter marry a foreigner, a total stranger, an American capitalist whose family grew flowers. He would have to know more before he would give his consent. He was not so easily convinced, but his Regina was steadfast.

XXVI

The wedding took place in August in a small chapel in the quaint village where they had met her parents the previous week. The day was steeped in family tradition and Catholic ritual. Her family was represented at regimental strength: father, mother, siblings, cousins, aunts, uncles and everyone who lived and worked on the bodega. There was little hope that Sloan would remember the names of all his new in-laws.

The Abernathy clan was not represented. Sloan explained that his family was too old or too poor to make such a long journey on such short notice.

Regina ran her fingers down the chest of his Army dress uniform, "So handsome."

She wore a white wedding gown passed down from her mother and her grandmother before her. Regina's mother could have still worn the dress. She was so wonderfully slender and delicate. Long days in the sun tending vines had done little to tarnish her natural beauty. He found it reassuring that Regina would retain her beauty long into her life.

She held out her arms and did a pirouette. "You like?"

"Beautiful," he admitted. He wondered what Abigale would have looked like on their wedding day. She would have worn something starched and proper with pearl buttons, perhaps.

Sloan asked Captain Jameson to be his best man, which seemed fitting considering he had introduced the couple that night in Madrid. Regina was attended by her sisters, a cousin and three girls from the village.

The couple stood before the priest who had known Regina all her life.

Sloan wondered if Regina had confessed their night of debauchery. If so, would the father reflect on her confession as he proceeded with the wedding ritual? Perhaps it was the priest who had insisted she pursue marriage as a solution to her dilemma. Sloan's paranoid nature drove him to suspect that Regina had somehow stacked the deck. Like Daddy always said, "Every hand's a winner."

"Lieutenant Abernathy, do you take as your wife, Regina Gonzales?"

"Yes—si. I do."

This was the day everyone looks forward to for most of their lives, but Sloan felt trapped as the priest read and the couple recited their vows. He thought of Abigale and how this day would have been different if she was standing there all in white, starched and buttoned down. Mr. LaHolm would be standing behind Sloan and patting him on the shoulder. *Sloan's such a fine young man*, he would have said.

"Yo los declaro marido y mujer, Lieutenant. You may kiss your bride."

And he did.

By family tradition, the bride and groom would spend their first night in the family compound. In earlier times, the mother of the bride waited outside the bride's chamber to receive the bloody sheets as testament to the bride's virtue.

Sloan was not sure what was expected of him nor did he feel affection, let alone lust, for his bride. He was overcome by guilt for having betrayed Abigale and for being an interloper in the Gonzales family. He was the jackal who had dragged their lovely daughter into the thicket of a loveless marriage, an unholy union between strangers, consummated for the sake of an unborn child.

"So, my darling Sloan," Regina said, closing the bedroom door, "if you want to have some fun with my family tomorrow morning, all you have to do is prick my finger, or if you are a true gentleman, we can prick yours."

He was relieved when Regina complained that she was exhausted from the day's events and that she was uncomfortable making love in the upstairs guest room of her family home. She imagined cousins and siblings lurking outside their door in hopes of hearing telltale sounds. "I know, I was right outside this door when my older sisters got married, God forgive me, I heard everything. Believe me she was no virgin."

They dressed for bed. Regina dropped off almost immediately. Sloan stretched out on his back in the dark, stared at the ceiling and wondered how life really worked. It seemed to him as if the unborn child was in control. Was it a new soul that demanded a body for its habitation?

Regina had little knowledge of contraception beyond the rhythm method and her family or church would not have condoned its use. Was this little soul, the one living inside her body, one that had tried to make the journey from Sloan's loins to Brenda's womb only to have been denied by a chemical in Brenda's body? Was this soul resolute in its determination to have a life, having found its way to Regina's womb? Who could say how it all worked? Should Regina lose the child, what then? His relationship with Abigale was in ruins. He was in a marriage with a woman who was not his true love. In fact, there was no spiritual connection between them whatsoever. He did not see her from across a crowded room. She was just one more face in a smoky crowded bar.

The next morning, the newlyweds appeared in the main dining room for breakfast with the family. Sloan was conspicuous with a tidy bandage tied around his index finger. Everyone at the table giggled and smiled knowingly.

After breakfast, the couple departed the Gonzales family home back to Madrid where he had located and rented a cozy bungalow near the base. The cottage, built around 1900, was constructed from stone harvested in nearby fields. The interior revealed evidence of repairs made to the east wall as a result of a bombing raid that took place during the Spanish Civil War.

The structure was located at the end of a long drive that made a circle in front of the house. English gardens bordered the drive. These exquisite gardens would provide an outlet for Sloan's love of gardening. As a boy, he had grown vegetables in his back yard and had come to enjoy tilling the soil and tending the plants.

Sloan had no money for a honeymoon nor did he have sufficient leave accrued to take time away from work. He had managed a three-day pass for the wedding and a promise from Gibbs to keep him off travel status for a few days.

As they arrived at the house in the borrowed Jeep, they spotted an envelope stuffed in the crack of the front door. Sloan opened it and read a message from Sergeant Tobin:

Lieutenant Abernathy,

Your leave has been canceled.

Report immediately to HQ with full travel gear.

Plan for an indefinite stay at your temporary assignment. A shuttle has been arranged to take you to Madrid International for a MATs to Hong Kong.

Duration of assignment is unknown.

Happy honeymoon,

Sarg.

He handed her the note. "Looks like the honeymoon's over. So much for Gibbs' promise to keep me off the road for a few days."

"Short honeymoon, huh, Sloan," she pouted. "You could pretend you didn't find the note until tomorrow."

"You don't know Gibbs. We have just enough time to walk around, have a look and talk about sleeping arrangements."

"Nobody sleeps on their honeymoon," Regina said. She smiled then laughed out loud. "Guess we already had our honeymoon and the bandage to prove it. We will have to postpone our next one 'til you return."

Sloan took her on a quick tour of the bungalow.

"This is the main bathroom, also the only bathroom. We'll have to share it."

"No problem. As long as you put the seat down."

The bathroom had a cast iron tub and a shower attached to one wall. The shower and tub were as old as the house itself.

"And through here is your bedroom. You can have the biggest one, you'll grow into it."

"Very funny, soldier boy."

"I'll take this one. I have a room at the base if I need more space."

She propped her knuckles on her hips. "Sloan, have you already forgotten that ceremony at the church? We are man and wife and in Spain that means we share a bed."

"I hope you understand. I'll need some time to get used to the idea, that's all. You know I was planning to marry my college sweetheart. I can't just turn her off like a light switch. It's not as easy as that."

"Never thought you'd treat me like extranjero, house maid. This is all very sudden for me too, and it was not all my doing." She grabbed his hand and placed it on her stomach. "You were as eager to go to my apartment that night as I was to take you there."

"And I accept full responsibility," Sloan said. "Had it not been for that full moon, none of this would've happened."

"So, now you blame the moon? No good, Sloan. We have the culprit right here," she laughed and faked a punch to Sloan's gut.

He caught her hand in his fist. "Look, Regina. I've made a commitment to raise our child with you and I will live up to my end of the bargain. Anything else, if it happens, will take time. Our baby will be here in about seven months. That should give us time to decide if it's love or lust that has brought us together."

"I hope a little of both," she said.

XXVII

Captain Jameson was in charge of the mission to China. Sloan was second in command. In all, there were three men from allied forces and five Americans. Among the Americans was a lovely young Tech Sergeant named Margret O'Shannesy, who spoke fluent Chinese. She was born and raised in a small ranching community in Montana and joined the Army in hopes of seeing the world. With a Chinese mother, Margret was a natural to become a linguist. She also spoke fluent Spanish, and when she learned that Sloan had a new Spanish bride, she offered to tutor him.

For thirteen days, the team hung around the airfield at Qingdao with little to do but get acquainted. The objective of the mission was unclear to Sloan or to Jameson. For Sloan, little was gained beyond learning that Jameson shared an interest in sailing. They agreed that, upon returning to Spain, they would venture down to the Mediterranean for a charter and some sailing lessons.

The entire team, along with three helicopters and two single-winged reconnaissance aircraft were billeted in one large hanger. Sloan slept on a cot next to Jameson on his left and Margret on his right. Long after the crew had turned in for the evening Sloan lay on his back and stared into the rafters of the hanger. Pigeons roosted directly above him. He thought about the twists his life had taken since leaving school. He was married to a woman he barely knew, and she was carrying his child or, by all accounts, it was his child. He was sleeping on an Army-issue cot in the middle of a very foreign country, side by side with a woman whose Irish Catholic name he could not, without some difficulty, pronounce. Thus far, Jameson was one of the few constants in Sloan's life. He had introduced him to Regina and later had acted as best man at his wedding.

After almost two weeks of unproductive time in China, the team grew short on patience and sick of Chinese food. Jameson contacted Gibbs in Madrid and requested permission to return to the base. Permission was granted. Sloan located a MATS flight that took the contingent back to Spain. When the taskforce arrived in Madrid early the following day, Sloan called Regina from the base to forewarn her that he would be home for dinner that evening. He arrived home to find the cottage swelling with the aroma of spicy Spanish food. A cozy fire added warmth to their home.

"Sloan!" She screamed with delight and threw her arms around him. "I thought you were never coming back. Where have you been for the last year?"

"Month. It just seemed like a year."

"So, you missed me?"

"Well, I sure as hell missed your cooking."

"You don't really think I can cook do you?"

"Told your mom you could. Anyway, it's gotta be better 'n Chinese."

"Do Chinese really eat cats?"

He decided not to answer her question. "What did you do to fill the time?"

She spread her arms. "Just open your eyes and look around. Don't tell me you can't see what I've done." She doubled her fist and playfully poked him in the stomach. "Damn it, soldier boy. I got so lonesome I started inviting the neighbors in."

The old house had come with the basics: beds, curtains and cooking utensils. She had hung paintings and family pictures that transformed their drab bungalow into a cozy casa.

Thanks to Margret's tutoring, Sloan understood more of Regina's Spanish. After the separation, he was drawn to Regina's creamy complexion, her black eyes and her warm smile. He was mesmerized by her as she glided stealth-like through the house. Regina would never replace Abigale, but two weeks of barracks life and Chinese food had taken its toll on Sloan's morale.

He remained puzzled by her command of English. It seemed to come and go, but as she led him through the bungalow by the hand, she spoke and understood him perfectly. Perhaps she had been studying too.

"Mis padres gave us this wonderful bottle of vino, and I make us yummy dinner. Sloan, my darling, will you uncork the vino, por favor? I will serve our cena."

The table was set and candles lit. Sloan forced the screw into the cork to free the rich red wine. They had been given two crystal glasses as a wedding gift. Sloan decanted two servings; they touched their glasses in a toast. The crystal rang true.

"Salud," Sloan said.

"Salud." Her warm smile made him feel good. He found himself snuggling back.

She set plates of food in front of them. He pulled out her chair and scooted it beneath her. He gently touched her shoulder, stroked her hair and kissed her neck.

"My mother came for me and I spent a week at home. Is that good?"

"Good?" he said. "Do you mean, was it okay?"

"Si, okay, por favor?"

"I'll be gone for long periods with my work at the base. I see no need for you to be here alone all that time."

They finished their salads and Sloan poured a second glass of wine for himself, but Regina refused a refill.

He took her by the hand and led her down the hall to the master bedroom. They stood at the side of her bed. He caressed her and kissed her. He released the clasp that held her dress together at the back. Her silk frock fell to the floor in a pile at her feet. He kissed her again, lowered her onto her bed and joined her there.

"Do you love me?" she asked.

It was a fair question, but one that came with enormous conflict. Circumstances and chemistry had brought them together, and a ceremony in the presence of God had bound them till death would part them.

She needed to know that he had feelings for her. It was inalienable.

"Sí te amo. Till death do us part."

XXVIII

Sloan answered the phone in his office and was greeted by heavy breathing and snorting followed by dead silence. He leaned back and put his boots up on the desk. "Hello, Jake, you old whore. What're you up to besides wasting my nickel?"

"How'd you know it was me? It could've been another one of them Spanish bitches calling to say you'd knocked her up."

"Hardly," Sloan said. "So, what's up with you?"

"You're talking to a freshly minted college graduate just out of the FSU School of Engineering."

"You mean you finally got the skin? Only took you, what, eight years?"

"Eight, my ass. Five. Graduated in the top half of my class."

"Got your orders yet?" Sloan asked.

"Yep, and that brings me to why I'm calling. I just might be comin' your way."

"Spain?" Sloan said. "I doubt that. We got no use for construction types here in snoop town."

"Are you kidding man? They tried to send me there, but I wouldn't have it. I did a whole hell of a lot better 'n Spain, that's for damn sure."

"What could be better than Spain?" Sloan said.

"Germany. I'm on my way to—"

"Germany? Man, it gets colder 'n a witch's tit. What 'n hell are you gonna do there anyway?"

"They got some old hospitals, you know, left over from the war that need to be overhauled. I'm gonna head up the whole damned operation."

"So, you're in over your head from the get-go?"

"Nothing new there. I'm thinkin' maybe I can swing by Madrid day after tomorrow on my way to Berlin. Think you could buy me a few drinks and let me meet your squeeze?"

"Just let me know your timing and I'll see what I can do. I know this little place close to the train station where I can get you a passable warm beer."

On Friday, Sloan checked out of the office early and made his way to a tavern a block from the train station in downtown Madrid. He was sipping on his third Scotch when he saw Jake's reflection in the mirror behind the bar. He looked taller and leaner. His hair was freshly cut, and not by that cadet down the hall who made his spending money sheering his fellow students. He stood silhouetted in the barroom door. Sloan swiveled on his stool. "Welcome to the European theater."

Jake swaggered into the dimly lit bar as if he'd been there a dozen times. "Thank you, Suh." Jake postured like MacArthur and pretended to be smoking a pipe.

"This peacetime duty gets mighty boring, if you ask me. What we need is a nother war." Jake rested his palms on the bar and shouted good naturedly to the barman. "Hey what's a man gotta do to get a drink around here?" The waiter set a glass in front of Jake, filled it with Scotch and topped off Sloan's drink in the same smooth motion.

"Been waitin' long?"

"Couple of hours," Sloan lied. "Expected you'd be late, Suh."

"Why would that change just 'cause I graduated college. Wouldn't want to lose that Southern charm. So, where's this Spanish beauty I been hearin' so much about?"

"Didn't bring her. Getting too big around the middle to be any fun at a party."

"So, it's true then. You got a Spanish wife and a kid on the way?"

"Think I'd make it all up? Shotgun weddings aren't the kind of thing I joke about."

"Man, how things change. When you left for Spain it was all about Abby, and now you're all married up to a Señorita. My God, man, I hear these black-eyed beauties have great power over men, but shit, this tops it all."

"Power?" Sloan reflected soberly on the meaning of the word. "You could say so. I know it looks strange, but it happened. We met at a dinner party. One thing led to another and we ended up at her place. I thought I was being gallant, you know, seeing she got home safe, but she had a different idea."

"Now I get it," Jake said. "She held you at gunpoint and forced you into bed."

"If I told you that was true, would you buy it?"

"No. I get it that you slept with her, but what made you think you had to marry her?" Jake leaned back and hooted at the ceiling. "Must a been damned good!"

A couple at the end of the bar moved to a private table to avoid being drawn into their rowdy discussion.

"Yeah, well, I told her I was engaged and she understood and agreed not to bother me.

"I like your hang out," Jake said. "Bet you could pick up some lovelies in this place. So, what happened next?"

"That was the end of it 'til about a month later when she called and wanted to meet up with me for a talk."

"Oldest scam in the world and you fell for it. How'd you know she wasn't one of them CIA operatives checking you out for your clearance?"

"That's crazy talk, man. Where 'n hell did you get such an idea?"

"It happened to some guy in our outfit who went to Italy."

"And just how'd you find out?"

"Grapevine, story that was going around the barracks."

Sloan reflected on Jake's line of crap. Suppose she could've been lying, but I couldn't chance it." Sloan gave in to scratching a nervous itch on the back of his neck.

"So, you dumped Abby 'cause this black-eyed beauty *said* you knocked 'er up."

"Like I said, man. I couldn't take the risk. I had no choice."

"Let me guess. She's a good Catholic girl, not on the pill."

"You're right about that. Pill hasn't made it over the pond except on the black market, and yeah, most all of Spain's Catholic."

Jake spun on his stool to survey the prospective ladies. He stopped with his back to the bar and both elbows on it. "Most men I know would insist on an abortion rather than marry someone they just met and fell in the sack with. Happens all the time." Jake stared reflectively into empty space and stirred his Scotch with his finger. "Remember all those nights in the dorm when we argued about abortion, premarital sex and such things as when a fetus becomes a person and therefore entitled to vote? You argued that we all had souls at conception." Jake shook his head. "Your old man sure must've done a number on you."

"The pill was a game changer. You can't deny that it gave single guys like us an out that circumvented the question." Sloan said.

"When push came to shove, I thought you'd take the easy way out, like the rest of us. You're the last one I expected to man up."

"Listen man, we're talking about my wife here and the mother of my child. I'm likely to spend the rest of my life with her, so I *have* to accept it."

"Then you better, by God, make the best of it." Jake said. "She got any sisters? Maybe I can come back on leave and she can fix me up."

"Don't hold your breath."

"What'd you tell Abby?"

"Abby? Nothing."

"You mean you lied to her?"

"Well, no. Not exactly."

"Then, exactly what *did* you tell 'er?"

"I called her right enough, but once I got her on the phone, I couldn't get it out, so I took the coward's way out and wrote her a letter. I figured in a letter she couldn't interrupt me before I was finished. You know how headstrong that woman can be."

"How could you be such a jerk?" Jake said. "You're not the man I shared a room with. Where's the guy who went through life looking for his true love and all that crap? The man I knew wouldn't do what you did—dump his true love without a word or a second thought. That guy would've found a way to get around it. I know for a fact she would 'a stuck with you."

"Nothing you can say I haven't already thought of. Now, let's just forget about—barkeep, another round por favor."

"Okay, I'll come clean. I see her on campus from time to time. A few weeks back we had coffee. She was all torn up. Hadn't heard a peep out of you in over a month. Hey barkeep, can you burn us a couple of big steaks?"

Sloan moved to the edge of the bar. "Damn it, Jake. What'd you tell her?"

Jake saw the misery on Sloan's face. "Same crap as you. That you was on some secret assignment and couldn't contact anyone. Incognito, national security at stake. Just bullshit."

"She buy it?"

"What's the difference? She's out of your life for good."

"¿Qué tan grande le gustaría esos filetes, señores?" The waiter interrupted.

"She got my letter, right?"

"Didn't mention no letter."

"¿Cómo quiere que sus caballeros filetes hacer?"

"Make mine burnt on the outside and raw inside," Sloan said.

"Burn 'em both to a crisp," Jake repeated,

"Think, man. It's important. Don't you see? If she didn't get my letter, she might think it's still on with us."

"Don't see how much could change," Jake said.

"Hell, man, I could arrange a trip back to the states on Army business. It would be great to see her."

"You'd best forget that horseshit. She's likely to take a hammer to you."

"So . . . will you tell her for me?"

"No way 'n hell, good buddy. I'm stayin' on her good side." He swirled the ice in his glass. "Never know when I might put some moves on 'er myself."

"You'd do that? Put the make on your best friend's woman?"

"Not like you're gonna be back at her for a while yet. Maybe twenty years and by then she'll be old news. Course, she might just surprise you and show up."

"Here, in Madrid? What 'n hell are you—"

"Nothing. Forget it. Forget I said anything."

"While you're working on them steaks we could us another couple of drinks," Jake said.

"Sí señor, señores."

Jake and Sloan gnawed through tough steaks, drank more Scotch than they needed, and relived some of the great moments of their college days. For Jake, it was all about the women he wished had come in and out his door. Sloan played along, but his heart wasn't in it. They spoke no more of Abigale and the mess Sloan had made of his life with her.

Along about midnight, Jake checked the time. "Damn it. Got to catch that train to Heidelberg."

"Heidelberg, hell. You ain't fit to go nowhere. Better take you home with *me*." Sloan was drunk enough to agree to most anything. The whiskey was doing all the talking.

"I do wanna meet your bitch but not when I'm half in the bag."

"Trust me, old stick. You're all the way in the—better go with you to the station. It may take us both to pour you on the train. Grab some empty seats and sleep it off. You'll be in Berlin 'fore you sober up."

"By the way, Brenda, says hello."

"Brenda? You mean—you son of a bitch."

"I couldn't see lettin' that nice apartment go to waste. Besides, like you said, she had a prescription."

XXIX

The conductor shook Jake hard, but he didn't so much as move or open an eye. "Der Dirigent schüttelte ihn kräftig. Hier können Sie aussteigen. Das ist Ihre stoppen. Ihre Basis ist nur fünf Meilen von hier. Nimm ein Taxi. Er wird genau wissen wo es geht"

Finally, Jake blinked and tried to focus on the rude old German who was rattling his brains. "Can't understand a word you're saying. Cheap Scotch must've affected my hearing. You talk any 'merican?"

The crotchety old conductor gave Jake one last shake and shouted, "Get off train, take taxi to base. You make tip now, okay, please?" Jake made it to his feet and hoisted his duffel onto one shoulder.

Not sure which is heaviest, this duffel or my head, he thought. He dug in his pants pocket for some loose change and handed it to the porter who stared at his palm as if Jake had spit in it.

Jake struggled to the door of the passenger car and threw his duffel onto the landing. An eager driver grabbed it, and without exchanging so much as a greeting, threw it in the back seat of his hack and motioned Jake to join him in front.

He fumbled through his pockets for a copy of his orders to show the driver his address. "Here," Jake said, pointing to the base address. "Take me here."

The old driver nodded and sped away. Jake's head rocking back and forth on the seat, he dozed until the cab pulled up to the guard shack in front of Berlin Brigade Headquarters. Jake opened his wallet where he had squirreled away cab fare in German marks. The driver seemed chagrined as he was accustomed to taking advantage of soldiers who failed to convert their dollars to marks.

With a copy of his orders in his teeth, Jake dragged his luggage out of the back seat and made his way to the guard shack. The MP saluted, took Jake's orders, and got on the phone to make arrangements for someone to escort this newly minted, still intoxicated lieutenant onto the base.

Lugging his duffel, he followed his escort past the security gate and down a long corridor to the BOQ. The sergeant unlocked his room and held the door until Jake could dump his baggage in a heap on the floor.

"What do you guys do for excitement around here, now that Elvis went home?"

The young sergeant removed the key from the door and handed it to Jake. "Well, Sir, you just missed Oktoberfest. Everyone big enough to hold a beer mug spends two weeks in the beer halls, singing, dancing and sampling the local brews. First time in my life I woke up in a beer hall and started getting drunk all over again."

"I'm gonna like it here."

"You look like a man who could hold your own at a fest. Hang around until next year and give it a whirl. Several of us are going down to Checkpoint Charlie on Saturday. You're welcome to come along. We'll show you around."

"What'll we do there?"

"Hang out. Make a nuisance of ourselves. Some college girls will be marching around with signs. You know. Tear Down This Wall, Yankee Go Home, the usual shit."

"Sounds like a good way to meet women." Jake peered up from the bed he suddenly found himself sitting on. "Unless they're that angry type."

"No, Sir. They're usually pretty cool. And by the time the day is over, most of them are ready for some real excitement, if you get my drift. By the way, Sir, my name's Ed. If you need help gettin' settled, I'm your man."

Jake shook the hand that was thrust at him and fell asleep sprawled back on the bed fully dressed.

Jake's first free weekend came none too quick. After that drinking bout with Sloan and an intense first week on the job, he needed time to adjust to his new surroundings. Hanging around a few pubs and sampling the local brew was in order. Who knows, he might make the acquaintance of one of the local beauties, all tired out from carrying her heavy sign. He walked the streets, surveying the crowds. The pile of demonstrators' posters in the foyer of one bar was his clue that a thirsty crowd had decided to end their day of protest and start some serious demonstrating. He took a seat at the bar.

"Die Partei ist dort hinten im Garten," the bartender said.

Jake fumbled with his tourist dictionary, but before he could locate the right passage, the barkeep interrupted him, this time in perfect English, "Go on back to the Garten. They're a friendly lot. I'll bring you a beer."

This is like walking into Joe's, he thought. The music was more oompah than Willie Nelson, but holding the girl was the best part of dancing in any language. Jake had never been shy about talking a girl into his arms. In the hours that followed, he managed to meet several damen. Some spoke English with a cute German accent that they had learned in school or from dating American servicemen.

Between dances, he straddled a stool at the end of the bar and scanned the room and the ladies as they came and went. He'd been there a couple of hours when a pair of beautiful blue eyes stared back at him from the other end of the bar. He slid off his stool and made his way down the row to where she was sipping an iced beverage.

"Hello, blue eyes. I'm Jake."

"Pull up a chair, Jake. I'm Edie."

"Great. You speak English. I'm new here. Attached to the Army Corps of Engineers."

"Cold war soldier boy, eh? I'm third year at University."

"Rather think of it as peacetime occupation," Jake said.

"Is there a difference?" Edie said.

"What're you studying?"

"Government. I want to be a diplomat."

"What's the demonstration all about?"

"We want the Yanks to take their shit and go home." Her blue eyes danced as she spoke.

"Sounds good to me. But as long as I'm here, let's get some dinner."

"Not so fast, Mr. Army man. First, you should know something about me."

He propped his chin with the heel of his hand. "Okay . . . so, tell me. What is the one most important thing I should know about you?"

"My father was in the war. He was a fighter pilot. Might have shot your father. Does that bother you?"

"It was war. Your father did what was expected of him. Now, blue eyes, how about dinner? You pick the spot, not too pricy, now hear. I'm a poor sorry-ass GI."

"Spot?" she said. "You want to have dinner in a spot?" Her blue eyes sparkled in the afternoon sun.

"Restaurant, place to eat? You know, spot."

Jake and Edie spent the evening wandering the streets of Berlin. They talked about their lives and their dreams. Almost before they knew, the sun was gone and a harvest moon was lighting their way down the streets of Berlin.

Jake hailed a taxi to take them to Edie's dorm where they made a date to meet the following Saturday.

"Look, soldier boy, when you come for me next week, I'll have our day all planned. We will visit a war museum. You will enjoy, I think. We'll walk the streets of historic Berlin and have real German food at nice little *spot* I know."

Jake leaned down for the goodnight kiss, but she offered him her cheek. "Not so fast there, Army Man."

XXX

Mr. LaHolm glanced at his daughter in the passenger seat. "Are you sure you want to do this?"

"Yes, Dad. I have to go. If he really is on a secret mission I'll have egg on my face. No big deal. At least I'll know where I stand."

She kissed her father's cheek and walked into the terminal where she boarded a red-eye flight to Madrid. She was traveling light. One carry-on and a large purse with everything she would need to put herself back together after a long night in a coach seat. She did not anticipate a protracted visit. She knew Sloan had a job to do and might not have free time to spare. She expected to be away for three days, no longer. She would locate him and make sure he was well. Maybe the trip was crazy, but it had been over a month since his last phone call when he told her of plans to go on a long mission. Fine, she got that, but the last time she had received a letter was more than a week before that phone call. She had every right to be concerned.

Perhaps he was ill or had been injured in the line of duty. He may have been the victim of a traffic accident. Damn Spaniards probably drive on the wrong side of the road. Anything could have happened. Once she located him, they would renew plans for their future, the date of the wedding and where they would live.

Brad had bet her a quarter that Slag had taken up with a local woman, but Brad was an impertinent ass who thought he knew everything. She knew that Sloan would never do that . . . but suppose he *has* found someone new and there I am looking like a fool.

She waved to her father from the entrance to the ramp. "Thank you, Daddy. Here goes nothing."

Her flight arrived in Madrid just ahead of the sun. She cleared customs and found her way to the curb. She had told Sloan in a letter just last week that she would arrive on flight 3555. She expected that he would meet her outside at the curb.

Fumes from motor vehicles bellowed up in her face, robbing her of fresh air as she moved through the terminal.

After almost forty minutes, she gave up, hailed a taxi and handed the driver the address to the base.

"The trip would requieren una media hora," her driver said as he stowed her luggage in the rear.

"Perfect." A half-hour would give her time to freshen up and think about what she would say to Sloan. Why in hell weren't you there to meet my flight? Didn't you get my letter? She dug her compact mirror out of her purse to survey of the damage. She ran a brush through her hair then found lipstick and rouge. Her hands trembled as she made quick repairs.

She slid her sunglasses on, pulled her large-brimmed hat down over them and settled back to relax, but her nerves would not cease their jittering. *Relax.* She could not.

She held the ruby sea glass pendant that hung from a chain around her neck. She longed for Sloan's warm smile and strong caress. She wanted to crawl into his arms and spend the day. She worried that coming to Madrid might have been a mistake, but she had written him only last week without a response. Her gurgling stomach served as a reminder that she had turned her nose up at the breakfast they offered her on the plane.

The driver brought the taxi to a stop in front of the main gate of the military complex and hurried to open her door.

"Espera por favor mientras confirmo que mi amigo está aquí," she said.

"Yo comprendo, señorita."

Her heart was pounding as she entered the visitor's lobby. She felt a twinge of anxiety as she approached the reception desk.

"Good morning, Sergeant. I'm here to see Lieutenant Abernathy. Can you please tell me where I can find him?"

"No, Ma'am. I got no idea. After the wedding he moved off base and I kinda lost track of him."

"There was a wedding?" Her voice cracked. "Who got –did one of his friends get—"

"That's right, Ma'am. Lieutenant Abernathy," the sergeant broke in, "some local girl. A real babe, I hear."

"I'll be damned." She grasped the ruby sea glass medallion as though it would prevent her from falling into a crevasse.

"Tied the knot 'bout two months back."

"Perhaps I'm not being clear. I'm looking for Lieutenant J. Sloan Abernathy. Six two, athletic build, brown hair, cut short. He turned twenty-three just last month."

"That's him to a tee. Might be at home. You can try and catch him there. Pretty sure he's been on assignment for at least a week."

"Assignment? To where?"

"Sorry, Miss. Can't say. Classified."

So, he *has* been on a secret mission. This trip might have been for naught. This wedding thing might be part of his cover or something like that. She felt herself being drawn into some international intrigue.

"There must be some mistake," she said. "There just might be more than one Abernathy in this man's Army?"

"Look, Miss. You want his address or not?"

"His address? Uh, sure, that would be most helpful. Thank you, Sergeant." Beads of nervous perspiration formed under the broad brim of her hat.

The sergeant jotted the address on a note pad, ripped off the page and handed it to her. "Easy to find if you got wheels."

"Yes, I have a car waiting. Thank you." Cheeky bastard.

She turned and marched back to the street and her waiting taxi. She handed the note to her driver. Her hands trembled.

He steered his taxi through narrow cobbled passages until they arrived at a small bungalow in an historic district of Madrid. The taxi slowed to a stop at the curb in front of a modest dwelling.

There stood Sloan with a large can, pouring water over pink roses in a lovely English garden.

A tallish slender brunette came out of the house and walked toward Sloan with an iced beverage, tea perhaps, or sangria. She appeared to be in a family way.

Abigale watched as the brunette handed the drink to Sloan then put her arm around his neck and kissed his cheek. Sloan took the drink from the Spanish beauty. He sipped from the frosty glass and turned his gaze to the taxi.

"Please driver, take me to el aeropuerto rápido por favor."

The driver put his car in motion.

Sloan ran in the direction of the taxi as it pulled away from the curb. Abigale tried to stop the cab, but could not formulate a timely sentence in Spanish that would convey her wishes to the driver. She looked through the rear window. Sloan stood on the curb, holding his beverage and shading his eyes as if trying to identify the mysterious passenger in the rear seat of the black taxi.

The driver steered his car through the city and onto the airport access road. All the while, Abigale tried to make sense of it all. Sloan was cohabitating with a Spanish woman—quite beautiful, but in a family way. There must be some explanation. He might have recognized her except for her dark glasses and wide-brimmed hat.

Son of a bitch. Brad was right all along.

Abigale stared out of the portal of the 747. She saw the top clouds and an endless expanse of black water below. The huge airliner was making its way across the Atlantic, floating on rarefied air high above the earth. An ocean liner, looking no bigger than a toy, was en route to New York or Miami. Other airliners and large aircraft crossing the pond traveled tangentially to hers, all carrying passengers who were traversing this great ocean to be reunited with loved ones or friends. She wondered how many would find a surprise. She wanted to cry, but it was not her style to resort to tears just because her life had taken a wrong turn.

If she could get her portal open, she would fly through it and let the wind blow her soul to some far off place, or allow it to sink to the depths of this vast ocean never to be matched with its mate . . . if such a thing even existed.

Her misery was interrupted by the man who had taken the seat next to hers.

"You look like you could use a friend and a drink," he said.

She turned to inspect the handsome stranger in a dark blue suit and an over-starched white shirt. The cuffs of his sleeves were neatly folded back. A crimson silk tie hung loosely around his neck. His rimless glasses were parked neatly on the bridge of his nose. His close cropped brown hair was beginning to show signs of retreating from his bushy brows, giving him the look of a man who earned his keep in a clean, well-lit, air conditioned office. This man was no roughneck nor was he an athlete.

"Sure, why not? I'll have a glass of Mogen David."

"Would that be white, red or pink?" he asked, with a broad smile.

"I love it all." She forced an answering smile.

"I'll see what I can do. I doubt they have too many calls for MD in first class. Not that it isn't a good choice, understand."

He extended his hand. "Name's McIntyre. Charles McIntyre."

"Abigale LaHolm. Gale to my friends." She took his hand and forced another smile. She knew she looked a fright. Her state of mind was compounded by too many hours without sleep.

"Have you been vacationing in Madrid?" he asked.

"No. Sick friend," she said, "been visiting a sick friend."

Charles frowned slightly showing his disappointment. "He doing okay?"

"Yes, he's fine, thanks. And dandy, just fine and dandy. And you, what took you to Madrid?"

"Business, actually. I'm in international finance with a firm out of Frisco. What line of work are you in?"

"Doing undergraduate work at Florida State. Hope to finish in a few weeks. I have no immediate plans beyond that. I was planning a visit to Spain for an extended period, but now that my friend is, uh, you know . . . better, there's no need for me to—"

She turned to face him. He seemed so calm, reassuring and easy to be with.

"Curing sick friends? That a sideline, Gale?" He continued the charade.

She ignored his question. "Tell me, Charles, is that a Harvard ring you're wearing?"

"Harvard Law, actually." He looked down and turned the ring on his finger. "Followed in my father's footsteps, and his father too."

"So, you're a third-generation preppy."

He laughed. "Yes, guess so. At least, I was at one time. Shadyside Academy, but that's ancient history."

The flight attendant served them white wine. "Sorry, sir. We don't have Mogen David,"

"So, Gale—okay if I call you Gale?"

"Sure. At this very moment, Charles, you're the best friend I have in the whole world."

"Where are you getting off?" Charles asked.

"Miami. My parents are holed up in Vero Beach for the winter. If I'm lucky, my father will meet me at customs."

They whiled away the hours exchanging stories and drinking wine. Charles helped keep her mind off what she had seen in Madrid and her impulse to dive through the portal into the vast nothingness. Four glasses of wine into the evening, she realized that at this moment, Charles was the single thread that held her to this life.

Charles walked with her to the gate where Mr. LaHolm was waiting. Abigale threw her free arm around Charles's neck and kissed him on the cheek leaving a crimson lipstick mark to rival his red silk tie.

"Thanks for keeping me company. You just may have saved my life."

"Call me if you ever get to the left coast." He pressed his card into her hand. "We'll share another bottle of Mogen David."

Mr. LaHolm retrieved her luggage from the conveyor and led her to the car.

They sat without speaking. He glanced in her direction from time to time, but did not press her for details about her trip and she didn't volunteer them. He knew she would open up, when *she* was ready.

"So, who was that handsome guy you were kissing at security?"

"Name's Charles. He fed me wine and listened to my tale of woe for seven straight hours. He's a very special man."

"It's good you had someone to pass the time with. Those long flights can be brutal."

"Haavard Law. Graduated cum laude. He knows all our favorite haunts in Cambridge and Boston. His favorite is Anthony's. When I told him you were a lobster fisherman he just about flipped."

"Sounds like a nice guy. Gonna see him again?"

She had no idea what she'd done with that business card and didn't care. "Right now, Daddy, you're the only man I want in my life."

"Yeah, sure."

After some miles and silence she drew a deep breath and said, "So, don't you want to know what our boy Slag's up to?"

He rested his elbow on the center console and leaned in to her, "If you want to tell me, sure."

"Married. He's married to some local bitch."

"I find that hard to—I'm sure there's a good explanation." He spoke in his best father-daughter conciliatory tone. "What did he have to say about it? Did you actually speak with him?"

"Did I speak with him? Sure! We had dinner and tossed back a few for old times' sake. You know, talked about the good old days. No Dad, we didn't talk, but I saw them. I'd cry, but I'm just too damn mad. If I could get my hands on him this minute, I might do something violent."

The automatic gate swung open and he brought the car to a stop in front of their garage. Abigale jumped out, waved him on and made her way down to the beach where she kicked off her shoes and marched onto the sand and into the surf. The cool briny water on her feet and the salt spray on her face helped to clear her head.

She thought about wading out beyond the surf and sliding beneath the waves to find rest and relief from her hurt and anger, but doing so would be declaring Sloan the winner and she was not ready to concede.

"Every hand's a winner, ain't that right, Sloan!" She shouted into the wind.

She wandered along the beach. Waves licked her feet. The last of the harvest moon illuminated the vast Atlantic and glistened on the crest of the waves as they broke on the sand. She had the whole world to herself and her whole life ahead of her. She had hit a bump in her road, but by no means was she at the end of it. Sloan had destroyed her happiness and she would not soon forget how he and that Spanish bitch had made her feel.

She gripped the ruby sea glass medallion and gave it a tug. The clasp gave way under the strain and the necklace came off in her hands. She held it and studied it briefly. She loved the way it glinted in the moonlight.

"Sloan, you no-good son of a bitch. I wouldn't marry you if you were the last son of a bitch on earth. Here, take back your crappy engagement present. I no longer want it."

With all her strength, she threw the medallion into the ocean. As the shard of glass passed her fingertips and flew out of her hand, the broken clasp caught the sleeve of her sweater and the pendant was left dangling from her arm by a thread.

She looked down to see the shard of glass dangling over the surf. What the hell, I'll keep it, to remind me of what a fool I've been. She stuffed it in her pocket. Damned if she was going to wear it.

She walked back along the beach to the condo and the cleaning station where she used mineral spirits to remove tar from the bottoms of her feet. The odor of the cleaning chemical overpowered the salt air, her own fragrance, and even the memory of Old Spice that still lingered as a final reminder of Sloan. The smell of her new life was clean and harsh and raw. She'd better get used to it.

Hot coffee and toast with her parents brought her back to some semblance of normal, but they looked at her as if she was a wounded bird. Their pity was not welcome.

She packed her things, threw her luggage in the boot and drove to Tallahassee. In a matter of months, she would finish her bachelor's degree and be ready to tackle the next big thing that came her way.

As she put the miles behind her, she wondered about Brad. She had been abrupt with him at his apartment last week, so he might have discarded her as a prospective conquest. She could have been kinder. He was having some rough times, not being on a winning team for the first time in his football career, and she wasn't doing all that great herself. Maybe they could cheer each other up.

She pulled into the parking lot behind the sorority house and struggled up the stairs with her luggage. She exchanged cursory greetings with friends and sorority sisters.

On her pillow she found a pile of phone messages. Several were from Brad, some with short notes: Joe's at 7. Bike ride on Saturday. Where in hell are you?

She contemplated the stack of messages. Perhaps it's time to give second string a chance. Brad just might have another winning season in him after all.

She found the phone and dialed his number.

"Miss me?"

Later that evening, they went to Joe's for fried shrimp and beer. After she had stared down every bubble in her third mug of Coors, she said, "Bet you're dying to know what's going on in Spain?"

"Sure. When you're ready."

"Slag's married." The words came easy, thanks to Adolph Coors. Telling Brad seemed to make it easier for her to accept.

Brad rolled up a napkin and artfully launched it at a passing waiter's tray. "Touch down!" the waiter shouted.

"You know, I'm not surprised. And that would be Sloan. His name's Sloan, remember," Brad said.

"No, you were right all along. He's nothing but a big piece of slag."

"You sure they're married? He might be hanging out with one of the local ladies as a matter of convenience. I hear guys in the military do that some."

"They're married, all right. The man at the base told me."

"So, you never actually saw Sloan?"

"Sure did. And his pregnant wife too. She was sticking out to here." She exaggerated the size of Regina's belly.

Brad reached across the table and took her hands in his. "Are you okay with all this?"

"Long as I don't ever see him again. And if I do, I want to have a gun handy."

"What say I take you home? I think you've had enough fun for one day."

XXXI

There were movies, bike rides, and walks on the beach at St. George Island. Brad knew Abigale was on the rebound, but he didn't care. He had been in love with her from the first time they met. Now it was his turn, and he sure as hell wouldn't screw it up the way Slag had.

For Abigale, images from all those hurtful experiences began to fade and were replaced by great times with Brad.

They enjoyed dinner at Joe's, followed by visits to his apartment.

Brad was aggressive on the playing field, but off the field he was compassionate, tender and understanding. He gave her all the space she needed to grow in her love for him.

She felt herself coming under his spell. Perhaps when her biological alarm began to chime, it didn't much matter who was there to shut it off. This whole mating thing was more about hormones than feelings. If Brad had behaved differently on their first date, the outcome might have been different. At that time, he was getting so much attention from adoring fans and admiring teammates, it was difficult for him to discern reality. His true persona may have been masked by all that adoration from fans who fed on the excitement of winning. Could it be that he had lost sight of the adage: "To thine own self be true"

On Thursday evening after dinner in the school cafeteria, Abigale and Brad took in a basketball game. FSU won by three points in the last thirty seconds.

They drove back to Brad's apartment and went upstairs. She made herself comfortable on the sofa while he uncorked a bottle of red wine, poured two glasses and put on some soft music.

They exchanged small talk about the game and what was coming up in the next week. Brad had received several good job offers and was favoring a terrific opportunity in Anaheim, California.

Glass in hand, he joined her on the sofa.

"What do you think of the Anaheim offer? Should I take it?"

"What in hell do I care if you go to California? Good riddance. Take a job in hell for all I care." She smiled and stuck her thumb over her shoulder.

"Well, you could come along and keep me company."

"Right, I could be your assistant. Get your coffee and open your mail."

Brad reached into his jacket pocket and came out with a ring box. He popped it open to expose a beautiful but modest emerald-cut diamond ring.

"You could slip this on and have a steady job."

"Brad! What in hell? We never —"

"You know I'm crazy about you."

"Kinda thought, but—"

"So, will you marry me? Be my wife, my partner?"

"This is so sudden. When were you thinking?"

"Right after graduation, very next day."

Brad wasn't sure she was over Slag. She seldom mentioned him. When she did, it was with a reference to his sleazy behavior or his infidelity or how she would never tolerate such a man in her life again. But now that he was holding out the ring box, he knew he was taking a risk. His palms began to sweat as he awaited her answer.

"But, maybe you're not ready for—"

"I will be; I am ready. But where? Have you thought about this at all?"

"We could do it right here. I'm sure we can get the chapel for an hour or two. I still have *some* pull on this campus. Three conference championships count for something. Beyond that, no. I've done my part. I got the ring and popped the question. The rest is up to the bride. I figured you and your folks would put something together."

Abigale gave the matter a moment's thought. "One thing's for sure, I can't put on a wedding the week before I graduate."

A protracted silence grew between them. Abigale was the first to speak. "Hand me that phone."

He raised his eyebrows as she dialed, "Who are you—"

She held up a finger. "Mom, I got good news and I got bad news. Which one do you want to hear first? Uh huh. No, Sloan didn't turn up in a prison hospital. The good news? You sitting down? I'm getting married to Brad. You remember him. The smart aleck football player . . . right, Mom . . . no, Mom . . . more than anything in the world. I know it's sudden, but will you help us? . . . Thanks, Mom." She handed back the phone. "Okay, big shot. My part's done. Where we spending our honeymoon? Niagara will do nicely."

"How about a cross country motor trip from Tallahassee to Anaheim in the Voodoo Vette?"

"Sure, if you agree to sell that piece of shit car the minute we get there,"

"Agreed. We can use the money for a down payment on our first house."

On Monday, the LaHolms drove to Tallahassee to take charge of the wedding. They settled on the campus chapel for its central location to their families and college friends. Within days, invitations were extended, the dress fitted, a florist was under contract. Everything was in motion and Abigale had not missed a class. Even Sloan couldn't have beaten that.

She chose a white, ankle-length gown with a train that touched the floor. The men would wear blue tuxedoes, and the five bridesmaids would dress in blue, knee-length dresses.

Early on a Friday morning, just a week before the wedding, Abigale was awakened by the ringing of her phone.

"I didn't call too early, did I?"

"I guess that depends. Who in hell are you?"

"Charles. It's me, Charles McIntyre. We met on a flight from Madrid a couple of months back."

"Charles, you rascal. What do you mean calling me at this hour? You know us sorority girls are getting our beauty sleep."

"Should I call back later?"

"Haavad man—can't you take a joke? You really don't have a clue do you? So, what's on your legal-beagle mind this fine May morning?"

"It just so happens that I'm coming through town on business and thought we might have dinner."

"Man, is your timing rotten. Since we met, I've accepted a marriage proposal. Not that it would change anything between us. We *are* just friends."

"I find it hard to believe you're getting married. When we met on the flight from Madrid, marriage was the last thing on your mind. Your sick friend must have had an amazing recovery."

"Him? Hell no. He died. I have a new lease, much happier than I was that night we met."

"I still want to see you. That is, if it's okay with your fiancé."

"I'm still my own person. Don't need anyone's say on what I do or who I see."

"I wouldn't expect a marriage proposal to change that," Charles said. "I'll drive over Wednesday and pick you up at your sorority house. Look for me around six?"

"Plain or fancy?" Abigale asked.

"Fancy. You pick the restaurant."

"Ever been to Ricardo's?"

The organist played the Wedding March. Mr. LaHolm gave his arm to Abigale and together they marched down the aisle. Each step took her closer to Brad and further from Sloan.

This should be our wedding. Slag should be waiting for me at the altar not this ego maniac football hero. It should be Sloan, not Brad, who takes me by the hand.

She'd tried to set her world right, but it continued to wobble on its axis. Tears began to find their way to the corners of her eyes and down her cheeks where she captured and hid them in her lace hankie. She hoped Brad would not realize that they were tears for Sloan.

"Abigale LaHolm, do you take Brad Hager to be your lawful wedded husband? To have and to hold until death do you part?"

"I do." Damn you, Slag.

"Brad, you may kiss the bride." And with that kiss, her world became real and she became one with Brad, her true love.

XXXII

Regina shook him hard. "Go back to sleep," he mumbled. "Everything is fine. Tell me in the morning." He cuddled closer to her.

"Wake up. I think my time is here."

"Time for what, my darling?" He tried again to pull her to him.

"Para ir maldita sea. Wake up!"

"You mean, now?" Sloan threw back the blanket and flipped on the overhead light. He saw two piles of neatly folded clothing and a satchel packed with everything they would need for their stay in the hospital. He jumped into his clothes and grabbed the satchel. Regina sat back on the bed, held her stomach with both hands, whimpered like a cold puppy and held up five fingers.

"Five minutes apart?"

She nodded.

If his calculations were right, they had an hour to travel the nine miles to the hospital.

Regina telephoned her mother who agreed to meet them there. Sloan called the number he was given for the emergency room to alert the doctors and staff.

"Five minutes apart," he said. "Sí cinco minuto de diferencia."

Sloan heard the blast of the taxi's horn. "It's all right," he whispered, as he led her to the door.

It was an early morning in May. Light dew had settled on the rooftops and shrubs along the drive. He lowered her into the back seat of the cab. "We have plenty of time."

She held up three fingers and moaned.

"Still plenty of time," he lied.

The taxi arrived at the emergency entrance and parked under the awning. Regina held up two fingers and emitted a short shrill scream. Sloan felt panic set in. An orderly helped Regina into a wheelchair and rolled her to the elevator. Sloan's job was done. He had delivered her into the hands of the professionals.

Sloan and her father Jose settled into the waiting room for the duration which, according to Sloan's calculations, might be as long as fifteen minutes. Morning faded into mid-day and then afternoon, Sloan had exhausted his supply of coins for the vending machine.

Sloan was lucky. He had found Abigale, but through his own missteps he had lost her. Abigale had been replaced in Sloan's life by Regina whom he had come to love.

The last nine months had not been so bad. At times it had been great fun. He could even admit that he loved her, perhaps not in the way he had loved Abigale.

He had shared Regina's bed. They made love almost every night until she became too large to comply. Then he lay next to her with his hands on her stomach and felt their child move about in her womb.

Before this day ended, they would be a family. He would—they would—have a child. A Wendy or a Sloan Junior. It didn't much matter to him. He prayed that Regina would be okay. He was amazed that he could care so deeply for a child he had never met.

Just as the hour passed three, the door to the visitor's lounge swung open.

"Where is Lieutenant Abernathy, por favor?" asked the attending nurse. Her shrill voice jerked Sloan back from a nap and brought him to his feet. "I'm—"

Her cap askew, the nurse gave him a tired smile. "Felicidades Sr. Teniente-uh-tiene una niña."

"A girl! Wendy," he said. "When can I—"

"We can go now. Just follow me. Usted no can stay long. Five minutes solo . . . esposa e hija están muy cansados."

Sloan jostled Jose.

"Wake up, old man. You're a grandpa."

The nurse led the two men down a long corridor to the maternity ward where he found Regina sitting up in her hospital bed, propped on pillows and holding their child. Jose stopped short and waited at the door to be invited into the room.

Regina had brushed her raven black hair and touched her full lips with rouge. Her eyes glistened like black opals. She put out her free arm to offer a hug. Sloan embraced her warmly, kissed her and stroked her hair. In her arms was their tiny swaddled bundle. "Thank God, you're both okay."

"Here, Sloan. Say hello to your daughter. Wendy, this is your papa."

Wendy had been nursing from Regina's swollen breast when the nurse pulled her away and handed her to Sloan. He cradled her in his left arm and gently jostled her as he had seen his brother do when *his* first child was born.

He stopped for a moment and peered in at the wrinkled, red and swollen face. He was assured by the nursing staff that she had arrived with a full complement of fingers and toes. He could see she had arrived with a full head of raven black hair which had been combed into one large kewpie doll-like curlicue on top of her head.

"My God," he gasped. "This is amazing."

Regina's parents hovered over their new granddaughter as though she was the heir to the family throne when, in fact, she was the fourth grandchild to be born into the family. Wendy's claim to family notoriety was that she was the first in the Gonzales family to be fathered by an American or any man not born within walking distance of the family vineyard. Wendy was an Abernathy.

After five days of hospital care Sloan collected his new family from the maternity ward and took them home. They arrived late in the afternoon. Sloan flung open the front door so Regina could enter carrying their daughter.

"I've tried to think of everything," he said. "I made dinner and your dad gave us a bottle of red to toast the new addition to the family."

"That's wonderful that he thought of us, but I will not have wine today, por favor. But you may enjoy it. I don't think I should pass even my father's best vino along to Wendy. Please Sloan, you should call him Papa or Father. Dad must be an American title. His name is Jose. He would love for you to call him Papa."

"Right. Jose gave me a vintage bottle of vino rojo, but why aren't you—oh, I get it. Wendy would be getting the wine. How long will that go on? You know, the nursing thing?"

"A year or so," she said. "Come on, Sloan." She put her palm on his cheek. "We got to start thinking like a family, por favor."

"Sure, I'm ready. We have the rest of our lives to drink wine. This is the only Wendy we will ever have. I'll drink your half. I need it to relax. Becoming a father has been stressful."

"Pobrecito, has it been hard? Not having me to cook and clean, huh, Sloan?"

"Mess hall food is getting old. I have to admit, these last few months you have done your best to spoil me."

"Spoil?"

"You know— estropear."

"For me is labor of love," Regina said. "You should try it sometime."

Sloan saw a glint in her eye as she touched on that delicate, omnipresent topic of separate bedrooms.

"I think that as long as Wendy is sleeping in her crib, we should share your room, don't you think? That way, if she wakes up at night, we can flip a coin to see who has to get up."

"Heck, Sloan, with that lucky dollar of yours I'll never win. Besides, there's not much you can do about feeding her. Your job will be to keep the bed warm." She closed her eyes prayerfully.

He looked at this woman whose bed he would now share. Over the past nine months, some of Regina's raw beauty had been replaced by the radiance that so often accompanied a woman with child.

"So, what's for dinner?" she said. "I'm starving."

"Lasagna and salad, and once I warm it, pie for dessert."

"You made pie? Sloan, you darling. Para me?"

"Would you believe me if I said yes?"

"You buy it from the market?"

"But I did make the lasagna. Would you like to tuck Wendy into her crib while I start a fire?"

Sloan had prepared Wendy's crib with sheets, blankets and pillows and three changes of pajamas, neatly folded on the sideboard.

Regina put the sleeping infant into her crib, but as soon as she was tucked in, she awoke, hungry and crying. Regina fed her, wiped her face with a soft damp cloth, put her on her shoulder and lovingly patted her back in hopes putting her to sleep. No such luck. Regina returned to the kitchen holding Wendy on her shoulder, talking to her softly.

"I think she wants to join us for dinner."

Sloan slung a dish towel over his shoulder. "It'll be three for dinner." He sat Regina's plate in front of her.

"How're things at your work?" Regina asked.

"Crazy. Captain Gibbs wants me to go to China again as soon as you can manage on your own."

"Then go. If I need help I'll call a neighbor or my mother. Mi Madre wants to help, and if I don't let her it will only hurt her feelings."

"I can hold him off for a few more days. He still owes me a honeymoon, and your mom has been great, spending all that time at the hospital while I catered to Gibbs."

No longer did Sloan see Regina as the sexy Spanish bombshell he'd met in a bar and hustled away for a night of debauchery. She was wife, homemaker, mother and caregiver to their daughter. He wanted to be at home.

XXXIII

Sloan sat with his feet up and stared out the window onto the main command post. Wendy had just celebrated her first birthday and was trying to make sense of standing and walking, although her favorite mode of locomotion was crawling.

Part of him wished he would draw an assignment so he could get out of town for a few days, and part of him wished the day would end so he could join Regina and Wendy on a trip to the park and the playground.

The mail clerk poked his head into Sloan's office. "Sorry to wake you, Lieutenant, but this Twix just came for you. Must be important. Comes all the way from Berlin."

Sloan ripped open the envelope. The message read:

Roomie:

In a mess of trouble. (STOP)

Need your expert guidance (STOP)

Call me at this number ASAP (STOP)

Jake. (FULL STOP)

Sloan dialed the number and Jake's voice came over the receiver.

"You in jail or what?" Sloan asked.

"Pretty much. Truth is, I'm in bad need of a best man."

"Oh, God, man. What've you gone and done?"

"Something about missing a period. Thought maybe you could explain it to me."

"Oldest trick in the—"

"Can you get here on Saturday? Wedding's at seven. That is, nineteen hundred hours."

"Don't see why not."

"Bring your whites. We're having a little do at her mom's place after. By the way, you'll need to make a toast."

"I can handle it."

"None of that crap about weed farmin', okay?"

"We'll catch the first train Saturday morning."

"We? You have to bring 'em both? Thought maybe me and you could do some serious celebrating. Besides, I still owe you a three-day hangover from that night in Madrid."

"Can't just put the baby in a kennel. She's not a poodle."

"How'll you manage her on the train?"

"Look, Jake. All she does is sleep and poop. She don't need a suite at the Waldorf for that."

"Waldorf? Oh yeah, reminds me. I reserved a guest room at the base for you. When you get to the gate, mention my name and pay 'em a hundred marks."

"Thanks, man. You really went all out."

The Abernathys arrived at the base around five on Saturday. Regina was pushing the stroller. True to form, Wendy was sound asleep. "We're here for a wedding. I'm Abernathy and this here's my wife and daughter."

"Let me check." The clerk ran a finger down a sheet on a clipboard. "Nothing on the ledger by that name and I never heard of you, so maybe you got the wrong day."

"Oh, great. That's just—Jake dropped the ball again."

The MP smiled then broke into laughter. "No, Sir. Jake told me I could give you a hard time. You're in room 44, right down that hall. Key's in the door."

"So," Regina said, looking around their room, "this is what a BOQ looks like from the inside."

"Yup, pretty much. Guess they're all the same," Sloan said.

"Here's one difference," she said picking up a note off the bed. "Your old drinking buddy wants to meet you for a few stiff ones before the execution takes place. His words, not mine."

"Can you manage on your own for an hour or so?" Sloan asked.

"Sure, I'll feed Wendy and join her for a nap. Just you remember, Sloan. It'll be a long night. Don't drink it up before the wedding even starts."

Sloan found the Officer's Club and strutted in expecting to see a hoard of drunken soldiers and Jake riding around the bar on the backs of two barmaids. To his dismay, Jake was sitting alone in a booth nursing a beer.

He didn't speak or stand, but simply put up a hand to be shaken or slapped.

Sloan gave his hand a slap and slid into the booth opposite him. "Man, you don't look like a guy who's about to get married." He waved two fingers at the barman who made two glasses of Scotch appear at their table.

"You're looking at one shit-scared son of a bitch. Can you get me out of here? To the Foreign Legion? They're just over there in France, ain't they?"

"Calm down, sculler. Being married and having kids isn't so bad. Look at me. I got my first kid and I am crazy about her. Believe me, I got off to a rockier start than you. You don't have an Abigale to deal with."

"Not so fast there, Lieutenant. You do remember Brenda?"

"Yeah, but . . . You didn't tell her you—"

"Afraid so, man. She's so freaking hot, I couldn't help myself."

"You didn't promise her . . . did you? Anything you weren't willing to deliver?"

"You know how I am when I've had too much. I'd a promised most anything just to get in them knickers one more time. Once I told a girl I was an astronaut in training."

"Only you could make up that kind of crap," Sloan said.

"When I shipped out, she went back to Melbourne and got on with that big aerospace outfit where her daddy works. She said she was waitin' for me, but hell, by now she's probably screwin' the boss."

"So, you dodged one bullet and took another one from Edie. But look, man, things with me and Regina are gradually coming together. She has kept her side of the bargain, and I'm beginning to understand what being a husband and father's all about. I provide a home with security and food and all that crap. I get that and I embrace it. Being a parent is an awesome responsibility."

"Still think about Abby, do you?" He pushed the stale beer aside and took a long drag on the Scotch.

"No. Not much . . . Well, some. At the end of the day when the girls are asleep, I sometimes sit on my porch and wonder what might've been."

"But hell, man, she's moved on," Jake said. "She and that Brad guy hooked up."

"Hooked up? You mean they got married?"

"Yeah. Didn't know if I should tell you."

"It's kind of a relief," Sloan said. "At least I know she's moved on."

"Nice weddin', too."

"You went to the wedding?"

Jake looked away from Sloan to avoid his scorn.

"What the hell, man? I got an invite. Would not uh been polite not to go."

"You turncoat son of a —"

"Hey, they had an open bar and hot bridesmaids. What would you have done?"

XXXIV

Wendy grew from a tiny infant, to a crawling toddler, to a running, screaming child. Almost before Sloan knew it, she was a precocious two-year-old who spoke Spanish and English equally well. Sloan hoped she would learn to read at an early age. Reading had been difficult for him. He had no reason to worry as Wendy was a quick study. She watched programs on TV and learned the characters by name. She could follow the stories from one week to the next, and when he came home in the evenings she would explain the plots.

Sloan spent his free time with Wendy: teaching, showing and playing, always in English. When he was at the base or traveling, Regina read to her, taught her songs and told her stories about when she was a child playing in the vineyard. Most of Regina's communication with Wendy was in Spanish.

At times, he still thought about Abigale and all those things he had told her about true love, love at first sight, being soul mates. And what of his promise to marry her? Abigale had most likely thrown the ruby sea glass medallion in the trash or back into the sea. He could not blame her if she had.

Sometimes Regina caught him gazing into the distance. "That woman, she is still on your mind?"

"Not much," he'd say. He had to be honest, but he could tell it hurt her. He tried, but he couldn't completely let go.

His work at the base was challenging. A great deal of his time was spent on assignments in other countries, something he resented because it took him away from his girls. But Gibbs managed to find work for him in remote locations around the globe. He often spent a week at a time in Australia, Egypt, China or South America. Hardships brought on by this extensive travel were not Gibbs' concern. According to Gibbs, if the Army had wanted him to have a family they would have issued him one.

Sloan finished a project in Australia and caught a MATS flight back to Madrid. He would be arriving a few days ahead of schedule and hoped to enjoy a few days with Regina and Wendy before he had to return to the base and start his next assignment.

He arrived home just past midnight and let himself in the front door. His normal routine was to call ahead so Regina would have ample warning in the event the house was a wreck, but the late hour left him no choice but to arrive unannounced.

He crept quietly through the darkened house to Wendy's room where he heard her whimpering in her crib. He put her on his shoulder and patted her back, all the time whispering to her.

"Wendy miss Daddy?"

She hugged his neck. "Daddy been wokin'?" She whispered as if Sloan's arrival at home was a big secret shared only with the two of them.

"That's right. Daddy's been working, far, far away. Let's surprise Mommy."

With Wendy in his arms, he made his way down the narrow hallway towards Regina's room. As he approached her door, he heard voices and laughter emanating from her semi-darkened bedroom.

"Uncle John," Wendy whispered.

Sloan recognized the man's voice.

His mind whirled, confused and in shock.

"Better still, let's put you to bed," Sloan whispered to Wendy.

He made his way back to Wendy's room, careful not to step on the squeaky board in the hallway.

He tucked Wendy into bed and softly patted her back until she went fast asleep.

He drew his service revolver, still strapped to his side as it had been for the past week of field duty. He made his way back to Regina's room, trusting that the boards in the antique floor would not betray him. It took an hour, or five seconds. Time lost all meaning. The world may have stopped turning. He could not say for sure.

He stood outside the door of her bedroom, the one he had come to think of as *their* room. His hands trembled as he gripped the pistol. From the shadows, he raised the weapon shoulder-high. Two steps into the room would place him at the foot of her bed. He would fire into the darkness.

He heard laughter and what he believed was heavy breathing. The bed creaked amid the rustling of sheets or clothes, he could not say for sure.

In an instant, sounds of lust would forever be silenced. His pounding heart would not be heard over the echoes of the shots as they rattled the walls of the old stone house.

His hand on the knob, he rested his forehead against the cool wood of the door. He imagined walking toward the gallows side-by-side with an old padre.

His knees turned to jelly. His legs would not support his weight. His arms fell to his side

He might have to crawl into Regina's room on his hands and knees.

Once again he raised the pistol shoulder high and supported it with both hands. The weapon felt light, too light.

This damn thing's not loaded, he thought.

Sloan stood trembling at Regina's bedroom door. Thus far, his presence had gone unnoticed. Regina and Gibbs were too engrossed in one another to have heard a board creak or Sloan's heavy breathing over the pounding of their own hearts.

Sloan holstered his pistol and retraced his steps to the front door.

He climbed into his Jeep and turned the key. The engine caught on the first turn.

He eased the crude machine into gear and started it rolling down the circular drive passed another base vehicle parked in the shadows.

Sloan steered the lumbering Jeep past the dozing MP, parked it in front of the BOQ and went to his room. He needed time to think. Once inside his quarters, he could relax.

He had come to care for Regina. Why had she chosen to cheat with Gibbs? Hell, if it weren't for her, he would've married Abigale. If it had been Abigale with another man . . . for sure, he would have gone back and shot them both.

He drew his sidearm and brandished it at the shadows, then stretched out on his bunk and tried to get his head around all he had witnessed. Gibbs was not about to make a permanent move, divorce his wife and marry Regina. He had too much at stake. He would be putting his precious career on the line. "The Corps, the Corps, the Corps!" Regina was just a fling. He was sure of that. If he went back and shot them both, Wendy would be the big loser. Captain Gibbs was married with children of his own. No one would win, least of all Sloan.

Now, all those pointless missions made sense. Gibbs sent him out of town so he could make it with Regina.

He rolled off his bunk and opened his fridge. The light flooded the darkened room. He grabbed a beer, kicked the refrigerator door shut, flopped down on his lounge chair and sat in the dark room staring at the ceiling. Gibbs was taking advantage of Regina's need for companionship brought on by Sloan's long absences from home, and by the fact he had never been the husband she deserved.

But, hell, did that give her the right to? He wondered if he was being shoved aside for the big man on campus. He swore it wouldn't happen—not this time—not to him. He had learned a hard lesson from Jackie and he'd never forgotten it.

Regina had broken their wedding vows, so he was no longer bound by them. "Till death do us—or till she goes to bed with my CO."

He discharged his empty weapon at the shadows. Click-click-click. "Take that you bastard." He threw the impotent piece at the empty chair across the room. It bounced and fell to the floor and exploded as it discharged a single round. The 45-caliber slug pierced the cushioned arm of the chair and lodged in the wooden frame.

"Shit." He fell to the floor unsure if the round had passed through his body. His mind went blank.

His nostrils filled with the smell of brimstone.

He heard footsteps in the hall then a hammering on his door. "Open up! MPs! We heard shots!"

Sloan struggled to his feet and checked his body for holes. He examined the floor for a pool of blood.

"Nothing serious. Dropped my weapon and it went off."

He made his way to the door where he found Sergeant Tobin and a short, burley MP. Tobin wore the armband that designated him as Officer of the Day. "What happened here?" he demanded. "Sloan, thought you were down under."

"Got back a few hours ago and decided to stay here tonight rather than wake my girls. I tossed my gun belt on the floor and an errant round discharged. Scared the be-Jesus out of me."

"Errant my ass," growled the young MP. "You're in violation of code W-332, loaded firearm on base."

Tobin interrupted the overzealous MP. "Hey, shit happens. That model of sidearm has a tendency to get a round jammed. Next time you check out a pistol, make damn sure it ain't got one stuck in the chamber. They use these pieces at the target range so you never know who had it last."

"Thanks for the warning. I'll be more careful."

"I'll have to make an entry on the Daily Report. Gibbs is bound to see it. He don't miss much. You ain't due back till tomorrow and that'll piss him off more 'n if you'd shot yourself. He hates it when his people don't stick to their schedule."

Tobin made a few notes, handed the pistol back to Sloan and left him to his troubled evening.

He knew this much. Wendy was now his first priority. For her sake, he would do what he had to do to maintain a happy home. He would chew his pride and gulp it down. When the time was right, he would blow this thing open. But on *his* terms, when *he* was ready. When Wendy was old enough to stand on her own, he would cash it in. Every hand's a winner, right, Daddy?

At first light, he rinsed off in the shower, pulled on a clean set of fatigues and made his way to the officer's mess. Captain Gibbs was already there enjoying breakfast with several other officers. Monday mornings in the officer's mess were a time for informal gatherings to catch up with the other units.

Sloan piled his tray with the standard breakfast fare and made his way to Gibbs' table.

"Morning, Sir," he said, over the hum of mess hall clatter.

"Abernathy, what 'n hell are you doin' here? Wasn't expecting you for another day or so."

It all came clear to Sloan why Gibbs was a stickler when it came to his officers staying on schedule.

Sloan swung a leg over the chair and sat down opposite Gibbs. "Finished early and came back when I could hitch a ride."

"I see," Gibbs said.

Sloan wondered if Gibbs had seen the morning report and noted the shooting incident in the BOQ.

"Good weekend, Captain?" Sloan asked.

"Played golf on Saturday. Hit 'em long and straight. How about you? Oh, that's right, you were in the field."

"That's right, Sir. Australia, for over a week. That *special* mission. You know, the one you arranged for me."

Sloan nodded to the other men around the table. "Finished early and came home to see my Spanish bride." Sloan stirred his coffee then poured milk over his cereal. His hand shook as he sipped his coffee.

"Man, am I starving. Nothing new to report about food service on ATS flights. Like, there ain't any." He forced a laugh but could not disguise the case of nerves.

Another officer pretended to find humor in his comment. He chuckled politely and followed up with his own anecdote.

Sloan inspected Gibbs' face for signs of guilt.

"Got in around 0100." Sloan volunteered. He thought he could read relief on Gibbs' face.

"If it meets your approval, Sir, I want to take a few days and ditch my jet lag."

"Sure, take some time. Long as you get back here tomorrow. We got a Cold War to fight. Might need you in Amsterdam on Wednesday."

"Thank you, Sir. I could use a timeout. Haven't seen my girls in over a week."

Gibbs gave Sloan his standard line about how the Army didn't issue him no family, so he shouldn't make them his problem.

"No, Sir, I wouldn't expect the Army to take a personal interest. Sir—no, Sir."

Gibbs stared at him for a moment and then dug his fork into his pile of eggs.

Sloan half-listened as Gibbs regaled about the Aussies and how they were real party animals. "Bet they kept you out every night," he said, "and how 'bout those big-titted Aussie gals? Man, oh man." He flashed a lecherous grin at Sloan and the other men as he chewed a link sausage.

"Not as good as here, Sir," Sloan said. The inference ricocheted off Gibbs like a volley of machine gun fire off a Sherman tank.

"You meet the one they call Cantilever Katie?" Gibbs continued.

"Yes, Sir, as a matter of fact, Sir. Nice girl."

Gibbs leaned in. "The engineers at the base joke that she needs a bra with special support to hold them out in front. A cantilever bra, get it?" Gibbs laughed. Some of the men chuckled. "Don't see how she can stand up straight."

Sloan was offended. For all he knew, when he wasn't around, Regina might be the brunt of Gibb's bad taste or the subject of one of his wild tales.

Gibbs leaned back in his chair and looked at the ceiling. "Met her at a party and got the green light. Had to do 'er. Man, was she—damn!" Gibbs shook his head, but provided no further details to his eager audience. Several men were on the edge of their chairs.

Sloan wondered if the other men knew about Gibbs and Regina or other women whose husbands were being sent on extended missions for little gain beyond making friends with the locals and leaving their beautiful wives at home for Gibbs to ravage.

Gibbs set the front legs of his chair down with a click, leaned on both elbows and pointed at the morning report on the table in front of him and tapped it hard with his finger. "I see here we had a shootin' in the BOQ last night. Who knows somethin' about it?" he asked. "According to the DR, the OD couldn't determine exactly who fired it. Abernathy, it looks like it was down your hall or thereabouts, but you was still in the air at 2300 hours. Ain't that right, Lieutenant?"

"That's correct, Sir. I was out over the Atlantic."

Tobin had jimmied the Daily Report in such a way as to *exonerate* him and, in the doing, it gave him the alibi he needed to explain his whereabouts the previous evening.

"So, what's new around here?" Sloan asked. He wanted to change the subject, but little was offered. One by one, the men finished their breakfast and left the dining hall. Before long, it was just Sloan and Gibbs.

He didn't try to stare the Captain down, but hoped that his presence was making him uncomfortable—if the man had a conscience. After all, a few hours earlier, he'd most likely been pouring the coal to Regina. Gibbs didn't know how close he had come to being a statistic.

Army Captain and Lieutenant's wife found slain. Jilted husband held as prime suspect.

Sloan waited until Captain Gibbs finished his coffee and stood to leave. Sloan drank his last sip and followed Gibbs out of the dining hall, one step behind and in lock step, which was in strict accordance with military protocol. Without speaking, they walked to Gibbs' office.

"See you later," Gibbs said. He quickly closed his door, leaving Sloan just outside his office.

Sloan didn't know how long he could tolerate the situation but, for now, he had to keep all this bottled up inside. He hoped the Captain was riddled with guilt over his conduct with Regina, but he doubted it.

XXXV

Two years had passed since Sloan arrived home unannounced and found Gibbs with Regina. Wendy was four and attending kindergarten on the base.

Sloan's dealings with Gibbs had become strained. He had done his best to eliminate or minimize his interaction with him. Twice he had extended his tour of duty, which he considered to be in Wendy's best interest. Once he took her to the states, he wanted to be sure she was ready to make the adjustment both socially and academically.

His long-term plan was to resign his commission, return to the states and build a new career in the electronics industry, but until that opportunity presented itself, he would continue to maintain a working relationship with Gibbs and some semblance of a marriage with Regina. Sloan knew this was too many balls for any one man to juggle indefinitely.

He had developed true feelings and genuine love for Regina right up to the moment he walked into the house and heard Gibbs making passionate love to her. His feelings for Abigale had faded to the point that thinking of her was no longer painful. He loved Regina in every sense of the word.

He sometimes wondered how different things would have been had his sidearm been loaded. Would he have had the guts to murder them in cold blood? On that night, his life had taken a turn. He began sleeping alone once again. When Regina questioned his sudden change in behavior, he complained that she snored and disrupted his sleep, or he had developed a rash from his contact with a virus prevalent in North Africa and needed time to recover before he risked passing it on to her.

When he could no longer hold out, he relented and joined her in bed. After all, he was a virile, needy man and she, an incredibly beautiful woman. But, sleeping arrangements at home were seldom an issue as Gibbs kept Sloan in the air and on assignment most of the time.

Sloan was enjoying a rare week in Madrid when news came that Gibbs had requested an audience with him at 0900 the following day.

Sloan arrived at Gibbs' office shortly before nine. He sensed excitement among the staff as they moved around the area in pursuit of their duties. The Army grapevine was an excellent source of information, but on this occasion Sloan was out of the loop. The meeting had an air of foreboding. His mistrust of Gibbs had only grown in the four years they had been colleagues.

Gibbs motioned for Sloan to sit while he studied some paperwork from European command. He chuckled under his bushy mustache. "Guess you're wondering why I asked you here?" He seemed pleased that he had drawn a parody on a movie that had recently shown at the base theater.

Sloan remained stoic. "As a matter of fact, Sir, yes."

Gibbs dropped the papers on his desk. "Relax, Lieutenant. This here's a happy occasion. Command has seen fit to recognize us for the great job we do. First thing I want to report is, due in large measure to you and others under my command, the General has seen fit to promote me to Lieutenant Colonel." He smirked, obviously pleased with his accomplishment. He stroked his bushy mustache in a manner Sloan thought unmilitary.

"Explains the hubbub in the halls," Sloan acknowledged in a matter-of-fact tone.

Gibbs had beaten the odds of a field-commissioned officer.

"With this here promotion, I'm one step closer to Brigadier," Gibbs said. "But you know, man, I can't take all the credit. Guys like you, Jameson and a few more are making me look damn good."

Gibbs' success was, in large measure, a result of his shotgun approach to covert operations. There were times when he had no rationale for deploying a task force, so he fabricated one. Command usually went along because it was difficult to say for sure if there was a need that warranted the expense or Gibbs was just blowing smoke or taking a shot in the dark.

"Can't put a price on national security," Gibbs said. "I'll bet you're thinking I asked you here just to tell you I'm makin' Colonel, bragging son of a bitch that I am. But, no. Here's the whole deal. Now comes the good part. In the same petition," he swept up the documents, waved them at Sloan and swaggered from behind his desk, "you, Abernathy, are being promoted to Captain." His smirk changed to a boyish grin as he watched Sloan's face for some reaction to the news.

"Me, Sir? Why?" In Sloan's view, anything Gibbs said or did had to be motivated by his interest in Regina. Promoting Sloan would keep him engaged in the mission and Regina available for his liaison. In other words, business as usual.

Most of the missions Sloan was given lacked substance or, in his view, were outright bogus. A few had offered such enormous challenge that no one up the chain expected tangible results, so any result at all was viewed as progress. Sloan often went beyond what Command had expected of him in order to produce some tangible result.

Gibbs winked and shook a finger in Sloan's face. "The General thinks you're ready for more responsibility, and that means advancement outside of normal time in grade. He's promoting you to Captain and giving you responsibility for directing all field operations out of Madrid. Hell, Abernathy, they're singling you out as an example to other young officers. They want to show what hard work and motivation will produce."

In this move, Sloan had left several West Pointers in his dust and, by damn, he had earned it. When Gibbs had given Sloan a lemon, he had given him back a spy ring or a covert operation—the stuff heroes were made of.

Gibbs came around and sat on the edge of his desk. "Here's the deal, *Captain.* You will take over some of my duties and my role will be expanded to new territory and greater authority. I have kept this hush-hush, knowing that—in part—if I brought you into it, you'd see it as a re-up pitch. Which, by the way, it is. Hey, I know you've been entertaining thoughts of heading back to the states. Well, here's a job with some real profile. You can get great visibility at Command and throughout the Intel community and the best part is, you'll be home for dinner damn near every night."

Now, Sloan was confused.

Gibbs returned to his military monotone, "There's a handful of companies out there that'd hire men out of my unit just for the experience they bring. Most of them are half as quick on the uptake as you. Me, I get offers all the time, but I like it right here. I'm a lifer through and through. But soon's I get that first star, I'm outta here."

"Sure. I'll take the job," Sloan said. "Can't think of a reason not to, but I'm not promising it will turn me into a lifer."

"Only thing I need from you is your commitment to extend for another year."

"So, this *is* a re-up pitch."

"Gotta give a little to get a lot. Hell, man, looks good on your resume. Come on, Captain, just put your John Hancock right there."

"Damn you, Gibbs," he swore under his breath as he signed the commitment agreement making sure it specified one year.

Sloan wondered if his competence and achievements had led to the promotion. Advancing beyond First Lieutenant would have been impossible for someone with Sloan's unmilitary mindset had it not been for Gibbs and his impossible assignments.

Now, it was Sloan who would send other service personnel on assignments around the globe. His own travel would be limited to locations he chose to visit as part of his administrative oversight, although his new duties made him wonder about Gibbs and Regina.

XXXVI

That next year was enjoyable for Sloan and his girls. With his new rank and position, he was allowed to sign out a vehicle for a day or a weekend. This new privilege allowed for motor trips to interesting and scenic locations around Madrid.

Peace reigned in the Abernathy household. Sloan made frequent trips to Regina's room, some lasting for days. He was reconciled to the notion that, if there was anything going on with Gibbs, it had long since run its course. While he was far from forgiving and forgetting the events to which he was a witness, he had rationalized that it was not an issue he needed to deal with while Wendy was still at home.

While in Paris attending a conference on electronic intelligence, Sloan was contacted by the president of a small electronics firm in California. As he checked into his hotel, the desk clerk handed him the key to his room and a message that read:

Captain Abernathy: Can you meet me for lunch in your hotel lounge at 1300 hours today?

Ask for me at the door.

Tom McNaire

President, Vortec Electronics.

He turned the note over and scribbled a response:

Can do.

Sloan Abernathy

Captain, U.S. Army

This was the first of three meetings between the two men. On the last day of the conference, they met for a third time over dinner, brandy, and cigars. Tom made Sloan an offer of employment that he found irresistible. With two months left on his commitment to the Army, the job offer was the right opportunity at the right time.

On Monday, Sloan returned to Madrid and proceeded to file all the necessary paperwork to resign his position and return to civilian life. The Army bureaucracy ground to a halt. Three months passed before Sloan was notified that Colonel Gibbs had requested a meeting with him.

"What brought on this sudden decision to head home? Word on the street is you landed yourself a great job in California. So, what's the scoop? How'd you come across such a sweet deal?"

"You sent me to a conference in Paris where I met the President of Vortec."

"That'll teach me to send my top people off to those expensive conferences," Gibbs growled. "Probably no point in goin' over the reenlistment pitch again, but I would be remiss if I didn't try."

"You're right, Gibbs. There *is* no point. I've made my decision. I'm headed stateside."

"Okay, I'll can the bullshit. But you know, Sloan, keepin' you 'round another year would be good for both of us. We might both make another stripe. That Eagle would look mighty good on your epaulettes. Truth is, Old Sport, I have the go-ahead to offer Lite Colonel as an inducement."

"Colonel!?" he whispered. "Colonel. . .the General okayed Colonel?"

He pictured wearing the eagles on his lapels. "You know, Colonel, that's damned tempting, but it's time I was getting back while I have this good job lined up."

"Man, I can tell you, if you got the military side of your career on track—you know, be a little more corps happy—you could earn a star in no time. In this outfit, they hand 'em out like candy. Needless to say, getting you to re-up would look good on *my* record too," Gibbs said as he pushed his half-eaten cigar to the other cheek. "To tell it like it is, Abernathy, you've done well. Perfect service record, married into the community, made Captain in record time. You have a great future ahead of you in this man's Army. The duty's great and the retirement pay is hard to beat once you make bird."

"The Army *has* been good to me. No complaints on that count."

"Then stay, man." Gibbs' desk chair creaked as he leaned forward. "Your *country* needs you."

"Sorry Colonel, my country will just have to make do with me as a taxpayer from now on."

"Ah, hell Captain, you'll do fine as a civilian. I'm sure of it. Just hope you'll stay in touch. Never can tell when I might need one of them cushy stateside jobs myself." He pushed back from his desk. "Guess you're all packed and ready to get out of town, huh, Captain."

"That I am, Sir. When I walk out that door I'll be a free man. We leave tonight for London and next week, Los Angeles."

"Don't let the door hit you in the ass. I've cut you slack long enough."

Sloan stood to leave.

"Wait. I got just one last thing before you go. Back when you first got here, we made a practice of inspecting mail that came in or went out from the base."

"Yes, Colonel, I'm well aware of that."

"It was done in the early days to screen those communications channels for inadvertent security leaks. You know, careless comments that might convey info that we didn't want on the street." Gibbs almost sounded apologetic.

"I know all about the practice. So what's your point. Why bring it up to me now?"

"Nothing really. It's just that I was cleaning out your files and came across some old letters from when you first got here.

It was left up to me to hold 'em or let 'em go through. I'll be damned if I can remember why I pulled 'em." In one smooth move, Gibbs pulled a file drawer open, extracted a folder and handed it over to Sloan.

"Anyhow, it's water under the dam. If you want 'em, take 'em. Otherwise they're headed for the incinerator."

Sloan examined the file and found three envelopes. He recognized his handwriting on a letter he had sent to Abigale. The other two were *from* Abigale. His hands trembled as he pulled the one-page letter from its envelope.

Hot Irish blood turned his face a deep red. "You've had these letters for five years?"

"Time sure flies, huh, Captain? Guess I forgot to give 'em back . . . Hope they weren't too—"

Sloan reached across the desk and grabbed Gibbs by his lapels, spun him a quarter turn and planted his fist squarely in the Colonel's face.

Gibbs fell backwards, landed hard against the window sill and slid to the floor. Blood leaked from his nose onto his tie and lapels. He wiped his nose with the back of his hand and saw blood. He shook his head to refocus his eyes. "Damn it, Captain! I'll have you brought up on charges."

Sloan went down on one knee, grabbed Gibbs' shirt front and pulled him up close.

"And I'll tell the AG how you sent me on all those bogus missions and entertained my wife while I was away." He grabbed his out-processing file off Gibbs' desk and shook it in Gibbs' face. "You're talking to a civilian here, man. I out-rank you."

"Huh?" Gibbs shook his head again and pinched his nose to slow the bleeding. His eyes focused then crossed, "Strictly business, man. That was—just business. Thought you knew." He wiped at the blood trickling from his nose and mumbled under the pain of Sloan's hard fist. "I got no interest in your bitch. Got better at home. . . Harsh, ain't it, Captain, for a couple of Dear John letters?"

Sloan left Gibbs' office and headed back to his bungalow, but he was too upset to be around his girls. He walked through the compound until he found a bench and sat down. He tried to calm his nerves. He pulled the letters from his jacket pocket and removed one from its tattered envelope:

My Dearest Sloan,

It has been several weeks since you received your clearances and raced off on some secret job. I do hope you are safe and well. You did warn me that you might be away for some time but...

The second letter read:

My Darling Sloan,

I have made repeated attempts to contact you or learn your whereabouts from your CO. I believe his name is Gibbs? Since no one is willing to disclose any information regarding your whereabouts or well-being, I have decided to come to Spain and learn firsthand why I can't reach you. On Tuesday of next week, I will fly to Madrid and arrive early on Wednesday morning. If you receive this letter, please meet me at Madrid International, flight 3555.

Son of a bitch, he thought, I remember that day. Regina was about six months along. A taxi pulled up at our house. It sure as hell looked like . . . must have been. He dragged a hand down his face.

He tucked the letters in a side pocket of his briefcase and headed back to their cottage where he found Regina making last-minute preparations for their trip to the states. She was squeezing between boxes and crates to make breakfast. Sloan watched as she buttered Wendy's toast.

"They want me to stay."

"Course they do, Honey. You're a real bargain."

"Gibbs offered me Colonel."

"Gibbs is so full of caca."

"Should I take it?"

"And not go to California? No way. We're packed and we're going."

Gibbs had said it was 'just business.' What could he have meant? At least Sloan knew the identity of the stranger in the large-brimmed hat.

XXXVII

The Abernathy family departed Madrid for a new life on the beaches, in the sun, and amidst the Southern California traffic. On their first day, they located and rented a three-bedroom apartment in Redondo Beach near the Vortec offices. The three toured their new home and discussed the sleeping arrangements.

"What say I take this room," he said, pointing to the master suite. "I know it's bigger than the other two, but I want to get up and out early and this is closest to the door. I want to be at work by seven and both you guys will want to sleep in."

"That works for me," Regina said. "Which closet is mine?"

"Don't think you quite understand. You can have the room down the hall. You'll have more privacy there."

"No thanks," she said jovially. "I'll have all the privacy I need right here. I'll get up and make your breakfast every morning. A working man has to have a good breakfast before he puts in a hard day at the office."

Wendy hung onto her mother's leg. "Sure, Daddy. Mommies and daddies sleep together. Right, Mommy?"

"Regina roughed up her daughter's short wavy hair. "But you know, you're right. Mommies and daddies *are* supposed to sleep together. Aren't they, Sloan?"

When Wendy and Regina joined forces, Sloan seldom won the argument so he agreed to try Regina's sleeping arrangements. He wanted his girls to be happy and adjust to their new surroundings. He was willing to put the memories of that night in Madrid on the backburner.

Sloan was concerned that the adjustment to California life would be difficult for Regina. She was in a new country, a strange city and among foreign people.

"Compared to Madrid, this place is the moon," Regina said, staring out of the window at the stark asphalt parking lot.

In Madrid, bicycles were a suitable means of getting to and from the base and the market, but Sloan could not expect Regina to ride a bike in California commuter traffic, so he parked his girls in their new home and went in search of affordable transportation. He bought a vintage Ford pickup truck with good tires, clean oil and very little rust.

Sloan pulled into the parking lot adjacent to their apartment to show off his new ride. Regina took one look and pushed up her nose with her thumb. "You call this a car?" But she could not argue that there was room for three on the bench seat and a place in back for bikes and picnic supplies. The old truck would serve them until they could afford a late model car.

"When do I get to drive?" Regina pleaded.

"When you get your learner's permit and figure out how to manage a five-speed gear box."

"Sloan, you ever work on a farm? I was driving trucks and tractors around the vineyard when I was maybe ten years old."

"Primer día del resto de nuestras vidas . . ." Sloan said.

"Yeah, sure. I just hope someone here speaks Spanish."

"No problem on that count. Spanish is the language of choice in this part of America. Remember Jake and Edie?"

"Sure. We went to their wedding in Berlin. He's your old drinking buddy."

"They came here from Germany about three years ago."

"Jake and Edie?" Regina said with a ring of surprise. "When can we see them? This place is lonely like the moon."

"Soon as our house is settled and we're ready for company."

"How many kilometers is that to where they live?" Regina asked.

"I don't know, fifty or so. Over here, we measure distance in miles. Every kilometer is about six-tenths of a mile."

"Oh. Too far to ride my bike. I must learn to drive the truck."

Regina was determined to learn to drive and take control of her life. Sloan admired that in her. In the coming weeks, Sloan and Regina spent Sunday afternoons on back roads and parking lots where Sloan taught Regina to drive on California streets.

XXXVIII

Early on the morning of his first day at Vortec, Sloan was rummaging through his closet for suitable business attire. As a soldier, he had two choices: class A's or fatigues. He found a jacket, trousers and shirt that had a common color scheme: blue. His military-issue black shoes looked good. Despite his desire to rebel against it, his five years in the Army had softened his penchant for individuality in dress. He had become comfortable in the sameness of the uniform since it served his primary goal, which was to achieve something every day of his life.

True to her word, Regina was up and in the kitchen. While Sloan showered, she stirred eggs, fried bacon and slid three slices of bread under the broiler.

Sloan had been instructed to arrive around nine o'clock. The drive would take twenty minutes. He poured a second cup of coffee and passed an hour rereading the Sunday paper.

Regina grabbed him by his tie. "Do good today and come home quick. I already feel lonely." She kissed him hard on the mouth. There was victory of sorts for her. She had finally regained her place in his bed. She too had been promoted.

He drove to the Vortec parking lot and pulled into the first vacant, unmarked space where he killed some more time rereading the Vortec company propaganda. Around eight-thirty, a car pulled in behind him and honked. A well-tanned young man with surfer-blond hair leaned out the driver's window. "Hey, man. You're in my spot."

"Sorry. New, first day."

The young man pointed to the back of the parking lot. "Newbies park back there behind the fence."

"Sure, okay."

Sloan had never visited the facility or met any of his fellow employees except Tom. He parked behind the fence and walked a half-block to the main entrance where he approached the receptionist and asked for Bob Martin. The receptionist looked past him and pointed to a man in a dark suit and silk tie. It was the man who had told him to park a block away.

Bob held out his hand. "Sorry to chase you out of my parking place, but you threw me a curve with that old truck and that military tie. I had no idea you were our new Director of Product Development. Didn't mean to be rude. Got a dose of the Monday blahs. Had too much fun this weekend. Not quite ready to put my nose to the grindstone."

"Forget it. I'll learn the ropes soon enough," Sloan said.

"The management team meets every Monday at nine. When you're ready, I'll take you there."

"Always ready," Sloan said.

"You know, they're expecting a full presentation on your background and the product plans you and Tom discussed in Madrid—the whole nine yards. Be forewarned, not everyone will lay down for you. Some people hate Tom and hope he falls on his ass and takes you along with him. They're giving you enough rope in hopes you will hang yourself. That conference room is a shark tank. Still say you're ready?"

"Don't worry about me, Bob. I'm bulletproof." Sloan comically pounded his chest. "A room full of Generals and Senators didn't scare me."

Bob ushered Sloan into a spacious conference room. Eight men and five women were seated around a large oval table.

Inexpensive art decorated one wall of the lackluster meeting space. The outside wall of glass framed the buildings next door.

Bob stopped at the door to introduce Sloan to the group. Tom sat at the head of the table. "Good to see you again, Sloan."

Drake Hammett, Vice President of Engineering, sat next to Tom. On the org chart Sloan would report to Drake, but it was clear from the outset that Sloan would have Tom's ear. Drake might well be the subject of a lateral arabesque.

"Take a seat, Sloan." Tom pointed to a vacant chair next to Drake. "We're about done with our weekly agenda, so you're up." He turned to the group. "Sloan has prepared a briefing on a proposed new product plan. We've been working long distance on this plan since he hired on three months ago. We're anxious to hear your report from the field on our products and your thoughts on new markets for our technology."

Sloan dragged a whiteboard to the center of the room. His throat tightened. He just might be in over his head. He had no prepared slides or charts. He would have to use the whiteboard and take questions from the group to make his points.

Beads of sweat popped out on his forehead. He looked at his audience and counted four friendly faces. Among them were Tom, Bob and two of the women.

"Ladies and gentlemen." His voice cracked and garnered supportive laughter from the few who were pulling for him. Then everyone else chimed in and the ice, like his voice, was broken.

He charged ahead, "To date, Vortec has focused on military applications for GPS and some sophisticated communications gear. You have done extremely well, thanks in large measure to the voracious appetite for your products. But, in my view, the military market is only the beginning. A time will come when every vehicle on the planet will be equipped with a GPS. Hikers will carry a unit into the wilderness. Every ship will be equipped with navigation tools augmented by geo-positioning technology. War will be waged on the strength of a nation's ability to track their enemies. Two factors will drive the market: accuracy in locating a target and cost. With today's technology, we can locate a target to within a hundred meters. We can and must drive that accuracy toward one meter."

"One meter?" Drake tapped his pencil on the table. "And just how in hell do you propose we do that?"

Sloan grinned. "One centimeter at a time, just like I-Tel and their microchip development. When they release a new chip, they already know how fast they can make the next chip operate. Their planning goes out several years in advance of the technology. Soon as a chip saturates the market, they bring out a faster one."

"All it takes is money, brains and the guts," Tom said.

Drake pounded his knuckles on the table. "And that's a butt load of money. Any idea where we're gonna get even the first hundred million? You're talking more risk than a serial killer. Money's a little harder to come by in the private sector." Drake moaned and looked over his glasses and down his nose at Sloan. "Here, we can't tap into Uncle Sam's pocket anytime we feel like it. Perhaps you should've stayed on Uncle Sam's payroll where you could spend our tax dollars."

Sloan leaned forward, his palms on the table and eyes on Drake. "Nothing of value comes without risk. Cost and risk can be mitigated by recruiting the right investors. Today, the capital investment required to track or locate a target is prohibitive for the commercial market, but as this technology grows in popularity, the cost per unit will approach five hundred dollars or even less."

Sloan pulled out his freshly ironed handkerchief and dabbed his forehead. Regina had dashed it with perfume. He lost his focus.

"Think you're being just a tad optimistic?" Tom said.

"Maybe. But we won't know till we try."

Sloan was on a roll. He was back in the briefing room in Madrid, staring down a hoard of skeptical generals. Drake had continued to try to knock him off his game, but Sloan managed to stay on his feet. Tom ran friendly interference for Sloan. He was asking some of the hard questions before the sharks had a chance to take bites out of his new protégé.

Sloan's vision for the GPS market brought an onslaught of criticism and skepticism. Setting a new market direction for this little company would be fraught with peril. He might have served his girls better by taking Gibbs' offer.

Tom stood to wrap up the briefing. "Now, I ask you, who better to exploit these markets than us? We're small but agile and forward-thinking. And if we play our cards right, there's no reason we can't be a major player."

"I'd like it too," Drake said, "if I had a magic wand. Where in hell are we gonna get all that money to develop those pie-in-the-sky high-risk products?"

Sloan would leave the debate over money with Drake or technology to Tom. Sloan continued, "And as long as we stay on the leading edge and stand behind our products, we can dominate the market. We should envision the end product and set a course towards it. For argument's sake, let's use my numbers, one meter and five hundred dollars. With those numbers as our targets, we can chart a course. Time is the only dimension about which we must debate. Every year we will announce a new and improved product."

Drake rose to his feet and butted in. "We could lose our shirts and our retirements and screw our investors in the process,"

Body language around the table told Sloan that several of the executives at that table were feeling threatened and were siding with Drake.

Tom attempted to diffuse the debate. "We have a meeting of the architectural committee scheduled for Thursday at ten. Everyone should come prepared to defend their position. Sloan, that means you too. I'll have lunch brought in so we can make a day of it. for now, let's get on with our week. . . see most of you on Thursday."

XXXIX

Friday night dinner with Jake and Edie became a tradition, each taking turns preparing the meal. Regina, Edie and the girls all pitched in to clear the table while Sloan and Jake retreated to the patio or out by the pool to swap lies about their week and to finish off the wine or open one more beer. On special occasions such as a promotion or birthday, they splurged on a bottle of Scotch that seldom survived the evening.

"Trouble with this high tech life is that I never get any exercise," Sloan said as he and Jake sat in poolside lounge chairs, drinking. "You ever watch Sea Hunt when you were a kid?"

"Yeah, sure. Lloyd Bridges got damn-near killed every week. Someone always managed to cut his air hose or trap him fifty feet down with a sea monster."

"But he always managed to survive at the last minute," Sloan said. "Ever thought about trying it?"

"Drowning?"

"No stupid, diving."

"Not really—no—not my thing, down there with all those sharks."

"A dive club I know teaches classes. I thought I might give it a try." Sloan lifted his glass. "I wouldn't mind some company if Edie would let you out of the house."

"Count me out. I can think of better ways to make her a widow. What do you need to get in? The class, I mean."

"A pulse and you need to know how to—you *can* swim, right?"

"Swim team in my junior year. You think you can crew without knowing how to swim? I'm more worried 'bout you. Was there enough water in west Texas to swim in?"

"Do I hear a challenge coming on?" Sloan said.

"Me, I'd rather play golf," Jake said, "but getting close to a course on weekends is next to impossible, and I can't see taking off during the week. My new boss might think I wasn't serious."

"This dive club thing might be just what we're looking for. The classes are at night and the dives are on weekends. It'll set us back a hundred bucks for the class. Can you handle that?"

"Just money." Jake drained his glass and grinned. "And hanging out with sharks. But heck, I do that every day on the job." Jake had talked himself into learning to dive.

Tuesday nights for the next eight weeks, Sloan and Jake surrendered to the scuba instructors. In the first session they were tested on their swimming ability and endurance.

"I won," Jake proclaimed as he dragged his exhausted body halfway up the ladder on the shallow end of the indoor Olympic-sized pool.

"My ass," Sloan argued. "I've been sitting here waiting on you for at least five minutes."

"You cheated on the treading part," Jake said. "You must a cut that short."

"I lapped the pool twice under water. You only did one." Sloan said.

It was a cool Sunday morning in early summer after eight weeks of intensive training, Sloan collected Jake and his gear and the two made their way to Long Beach Harbor and boarded a boat to Catalina Island. They arrived early and stacked their gear on the deck of the eighty-foot dive boat.

A smattering of fog lay out along the horizon, and to the north and east they saw a thick layer of brownish yellow smog pushed up against the mountains. A gentle breeze moved in off the ocean. Sloan, Jake and forty-odd eager divers were greeted by the aroma of fresh-brewed coffee floating on the salty morning air.

Sloan watched as the captain fired up the two enormous diesels, freed the boat from her berth and steered the huge vessel away from its moorings and into open water. The throaty engines moaned and sputtered as the big boat pitched and rolled on the glassy morning sea.

"Hey man," Sloan said. "Your lips are turning green. Don't you like boats?"

"Got this tendency to get . . . you know… barf."

"Ain't that a helluva note?" Sloan quipped.

"Why'd I ever let you talk me into—" He pressed a hand to his mouth.

"What? How you gonna manage when we get in open water?"

"Who the hell knows? Why'd I let you talk me into jumping in the ocean at this ungodly hour on a Sunday morning?"

Sloan stood by as Jake hung over the bow rail and spat his breakfast into the sea.

"You gonna be alright? Want me to ask him to turn around? I read once where staring at the horizon helps."

"Worth a try." Jake felt his head start to swim. He slid back over the rail and sat on the deck. "Hell, we shoulda taken up skydiving. Woulda killed us quicker 'n drowning. Just think, we could be on the first tee at Anaheim Public, waitin' for the sun to come up."

"Along with a thousand of our closest friends," Sloan said. "See that ocean and this big old boat? They're what I call people buffers. On this boat, we have just forty or fifty other folks to contend with who don't know us or want to talk to us, and when we get down thirty feet, we will have only each other, and when I shut off your air . . . I'll have it all to myself. How's that for anonymity?"

"Until *your* air runs out," Jake grinned.

"Nothing in life is forever."

The exhausts from the diesels gurgled and coughed. The big boat labored side-to-side as she made her way out of the harbor and onto the blue Pacific. The morning sky was clear, and Catalina Island appeared so close Sloan could scarcely believe it was over thirty miles away. He felt he could reach out and touch it.

Sloan watched as the experienced divers curled up on the fantail to squeeze a few more minutes of sleep out of the morning. He found a vantage point on the bow and settled in to enjoy the ride. Once they passed the last buoy, the captain revved the diesels and powered the heavy vessel to a top speed of about ten knots.

From his perch, Sloan witnessed the raw beauty of the ocean. The big boat rocked fore and aft. The salt spray came over the bow and soaked him to the skin. It felt good. He knew his clothes would dry stiff, but he didn't care. He watched shorebirds as they followed behind, looking for scraps cast overboard or a tasty fish kicked up by the props.

A pod of dolphins joined the chase, playing and diving off the bow. Their grey bodies glistened in the morning sun. Sloan had read that dolphins mate for life.

Is it love at first sight for dolphins? he wondered.

He sat in self-appointed dominion over all that he surveyed. At times, he was overcome by the sense that he still felt a bond with Abigale.

The captain piloted the lumbering craft into a protected cove off the southern tip of the island. The crew dropped anchor and the captain backed the vessel until the anchor was lodged on the rocky sea floor. Divers donned their wetsuits and tanks.

Jake put a hand over the side. "That water feels like forty."

"Sixty-five, most likely," Sloan said.

The dive master shouted instructions to the class. Sloan felt a hit of adrenalin course through his veins.

"Class, listen up. We'll be making two dives. The first'll be with a coach. Together you'll go down to about thirty feet. Visibility is good today."

Jake shouted, "Hey, can I trade my buddy for one of the ladies? You know, just in case I need mouth to mouth."

"No," the instructor grinned. "But thanks for that good question. When the bar opens tonight and you've made it back on board, you can shout the first round."

"And if he don't make it back?" Sloan asked.

"He's still buying the first round."

Nervous laughter spewed from the beginners who weren't sure how to take their instructor.

There were no more questions.

On the first dive, the coaches let the novice divers take their time and enjoy the scenery. Sea urchins and abalone clung to the seafloor. Fish of every imaginable size and color swam around them all members of a common clan. Sloan looked up at tall stalks of kelp that seemed to reach for the sky. Small, curious fish peered into his mask. He felt like an interloper in a world not normally available to humans. The only sounds he heard were pings and crackles that were the soundtrack of the bubbling of his breath as it escaped his regulator and wobbled ever expanding to the surface.

One by one the student divers floated to the surface and climbed back on the boat to prepare for their second dive where they would be paired with another student in the buddy system.

For the newly minted divers, the day passed quickly. It was three o'clock and the captain was hauling the anchor back on board and revving the engines for their return trip to long beach. Sloan stored his gear and bought a beer from the concession in the galley.

The crew freed the anchor and winched it back on board. Within minutes, the captain set a course for Long Beach Harbor and the dive boat was underway.

The return trip was an occasion for drinking beer and raising hell. Everyone joined in celebration having earned the distinction of *certified scuba diver*. Several divers coupled up, fell temporarily in love and snuggled together on the fantail or on the bunks below deck.

Sloan was relieved and proud that he had completed the class. Jake fell asleep in the galley with half a bottle of beer in front of him.

Sloan returned to his favorite perch where he was witness to a different ocean than the one he had traversed to the island eight short hours earlier. Afternoon winds and six-foot swells provided a ride that was poles apart from the slick, finished ocean they enjoyed that morning. The dolphins were nowhere to be seen. Strong currents and stiff seas had long since sent them packing for shelter.

XL

Sloan was coming up on his first anniversary at Vortec and his job had come to dominate his life. His days often stretched into evenings and weekends. Monday had been an unusually slow day as several of the executive team were on international status. Sloan was looking forward to getting home at a reasonable hour and enjoying some quiet time with a cold beer or a glass of wine, but when he arrived home Wendy greeted him at the door. "Daddy! Daddy! Guess what. Mammaw wants me to come see her on the jet plane all the way to Texas America. Can I go, Daddy? Please, can I? Mommy says yes if you do."

"Hey, slow down. This is the first I heard about a trip on an airplane without Mommy or Daddy."

"Mammaw called today! Wants me to come see her. My cousins will be there, too. Is it okay, Daddykins? Can I go? Huh, please."

"Maybe, but first you must promise me you will never call me that again."

"Daddykins? It's my new name for you. I made it up all by myself. Mommy says it's cute."

"Well, but only when we're alone, okay? Not in front of people. Not when Uncle Jake is here, for sure."

She tugged at his arm, dragging him toward the phone. "Call Mammaw and tell her I can come! Now. Okay, Daddykins?"

"Tired, Honey. Daddy'll call tomorrow and arrange for a flight."

"No, Daddykins. Do it now, please! Please, Daddykins, please!"

"Sure you're old enough to be going off without Mommy or Daddy?"

"I'm six. Going on seven!" She clasped her hands like she was praying to him—something she'd have to do a lot of if she was hanging out with her Uncle Wayne and his kids. "Please, I got the most gold stars of anyone in my class!"

"We had better make sure all this is okay with your mother."

Regina appeared from the kitchen with two glasses of wine. "She's begging you, right? You look like you could use this. I've been putting up with this since your mother called this morning."

"Are you good with putting our daughter on a plane to fly halfway across the country?"

"To Texas America?" she smiled.

She handed him the glass of wine and hung her arm around Wendy's shoulders. "Wendy, are you sure you won't be homesick and want to come home?"

"Don't be silly, Mommy. You know I'm a big girl now. I can read and everything and jump rope. Last summer, I learned to swim." Wendy grabbed Sloan's sleeve and dragged him toward the phone.

She picked up the phone and dialed. "They said yes, Mammaw!'

"Well," Regina said. "Does the same deal go for me?"

"What? You want to go to Texas America, too?" Sloan said.

Regina posed pensively with her finger on her chin. "You are working all the time."

"Oh, I see. You want to go back to Spain for a while? Sure, I would be okay with that. It would give me some time to focus on work and take a few dive trips with Jake."

"Just like that? No argument?" Regina looked sad. "All right then. Good. If I'm not needed, then I should just go home and stay."

She was the one who had said it, but he realized that she had been needed_less as Wendy grew older. When school was in session, Wendy dressed herself and walked to the bus stop on the corner. Regina, like her tennis buddies, preferred to dispense with household duties in the morning and leave the afternoons free for tennis and cocktails before rushing home to throw a meal together. Sloan wasn't complaining. When he returned home from his day of toil, she had dinner waiting and the house was always clean, but it wasn't a full-time job.

"Of course, I'll miss you both. But I'll manage somehow," Sloan said, smiling.

"You always do, Sloan." Regina shook her head, her eyes shiny. "You always do."

On Saturday, Wendy was up, dressed and waiting at the front door three hours before her flight was scheduled to depart. Regina lacked her daughter's enthusiasm for early, but she had managed to pack and set her alarm in time to make her flight to Madrid.

"Sure you're going to be okay without me, Sloan?"

"Oh, hell, it will do us good to be apart for a few weeks. Give us a chance to miss each other," he joked.

"Won't forget me, will you?" Her fingers trailed across his back as he carried her suitcase out the door.

Sloan loaded their luggage in the truck and drove Regina and Wendy to the airport. He pulled into the passenger unloading area, double-parked and offloaded Regina's luggage into the hands of a Red Cap who checked it through to Madrid. She stuffed four dollars in the porter's hand and hugged and kissed Wendy goodbye. "Be a good girl. Do what you're told." Regina flung her arms around Sloan and kissed him hard on the mouth. "You be good, too. And try to miss me." She smacked Sloan on the butt for good measure and, with that, she turned and ran for the terminal.

Sloan parked Wendy in a plastic seat near the gate and went up to the desk to double-check her boarding arrangements. "Don't you worry," said the gate agent. "A flight attendant will make sure she boards ahead of the rest and that she is united with her grandmother in Odessa."

"Hey, Wendy," a woman in a flight attendant uniform called to her. "Would you like to meet the pilots and see where they sit when they drive the airplane?"

"Really, can I?"

"Sure, give me your hand. We can go aboard right now." Sloan watched the flight attendant, a complete stranger and his precious daughter, proceed down the ramp and disappear into the huge silver bird without so much as a wave or a glance in his direction. He felt abandoned and displaced. Wendy had opted for the company of strangers over the prospect of hugging her father's neck one last time before she left on her summer vacation. She might have shed a few tears to show that she'd miss him. Sloan got none of this, and for a second he remembered a brash young lieutenant hanging a pendant around the neck of his intended and disappearing into a similar plane without once looking back. Was his life coming full circle?

The remaining passengers boarded. The large hinged portal swung into place and the silver machine rolled away from the boarding ladder. He rushed to the windows to watch as the lumbering airliner paused briefly to fire up the Rolls Royce engines that would propel Wendy to the same small town Sloan had known as a child. She would learn what it was to be a small child in a hot, dusty, West Texas town.

He hoped she would take a window seat on the port side where he might have one last look at his precocious daughter.

He saw a tiny face peering from a portal. A small child that resembled Wendy was waving at no one in particular. He waved back. He hoped it was her.

Would she still be his little girl when she returned home, or would she become worldly, wise and smart of mouth? She might no longer need a father to guide, teach, and be her hero. Even if she did, the day would come soon enough when she no longer needed him or Regina. Was Wendy the glue that held their family together?

He thought about Regina and her trip back to Madrid. In spite of what transpired that night when he found her with Gibbs, his feelings for her had changed and grown. He remained puzzled about the circumstances that surrounded that evening and the reaction from Gibbs after suffering a broken nose. What did he mean—strictly business? Don't men usually tell the truth in such situations?

Regina was a beautiful woman, not yet thirty. He wondered if, in the month that she would be footloose in her hometown, she would be receptive to male companionship. Would she renew old acquaintances from school or church, or would she drop by the restaurant where they met? Some of her old friends might still be hanging out there, doing their part to cement international relations with the troops. Gibbs may have moved on to DC or Maryland. If he'd played his cards right, he had a shot at Brigadier General. It was unlikely he was still in Madrid. Sloan hoped their altercation at his exit interview had created some havoc in his career advancement.

He reflected on his farewell kiss with Regina. It was nice, pleasant. Had it not been for that night, he would have felt different about her. They had been well on their way to a solid marriage when he'd caught her in the act with Gibbs. She could have filled a huge void in his life, but as it stood, their life together was a compromise riddled by mistakes they'd both made, and he saw no way to rectify their situation short of a divorce. He knew Regina sensed that things were not right, and it hurt her. She often looked at him as if she wanted to ask him, but could never quite formulate the question.

Sloan would not consider becoming involved with women on a casual basis. He did not want to be encumbered in some sordid physical affair. Such indulgences had never worked for him. With his luck, he would contract a disease or incur the wrath of an irate husband who packed a piece.

Part of him still believed that Abigale was his soul mate—if such a thing exists—but that ship had sailed. There was little likelihood that he would ever see her again. As far as he knew, she was off on her own track, happily married to Brad.

He would have to persevere. When Wendy was eighteen or so, he could once again think of his own happiness. Until then, he would focus on being a good father, his career, some diving, and down the road, when he could afford it, a sailboat. A pretty poor substitute for happiness, but it was the best he could manage.

XLI

Annual visits to Mammaw's house for Wendy and to Spain for Regina became a tradition, and Sloan looked forward to that month or so every summer when he had his life to himself. On several occasions, Regina's parents came to California for an extended visit or Sloan accompanied Regina to Spain. But he always returned before she did, so he and Jake could do some serious diving. Almost every year, they signed on to week-long trips to Mexico and Central America.

Wendy passed into her teens and began to struggle with the classic symptoms of raging hormones, social acceptance and all the adjustments that accompany puberty. Sloan had observed a tendency in Wendy to stay to herself, particularly in social or public settings when Regina and he were present. He feared that she would make bad choices and become entangled with a crowd of misguided youngsters.

Regina had spent her formative years in a male-dominated family and society that left her woefully ill-prepared to raise a twentieth century California teen. When it came to parental guidance for Wendy, Regina depended on Sloan to make all the decisions, but he found his experience with child rearing was distorted by growing up in a culture of hero worship that had pervaded his high school years.

At the tender age of fifteen, Wendy was invited to the all-school dance. Before he granted permission, he contacted the school to insure that the event was well-chaperoned. He offered to drive Wendy and her date to the shindig but she flatly refused, so he contacted the boy's parents to make sure *they* understood how seriously he took his daughter's first real date.

In his youth, Sloan had spent time with his dad at the pool hall down on Main Street where his father coached him on the finer points of the game and on the facts of life. Sloan had no pool hall to offer Wendy, and she would have rolled her eyes at the suggestion that they take an afternoon and shoot a game or two and toss down a few brews. Talking to her about the facts of life was not a task for a father. How could he explain birth control, weed farming, or the jokers at condom factories? The best guidance he could give her was to look for true love and save herself for that one special person. If she asked about Regina, he would lie.

Since the days when Sloan and Jameson chartered sailboats to explore the Mediterranean, he had dreamed of owning his own boat. He could teach Wendy to sail. The sailboat would be their pool hall.

Vortec sold stock to a venture capital firm in order to finance the company's expansion, and the sale had provided shareholders like Sloan a path to liquidity. The sale created a war chest of cash that he could apply to the purchase of a badly needed car, investments and a sailboat. He could manage these purchases without going into debt, provided his appetite for driving and sailing hardware was not too extravagant. He located a vintage WestSail 42 in a marina close to work and near their new home on Palos Verdes. She was equipped with the latest in communications and navigation gear and rigged for single-handed sailing. After several meetings with the owner and an all-day shakedown cruise, they struck a deal.

Sloan began his sales pitch to Wendy by talking up sailing as an exciting pastime, one that was not available to other kids her age. Wendy responded with a blank stare and a look of puzzlement. "Must be right up there with watching paint dry," she said. Jake had given him the same look when he mentioned the WestSail to him. Getting Wendy and Jake hooked on sailing would prove more difficult than he had anticipated.

Jake had been slow to warm to the idea of sailing until Sloan sweetened his interest with private dive trips. They would be much cheaper than riding cattle boats to the islands as they had been doing for the past ten years. Sloan's scheme to get Jake on board involved an extended lunch to showcase his new toy. If he could sell Jake on sailing with an impromptu afternoon cruise, he would then try the idea on Wendy.

Jake was led to believe they were meeting women for an afternoon of drinking. He should have known that was the last thing on Sloan's mind but the ploy got him out of the office for the afternoon.

Sloan stopped in front of Jake's construction trailer and honked. "Get your ass out here. Lunch is ready."

Jake shot out of the trailer in a dead run, jerked open the passenger door of Sloan's late model Mercedes and climbed in. Sloan steered the sleek coupe onto the Santa Monica Freeway and headed for Marina Del Rey.

"What's the damn big rush? We got hot dates or what?"

"Yeah. With a real lady," Sloan said.

"Real ladies don't sound like much fun."

"I had to fire one of my salesmen," Sloan said.

"Not making his numbers?" Jake said, showing a willingness to go along with the gag.

"Numbers, hell, he parked in my private parking space."

"The nerve of some employees," Jake said. "Where you taking me for lunch?"

"You'll love it. All you can eat and drink and it's all on me."

Sloan pulled into the marina and rolled up to the security gate. "Where do I park?" he asked the gate attendant.

"Take any slot that's convenient to you, Sir."

"We'll be out late. Any problems getting back in?" Sloan asked.

"Nope." The security guard grinned at Sloan's naiveté. "We're here twenty-four seven."

Jake peered through the windshield. "We talkin' fish and chips out of a rolled up newspaper?"

"Nothing that fancy." Sloan pulled forward to the gate and the guard swung it open. Sloan passed through to the private parking and loading zone.

Jake's jaw went slack. "What 'n hell are we doin' here? Gotta get back. Big important meeting at two."

Sloan threw Jake his mobile phone. "Better get them on the phone and reschedule. We'll be out the rest of the day. Damn it, Jake, I told you that." Sloan realized that Jake was most likely faking the meeting to give the impression he was important, in control and indispensable at the construction site, or else it was his comeback for Sloan's story about firing the guy who'd parked in his spot.

Jake fumbled with the new mobile phone. "Never can get these things to work. This better be good."

Jake spoke into the mobile phone. "Something's come up, need to reschedule that meeting with the carpet vendor. . . Great, thanks. Later, yeah. . . Me? Have fun? I'm with customers all afternoon. You know how boring that can be."

Jake turned back to Sloan and tossed him the phone. "Got a pass for the rest of the day. So where's the ladies you promised?"

"Lady," Sloan repeated.

"Meetin' her here?" Jake said. He looked over the big sloop. "Who owns this barge?"

"Guy I know."

"Know how to drive this thing?" Jake chided Sloan.

"Easy. Just point the sharp end into the wind. She does the rest."

"Don't forget, Old Stick, I sailed with you in Spain. So what about putting up sails and finding your way home after three days at sea?"

"Well, there's always that too," Sloan said.

"How about if we go aboard," Jake said. "Long as she's tied to the dock you can show me around."

"Not so fast there, coarse construction worker. You can't board this beauty in those hob-nail brogans you wear on the construction site. Grab that duffle out of the trunk. You'll find a pair of Dockers just right for your oversized . . . gift to you as first mate in training."

"Free shoes? Great!" Jake said.

Boat shoes laced, Jake knelt on the dock and ran a hand along the gunwale. "So, this guy you know, he know we're stealing his boat?"

"Won't be stealing when my friend James shows up with the bill of sale."

James, a crispy British gent appeared from below deck. "Afternoon, Sloan. Soon as you guys get aboard and stow your gear, we're ready to cast off."

Jake, who seldom missed an opportunity to make a mockery of his years in the Army, stood at attention and saluted with his left hand. "Permission to come aboard."

Sloan ignored him.

"This here's James, the soon-to-be-former owner of this fine vessel."

Jake abandoned his ruse, climbed aboard and shook hands with James.

"Done much sailing?" James asked Jake.

"Almost none. Mostly Sloan and me ride them big cattle boats out of Long Beach for diving. When I was stationed in Germany and him in Spain, we chartered a few times and explored the Mediterranean. We sailed some, but mostly we drank and whored around."

"Speak for yourself," Sloan said.

"Can't say I learned much sailing. Sloan was a real student of the sport and not half bad 'til he got drunk."

"No worries, mates," James said. "I'll go along today and show you the ropes and how to manage her in and out of the marina.

The rest is up to you. Sloan has had her out three times, so he's ready to go for his ticket. First, let's make it official. I have the bill of sale ready for your John Hancock any time you're ready. Have you decided what you're gonna call her?"

"She'll sail under the name of *Akubra.* That's A-K-U-B-R-A."

"Where in hell did you come up with that?" James asked.

"It's an Aborigine word. Means cool safe, shady place, a place for relaxing."

"If you say so." James printed the name of the vessel in all the appropriate places on the documents. They signed the bill of sale and Sloan handed over a cashier's check. Jake grabbed the camera and snapped pictures of the two men signing the document.

"You know, Sloan," James said, gazing at him, "changing the name on a vessel is bad luck."

"Don't believe in luck, bad or otherwise," Sloan said. "When it comes to luck, I make my own."

"Don't talk it down. Luck can come in handy when you're at sea," James said.

The three men made the boat ready to leave the dock. Sloan took the helm, James untied the dock lines and Jake took more pictures.

Beneath the last rays of the summer sun the three men tied the *Akubra* to her moorings, and under Sloan's close scrutiny, they rendered the vessel spotless. After shaking hands, James offered Jake a lift back to the construction site, which he gladly accepted.

Regina had retired to bed where she was engrossed in a late night talk show. Sloan's evening meal was wrapped in foil and waiting for him on the small dining room table. He searched the fridge for a cold beer and sat down to unwrap his dinner.

Wendy came down the stairs, pulled out the chair across from Sloan and plopped down, "Can I join you?"

"Sure, long as you're not hungry."

She eyed Sloan's frosty bottle of beer. "Had dinner, thanks, but I could sure do with a cold brew."

"Sure, help yourself, but first, you had best let me check your I.D."

"Come on, Daddykins. You know I'm almost old enough."

"Just trust you, eh?"

Wendy stared while Sloan tried to enjoy his meal and his beer. "You don't look like you've been working. Too much sun on your face and I never knew you to play golf or tennis. So . . . what gives?"

"Been at play, right enough. With the greatest toy ever." He put a forkful of spicy chicken in his mouth and talked around it. "Bought a sailboat today."

"So, you finally did it. Got yourself a hole in the water to pour your money in? Now if you only knew how to sail."

"I sailed some in the Mediterranean, while we were in Spain. You were too young to remember."

"Think you learned anything? Mom says those were mostly drinking parties."

"She's mostly right, but they write books on the subject. I'll just read one or two."

"Your answer for everything, huh, Dad?"

"Would you like to try it?"

"Maybe." She snagged a fried potato out of the bundle on Sloan's plate. "Will you let me drive?"

"Steer. When you learn, sure. You can go with me and Jake on Saturday if you aren't too balled up with what's his name?"

"Jimmy? We're just friends. Besides, I'm not likely to have any real dates until you come off that ten o'clock curfew." Wendy eyed another fry.

"Won't happen anytime soon." He shifted his plate away from her. "At least I don't sit behind you at the movies anymore."

"Yeah, that's real progress. Can you just hear the guys talk when I walk by at school?"

"Having a father who owns a forty-two-foot sloop should be a drawing card."

"So, they'll date me just to get on the boat, is that it? Just what every girl wants to hear."

"Did I mention that a yacht club membership comes with the deal?"

"Oh, great! Talk about snob city."

"There's just no pleasing you, is there?" He reached in his briefcase and came out with a large book on sailing and thumped it down on the table. "If you're serious about sailing, all you have to do is read this book by Saturday and I'll let you come along with me and Uncle Jake."

She lifted the book, weighing it in her hands, then flipped to the last page to see how many there were. "Have I been set up or what? You had this planned all along—the book and everything."

"Who, me? Just remember, if you ever call me Daddykins on my own boat, I'll cut off your allowance."

"And just which allowance would that be?"

"The one I might start paying you for cleaning my boat."

"Our boat," she said.

He grinned. "Okay, our boat."

Early on Saturday morning, three sailors boarded the *Akubra.*

"Come on. Let's get this sloop underway," Wendy shouted. She was exuberant, and Sloan was pleased that she had gotten far enough in the text to know the *Akubra* was a sloop. Jake was still back on the first chapter where they talked about wind, tacking and basic seamanship.

Sloan cranked the diesel. The odor of burnt fuel lay on the water. He directed his fledgling crew to make the *Akubra* ready to motor out of the marina. Once they had cleared the last channel marker, he shut down the engine and they hoisted the main and then the Genoa.

Sloan watched with pride as Wendy pulled and tugged at the sheets to bring the sails into nearly perfect trim.

"Hey, Pops, this is kinda cool."

"Beats hell out of wandering the mall with the gang on Saturday morning, huh?"

"Nothing wrong with a little mall wandering ever now and again, huh, Daddykins?"

Sloan took the helm and pointed her as high on the wind as he dared without giving his novice crew the sense that the *Akubra* was about to tip over. He wanted Wendy to experience the thrill of sailing, but not be afraid the boat would capsize. He would wait until she had more experience before he pointed her high enough into the wind to put the rail under water. Sloan steered the sloop toward open water—free at last. Jake settled back against the mast with a steaming cup of coffee and Wendy joined Sloan in the cockpit.

"My turn to drive."

"Climb in here and put both hands on the tiller. And it's called steering. Hold this course and point high enough to keep the sails full of wind."

"I know when you're full of wind, but how can I tell the main is?"

"By listening," Sloan said. "If she starts to luff you can hear her."

Wendy was quick to catch on.

"In a couple of months, the club's having a father-daughter race. What do you say? Want to enter?"

"You mean I could meet some yacht club snobs?"

"Who knows, there might be one or two in the bunch worth knowing."

"Think we can win? You know, Daddykins, you're not much of a sailor. Leastways not yet. And I really don't want to enter if we can't win."

"Listen to you. First day on the boat and you're already talking like a sailor."

Over the next few weeks, Wendy came to love sailing and went often with her father and Uncle Jake. The very idea of being blown around on the ocean powered only by the wind seemed to appeal to her sense of independence, love of freedom and her spirit of adventure.

On long weekends, they crossed the channel and spent the night in a beautiful cove on Catalina Island. On these special occasions, Regina, Edie and Jake's daughters joined the group.

Spending an afternoon heeled over with a rail in the water was not Regina's idea of fun. Lunch and a movie, a few sets of tennis with the girls or cocktails in the club bar was more to her liking. After one scary sail, Regina swore she'd never come again unless Sloan promised not to lean it over, but in Sloan's view, sailing, like life, was meant to be enjoyed with a rail in the water, Otherwise, why bother?

Wendy enjoyed their outings, but soon became bored with conversation that Jake or Sloan could provide. The generation gap was never more evident than when the two men engaged in discussions about work, diving or getting ahead in the world. Edie and their girls provided Wendy with an audience to show off her sailing skills. Edie was a game sailor as long as she stayed below in the galley. Her contribution to the outings was making lunch, coffee and snacks that she would pass up the companionway to the sailors.

One Saturday afternoon as they were motoring through the marina to their slip, Wendy approached Sloan with a proposition.

"You know, Pops, this sailing is a great way to get to know you two old dudes but it sure would be nice to mix it up a bit."

"Like what?"

"What would you say to my bringing some friends along?"

"Sure," Sloan said. "As long as they wear proper shoes and do their part of the cleanup."

"I'll be sure to invite a galley slave or two."

"And you address me as Father or Captain, but not —"

"It's a deal, Daddykins. Next week I'll be in charge of shanghaiing the crew."

Saturday morning, Wendy, two girls and a guy showed up on the dock ready for their first sailing lesson. Derrick had sailed before, but the two girls giggled and confessed total ignorance and little interest in learning how to sail. "If you don't mind, we're going forward and work on our tans."

They entered open water and Wendy went forward with one of the novice girls to hoist the mainsail. Wendy then came aft and manned the tiller while Sloan took Derrick to the bow and demonstrated the procedure for hoisting the jib. Sloan wondered how it would have been to have a son. He would probably be in a smelly, smoky pool room on Venice Beach.

The *Akubra* was heading into a fifteen-knot breeze out of the Northwest and on an even keel at about fifty degrees off the wind, enough to move her along but not enough to make his fledgling crew uncomfortable.

Toward early afternoon, they began to show signs of boredom. Sloan lost track of Derrick and one of the girls. He turned the tiller over to Wendy and went in search of the missing couple. Through the starboard portal, he could see them in the aft salon. Sloan threw a bucket overboard to collect a gallon of cold seawater. He lifted the stern hatch and doused the pair then quickly dropped the bucket in the cockpit. The two doused lovers scrambled out of the cabin and up the companionway swearing at anyone who might have perpetrated such a prank.

"Wendy, you bitch. I'll get you for that," the young girl shouted as she readjusted her halter top.

Wendy casually pointed at Sloan. "Don't look at me. I told you, he's a real square."

The girl spotted the bucket, hooked it to a loose halyard, tossed it overboard, pulled it back into the boat and dumped it on Sloan's head. She threw the bucket down and ran to the bow hoping to escape.

Sloan contemplated his alternatives: escalate or capitulate. He dropped the bucket on the deck and laughed. "Okay, you win. Without another word he brought the *Akubra* up into the wind. "Wendy, haul in that jib," he shouted.

"Aye, Captain." The starboard rail disappeared beneath the surface. What had been a joy ride suddenly became a carnival ride. Everyone scurried to get a firm grip.

"Hey, wow, Mr. Abernathy," Derrick shouted, "this is great! Can I try my hand at the tiller?"

Winning Wendy over to sailing was a victory for Sloan. She was committed to the exclusion of many activities that normal healthy teenagers were involved with. She had come to believe that Sloan bought the *Akubra* just for her and, in a way, she was right.

XLII

Abigale rose early on Thursday morning of what might be the final day of her month-long job search. She had narrowed the field of prospects to two high tech companies: Elcon and a much smaller, but very successful company by the name of Vortec. Last week, she'd had three meetings with Elcon but thus far, no offer had been made. Today she was scheduled to meet with the hiring manager at Vortec, a man about whom she knew very little. She arrived early and approached the reception desk in the main lobby.

"Please have a seat, Ms. Hager. Mr. Abernathy will be with you as soon as he gets off the phone."

Abernathy? No, it wasn't possible. Plenty of Irish immigrants with that name had crossed the pond and settled on the west coast. She took a seat in the outer office and nervously thumbed through last month's issue of *Fortune* magazine.

"He's off the phone. You may go in now."

Abigale stood and collected herself. She pulled at her skirt and smoothed it behind her. Poised, she entered the hiring manager's office and was greeted by a tall slender man standing behind a large oak desk. He posed with one hand on his hip as he studied her resume. His blue suit, white shirt and a brilliant silk tie, accidently pulled to his left, gave him an air of sophistication. There was a familiar, stubborn set to his jaw. A wave of apprehension washed over her.

He gnawed the earpiece of his horn-rimmed reading glasses. The morning light shone from the window and illuminated the pages of the cover sheet, but left his face darkened. Only his voice offered a clue to his identity. Still looking down and out the window, he spoke without turning to face her fully.

"Please," he said, "have a seat. I've been traveling and just this morning returned to the office. I need another minute to review your file."

Abigale realized that there was an amazing thing about voices. Everyone would recognize Elvis Presley's voice even though they'd never met him. Or John Wayne. Anyone who had ever seen a John Wayne movie would recognize his voice.

She'd last heard Mr. Abernathy's voice on the phone when he called her from Spain to say he was going on a secret mission. The last time she had seen him was in Madrid when he was having sangria with his beautiful, pregnant, Spanish wife. The last time she'd heard this voice in person was when he ran up the boarding ramp at the Miami airport to give her a ruby sea glass medallion.

"Means we're engaged," he'd shouted over his shoulder as he ran back down the ramp into the plane.

"Sloan? Sloan Abernathy!" She realized she was shouting, but she could not help herself. "You son of a bitch. What 'n hell are you—"

He turned to face her. For the first time in fifteen years their eyes met. She returned his gaze with hatred and disdain.

"Your résumé—I thought maybe, the name. . . so. . . hey . . . it's great to . . . how are you—"

"Oh, just *dandy.* Haven't been jilted in years."

"Heard you married that jock . . . Brad somebody."

She lifted her chin. "Damned straight I did."

She often wondered what she would say if she ever saw Sloan again. Now that he was standing before her, she couldn't conjure the words she had rehearsed so many times.

"Abby, just sit down. I can—"

"Explain? I'll bet you can! When I saw you in Madrid you were—"

"You saw me in Madrid?"

"Sure as hell did, all doodled up with some Spanish bitch. You didn't even have the decency to write or call. Now—you can explain?"

He came from behind his desk and rushed to her and grabbed her arm. His sudden motion startled her and she pulled away.

"Abby! Please, let me."

"*Don't Abby me,* you scumbag son of a bitch. I thought you were dead, or worse. Then I find you married to some Spanish—good PR for the Army, huh, Sloan? How many in the brood by now? Six? Seven? Got your ball team yet? I hear those Latin women are regular baby machines."

She turned and marched toward the door. The receptionist was startled by the commotion. "Anything I can do to—"

Abigale strode past her and into the open elevator.

Sloan took the stairs and caught up with her on the street. She swung at him with her briefcase, fully intending to break it over his head. He ducked to avoid taking the blow across his nose.

"I'll scream."

"Abby, please try to understand. What else could I do? I couldn't face you after the mess I—listen, can we just please have some coffee and talk?" He took her by the arm again, gently, and steered her toward a small café. "This is a nice spot where we can sit and talk."

"Coffee? Sure. One cup. You pay and your story had better be damned good." They found a small table on the patio.

"Please bring two coffees and some Danish, thanks."

He scooted her chair underneath her.

She stirred cream into her coffee, regained her composure and even began to see humor in their meeting. She wasn't the heartbroken girl who drank herself silly with Charles on that transatlantic flight from Spain.

"So, Captain Abernathy, what have you been up to all these years since you jilted me? What's the story? I just can't wait to hear it." She crossed her legs under the table and put one elbow on the glass top, ready to hear the long tale of Sloan's life since the day he dumped her.

He searched for just the right words and the best place to begin. She sipped her coffee, tore a muffin into pieces soaking each piece in her brimming coffee, a habit he knew she had learned from her father.

Sloan cleared his throat. "Look, Abby—"

"Damn it, Sloan. I told you not to call me Abby. Reminds me of an old sweetheart, a man I trusted with my heart and he pissed on it."

Sloan squirmed in his chair. "Okay. Sure, Abby . . . Gale. Here's the whole truth. I met this lady at a dinner party. I was lonely, homesick and missing you."

"Oh, so, it was all my fault." She pointed a thumb at herself.

He ignored her caustic remark.

"Later that night, we went to her apartment. She'd had a lot of wine and needed help getting home. Things got out of hand. Actually, I had a lot too. I know being drunk is a feeble defense for my behavior. Who would've thought she would get pregnant?"

"Really . . . who'da thunk it?" Abigale pushed back in her chair, crossed her arms and glared skeptically at Sloan who shoved both hands in his trouser pockets.

"Once I learned she was carrying my child . . . Wendy, my daughter, I felt I had to take care of her. Wouldn't have been right to let her fend for herself. Wendy's the best thing in my life, my pride—"

"You are such a white knight! You let me take the fall and then steal *my* choice of names for your daughter. You scum—"

"Oh, you mean Wendy? Guilty on that count, too. I remember that night on the beach when you suggested it for our daughter. So yeah . . . I did."

Abigale sat up straight. "Why in hell didn't you tell me all this?"

"Couldn't face you. Took the coward's way out and . . . wrote you a letter."

"Oh, now I get it. You wrote me a long newsy letter and simply forgot to mail it or you couldn't afford a stamp on Army pay."

"The letter and what happened to it is another story entirely."

"Let's hear it, Cowboy. If you can afford a second cup of coffee."

"My CO intercepted the letters I wrote you and the ones you wrote me."

"Intercepted? How does one intercept a letter? Is that a football term?"

"The Army inspected our mail. It was done at the discretion of my CO who, I believe, found sadistic pleasure in screwing with the lives of his subordinates. He returned your letters to me on the day I mustered out. Sadly, it was too late to change the outcome between you and me."

"I'll say!" She hung one arm over the back of her chair and looked him straight in the eye. "Look, Sloan, I'm not buying this. You've had fifteen years to concoct this load of crap. Truth is, old man, it's all my fault. I should never have fallen in love with a Texas roughneck in the first place. I should have known better."

"Don't I deserve *some* credit for at least trying to do the right thing . . . for my daughter and her mother?

"Give yourself a gold star." She leaned toward him. "You should've told me, you bastard. You owed me that. Do you have any idea how much you—"

"Wished a thousand times it'd turned out different, but as time passed it was more difficult for me. Guess I just went with the flow."

"Didn't you just—how'd you get here? To California?" she asked. She may have felt a modicum of pity for her one-time sweetheart.

"Vortec offered me a job."

"Oh? What's this job you want me for?" she asked.

"We're coming out with a new navigation system for maritime applications—"

"And, let me guess, you're responsible for the rollout."

"That's it exactly. So come on back to the office so we can talk more about it."

"To be honest with you, Sloan honey, the last thing I want is to report every day to a job that reminds me of the worst time in my life."

She stood and extended her hand. "Goodbye, Sloan darling, and thanks for the coffee. But frankly you can take your job and shove it."

She marched out of the little café like Patton.

Sloan arrived home around seven. Regina had prepared his evening meal and left it on the small dining room table. He poured himself a glass of red and sat down to the dish. Regina passed the dining room on her way out for the evening.

"I'm meeting Edie for a drink and a movie. I might be late."

"Great," Sloan said, without looking up from his dish.

"Great that I'm leaving?" she asked.

"No, of course not. It's great you're having some fun." After the day he'd had, he could not face her. He was relieved that she would be out of the house for the evening, leaving him with enormous guilt for what he was thinking about Abby.

He finished his meal, poured another glass of wine and settled into his favorite chair in the den. He opened his briefcase, located Abigale's résumé and reread it, searching for a hook on which he could hang further discussions about the job and for clues about how she had spent the years since they were together.

Wendy stopped at the door, "Hey, Daddykins. Is it okay if I go to Marlene's to study for tomorrow's test?"

"It's a school night, kiddo. Better not be late. Her parents at home?"

"Not to worry, Daddykins. Her parents never go out. They're even more boring than you, if that's possible."

"You gonna be studying or listening to that awful music?"

"Little of both." He didn't look up as he spoke to Wendy, the daughter who might well have been Abigale's.

He felt the weight of the years. Seeing Abigale had brought it all back. He stared at her neatly typed resume and thought about their meeting. She said no to the job, that's all. People often say no as many as three times before they say yes. It's human nature. I'll give her two more chances. He punched her number into the phone. He could be very persuasive when it came to getting what he wanted. They had not talked money and the job came with an attractive salary, great benefits and a generous bonus. She would be hard pressed to do better and she needed a job.

"Hello." Her voice was lyrical, as if she had completely forgotten all that had happened earlier in the day.

"Can we talk?"

"Oh, it's you. Sure, Slag. What's on your minuscule military mind? Thought I made it clear where I stood on your freaking job." Her tone of resentment had returned.

"Listen, please, just hear me out. You and me—we were close once."

"So now you want to get a little something going on the side, is that it?"

"You know me better than that."

"I know you all right. You're all about knocking up strange women and jilting your soul mate."

"Look, Abby, I don't expect you to forgive me. God knows I haven't forgiven myself. I just thought maybe we could be friends and perhaps you would reconsider the job. We haven't talked money yet and I can make the salary and bonuses pretty darned attractive. I have sole discretion over all payments."

"You just don't get it do you, Sloan. This is not about money. You've got your life and I have—let's just let it go at that. You leave me alone and I'll leave you—"

"How's the jock these days?"

"You mean Brad? He passed away over five years ago."

"Sorry . . . really. Don't mean to pry, but were you happy? You and Brad."

"Yes, and very much in love. We got married right after graduation and moved out here to California and bought this darling little house in Anaheim. Brad Junior was born that next year. Brad was working late one night when an aneurism took him. The janitor found him slumped over his desk."

Sloan could hear deep sadness in her voice. He thought that she had begun to weep.

"Must've been tough for you and Brad Junior."

"You can't imagine how he idolized his father. We both miss him. Not a day goes by . . ." Her voice trailed off.

"Yes, well, I'm sure Brad Junior makes it all bearable. Tell me about him. What kind of a kid is he?"

"Typical teenager. Plays quarterback on the Junior varsity."

"Chip off the old block?" Sloan said.

"He shows some skill, but not the passion his father had. He lacks the killer instinct that made his father a great athlete. Brad Junior has so many other fine qualities. Compassion for others, an interest in art and literature. It won't surprise me if he goes into public work of some kind. Unlike his parents, he's strong in science and math. He might be good in international finance or something like that." Her voice softened and he knew she was smiling. "There are times when I wish I could send him to talk to your old man. He's at that age when he needs one of those backyard talks or a trip to the pool hall. Not that they did you any good. You turned out to be a freaking weed farmer." Her caustic comment brought a long silence. "When I think about us, you and me, and those days at FSU . . . walks on the beach, looking for sea glass—"

"That necklace you were wearing today? Was that the shard of ruby sea glass I gave you as an engagement present?"

"Uh-huh. Want it back?"

"Abigale, please come work with me. It'll be fun."

"Fun? Sorry, Slag, but I don't need a daily reminder of the most heartbreaking day of my life. That ship has sailed. It's over. Let it go and bid me farewell. I'm sorry we ever met."

"What will you do?"

"Don't worry about me, big shot. I can take care of myself. Fact is, I've accepted a position with Elcon, just this afternoon actually. They made me a great offer. I start next week reporting directly to the president."

"Elcon? Damn it. They're my biggest competitor."

"Yeah, I know. I'm so glad you called. You've helped me unload a ton of baggage I've been hauling around for a lot of years. See you in the marketplace, huh, Slag?"

"I'm truly sorry things worked out the way they did. I hope someday you'll forgive me for making a mess of—"

"Someday, Slag, but not tonight. Take good care of that lovely Spanish bride. Loyalty is a fine quality in a mate. I hope you deserve it. Goodbye, Sloan."

There was finality in her tone and he waited for the click. Instead he heard her take a deep breath. "Listen, Sloan? Don't call me or try to see me ever again. I'm over you and that's the way I want it. Don't try to drag me back into a life you ruined for us. If you see me on the street or in the supermarket, walk right on by, just like the song says. Don't speak, don't smile. As far as I'm concerned, you don't exist. You're dead just as sure as Brad is, without all the happy memories."

He was left holding a phone, listening to the dial tone. He slid his desk drawer open and withdrew a folder labeled personal. He found the letter addressed to Abigale LaHolm at Florida State University. Before stuffing it in a larger brown envelope he would address to Mrs. Abigale Hagar, he scrawled a short note beside the address:

Dear Abigale: My Ruby Sea Glass.

Better late than never,

Slag

On Monday, Abigale began her new career as special assistant to the president of Elcon.

Sloan hired Marla Day as his Administrative Assistant. She was a newly minted graduate of business administration from Stanford. She was eager, ambitious and attractive. He hoped she would stay with him for a few years before she left in search of more responsibility or greater opportunity for financial reward.

XLIII

Remnants of the morning fog lay along the cliffs. The water was clear and calm. A pod of dolphins played around the sloop as she made her way into open water. Once clear of the last buoy marker, they sailed south and west along the coast to Newport Beach where they dropped anchor just a mile off shore.

Wendy had begged off the weekly sail to spend a long weekend with her mother in New York. Regina had arranged the trip to celebrate Wendy's sixteenth birthday. They planned to take in a Broadway show and do some serious shopping up and down 42nd Street.

Sloan and Jake pulled on their wet suits, strapped tanks on their backs and joined the dolphins in a day of play in the turquoise Pacific. Shafts of light from the mid-morning sun bored great holes through a forest of kelp that in turn provided camouflage for millions of fish. The kelp swayed rhythmically to and fro with the waves. Sloan rolled over on his back and opened his arms in thanks for the privilege to bear witness to such beauty. Without provocation, a dolphin swooped down and nosed his mask as if to kiss him and say good day. Jake swam by in hot pursuit of a lobster he had flushed from the foliage. He soon returned empty-handed. In fact, they harvested no game for the table, but it didn't really matter. It was a wonderfully scenic dive. For an hour out of their busy lives, they shared the experience, much like exploring another planet.

They climbed back on board and shed their tanks and wet suits. Sloan opened two beers and handed one to Jake, then tossed him a sandwich and unwrapped one for himself.

"What's that old structure along the shoreline?" Jake asked, shading his eyes. "Looks like an old pier or a dock."

"According to the charts on this area, there was a hotel and resort on this site back in the twenties. It was a Great Gatsby kind of place."

"Beautiful in its day."

"Not so bad today," Sloan said. He wanted to get around to a discussion of his upcoming plans but he wasn't sure how to start, so he jumped right in. "Love at first sight," he finally said. "Do you believe in that stuff?"

Jake had finished his Heineken and was digging in the ice chest for another. He looked back over his shoulder. "In what?"

"You know. Do you think it really happens that way?" Sloan took a slug of beer to wash down the last of his sandwich.

"I suppose so." Jake wiped the ice off a fresh bottle of beer. "Never happened to me."

"What about Edie? That was love at first sight when you met her, wasn't it?"

"I do remember seeing a pair of beautiful blue eyes looking back at me from the other end of the bar. And come to think of it, Edie was the only girl I spent time with after we met that day in Berlin."

"How long 'till you decided to get married?"

Jake closed one eye as if he could think better. "Six—maybe, I don't know. Could have been seven . . ."

"Months?"

"Weeks. No, it was no more than a few weeks."

"Don't take that long to flunk a pregnancy test?"

"Did I say weeks? No, months. It was a few months, maybe two. Let me see now, our oldest daughter came along when we had been married about eight months. If you ask me, that was close enough for guvment work."

"And it worked out great, right?" Sloan confirmed.

"Yup, I guess it did." He sat on the deck, knees bent, holding the bottle by its neck. "I remember the night when Edie leaned over and whispered in my ear. I said, 'the hell you are,' and a week later, you and Regina were in Berlin and I was standing in front of the Chaplain at the base." Jake took a long swig of beer. "I got no complaints, but that doesn't mean it was love at first sight or soul mates. Nothing like that."

"That all sounds like a load of crap to me," Sloan said. "It was you who told me sex was all about quantity not quality, remember? You were trying to nail as many babes as you could before the warranty ran out on your manhood, and if one of them got pregnant, there was always abortion."

Jake shrugged. "Back at FSU, that was true. In those days, you couldn't be sure who had been there before you. With Edie, I was pretty sure I was the only one she was interested in."

"Ever cheat?" Sloan asked.

"No, not really. Been known to wrestle around in the back seat with some babe after a dive trip or when I was out of town on a business trip. I talk a good game, but when it comes down to it, I fake it. Honestly, I guess I love the old girl. She puts up with my shit, so I count myself lucky."

"Bet you getting married to Edie took Brenda by surprise," Sloan said. "She was probably expecting you to come back for her."

"Brenda. Now there's a blast from the past."

"She think you were serious?"

"Can't remember," Jake said. "What's all this about anyhow? What's on your mind, all this talk about love and who screwed who? You ain't got something going on the side have you? You'd be crazy if you did. Regina is just about the best a bum like you could hope for. You should have ended up alone or in jail after you did Abby that way."

Sloan took his time answering. "In August, me and Regina will be married seventeen years and Wendy will be starting her first year at UCLA."

"Now you and the old lady can sit back and take it easy," Jake said. "The hard part is over."

"Maybe."

"Maybe?" Jake stopped with the beer bottle halfway to his face. "What's the matter with you man? Comin' down with a brain tumor or somethin'?"

"You're going to find what I'm about to tell you a bit of a stretch, so pay close attention. I only want to say this once."

"I'm all ears, big brother."

"This goes back a ways. As I recall, Regina and I had been married about three years." Sloan leaned back on the bulkhead, drained his Heineken and screwed his courage to the sticking point. "That's right. Wendy had just turned two . . . damn, she was cute. Anyway, I came home late and Regina was in bed with another man who just happened to be my CO."

"You're a lying sack of shit! None of that never happened."

"Told you this was going to be hard to swallow, what with you knowing and loving Regina like you do. I made myself a promise that I would stick it out for Wendy's sake, but when she was old enough to deal with it, I would pack it in on the marriage and that's what I intend to do."

"You outta your frigging—I can't even imagine you dredging up all that crap, what, fifteen years after the fact? Hell, man, you should've shot them both when you had the chance and been done with it. About now you'd be comin' up for parole."

"No bullets—or I just might have."

"What! You had a gun, but it wasn't loaded?"

"Something like that. I snuck out and went to my BOQ. No one knew I was back in Madrid until the next day when I met the CO in the chow hall."

Jake took another long draw on his beer and looked at the sky. "I've known you forever and never figured you for a coward."

"I've been known to take the easy way out in the past, but not now. Not this time."

"You know, man, a divorce is gonna cost you plenty, especially in California. You better sign the *Akubra* over to me or she'll get it along with everything else you own. Then I'd have to go sailing with Regina." Jake chuckled then laughed. "Now that has some possibilities."

"Glad you think this is so freaking funny," Sloan grumbled. He folded his arms and spat downwind over the lifeline.

"Hell, man, I know some guys at work who got divorced and they all live in one-room efficiencies so they can pay their alimony. You sure you've thought this through? What will come of our family friendship? Edie and Regina are damn near inseparable, and I even like you pretty good. Mostly because you let me sail your boat. We've had dinner ever Friday night for as long as I can remember. Guess from now on it'll be just Regina. Oh, you can still send over a good bottle of wine, but don't expect to stay for dinner. Hell, man it won't be long before she'll be bringing a new man over. With all your money, she'll have her pick."

"Hadn't thought about that," Sloan said. "Suppose all that will work itself out in time."

"Like I figured, you ain't thought this through at all. You know that little woman puts up with your crap and that's more 'n most women would do. Hell, man, you got all the freedom of a bachelor as long as you don't come home all stinky with perfume and such. If I had gone out and bought a sailboat without asking Edie, she would have locked me out of the house or had me committed."

"Grant you," Sloan said, "she's easy to get along with, but I always figured that was 'cause she had all that guilt, you know, wearing a hair shirt."

"Guilt? Hell, yes, she's got guilt. She's Catholic, ain't she? Rest assured she's been long since forgave for doin' your boss—if she ever actually did, which I doubt."

Sloan pondered Jake's logic, but would not be swayed. "I have it all figured out. Instead of lawyers, we'll hire an arbitrator. It'll be a damn site cheaper and I'll make her a fair offer. I've done well in the stock market and some real estate holdings, rental units and such that I bought over the years. In California, it's hard not to."

"Yeah, man. That house of yours on the peninsula is a beauty, but you can kiss it goodbye. She'll get the house and you'll get the payments."

"I *do* love that house," Sloan said. "What makes you say she'll get the house?"

"Unrecognizable differences." Jake replied.

"Irreconcilable—"

"Yeah, that too. You have to prove that you've got 'em and no judge will believe you. She'll most likely let you use the house for special occasions, providing you can afford the rent. Remember that country song? She got the goldmine, I got the shaft. Hate to be the one to tell you this, man, but you're the heavy in this scene. Divorce lawyers are just sitting there waiting for cases like yours to come along. You'll get some female judge who took it from her old man and she is out for revenge."

"It's not as black as all that. Besides, she doesn't deserve half. What did she do to earn half? On what I'm prepared to offer her, she could move back home to Spain and live a comfortable life. Course, if she stays here, she might have to get a job to maintain her lifestyle."

"Or marry some guy who has one." Jake added. "Her and this new dude will live in your house, he'll screw your wife and Wendy will call *him* Daddykins."

"Wendy will always be my daughter. Nothing's gonna change that."

Jake turned thoughtful and leaned back on the mast. "I think I'm getting this all figured out. Only one reason you would put everything you have at risk. You hooked up with Abby, didn't you? And now you want to wriggle free so you can pick up where you left off with her."

"Don't I wish? You're right about one thing. I did see her a while back. Didn't go well. She hates my guts. Her last words were, 'Screw you, Slag darling, and the horse you rode in on.'"

"Still think she's your soul mate?"

"Never doubted it for a minute."

XLIV

Saturday morning, Sloan was up early and found his way into the kitchen to brew a pot of coffee. He spread the paper over the kitchen table and managed to spend an hour browsing the business section.

From the upstairs bedroom, he heard a clatter and then footsteps as Regina began her descent of the stairs. She bounded into the kitchen and greeted Sloan with a kiss on the ear and an affectionate slap on the back as he was bent over the kitchen table with his elbows on his morning read. Her raven black hair flowed over her scarlet silk robe and was scattered in disarray over her shoulders and down her back. She found a mug and poured a steaming cup of coffee. "Why aren't you sailing?"

"No crew. Can't get a crew together. Jake's kissing up to his boss at some charity tournament and Wendy has a school assignment, so I guess I'll hang around and pester you."

"You could go into work and fire some people and make some more money for good old Vortec."

"Sounds like fun," Sloan smiled. "Or you could come along."

"To work? I'd rather go to the club and take out *my* aggressions on tennis balls. They don't hit back or sue for age discrimination."

Sloan winced at her reference to a legal battle that was brought on Vortec due to his overzealous handling of a dismissal.

"No. Sailing. We could take the boat out. You and me."

"Not on your—last time I went on that boat you leaned it over so far I about fell off."

"Heeled," Sloan corrected her.

She waved a hand in the air. "Heeled, leaned. What's the difference? Forget it, I'm not going and that's final." She took a sip, made a face and blew on the hot cup. "You know me and sailing."

"If I promise to keep her on an even keel?"

She set her cup on the counter and gazed at him thoughtfully. "I suppose I could. Have to cancel my match or find a sub. What time were you thinking?"

"Can you be ready in half an hour?"

"Promise you won't lean it over?"

"Promise."

A mile or so off the coast of Laguna Beach, Sloan dropped the sails and set the *Akubra* adrift. The afternoon swells were beginning to assemble. Each new roller was taller than the last. The stiff breeze put a frothy finish on every wave as it passed under the *Akubra.*

They settled back with deli sandwiches, cold beer and chitchat about the weather.

"There's something I want to talk about," he said. With a deep breath, he launched headlong into the undoing of his almost seventeen year marriage.

"Sure, what's on your mind? Is it that dive trip down the Baja?" She shrugged dismissively and swigged her beer. "I'm fine with it as long as you can afford it and that pathetic company of yours can manage for a month without their attack dog. Who would fire the people if you weren't around?" She handed him a well-squeezed tube of sunscreen. "Here, smear some of this on my back."

He obediently squirted the salve on her back and rubbed it in. "No, not that trip with the dive club. This is something that's been bothering me for years."

"Years?" She held the sides of her cover-up with one hand and twisted the drawstrings into a knot. "Do my lower back, too, will you, Hon, por favor?"

He squeezed the tube to free the last of the lotion. "Do you remember when I was on that long assignment to Australia? Wendy was two at the time."

His mouth went dry. He took a long drag on his beer. The refreshing bubbles escaped and hissed as he poured the cold liquid over his tongue. He had opened the topic, but would he have the nerve to see it through?

"Come on, Hon, you were on so many assignments, who can remember? That was so long ago, and besides, I never knew where you were. You could've been down the street for all I knew."

"I do," Sloan said. "I remember like it was yesterday. I came home late. Sometime after midnight." He looked out over the bow at the vacant sea in hopes he could collect his thoughts.

The *Akubra* rolled submissively from port to starboard.

"I came quietly into the house so as not to wake you, but I heard laughter and voices coming from your room.

Regina jerked and stood up as if struck by a bolt of lightning.

"That's crazy, Sloan!" She shook her fist at him. "You can't prove that. You didn't actually see anything—did you?" She covered her mouth with both hands as if she could catch her words.

He had taken her by surprise.

"Wendy knew who was with you. She called him *Uncle John*. Remember? Did you think you had lived it down? That I'd forget? You thought all that time and all those confessions to your priest would make it go away? Well, it hasn't."

She fell back on her cushion. "Honest, Hon, I can barely recall that night, or what happened. Fifteen years is a long time.

Okay, sure—you're right about one thing. He *was* there, but we weren't in bed. We were in the kitchen talking and drinking coffee. Nothing happened. Honest."

"Fess up, Regina. Gibbs already told me he had you."

"And you believed him over me? Men always lie about screwing other men's wives." She threw her half-eaten sandwich overboard. Bait fish attacked and devoured it. She took a long nervous swallow from her beer. Foam trickled down the corners of her mouth. She wiped her face on her sleeve. She stared out over the Pacific.

Sloan collected his thoughts. "Listen, Regina. I stayed in our marriage all these years for Wendy's sake. She's a senior this year, and if we go our separate ways she'll be okay with it. So . . . that's it. I want out. It's that simple." Sloan knew his words were hurtful, but he did not back down. He had to stay the course. "I want to be free to find true happiness while I still can."

"I get it," Regina said. "You've got something going with that cute bitch at your office, isn't that right?"

"No. That never even occurred to me."

"So, what then? You're not turning queer on me are you?"

"Don't you get it, Regina? Fifteen years ago, you broke our marriage vows, so I don't consider that I was bound by them. Since that night, my commitment has been to Wendy. I did what I had to do to make her life the best it could be."

"So, now you're kicking me out?"

"I'll see you're taken care of. I'll set you up with a trust fund. You'll have enough to be comfortable."

"What's a trust fund anyway? I trusted you and see what it got me."

"You can draw on it like a bank account."

"That sounds great. Why haven't you given me one before now?" She tried desperately to turn the whole situation into a joke, but Sloan was not laughing.

Regina straddled the lifeline and stared into the water. "What would I do?" She looked back at Sloan. "Where would I live? The only life I know is with you and Wendy."

"You could get a job, something you enjoy. You could go home to Spain and live like a queen or find a nice apartment where Wendy could come and stay. You've been a good mother and a good homemaker. I don't hate you or want to hurt you. I just want to make this easy for both of us. We have done the job we set out to do. We raised our daughter even though we weren't in love."

"What do you mean? I love you. I always have."

Her affirmation came as a surprise and brought with it profound confusion and guilt. Was it possible that she did love him? When they first met, her pregnancy was the condition that had altered their lives. In so many ways, they lived separately and at peace. She let him do as he wished, and he gave her as much freedom as she wanted. In spite of his insistence that they have separate bedrooms, he often paid her visits that lasted for a week or more.

The *Akubra* became too small for the two of them.

She ran to the bow.

Sloan followed close behind, fearful of what she might do. She had a wild, crazy look in her eyes.

She reached the bowsprit where she turned and sat on the pulpit. Was she considering his proposal? Telling her had been difficult. He questioned his motive.

The *Akubra* rolled up the front of a tall wave then pitched and rolled down the back side. The sudden motion tossed Regina in the air like an acrobat on a trampoline. When she came down, the boat and her perch on the pulpit had shifted to port.

She screamed like a panther as she landed feet first in the cold blue Pacific. She surfed bow to stern past the *Akubra* and disappeared behind a wave.

In a panic, he grabbed the bow line and flung it in the water.

"Regina!" he shouted.

He ran to the cockpit, switched off the engine and pushed the tiller hard alee. The *Akubra* obediently came back into the wind. The maneuver took off most of her forward speed.

He thought of jumping in to find her, but if he did the *Akubra* would follow the big rollers and be dashed to splinters on the rocky shoreline. He would have to swim a long distance. Under the best of conditions, he might not make it. He scanned the horizon but did not see her. He threw cushions into the water in hopes that she would surface and grab one. He ejected the man overboard buoy from the stern. It would help him keep track of where she had gone in.

Again, he scanned the surface of the water and again there was no sign of her. Thoughts raced faster than he could process them.

He needed to make a Mayday call, but she might surface while he was below deck and he would miss her. She might be okay if she did not hit her head on the way in.

Sloan started the engine and put the *Akubra* in reverse to slow her forward motion. The maneuver worked, but what if she was underneath the boat? She could be drawn into the prop. He shifted the engine to neutral and continued to scan the surface for some sign of her.

An hour passed. No, minutes. A minute—or less.

"Regina! Regina!" he screamed.

He heard a faint voice off the port stern. "Help! Over here!"

"Thank God."

The *Akubra* went slack and broached on the rollers. He put the engine in gear and maneuvered in her direction. As the sloop topped one swell, he saw her in the trough of the next wave.

When she was twenty feet from the boat, he ran forward to the rope locker and found a long line. He tied a bowline in one end and heaved it in her direction. Her black eyes were wide with fear. He switched off the engine. "Put the loop over your head and shoulders," he shouted. "I'll pull you to the boat."

Once she was back on board, he wrapped her in a towel and held her. Frigid water ran from her drenched body onto the deck and into the cockpit.

"Are you okay?"

She sponged her hair with the towel and looked up into his eyes.

"Still want a divorce?"

He held her close and patted her dry. In that moment, he realized that he had deep feelings for her, feelings that would make him sad for her loss. How could he have lived with her for seventeen years and *not* have feelings for her. He had shared her bed. They rejoiced in Wendy's successes. Regina had been there on thousands of mornings when he ventured out into the world to earn them a living. Had she brought love into their lives? Was he about to embark on a search for true love only to find it was already within his grasp?

"Go below and find some dry clothes," he instructed her, "while I set up the autopilot for our trip home."

Regina removed her wet clothes in the main salon and piled them on the floor. She climbed back up the companionway, exposing her naked bosom to Sloan.

"I can't find my dry clothes. Do you know where they're stowed?"

He could not take his eyes off her. Her waist-length, raven black hair lay matted between her breasts.

He gave the autopilot one last tug and went below. He stood facing her in the main salon. She put her arms around his neck and pressed her mouth to his.

"I love you, Sloan. Please don't make me go away. I can make it work for us. While I was bobbing around out there, I saw my whole life. I know I can make it better if you'll just give me a chance."

He kissed her again. She sat down on the edge of the starboard bunk and put her hands behind his neck. She lay down in the bunk and pulled him to her. He stooped and kissed her again.

Making love with her would be wonderful, he thought, but it wouldn't change anything. He would still want out.

He pushed her away and went topside. He released the autopilot and took control of the *Akubra.*

Fully dressed in her dry clothes, Regina came up from below. She wrapped herself in a blanket and curled up in the cockpit. She cast her dark eyes on Sloan. "You sure this is what you want?"

He nodded and turned his eyes to the horizon and home. He saw no way ahead but to hold to his quest for freedom and let the chips fall.

The *Akubra* touched the pilings and Regina jumped onto the dock and ran to their car. She sped away leaving Sloan to find his own way home.

"Hey, what about cleaning the boat?" he called out as she turned the key in the door and crawled in.

"Guess I can do it just this once," he thought.

He phoned Wendy and asked her to drive to the marina in Regina's SUV.

His attempt to put his life back on track had not gone well. She had left without any final words to indicate acceptance of his offer.

Wendy pulled into the parking lot and blasted the horn on Sloan's rusty old Ford.

"Why are you driving my truck?"

"No keys. Couldn't find the keys to Mom's car."

Sloan slid in behind the wheel and drove out onto the street and home.

"Look Daddykins, when you decide to get me a car, please don't make me drive this beat up old wreck."

"Not to worry, Hon. I'm not about to part with her. I like having a set of wheels no one else wants to drive. One day I'll have her rebuilt, and you'll be begging to cruise Rodeo Drive on a Saturday night."

"So, Dad, how is it that you needed a ride? Where's Mom?"

"She had an accident. Nothing serious. Fell overboard."

"Fell? Yikes, Dad, that sounds serious. Let me guess. You had a rail in the water?"

"No, nothing like that. We were adrift. She was out on the pulpit when the *Akubra* rolled just right to toss her in the water. She was shivering and unnerved, so I sent her on home and I stayed behind to clean the boat. Simple as that."

"She okay?"

"Guess so. Well enough to drive herself home."

"Probably brought an early end to Mom's sailing career, huh, Dad?"

"Probably."

"Wonder what she's making for supper?"

Supper, Sloan thought. On an ordinary day, she'd cook for the family. Sloan felt some regret having pursued this reckless course with Regina, but true to his nature, once he was committed to a course of action, there was no turning back.

XLV

Edie opened the door and stared wide-eyed at Regina. "My God, girl, you look like a refugee."

"Are you alone?" Regina asked.

"Jake's away at a celebrity golf tournament and the girls are at camp. So yeah, I'm enjoying some peace and quiet. At least I was until a drowned cat showed up at my door."

Regina's hair, usually well-coiffured, was little more than a black mop hanging over her ears. Her rouge and mascara were smeared on her face or left behind on the towel she was handed when Sloan pulled her from the sea.

Edie put her arm around Regina's shoulders, guided her to the living room and parked her on the sofa. Edie disappeared into the kitchen and returned with two glasses.

"Here, sip on this and get your head together. Now, tell me girl. What gives?"

"We had a quarrel."

"You and who, Sloan? Probably the first one in what—twenty years?"

"He wants a div—" She could not force the words past her quivering blue lips. She took another long drink of the cold chard.

"Divorce! You're kidding, right?"

Regina shook her head, pulled the afghan off the sofa and wrapped it around herself.

"On what grounds? You're too easy to get along with and you're just too damned beautiful?"

"I know you think we're the perfect couple, but there is más de lo que parece."

"English, please, my friend. My Spanish is pretty rusty and I don't want to miss one syllable."

"We've never really lived like a normal couple. Sometimes we sleep in separate rooms. Did you know that? He told me when we were first married that he loved someone else."

"But Regina, Honey, that must've changed over the years. Being so happy and all. So, tell me girl, what was this quarrel all about? What prompted him to—"

"He brought up something he says happened when Wendy was two."

"That man really holds a grudge." Edie smiled hoping to bring some levity to the situation. Once again, Edie put her arm around Regina's shoulders. "Come on, you can tell me."

Tears welled up in Regina's sad black eyes. Mascara, like black grease, ran down her cheeks.

"Okay, Honey, just calm down and start from the beginning." Edie pulled a tissue from a box on the end table and stuffed it into Regina's hand.

"We met at a party. We danced and talked. He wanted me to take him to my apartment. He practically begged and as the night wore on and we had more vino, I agreed to bring him home with me for one more glass. Morning came and he did not want to leave."

"Can't say that I blame him," Edie said.

"But I insisted. Sunday and I had mass."

"So, you slept with him that first night?"

"We had lots of wine. He wanted to come see me and I agreed. He asked me to marry him. It had been four weeks only and I was not ready, but he kept on telling me I was his soul mate. I must have started to believe him. My parents liked him, so I agreed. Good thing. I was pregnant."

"So, what's this grudge he's been holding all these years?"

"Not exactly a grudge. He was gone for weeks at a time to Australia and all over. I never knew for sure. He could have been down the street for all I knew. He told me I didn't have a need to know."

"One evening, I went to a movie with a friend. I hired the daughter of one of the men at the base to stay with Wendy. She was the daughter of Sloan's commanding officer. Gibbs was his name," she waved a hand, "or something like that. I didn't have a car, so he offered to drop his daughter off and pick her up. When he came for her, she was asleep on the couch. He hated to wake her, so I offered him coffee. All perfectly innocent. We were sitting at the kitchen table when, out of nowhere, Sloan barged in shouting at John—uh, Captain Gibbs. And he accused us of having an affair. He thinks I was sleeping with his CO."

"Well, were you?"

"Oh, please. You know I love Sloan."

"So, now he's using this as an excuse to ship you home?"

"Si! When I refused to go along, he pushed me overboard. I damn near drowned!" She held up her wet mop of hair as proof that she had indeed been for an unplanned swim.

"You're kidding, right?"

"He lost his nerve and came back for me. Yo tenía fear a la muerte and alone in my life."

"Please, Regina, English. I might miss something."

"I'll be damned if he'll send me back to Spain like some expatriado ayuda doméstica. I love Wendy, and I won't be separated from her. If it's freedom he wants, it'll cost him plenty. We have to break him." Anger flashed in her brilliant black eyes.

"Look, Regina, I'll help you get through this because you're my best friend and I love you, but don't put me in the middle of your quarrel. I can't imagine the four of us being divided, you and me on one side and Sloan and Jake on the other. We've been friends far too long. There are two sides to every story and you can bet it won't be long before Jake hears Sloan's side, if he hasn't already."

"Sure, Edie. I understand, but you may as well join me for a night on the town."

"Depends. What'd you have in mind?"

"Ever been to the Biltmore?"

"Can't say that I have."

"Me neither. But I hear it's top of the top. Grab your things and let's go. I'll call us a taxi. Or better still, a limo. A long, black one. We can leave the Benz in your garage. If you have a brush and a hair dryer, I'll put some of this hair back where it belongs."

A long, black limousine came to a stop in front of Edie's house, and the two expatriate housewives climbed in. A bottle of good champagne was open and waiting for them.

"Need a hand with your luggage, ladies?" the driver offered.

"We're traveling light. We'll buy what we need," Regina said.

"Not sure Jake would approve of that," Edie said.

"I've always believed that, if done right, armed robbery doesn't have to be an unpleasant experience."

Edie snapped her fingers. "I remember that line from a movie we saw last year."

"Thelma and Louise," Regina said.

"We don't have to drive the Benz off a cliff, do we? I can think of better ways to get even with Sloan and we can both live to tell about it. From what I'm hearing, you want to hit him where it hurts and that would be his bank account."

"Damn straight." Regina's Latin blood was starting to boil. She was growing a passion for revenge.

"On the tennis court, you're more about nurturing your opponents than defeating them, so I just don't get it. Where did *this* Regina come from?"

"Out of the icy blue ocean. He threw in the good little Regina and out came a witch, meaner than a snake."

The big limo cruised the streets of Hollywood. The women felt like Mafia Dons casing a new territory: Hollywood, Bellaire, Malibu, wherever the driver took them until dusk overtook them.

"Madams," he pleaded. "It's getting late. Perhaps we should find shelter for the evening and resume our tour tomorrow when the light is better."

"What a splendid idea. Take us to the Biltmore." Regina said.

"Yes, Ma'am!"

XLVI

Sloan turned onto the street in front of his house. A Mercedes coupe followed close behind. The headlights hit his rear-view mirror and he assumed it was Regina, but as he slowed to pull into his drive, the other car passed him and parked three doors down and across the street.

She must've arrived ahead of him, he thought. He rolled the truck into his garage expecting to find the Mercedes in its stall. Sloan could not fully appreciate the impact his life-changing proposal had had on her.

He imagined she would be contemplating her future as a single woman with a fully funded trust fund—like money was what this was all about.

His high beams flooded the three garage bays. He pulled the old truck into the left-most bay and shut off the engine. The coupe was not there.

"Darn, looks like we beat her home." Wendy said.

"Go check around by the pool. She was a tad upset from that dip in the ocean. She's probably drowning her nerves in a vodka tonic."

Regina was not by the pool nor was the Mercedes pulled around in back of the house.

"She's probably at the tennis club," Sloan lied.

"Or she's just out," Wendy said as she settled back into preparing for her college entrance exams. Wendy was unperturbed by her mother's absence. It happened all the time. "Got to hit the books, Daddykins. By the way, what's for dinner?"

Sloan attempted to reach Regina on the mobile phone. He tried Edie again. The evening passed with no word from her. Sloan became concerned that she might not be dealing well with his new plan for their lives.

The house phone rang and Sloan ran to catch it. "Hello," he shouted into the receiver.

"Thanks, man, but you didn't have to give me your car. I'll still go sailing with you."

"Jake, you whore. What in hell are you talking about?"

"I'm just home from the golf outing and found a brand new Merc coupe in the garage. So I just called to say thanks."

"Any sign of Regina?"

"Nope, nor Edie for that matter. She did leave a note though."

"Come on, man! What'd she say?" Sloan shouted with the last of his patience.

"Not much really."

"Just read me the damn note, will you?"

"Says she's off with Regina. Leftovers in the fridge . . . Don't tell Sloan."

Morning came, without a word from the angry, jilted, Spanish beauty or her sidekick.

The desk sergeant at the local police station explained that angry spouses often disappear for a day or so. "In most cases, it's punitive. Your wife is trying to punish you or make you worry. And it's working. Check with her friends and any boyfriends she may have. She might have checked into a hotel. If I had to guess, you had some kind of argument."

"We were talking divor—"

"Then you better give her a few days to cool down. If she doesn't turn up by tomorrow night about this time, give us a call and we'll do some checking."

"Thanks for your concern." The officer left Sloan with an empty feeling in the pit of his stomach. He called the local hospital emergency rooms. No accident victims that fit Regina's description had been treated anywhere in Los Angeles County The first clue to her whereabouts came when Sloan's credit card company called to verify that Mr. Abernathy was in possession of his card. Mrs. Abernathy or someone using her card had been making significant purchases. They wanted to make sure that the card had not been lost or stolen.

"As far as I know, the charges are legitimate. Tell me, where are these purchases being made?"

"All I can say, sir, is that Mrs. Abernathy has exceptional taste in clothes, jewelry, hotels and fine dining. Beyond that, I'm not allowed to disclose information about our cardholders. You don't happen to own a limo service by chance?"

"Not that I'm aware of."

"Want I should put a hold on your card?"

"No. She's entitled to blow off some steam."

He knew that if she was shopping, she was okay. Most likely, Edie was with her. All this news gave him some comfort.

Monday afternoon, Sloan's office phone rang.

"Hello."

"Miss me?"

"Regina!, where in hell—"

"Never mind where I am, Mister big shot. You'll get the bills, pronto."

"When will you be home?"

"And just where would that be? I've hired some lawyers. They're helping me prepare my case against you for mental cruelty. They are especially interested in how you threw me overboard and left me to drown."

"I never—"

"They are the best divorce lawyers your money can buy, so get ready to kiss your stuff goodbye. You'll be getting *their* bills, too."

"Look, Regina, we can do this without lawyers. I'd rather you get the money than some shyster."

"You had best learn to live small, Sloan, darling. When my lawyers are done with you, there won't be much left. I'll be back to *my* house this evening. Make damn sure your things are out of *my* room. I want the upstairs to myself. You can use the downstairs guest room or go live on that freaking boat of yours. I don't give a damn. Just stay out of my sight."

"Okay. Sure, that makes sense. You need your space. I get that."

"And that's not all. You can use the kitchen, but don't expect me to cook for you. I'll see to Wendy's needs, solo."

"I can manage on my own. But listen, Regina. Please . . . think about the arrangement I offered you. You'll be fine with it. It's fair. You won't have to struggle."

"Fair? You're talking fair? I'll tell you fair! Before I'm done, you'll be the one to struggle. You should not have pushed me off your boat."

"Pushed? No, no push. You fell . . . accident! It was an —"

"That was your one big mistake. You could go to jail. Attempted . . . whatever."

He heard clicks and his receiver went to dial tone. He realized that she was not alone. She had placed the call from her lawyer's office. Her demands and threats were presented well and thinly veiled. She was being coached by some shrewd shysters who were going to make the most of her having fallen off the *Akubra* and into their laps.

A few weeks had passed since Sloan's showdown with Regina. The home-cooked meals he had come to enjoy for almost twenty years had come to an abrupt halt. On the evenings when he came home, he tried his hand at making dinner. On weekends he sailed, so it was lunch from a deli on his way to the marina. He had put his plan into motion and it had backfired. Regina had proven to be smarter, more resourceful and more cunning than he had given her credit for. He was immersed in a profound sense of insecurity.

XLVII

Late on Saturday evening, a Mercedes coupe rolled up to the security gate at the marina. The two occupants smiled and waved to the guard. The yacht club insignia on the windshield earned them immediate access to the private parking area. The two figures, dressed in black, drove to a dark corner and from there ambled, or stumbled, down the gangway to slip B-57 and the *Akubra.* The two went aboard the great sloop and unlocked the companionway. They seemed to know their way around the darkened boat. They found the light switch, switched it on, and went below.

They were armed with small jars of red paint, fine-tipped brushes and a bottle of good Spanish red wine. Judging from the way the pair moved, they were well on their way to having a skin full.

"Let's see. What can I say to 'mi amado esposo' in his little 'carta de amor?'"

How 'bout "SCREW YOU, SLOAN DARLING."

"Great. Oh, perfect."

After writing several messages, the intruders climbed into the forward sleeping compartment to finish their wine and admire their handiwork.

"I'd love to see his face when he finds all this."

"Want to hang around till he shows up?"

"Think we should? He could come in and find us asleep in the forward bunk."

"Tempting. But, no, I think it's best we keep him guessing."

"Yea, like it will take him more than a New York minute to figure out who did this."

Arm-in-arm, the pair swaggered back to their car and drove away.

On Sunday, Jake and Sloan met for breakfast at the club. They finished their second cup of coffee and headed for the marina. Jake went ahead of Sloan to open the boat and put the sail covers away. Sloan made a stop at the ship's store for fresh water, sandwiches and beer.

Jake met Sloan at the gangway.

"We've been vandalized."

"How so?"

"Someone has writ crap all over the inside of our boat."

Sloan pushed Jake aside for a better look. "Not just any vandals," he said. "These vandals didn't know much English or they wanted us to think so."

"How do you suppose they got in?" Jake said.

"Most likely they were driving a Mercedes with a yacht club parking sticker on the windshield."

Sloan poured coffee from their traveling thermos and went below for a closer look.

"I take it this ain't nice stuff."

"Some of it you should recognize. Mostly, it's slang," Sloan explained.

"BESO MI ASNO; COMER MI CONO ; IR AL INFIERNO."

"Get the idea?"

Jake made a quick pass through the boat to further assess the damage. "Better come take a look here in the forward cabin," he said. "From the looks of that empty wine bottle and them panties, I'd say they had themselves quite a party."

"At least that's what someone wants us to think," Sloan said. "Those aren't panties."

"Coulda fooled me," Jake said.

"That's a calling card. See the monogram in the waistband? RA."

"We better clean this up before Wendy gets here."

Thankfully, Wendy was late so they had time to dispose of the most egregious evidence, but, unfortunately, most of the enamel paint was dry.

The three endured a lackluster sail and returned to port early in the afternoon, each having their own excuse for not being fully engaged in the day's adventure.

Sloan felt a sense of being violated. He credited the vandalism to Regina and one of her closest companions.

After sailing, Edie invited Sloan to dinner where she apologized ad nauseam for being a part of the wild weekend with Regina. She offered to repay him for what Regina had spent entertaining her, but he refused to consider any payment.

"In my view, you kept Regina out of serious trouble. Had she been left to her own devices, she might have landed in some bar on Venice Beach or, in her state of mind, she might have jumped off the Malibu Beach pier."

"You can thank *Thelma and Louise* for that," Edie said.

XLVIII

Sloan found that living under the same roof with Regina was like a poodle sharing the family pool with an alligator. Nights when he came home with a steak and the intention of throwing it on the grill, she might be making one of her famous Spanish dishes and setting the table for ten of her newfound friends who had come along with her new status of rich and soon-to-be-divorced. They were only too eager to enjoy a little slice of home in the luxury of Abernathy Manor.

It was clear the five thousand-square-foot house was not big enough for the two of them. Something had to give, and considering the way the settlement negotiations were going, Sloan was sure to lose the house, the cars and a large portion of his stocks and bonds. The private sale of Vortec shares a few years back had afforded him the opportunity to diversify his investment portfolio and he owned the *Akubra* outright. The bonuses he earned had gone into the house and late model cars.

Regina would not work with him to make things easier at home. She saw the house as her property, and the sooner he vacated, the sooner she could get on with her new life.

His only alternative, short of buying another house or renting an apartment, was to take up residence on the *Akubra.* He knew men at the yacht club who lived on their boats and it worked okay for them. There were showers and a laundry at the marina and large lockers provided him storage for his clothes. Considering the alternatives, he retreated to the marina. Cramped and uncomfortable, life on the *Akubra* was better than remaining at Abernathy Manor.

"Ahoy, the *Akubra,*" Jake called to Sloan as he jogged up the dock to slip number B-57.

"Come aboard, Mate. You can help me shoehorn my crap into the forward cabin."

"Kicked you out, eh?"

"It was my idea. Had to put some distance between me and her lawyers. Every day, they think of something else they want. At least here there is no phone."

"They come after the boat?" Jake looked over the side expecting to see a FOR SALE sign.

"About the only thing they didn't. She even wants that old antique lantern I bought from a street vendor in Madrid. Anything I place a value on, she wants."

Sloan sat down in the cockpit and draped one arm over the tiller as if to protect it from some imaginary lawyer. "And if I refuse, her lawyer reminds me of criminal charges for attempted murder."

"Should've finished the job when you had the chance," Jake said. "You always leave things half done and they come back to bite you in the ass."

Sloan pondered Jake's comment. "I'm beginning to wonder if I can afford freedom."

"Just a nuther word for nothin' left ta lose." Jake couldn't carry the tune, but he got his point across.

"Beginning to think Joplin was right," Sloan said.

"You'll be okay here, till it rains, and your claustrophobia kicks in."

"It won't be that bad."

"Do you think it'll ever get settled? This whole damn divorce thing?" Jake asked.

"I'll give it another three months. By then, I won't have anything left for her to come after."

"Except blood and body parts." Jake did his best Dracula imitation baring his teeth for effect. "We gonna get wet?"

"How about a nice peaceful sail? I need some R & R and Wendy's coming along. We don't have much time to chat these days what with all this divorce mess."

"How's she holding up under this parental fracas?" Jake asked.

"Amazingly well, but as far as I know, she has no idea what it's really about, and I hope to keep it that way. If she talks to her mom, she's bound to get a different story."

"Lying to her for her own good, huh?" Jake said. He shot Sloan a look of disgust. "Just how's that working out?"

Jake released the bow line and hooked it over a cleat for a quick getaway.

Wendy came running up the dock and gracefully jumped on board.

"Hurry, Kiddo. We're ready to shove off," Sloan said. "Jake, cast off those dock lines."

"Aye, Captain. Free at last, free at last." He put up one of his left-handed salutes as they floated away from the dock and left Sloan's troubled world behind them.

Sloan steered out of the marina, beyond the breakwater and onto the blue Pacific where they were greeted by steady breezes, perfect for a broad reach south by southeast and a little peace of mind.

Oil tankers made their way south toward Long Beach. Out on the horizon, a freighter was heading north to San Francisco or Seattle. Sloan was overtaken by the serenity of the open sea.

Wendy took the tiller while Jake winched the mainsail into place. Sloan rigged her jib and winched it up the forestay.

"Glad we decided to sail," Jake said.

Once all the cloth was up, Sloan took the helm and Wendy went below to brew coffee. She returned with three steaming cups and handed one to Jake. She found Sloan at the bow where he was settling in to enjoy the run down to Newport Beach. She sidled up next to Sloan.

"Okay, Dad. Time you did some explaining."

"Yeah, about what?"

"What's this divorce stuff really all about? Explain to your only daughter why she has to do without her parents and her happy home."

"Really kind of complicated."

"Let me guess. You got a hot babe on the side, huh? Is it that cutie who works for you, or is it some mysterious damsel from your dark past?"

"Nope. No babes, hot or otherwise. And I hope you don't think I'd get involved with someone at work. That's pure poison."

"I know you needed someplace to throw your money, so you decided to give it to Mom's lawyers?"

"That ain't funny, Kiddo."

"There has to be a reason, so fess up, old man. What gives?"

"Look, Hon, from where you sit, all this may not make perfect sense, but your mom and I had a sort of understanding."

"You sure she's in on this understanding? Because she's going crazy. She's running helter-skelter with all those strange people she calls amigos, you're living on your boat, lawyers are calling the house at all hours."

"That part I didn't plan on. Most of it I didn't plan on."

"You had a plan? Now that I'd like to hear."

"Yes . . . well, you see, when your mom and I first met, we didn't exactly plan on getting married."

"You just happened to say 'I do' and it got lost in translation?"

"If I told you that were true, would you buy it?"

"Look, Daddykins, I'm seventeen and we're living in the nineties. I understand what it means when people have to get married."

"So, why am I beating round the bush?"

"Damned if I know. Why don't you treat me like an adult for starters? I'm as much an injured party in this divorce as Mom. My home's being wrecked by the two of you. She's your wife, but she's *my* mother and I love her, so stop hedging. You should have consulted me before you decided to divorce my mother and wreck *my* family." She turned her head away from Sloan to hide tears that would change the playing field in a way he knew she wouldn't want.

"Here it is, plain and simple. We got married so you'd have a home and a start in life. We never—or at least, I never—intended it to be forever. Just 'til you were out of the house. That's the whole ugly truth. None of this is your fault and I don't want you to be feeling responsible."

"Look, Father dear, I *am* involved and I'm old enough to understand. Just don't try to keep me in the dark. Pisses me off."

"No way to talk."

She stared at him, deadpan. "Really? You're worried about the way I talk?" She grabbed his hand. "Remember when you first got the *Akubra*? The three of us used to go out for a Sunday sail? Those were great times. At first, Mom seemed to like it, too. And before that, we took those Christmas trips to Colorado for skiing. Man, were you terrible at skiing."

"Tying boards on my feet and sliding down a mountain of snow was never my idea of fun."

"We had some great times when I was growing up. Makes me sad to think there will be no more."

"Look, you're going to Mammaw's in a few weeks, and in the fall, you're headed for UCLA. That should get you out of the middle of all this fighting and squabbling."

"I don't want to go to Texas this summer. I think I'm getting too old to go to Grandmother's house on vacation."

"She's counting on you, but I suppose you could cut it short."

"What with all this divorce stuff going on and you moving out of the house, I just don't want to defend all that to Mammaw. That has to be your job. Just tell her I need to go to summer school. She'll understand. Besides, she's showing her age and getting more than a little forgetful. She might not be keen on having me there at all. My cousins are all working this summer, so they won't be there."

"She knows nothing about our situation at home. Your mom and me agreed to leave her out of it."

"Even worse! Now I would have to lie to her about what was going on at home. No thanks. I'm staying home this summer. This whole damned mess was your idea, not mine. You can make my excuses."

"Okay, sure. I'll handle it, but you might end up in summer school just to keep us honest."

"Like you tried to keep *yourselves* honest?" Her shoulders sagged and she stared into her lap. "When I think of how happy you and Mom were for most of my life and now all this. I don't think I can take it. I just might run away and live in Haight-Ashbury."

"Hey, come on, Kiddo. You're tougher 'n that. This will all be over soon and things will get back to normal, I promise."

"No, Dad. Things will never be back to normal. One more thing, while we're on the subject. Did you push Mom off the *Akubra*?"

"Fell. Honest to God, she fell overboard. She was sitting on the bowsprit when the *Akubra* surfed up a breaker, slid down the backside and tossed her in the water. Unfortunately, her lawyers and just about everybody else believes her version of the story."

"Okay, I can buy that. If you wanted your freedom, it would make no sense to risk it by doing such a stupid thing. Besides, you're my dad and I want to believe you didn't try to murder my mother."

"Thanks."

"The problem is, I want to believe you, but why would Mom lie?"

XLIX

The divorce battle raged on through that summer and into the next year. For Sloan, almost every day began with a call from Regina or one of her attorneys, making new demands for property, cash or altered behavior.

In June, Sloan's mother suffered a stroke and was under the constant care of an in-home nurse, so Wendy didn't make her annual visit to Texas. Sloan convinced her to attend a summer session at UCLA to prepare her for a successful freshman year. Wendy agreed, and for six weeks, she commuted to the main campus to attend classes in English Literature and Trig.

Late on a Tuesday afternoon, his private line lit up. He expected to hear Regina's voice but was surprised to hear his brother Wayne.

"So, how's the old girl doing?"

"You better come. She doesn't have long."

"Uhhu...so, what's the prognosis?

"If you believe her doctors...a few days...no more. Sometimes she doesn't even know me, or where she is for that matter. Yesterday, she had a conversation with Dad that went on for hours. It sounded like they were making plans to meet up someplace. This morning, she asked me who all the people in her room were."

"You tell her?"

"That's just it. We were alone... her and me."

"Look, Wayne, try to keep it together. I'll be there tomorrow. If I can get an earlier flight, I will."

"Can you bring Wendy? Mom's been asking for her."

"I'll try," Sloan said. "She's at school."

Sloan called Wendy at UCLA.

"Your grandmother's pretty sick. They don't expect her to be with us much longer. I have to go out there right away and I want you to come with me. This will be your last chance to see her. Throw a few things in a bag along with that black dress you got for that formal do last year. I'll pick you up in two hours."

Wendy tossed her bags in the boot and jumped into the passenger seat. Sloan pulled away from the curb and made his way to LAX.

"What's wrong with her, Daddy?"

"Your grandmother is getting old, Kiddo. It all has to do with that number on her driver's license. You mustn't be sad for her. We all do it. She's lived a long life and dying is a part of living. We just have to be sure we do a good job of both."

"Aren't you afraid?"

"Of what?"

"Dying."

"No, not so much. I'm more afraid I won't finish what I started."

Sloan slid his coupe into the valet parking at LAX and tossed the keys to the attendant. Wendy retrieved her carry-on and followed Sloan to their departure gate.

"You talking about all that wealth and anonymity hooey?" she said.

"And a lot more. At the moment, that stuff doesn't seem so important. I want to see you happily married and living a productive life with a few kids of your own."

"And what about graduating with honors?"

"I do want to live to see that. So don't take too long, okay?"

Sloan, Wendy and Wayne stood next to Mammaw's hospital bed where she was being comforted by two hospice nurses.

Sloan squeezed her hand. "We came as soon as we could." She was weak and pale, her eyes clouded by years of squinting into the smoldering West Texas sun.

She blinked and smiled at her sons and granddaughter. "There's my favorite granddaughter." She reached for Wendy's hand and spoke softly, but deliberately.

"Sorry I couldn't come for my regular visit last summer," Wendy said. "School is taking over my life and Daddykins here won't accept anything but A's." Wendy fought back the tears that welled up in her eyes.

"It's okay, Hon. Haven't felt much like having company anyhow." She gave her granddaughter a weak smile. "Wendy, would you mind waiting outside? You too, Wayne. Me and Sloan need to talk for a spell."

Sloan pulled a chair up to her bed and took her hand.

"So, what's all this I'm hearing about a divorce?"

"How's it you know about that? I agreed not to trouble you."

"You forgot to tell Regina. She called me a few weeks back, complaining about how bad you were treating her. Wanted me to talk to you about your behavior. Naturally, I don't want to take sides, but I'd like to hear yours."

"Pretty simple, really. We got married because of Wendy. We barely knew one another. Almost twenty years passed and now that Wendy is out of the house and away at school, there didn't seem to be much point in continuing the charade."

Sloan's mother stared into the distance as if she was trying to understand what she was being told.

"Hell hath no fury," she finally said as she squeezed Sloan's hand. Tears ran down her cheeks and onto her pillow.

"Yes, Mom, Congreve had it right, over three hundred years ago."

"Sloan, honey, are you sure you can work it so nobody gets hurt?"

"I'll do my part. Hope she does hers."

"You know, Son, in spite of all the neglect over the years, you're still my favorite. Oh, your brother's a good guy and I love him, but I always admired that you were out there meetin' life head on. Now listen up, you need to take control of my situation. I'm leavin' here quick as I can, but Wayne's coming apart. You'd think a priest could handle these things better."

"Too close, Momma. It's just too close for him. With his parishioners, he can be detached. With them, he's an advisor."

"Mighty charitable of you, Johnny, but the truth is, he needs help. Look, Son, this is all so simple. So's you'll know, I'm DNR. You understand what that means?"

"Yes, Mom. I do."

"Put my ashes in our family plot next to Daddy. Promise? After all these years, we can be together again."

"Okay, Mom. I'll see to everything."

Sloan fought back tears. He *had* neglected her, been too busy chasing the wealth and anonymity that didn't seem all that important now. All he could do now was be strong for his mother.

She stared into the distance, somewhere beyond time and space. She squeezed Sloan's hand and spoke with someone only she could see.

"Your daddy, my darlin' Tom?" she whispered softly. "He was the only man . . . never knew another . . . before or since. Loved him from the first minute. I can still remember the day we . . . like yesterday."

Sloan laced his fingers through hers and stroked her arm. She lay quietly then turned toward him, her gaze suddenly sharp. "What happened to that girl?"

"Girl? What girl?"

"You know. The one I met at your graduation."

"Abigale, name was Abigale LaHolm."

"Pretty gal and smart. Lovely . . . and crazy 'bout you. I could tell, you know?"

"Surprised you still remember her," Sloan said. "Went our separate ways a long time ago." His mother's cool hand squeezed his.

"Shouldn't have let her get away. You two had it bad. Think I didn't notice? She mighta been your one true love."

"I've often wondered about that."

"Listen, Johnny, I'm feeling like a nap. Don't mind if I—" She drifted off to sleep. He tucked her blankets around her and kissed her forehead. Now he could let go some of his own tears.

There is no good day for a funeral. Sloan hoped it wouldn't rain, but West Texas weather seldom included rain and this day—the day the Abernathy clan had set aside to say farewell to the family matriarch—was no exception. It was not a sad occasion, but somber. Sloan's mother had lived a long, comfortable and productive life. She had known true love and raised two fine sons. Her greatest sadness was the loss of Sloan's father, the love of her life. If what her younger son believed was true, she'd been reunited with him in the Kingdom of Heaven.

They bowed their heads in prayer. Sloan thought about his parents. His father had given him the guidance he needed to get through some tough times—would've gotten him through more if he'd followed his advice to the letter. His mother had loved him and set an example for Wendy throughout her formative years. He hoped Wayne was right. If there was a heaven, Sloan was sure they were both there, walking hand-in-hand across a green meadow.

The Abernathy family stood while the minister read John 3:16. "God so loved the world that he gave his only son . . ."

They lowered the urn into the ground next to the headstone marked

—Thomas J. Abernathy —Alice Sloan Abernathy.

"Goodbye, Mom." Sloan whispered under his breath, "Tell Dad we all say hey. Love you both."

L

The details of the hotly contested divorce were not widely known even among friends and fellow yacht club members. It wasn't until Regina was no longer a passenger on the *Akubra* for weekend outings and social events that the facts began to surface.

When pressed, Sloan would explain that they had decided to explore different aspects of their lives, an explanation that was sufficiently vague to cover almost any set of circumstances.

Regina, on the other hand, eagerly spread the news at her tennis club that a divorce was in the works, and that if she had her way, it was going to get ugly. She embellished and then freely spread the story about being pushed overboard when she refused to submit to his demands.

Those who knew Sloan did not believe that he had pushed his wife, Wendy's mother, overboard in order to end a quarrel or avoid a costly divorce. The consensus was that she had fallen or jumped during an afternoon of drinking. But some chose to spread Regina's version of the story—it was the more interesting—while others embellished the story to suit their audience.

After more than a year of haggling out of court, lawyer to lawyer, the parties were ready to sit in front of a judge and debate the merits of their respective complaints. Depositions had been taken that made clear the expectations of each party. There would be few surprises. It would be up to the judge to say just how Regina would be compensated for the indignities she had suffered at the hands of her cruel, vindictive spouse.

Sloan and Jake arrived at nine o'clock sharp. Jake took a seat in the gallery and Sloan took the seat next to his attorney. "We ready to win this thing?" Sloan said.

"Sure am, Mr. Abernathy. Just remember our definition of 'win' and we'll be fine." Sloan's milquetoast attorney was in his second year of a successful family law practice. Other more experienced attorneys were far more vindictive and aggressive when it came to attacking the opposition. Sloan was hesitant to retain such representation for fear of the damage they could do to Regina's reputation and standing in the community. While he might want to hold her accountable, he did not want her to suffer public retribution for her alleged behavior with Gibbs. When it came to public exposure of these private matters, his choice was to let that sleeping dog lie.

"Remember what we discussed at our last meeting. How we have won if you are still a free man after the hearing. That's my definition of winning. To be frank with you, Sir, if you don't end up in jail we will have won."

"Jail!" The word stuck in Sloan's throat. He looked across the aisle at Regina and her hot shot chick lawyer. Between them they exuded enough self-confidence to circumnavigate the globe in a wash tub.

The bailiff instructed the court, "All rise for the Honorable Judge Goldstein."

Judge Goldstein entered the courtroom from a door behind and to the left of the podium. She was a short fiftyish woman with a weight problem which she hid under her ankle length black robe.

"We are here this morning to adjudicate the petition for divorce of Abernathy vs. Abernathy. In part, the purpose of these proceedings is to equitably divide the couple's assets, taking into account the contribution of each to the accumulated wealth and the dissolution of the marriage. I will now hear arguments from the plaintiff."

Regina and her attorney were seated behind one of two tables in front of the judge's podium. Regina, beautifully coiffured and wearing a dark blue pinstripe business suit, sat beside her lawyer who, after an appropriate shuffling of papers, adjustment of her clothes and a whisper to Regina, stood and addressed the court.

"Good morning, Your Honor." She did not wait for a courteous reply. "If it pleases the court, I will proceed with the complaints lodged against Mr. Abernathy on behalf of my client."

"By all means, without further delay," Goldstein replied in a sarcastic tone. Sloan feared that her demeanor conveyed disdain for him and his alleged behavior toward Regina.

Regina's attorney peered over her glasses at the documents in her hand. "Our first complaint has to do with the fact that Mr. Abernathy relocated my client from her native home in Spain to a small apartment here in southern California. This move was made against her will, a move that took her thousands of miles from her family, her friends and familiar surroundings. I submit to the court that this heinous act constitutes emotional kidnapping." She paused, walked across the room and stood between Sloan, his attorney and the judge, blocking Goldstein from their view. She then proceeded to her table and whispered to Regina who eagerly scribbled a note on a yellow legal pad.

"I will allow the complaint, but I do find it capricious. Now, please proceed without further delay to the meat of this case." Goldstein seemed to be short on patience and visibly annoyed by the amateurish courtroom antics.

"Yes, of course, Your Honor. Our second complaint has to do with the defendant's insistence on the couple having separate bedrooms. This practice clearly deprived his expatriate wife, Mrs. Abernathy, the attention and affection normally warranted any hardworking, devoted mother and wife. We believe this behavior on the part of the defendant constitutes mental cruelty in its purest form, and we are prepared to render expert testimony to corroborate these charges."

Sloan shifted uncomfortably in his chair. He had always believed the arrangement was justified, but the truth of the matter would never be disclosed by him, at least not in this public forum.

"Your Honor, our third and, quite frankly, most egregious complaint is the charge of attempted murder."

The words echoed in the chamber.

Judge Goldstein's expression turned from boredom to shock.

"Surely, Counselor, you speak metaphorically."

"No, Your Honor. I do not." With shoulders back and chest out, the overzealous prosecutor continued. "When my client refused to grant her husband a divorce—a divorce, I might add, that he wanted in order to pursue an illicit affair with an old college sweetheart—Mr. Abernathy threw this helpless, defenseless woman, the mother of his only child, off the deck of their luxury sailing yacht. When he realized how bad it would look if she turned up days later, having swam ashore on her own, he returned to the location where he pushed her in and threw her a line."

The sparsely populated courtroom hummed with excitement.

Judge Goldstein sat back in her overstuffed leather chair and ran her fingers through her salt and pepper hair.

"Is there anything further you wish to add, Counselor, before I turn the floor over to the defense?"

"Yes, I have one more item, Your Honor . . . if it pleases the court." Her pause gave power to her words. "There's a charge of rape."

"Rape?" Judge Goldstein said. "Counselor, I don't recall rape mentioned. Do you intend to bring these charges up in a grand jury hearing? If so, I must advise you that rape by a legal spouse is difficult to prove and such a hearing would require a different venue. I am chartered to hear civil cases, period, so please confine your remarks to what is germane to this case.

Goldstein was, along with everyone in the courtroom with the exception of Sloan, awash in intrigue.

"Your Honor, we are well aware of your jurisdiction."

"So, this entire episode is strictly theatrics," Goldstein said.

Regina's attorney returned to her table and sat down, a tactic designed to deemphasize her allegation. "Once the defendant rescued Mrs. Abernathy, he took her below deck to the main salon of their *luxury* yacht and while she was in a state of confusion and shock, having almost drowned, he forced himself on her. She feared what he might do next if she did not comply. Given that he had tried to murder her, she felt she had to submit to his advances."

"Counsel for the defendant, what say you to these charges?"

Sloan's attorney shuffled his brief as if searching for the answers to these preposterous charges.

He stood and addressed the court. "Your honor, in light of these new developments, we choose not to rebuff these charges but recommend that the court proceed to the property settlement, the crux of this hearing."

Regina's attorney struck while her iron was hot.

"Your Honor, in light of these charges and in the absence of any rebuttal from the defendant's counsel, I respectfully request the court grant all the assets currently in possession of the couple to my client, with the possible exception of the security interest in Vortec, which we regard as a highly speculative investment and therefore of no value to my client. You will find a complete accounting of all assets in exhibit B." Regina's lawyer sat down.

"Your Honor," Sloan's attorney protested, "my client currently resides on his sailboat. At the moment, it is his primary, in fact, his only residence."

Silence fell over the courtroom as Judge Goldstein pondered the settlement. "Perhaps the court can exempt the sailboat."

Regina's attorney nodded, exuding generosity. "We have no objection, Your Honor, but now we must deal with the question of custody of the teenage child. Wendy is eighteen years of age and free to make her own choice in the matter of which parent with whom she chooses to reside."

"It is the recommendation of the court that Wendy Abernathy take up a permanent residence with her mother. She should spend time with her father only on those occasions when she is properly chaperoned. The court finds this man to be of unsound and immoral character. Therefore, I am placing Mr. Abernathy under a restraining order. At no time will the defendant come within one thousand feet of Mrs. Abernathy or the juvenile Ms. Wendy Abernathy unless he is properly chaperoned."

Sloan grabbed his attorney by the sleeve of his jacket. "Now I'm a child molester? Aren't you going to object?"

"Yes, but not here," he answered in a stage whisper. "Next week in an appeals court, we'll have a better chance. Trust me on this."

Sloan was thankful that Wendy was away at school and not present in court to hear Regina's lawyer refer to her father as a murderer, a rapist and now a child molester.

"Mr. Abernathy, will you please rise," Judge Goldstein said.

Sloan managed to stand. His chin rested on his chest.

Goldstein pointed to the rear of the courtroom. "Mr. Abernathy, do you see those doors?"

"Uh, yes, Your Honor."

"If I had my way, you would not be walking through them again for a very long time, but fortunately for you, this is a divorce hearing, and there is insufficient hard evidence to hold you on charges of rape and attempted murder. The best I can do is remand you to court-ordered, professionally supervised counseling. Mr. Abernathy, you need help to overcome your anger issues."

"Yes, Your Honor. Thank you, Your Honor."

"Case closed!" Judge Goldstein smacked the podium with her gavel.

"All rise for Judge Goldstein," the bailiff said.

Regina's attorney gathered their files and headed toward the rear door of the court room. Regina spotted Jake halfway back in the otherwise empty chamber. She ran to him and threw her arms around his neck.

"Oh, Jake, thank you so much for being here. What an awful day for poor Sloan. He sure got his comeuppance, though, don't you think?"

Jake disengaged himself from her embrace. "Someone had to bring him. You took his car, remember."

"He still has that old truck. We left him the old truck."

"Battery's dead, needs a new battery. Not like he has the bucks to pay for one."

Regina returned to the aisle and continued her victory march into the sunshine. Jake moseyed over to the table where Sloan sat with his head in his hands. His attorney stuffed papers and yellow legal pads back into his briefcase in preparation for vacating the premises.

"Like I said Mr. Abernathy, we won."

"Won? Just how in hell do you figure that was a victory?"

"You're walking out of here a free man, right? Isn't that what you wanted? You could have been held over on criminal charges. That was her strategy from the beginning. She had us going in. She knew we wouldn't make a counter argument with that hanging over us."

"I can't even see my daughter."

"Don't worry about that child custody thing. I'll file an appeal next week and get that reversed. I'm friends with the juvenile custody judge. Goldstein hates my guts."

"Fine time to tell me." Sloan winced from the thrashing he had taken at the hand of Regina's attorney.

Jake jingled the loose change in his pockets. "What now, Skipper?"

“Give me a minute till my head stops spinning. They just took everything I worked for all my life and left me with the mortgage on my house.”

“How ‘bout some lunch? I’ll buy,” Jake offered.

“You would have to. They just walked out of here with my last dollar.”

“Hey, man, you’re free. Just like Joplin said, you got nothin’ left ta lose.”

LI

Sloan pulled his vintage Ford into the Vortec parking lot and made his way to the front door. He had been traveling for a week and needed to catch up on things in the home office. Tom was just coming up the stairs, so they walked into the building together.

A broad smile crossed Tom's tanned face. "Judging from your ride, the divorce settlement is final and she got the Mercedes." Tom seemed to find it amusing that the Vice President of Marketing and a millionaire in his own right had been reduced to driving a circa 1960 Ford pickup truck.

"Go ahead, have your fun," Sloan said. "Someday I'll restore that piece of junk and it'll be worth big bucks."

"If our meetings with Elcon continue to progress, a new ride will be the least of your worries."

"So, the talks are going well then?"

"The next move is on you. It's time to unfurl our market strategy and you're the man for that job. I want you to put a presentation together for our meeting on Thursday. I'll get you some guidelines later today."

"I'm on it," Sloan said.

He wondered if Abigale would be at the meeting. The last he heard, she was the assistant to the president at Elcon, so it would generally follow that she would attend the meeting to help her boss stay on top of things. He pondered the possibility that she was involved with someone at her office then discounted it. She was not one to engage in a clandestine affair for the thrill of the moment.

Sloan closeted himself to prepare for the meeting that would become the closing argument in support of a merger between the two companies. He published a schedule of his work plan to Tom and the other members of the executive team. Sloan had a very short timeline to prepare the final draft, which left little time to think about Abigale and her role in the proceedings.

At 9:00 a.m. on Thursday, a contingent from both companies convened in the Elcon boardroom. Sloan was the last to arrive. He scanned the room for Abigale. Elcon's president had taken his place at the head of the table. Abigale was seated to his right. She glanced in Sloan's direction, but made no attempt to greet him or acknowledge that they were even acquainted. Her eyes passed over him as she might have passed a stranger in a crowded bus terminal.

He went about making final preparations for his presentation. He personally handed out copies of his report and introduced himself to everyone present. When he came to Abigale, he handed her a copy. She took it from him and spoke under her breath in a whisper, "Hello Sloan." She tapped her copy of the thick report with the eraser of her pencil. "Looks like you've been busy." He felt his hand tremble as he continued around the room.

God, she looks great, he thought.

Tom noticed Sloan's apparent case of nerves and spoke to him in a whisper. "Damn Sloan, what's the matter with you? You see a ghost or what?"

"You might say. I'll explain later."

His presentation lasted more than three hours. He extolled the virtues of Vortec, their technology, the markets they dominated and how their products would adapt to new markets outside the military and maritime space.

He reiterated that Elcon's market strategy for the new GPS system was similar to their own and by combining Vortec technology with Elcon's financial resources and private sector market presence, they would make an unbeatable team.

Time for the closer, he thought, looking around the room and making eye contact with the Elcon execs. "Ladies and gentlemen, a merger between our companies will constitute the embodiment of the true meaning of synergy. Two plus two equals five."

Abigale was in attendance during the entire presentation. She made pages of notes, some of which she passed to other members of the Elcon team. Sloan wondered if she was engrossed in the presentation and the potential merger, or whether the note passing was an attempt on her part to render him ill at ease. Knowing her cutting wit, she may well have been circulating snide remarks about his lack of knowledge or ineptitude as a speaker. Hell, she may have claimed his fly was open. To her credit, he saw no levity on the faces of those who received and read her cryptic annotations.

"Any final questions before we adjourn?" He turned off the projector.

The only body language Sloan could read from his audience was the nodding of heads signifying agreement. The placing of elbows on the table telegraphed receptivity to his proposal. The possible exception was Elcon's finance officer who had been punching numbers into his calculator since the day began.

Abigale vacated her seat next to her boss and stood at the rear of the conference room. Sloan tried not to read too much into her behavior, but her location would make it impossible for him to leave without walking past her. Still, if she had a vote regarding the merger, he could only hope her personal feelings would *not* be a factor in her business decision.

The Elcon president was the first to speak. "That was an excellent presentation, Mr. Abernathy. Can we offer you tea or coffee?"

"Coffee, thanks."

Abigale left her post at the rear of the room to pour a cup and walked to where Sloan stood behind his chair.

"Thanks Abby," he said under his breath as he stirred cream into the hot brew. "How've you been?" He noted that her ring finger was still naked, but he saw no sign of the ruby sea glass necklace.

"Don't push it, Slag. You're still on my shit list." She whispered too low to be heard by anyone else in the room.

"If this merger gets legs, we could be seeing more of each other," he said, also in a whisper.

"I wouldn't count on it."

"What? The merger?"

"No," she said. "You being around." She smiled demurely then turned and rejoined her group, chuckling casually with her boss as they sauntered out of the conference room.

Sloan spent Saturday in the office, cleaning up the mess left over from being out of circulation for the entire week.

He thought about Abigale. She looked great. She had gotten away from the Italian knit suits that were prominent in her college wardrobe. Now she seemed to favor sharp business attire, but she still looked fresh from Niemen's. If the merger went through, he would be seeing more of her. Perhaps she would soften towards him. They could do lunch or dinner and a movie. There was always a chance he could make amends. When she learned that he was divorced perhaps she'd see him in a different light. The hell he'd gone through with the divorce might be worth it. When he looked at her, even now, he saw his soul mate.

His private line lit up and then rang. "Hello," he spoke into the receiver.

"You blew it," Tom said. "You screwed the whole thing up for the rest of us."

"'Scuse me?" Sloan detected frivolity in his tone.

"Just had a call from Jonson, the finance guy over at Elcon. They have no interest in a merger."

"You're kidding, right?"

"No merger, Jonson vetoed it. They want to do an outright acquisition. . . stock and cash. Interested?"

"You mean I sold the whole company?" Sloan said.

"Looks like. We start negotiations Tuesday. Have a great weekend. Oh, by the way Sloan, how much for that rusty old truck of yours?"

LII

Two weeks had passed since his presentation to Elcon and the subsequent merger talks had begun. Sloan, his crew, and the *Akubra* were headed to the island for a weekend of sun and relaxation. Edie and Wendy were huddled against the morning chill, hot cups of coffee warming their hands. Jake moved about the deck trimming sails and coiling lines and sheets. Sloan was steering a course for Catalina Island. With good winds, they should reach the windward side of the island in time to relax or take a hike in the hills before cocktails and dinner with other members from the club.

A steady fifteen-knot breeze out of the northeast took them along the Palos Verde Peninsula. Through his binoculars, Sloan could see the beautiful home he had lost to Regina in the divorce perched high on a cliff above the Pacific Coast Highway.

She was just now waking up to start her day.

Jake caught him staring. "Water under the bridge. So, where we headed, Captain?"

"Cat Harbor."

"Around on the windward side?" Jake said, as he carefully coiled the main sheets and hung them on the mast.

"That's right, and up in the isthmus. We'll be meeting some of the regular crowd from the club, Bryson and Jones for sure. We'll raft up with them; anyone else who wants to join the party can paddle over."

"What say we get wet?" Jake said. "There're some big lobsters around those rocks just at the entrance to the cove. Remember that four-pounder I picked up there last year?"

"Sure I remember, just off Ballast Pointe. Amazing what that bug did for the taste of drawn butter."

Sloan was in a terrific mood and Jake could not contain his curiosity. "What's up? You get laid again?"

"Again? Like I'm out whoring around every night. I've been too busy with work to think about my libido, much less do anything about it."

"That's what they make whorehouses for," Jake said.

"With my luck, I'd end up falling in love," Sloan said.

"What's the latest on the merger?"

"More like a sale."

"You mean Elcon's gonna buy you out? That would explain that glint in your eye. It ain't sex, it's money that has you all lit up like a Roman candle." Jake shook his head. "Kinda sad."

"Sad my ass. We closed the deal yesterday. Did I mention Abigale works there—at Elcon? She's assistant to the head honcho. She seems to have his ear."

"Think you two might—"

"Doubt that. She hates my guts. Every time I try to chat her up, she throws Regina in my face. You know—how's your Spanish bitch? That sort of thing."

"Long memory, that woman. You make out okay? In the merger, I mean?"

"I came away with stock and cash that blew my freaking mind. No way would I trade places with Regina now."

"You staying on? You do still have a job, don't you?"

"For a year, as a consultant. They want me to transition my role to their marketing guy. It should be an easy year. I can set my own hours and draw down $300K for my trouble."

"That should take the worry outta being close," Jake said.

"Who, me?"

"Regina will throw a shit fit when she hears about the big one that got away. That should be sweet."

Sloan grinned. "I know. Can't win 'em all."

"The best revenge is doing well."

Sloan dropped anchors bow and stern near the center of a small cove. He left room for two boats to raft, one on port and another on starboard. Jake furled the mainsail onto the boom and secured it with bungees.

Wendy organized a hike for anyone who wanted to spend the afternoon exploring the island. She launched the small dinghy and paddled Edie and her girls the short distance to the dock. From there, they walked up the hillside and disappeared into the woods.

Jake ran the cocktail burgee up the mast upside down. Tonight, the party would be on the *Akubra.* Sloan watched as it flapped in the afternoon breeze, silhouetted against the clear, blue California sky.

"Who else knows?" Jake asked.

"Just you. I want to keep it that way. You know how Bryson gets when he smells money."

"How 'm I supposed to keep a straight face in front of all those people?"

"Just remember, if you don't, I'll leave you on that rock to hitchhike home."

"I get it," Jake said. "Mum's the word."

Sloan planned to catch some rays, do some reading and render the *Akubra* shipshape for the party. He felt like celebrating and he had stocked the galley with enough champagne to throw quite a party.

Toward late afternoon, the Jones' forty-five-foot Endeavor appeared in the cove and slid alongside the *Akubra.* Sloan flung them dock lines fore and aft, and they were soon lashed together. They dropped the lifelines on both boats to make it easy to traverse the two sloops. Within the hour, Bryson pulled alongside on his forty-two-foot Hinckley. He tossed Sloan a bow line. "Hope you haven't started drinking without me."

All three boats put down anchors fore and aft. The three boats would remain lashed together until the next morning when they would untie, hoist sails and race back to the marker buoy at the Marina Del Ray breakwater. The winner got bragging rights until the next outing. Bryson and his Hinckley almost always won.

"Hey, Sloan. How goes it?" Bryson shouted. "Don't think I've seen you since you tried to drown your old lady."

"Yeah, well, I've been missing you too."

"Finally beat that rap, did yuh?"

"By the skin of my teeth," Sloan said.

"Should have called me, man. I would a found you a *good* lawyer."

"Think you could've kept me out of jail?"

"Got to admit, that was a novel approach, pushing your old lady overboard. The right lawyer would've saved you a bundle on legal fees and settlement cost. I'm sure of that."

"What else am I gonna do with my dough, but throw it down a lawyer hole— sorry—rat hole?"

"I gotta tell you, man," Bryson said, "I miss having that fine-looking senorita on these outings. But enough bullshit. Tell me, how're things down at Vortec?" Bryson opened Sloan's cooler and helped himself to a cold beer and handed one to Sloan. "Here, have one on me."

"We're doing okay. Forecasting a flat year."

"I'm not talking revenue here, Old Stick. What's the skinny on this merger with Elcon? And don't tell me you don't know." Bryson took a long draw on his beer, stuck his hand into a bag of cashews and popped several in his mouth. "That dog won't hunt."

"No merger," Sloan said. "Ain't gonna happen."

Bryson shook his head. "Look, Old Man, it's in all the papers. Elcon opened sharply higher yesterday on the rumor that they would acquire Vortec for stock and cash. So, what do you say to that?" Bryson went for another handful of cashews and overstuffed his mouth.

"Hell, man, you know the press. Probably interviewed the janitor or our receptionist."

"Doesn't matter to me one way or the other, but I've been trying to get into both companies for years without any luck at all. How would it be if you put in a good word for me? I'm sure you guys spend millions on legal fees. I just want a piece of the action."

"Yeah, well, send me some of your propaganda and I'll make sure it lands on the right desk or at least in the right pile."

"You'd do that for me?"

Sloan had no intention of helping this bellowing barrister become ensconced in his company, but offering to do something seemed like the best way to shut him up.

By mid-afternoon, more than a dozen boats had floated into the small cove and put down anchors or tied to stationary moorings. The sun was over the yardarm and the crowd gathered on the *Akubra.* Sloan poured generous glasses of champagne as the party crowd climbed aboard the Hinckley or the Endeavor. He fired up the small charcoal grill on the fantail of the *Akubra.* He threw on some lobster tails and sliced abalone. Jones lit his grill on the Endeavor and laid on some burgers. The aroma floated across the cove and signaled to others in the flotilla to paddle to Sloan's party.

After everyone had devoured the grilled seafood and burgers, they all congregated on Bryson's boat where young Jimmy Bryson entertained with his guitar. The younger members of the group carried on while most of the adults found bunks below deck to sleep off the glow of Sloan's champagne. Others returned to their boats for some private time.

Fortunately, young Bryson was in plain view for most of the evening, relieving Sloan of his worry that Jimmy and Wendy might disappear below deck. She seldom gave Sloan cause for concern, but he knew there was some chemistry between the two, and he didn't want it to get out of hand. Wendy was just nineteen. In Sloan's view she was not yet ready to handle an adult relationship.

The serious drinkers continued into the evening. Sloan found a half-bottle of champagne and made his way forward to lean against the mast and sip the bubbly. He reflected on the events of the past few weeks. He was disappointed that there was no place for him in the new organization. Selling the company and ending up without a job was not an outcome he would have anticipated, but Elcon had a marketing guy and they must have felt he could handle everything. After all these weeks, it had begun to soak in that Abigale had said that he might not be around much longer and he wondered if she had anything to do with it. The notes she passed among the Elcon executives could have been his death knell. While he thought he was giving a killer presentation, the notes may have been about how, in the new scheme of things, he would be redundant.

Elcon had made a place for Tom, not with as much clout as he'd had as president of Vortec, but still better than $300K and the door they'd offered Sloan. What the hell. Sloan's bank account and net worth were at an all-time high and he was free, so why fight it? Acute anxiety swept over him when he wondered what he would do with his time.

He gazed at the bustling coastline on the horizon. Lights from the city were little more than dots. In that moment, it all seemed so far away: Regina, Abigale, and his beloved company which, he now realized, had never loved him back. He had been useful but expendable, like a paperclip or a swivel chair. Their need for him had been an illusion. Like water filling the place where a fish once swam, the void his departure created would be fleeting.

On the bright side, realizing his dream of anonymity was close at hand, but the prospect of not having a job scared him. Anonymity wasn't as appealing up close.

"Hey, Old Man, you look like you could use a friend."

He turned to see Wendy leaning against the boom with an empty glass. She turned it upside down, hinting that she was open to more champagne.

"Sure, if you brought your own libation. I'll need this one to finish drowning my joy."

"You know, Daddykins, it's all generational. My generation smokes their fun."

"Yeah, well, I still take mine the old fashioned way, from a bottle." He filled her glass and clicked it with his in a mock toast. He put his arm around her and pulled her in close. She fell against him. Wendy was a little high.

He marveled at how beautiful she had grown. She was blessed with her mother's looks and his passion for independence.

"Don't you miss her?" Wendy asked.

"Who?"

"Mom, of course. She was always so much fun on these outings. Since you moved out and I'm off at school, I think she's lonely."

"Well, she and her lawyers can cuddle up to all that dough and humiliation they dragged me through."

"With you Daddy, it's always about the money. Don't you have any feelings for her, or me?"

"For you, sure. When it comes to Regina, it'll take some time to heal."

"So, tell me Daddykins, to what do you credit your good humor of late? I can't remember when I last saw you in such a good mood."

"Sold my company, whole kit-n-caboodle." His tongue was too thick from the champagne to get it safely around anything more.

"My gosh, Daddy, that would make anybody happy. Funny, Mom always said Vortec wasn't worth a kilo of crap."

"Yeah, well, won't she be surprised?" Sloan smiled then laughed aloud and tossed the last of his wine into the sea.

Pride and love for Wendy welled up in him. He had been so busy these last few weeks that he had spent very little time with her, and since the divorce, she had been spending more time with Regina. They had formed a bond that transcended their mother-daughter relationship. He knew for a fact that on weekends when Wendy was home from school they frequented discos and nightclubs. On one occasion, Wendy was busted for using a fake ID to pass herself off as twenty one. It took most of the evening and a trip to the police station to iron out the situation with local authorities.

Wendy hugged her father and kissed him on the cheek. "I'm going below to find an empty bunk. You should do the same."

"I'm good right here." Sloan stretched out on deck under a blanket of stars and slept until dawn.

Morning came and with it an appetite for coffee, eggs and bacon. The Jones family hosted breakfast. Everyone congregated on their sloop with cups and plates in hand. By midmorning, all the boats were shipshape and ready to line up for the race to the mainland.

Every boat was given time to hoist their sails and luff up. Bryson blasted his foghorn and the race was on. Each captain steered hard-a-lee until they came a full 180 degrees and were on a tack for the marina.

The *Akubra* took an early lead but, in the first hour, Bryson had overtaken the fleet and Jones was closing fast behind Sloan. The *Akubra* finished a distant prideful third, a perfect end to a perfect weekend. The *Akubra* was no match for Jones or Bryson, but nothing could spoil Sloan's mood, not even losing a race to that smart aleck lawyer, Bryson.

On Wednesday of that next week, details of Elcon's acquisition of Vortec were disclosed in the press. Only then did the general public learn the facts of the deal.

LIII

Sloan's house phone rang. To his delight, he heard Wendy's voice coming over the receiver. "How would it be if I came to your place for the weekend? We could spend some time on the *Akubra,* assuming you don't already have plans."

"Nope, no plans, just my usual exciting stuff."

"Watching paint dry?" she said.

"That was last week. Why? What's up?"

"Truth is, Dad, I'm in bad need of a good father-daughter, you know, heart-to-heart. But not the one about weed farming again, okay?"

Such a request could mean several things: she was in love, pregnant or joining the Peace Corps. These possibilities left Sloan awash in anxiety. Since the divorce, he seldom saw Wendy except on holidays, semester breaks and birthdays. He had pleaded with Goldstein to relinquish the restraining order, but she refused, sighting the court's judgment. She was only forced to reconsider her ruling when Wendy appeared as a character witness on her own behalf.

Sloan reflected with remorse on all he had lost in the divorce. It was not the wealth and property he hated loosing. There was more where that came from. Rather it was a profound sense of family that had gone out of his life. It was the closeness with Wendy that he cared about most, and now she was estranged from him. She was nearing the completion of her sophomore year at UCLA, and she spent most of her free time on campus studying and enjoying campus life. When she felt like getting away for a weekend, she would visit her mother who was almost always at home relaxing and secluded in the sanctity of the Abernathy Estate.

Sloan was awakened by a ringing of the door chime. He bounded to the door to greet Wendy, lifted her duffel off her shoulder and gave her a hug.

"Come this way. I have you all set up in the guest room. The maid prepared your room and turned down the bed, complete with a chocolate mint on your pillow. You'll think you're in the Hilton."

"I'm sure this will do fine. Here, my good man. Please accept this." She pretended to tip her dad.

"Hungry, Madam?" Sloan asked, playing along.

"No, thank you, Sir. More tired than anything. How 'bout we call it a day? I'll munch on that chocolate mint and get some sleep. We can start fresh in the morning—if that's okay?"

"Well, the *Akubra*'s waiting for us anytime tomorrow or Sunday."

Saturday morning, Wendy was up early. She made coffee and warmed some Danish under the broiler. The aroma of the fresh brew and the clatter of dishes drew Sloan from his lair on the second floor. She poured two cups and curled up on the sofa in the living room. He sipped his coffee, sampled the Danish and waited patiently through the usual chitchat for Wendy to turn over the first card.

"Well, Daddykins, as I said, I'm in the market for a good heart-to-heart."

"Don't scare me, Hon. That ugly divorce and all that heavy business stuff has left me jumpy." He faked a shiver. "Bad as I hate to admit it, I'm half the man I used to be."

"And you might be stretching that some, but come on, Dad, it's been over a year. Don't you think it's time you put it all behind you and got on with your life? You need to get out there and start looking for your true love, like you're always telling me. With your dough and looks, you could have them lined up at the dock. 'Oh, Mr. Abernathy, won't you please teach me to sail?'"

"Okay, Kiddo. You didn't come all this way to talk about me."

"No, I didn't come all this way to give *you* advice on how to live *your* miserable life. I want to talk about *me* and *my* wonderful life, which is Sunday school stuff compared to divorce and being fired from your job."

"Fired? I wasn't fired, no way. We were bought out, acquired. There's a damn big difference, and I'm still needed there as a consultant and damn well-paid for my time, too."

"So, mister big shot consultant, when's the last time they called you in and asked for your help or consultation on something?"

"It was just last week, as a matter of fact. Had a call from Tom, my old boss. You remember him. After the merger he stayed on as VP of Operations."

"And what did he want, besides you buying him a drink after work?"

"How'd you know we went for drinks?"

"Call it a hunch. Any way you put it, Dad, they have no further need of your services. In my book that spells f-i-r-e-d, fired. It's time to move on, make a new plan. Sneak out the back. There are dozens of startup companies out there just craving the kind of leadership you could provide. Bet you don't even have a résumé, am I right?"

"My ass, here's the first draft." Sloan picked up a single sheet of paper and glided it across the cocktail table. Wendy took a quick glance, held it up to the light then laid it on the chair beside her.

"Kinda sketchy, don't you think?"

Sloan wanted to change the subject. "So, what's on your sophomoric mind, Kiddo? I'm sure you didn't take the whole weekend just to read *me* the riot act. Let me guess, you're joining the Peace Corps or you're flunking calculus."

She sipped her coffee and spread cream cheese on a Danish, cut it in half and shoved it over to Sloan. "You know, Dad, on the upside, you're one step closer to your dream of self-actualization. You no longer need other people or a steady income. That's all about wealth *and* anonymity, but it seemed a hollow victory. Not being needed or central to a process must be the kiss of death. Just for the record, Father dear, next year I'll be a junior and carrying close to a four point—and I have straight A's in calculus."

"Yes, I know. I write the checks, remember? And I expect a four point. Don't forget that."

"Damn it, Dad, why do you always have to make our conversations about money or grades?"

"The grades are a given. And money? Well, just try and get through school without it. Nobody wrote checks for me, you know. I did it all on my own."

"Really, Daddykins? Rotcie? Come on, not exactly the hardship route to getting through school. Now, just this once, can we talk about *me*?"

"These days, you seem to have a sharp tongue and an even sharper wit—or maybe I'm just losing my edge. So, what is it you want to talk about?"

"Trust me on this, Daddy. I'm not farming weeds, so you can breathe easy on that count."

"Good thing."

Wendy flashed him a warm and forgiving smile. "You're not going to believe it, but I actually met a boy—man—at school. I know you tried to keep me too busy studying to get out, but I managed to find time in spite of you."

Sloan crossed his arms. "Not joining the Peace Corps?"

"Give me a—"

"Not that Bryson kid, is it?"

"Give me *some* credit, Dad. Although he is rather cute. His father's richer than stink-o. But, no, it's not him. There are two things about my man that'll surprise and please you. First, he reminds me of you. At least before you had your train wreck—the divorce thing and getting fired."

"Damn it, Hon. I didn't get fir—"

"Whatever."

"So, he's good looking like me? That's a start."

"Better . . . *way* better. But there's more than looks. I think I'm in love with him."

Sloan dropped his Danish and it rolled off the table and onto the floor. "Like, he's the only man for me? That kind of love?"

"Almost from the day we met."

"How's he feel about you?"

"Same. He feels the same."

"Well, this *is* news. When can I meet this handsome devil?"

"What would you say to brunch at your club next Sunday?"

"Sunday brunch? Let me check my social calendar. Sunday looks clear at the moment."

"You do still have your membership in the yacht club, don't you, Daddy? Would it be okay if I invite his mother?

"Oh, sure. But wouldn't you rather we go sailing?"

"No thanks, Old Man. I want this first meeting to be civilized. I do *not* want them to spend the day clinging to the lifelines while you have the *Akubra* heeled over. Besides, you haven't removed that graffiti Mom painted for you. Am I right?"

"I'm thinking I'll leave it. Reminds me of how crazy—"

"Don't go there. She's *my* mother, don't forget."

"Lucky for me your mother and her lawyers didn't like boats or sailing—except when it came to adding a few decorations to the bulkheads."

"Daddykins, don't you think it's high time you put all that behind you? You're doing all right. You sold your company and raked in millions."

"So, what do I call this guy?"

"Brad. His name's Brad Hager. Oh, Daddy, you are just gonna love him!"

LIV

Sloan arrived early to make sure their table was ready and all was in order for brunch with Wendy, her new guy, and his mother. He could not believe his luck. After all these years of scheming to get back in Abigale's good graces, daughter Wendy was about to drop her right in his lap.

Wendy and Brad arrived at eleven sharp, but no sign of Abigale. Must be she'd figured it out, too. Time to act like a father, he thought.

Wendy held Brad's hand as they walked down the long corridor and into the main dining room. She radiated her love for Brad and her excitement for the first interfamily gathering.

Guilt washed over Sloan. He should have forewarned Wendy, but at this point, he felt it best to let the day unfold. He could hardly wait to see the look on Abigale's face when they all met for the first time.

"Daddy, this is Brad. Brad, this is my father, Mr. Abernathy. Call him Sloan."

The men shook hands. Brad was a stalwart lad, well north of six feet. He had the build of a football player but lacked the arrogance usually found in a gridiron athlete.

"Wendy has already filled me in on all the details." Sloan's words sounded corny and insincere.

"It's an honor to meet you, Sir." Brad seemed to struggle for the right words to make a good first impression.

"Welcome to my club."

"Nice, very nautical," Brad said. Again, he seemed embarrassed.

"Ever done any sailing?"

"No, Sir, but I want to learn. Wendy tells me it's really hot, especially when you're racing."

"Well, she can teach you plenty. She's been sailing with me since she was fifteen and she has taught me plenty, not all of it about sailing though. It's been good for both of us and it kept her off the streets and out of trouble . . . most of the time."

"That and having to make straight A's," Wendy said.

Brad glanced toward the door. "Mother lives in Anaheim. It's a long drive, so she may be a few minutes. Hope that's okay."

"Sure it is," Sloan replied. "Grab a seat."

Sloan began checking the door.

Never knew that lady to be late for anything, he thought, except our first date. "While we're waiting, we can get some drinks going. Mimosas okay for you guys?"

"Sure Mr. Aberna—uh, Sloan. Mimosas are great."

Sloan had spent the week wondering how he would feel when he met her face to face. Their last meeting had been cordial, but curt. It had been all business, as was appropriate for the situation, which was handing him the paperwork that terminated his employment.

Abigale entered the main dining area and asked the maître d' for directions to her party.

"That would be the Abernathy party," he said.

"Yeah, that's him," she said.

The maître d' showed her to Sloan's table where he was already standing to greet her.

"Well, Sloan, it seems you'll stop at nothing. What do I have to do to get you off my back?"

"Honest, lady, this wasn't my doing. I put it all together when I heard you were coming and my daughter was dating a guy from Anaheim by the name of Brad Hager. I'm sure there aren't too many of those around. But to tell the truth, I don't think the kids have a clue."

"Clue?" Wendy looked back and forth between them. "You two already know one another?"

"You might say we went to different schools together," Sloan said, eager to preempt Abigale with his version of the story. He hoped to get past the introductions with some flippant self-effacing humor, but none came to mind.

"Go ahead, Sloan. Tell them the whole sad tale."

For the third time since school, fate had brought them together, and Abigale found it amusing. Sloan was unable to form or utter a word.

Brad looked at Sloan and then his mother. "Mom, you already know Wendy's dad?"

"That's right, Brad. We met at FSU. It's been about two hundred years ago now, wouldn't you say, Sloan?" He squirmed silently as she continued her tale.

"It was at the end of his senior year, a sorority social. Sloan here crashed the gate pretending to be a fraternity brother. We danced, he asked me out and we started dating, fell in love and were planning to marry. Then Sloan here shipped out to Spain in the service of his country."

"ROTC, not like I had a choice."

She went on with her story. "We corresponded for a while and then his letters stopped coming . . . and his calls. I got worried and more than a little pissed so I went to Spain to find out what 'n hell was going on. I fully expected to find him in traction, or a coma, but no such luck. The fact is he had dumped me for a beautiful Spanish girl, who I presume, is Wendy's mother."

Brad's square jaw went slack. He turned to look into Wendy's unbelieving face. Abigale held up both hands as if to demand silence. She hurried to finish her tale. "Before I met Sloan, I had dated your father. I came home from Spain and bumped into him at the coffee shop. We started dating again, seriously this time. Right after graduation we were married. Now, Brad, you know how much I loved your father." She squeezed his hand, but was looking at Sloan. "I've never had a single regret."

"You jilted my mother?" Brad stared at Sloan in disbelief.

"Well . . . right. I never thought about it in those terms, but technically, yes. I had a good reason. It was justified. And, hey, if I—well you wouldn't have Wendy. She would most likely have grown up working in a vineyard in Spain or she could have been adopted or ended up in an orphanage."

"Oh, my gosh!" Wendy said. Light bulbs were coming on in her head. "You knew Brad's mom over twenty years ago?" She spoke with an air of clinical sophistication. "And I'm going on twenty one, so has it occurred to you that—"

"No, it hasn't," Sloan said. He poured a glass of champagne and handed it to Abigale. "Here, you look like you could use this."

"It sure looks like the timing was right, *Daddykins,*" Wendy persisted. "Could I be in love with my brother?"

Sloan glared at Wendy. "Thing about kids today, they learn arithmetic at such an early age. But no, Wendy, it didn't happen."

"How can you be sure? Brad and I—"

"Because, it didn't happen," Abigale interrupted.

Brad raised his eyebrow and looked into his mother's eyes. "Mom, what didn't happen?"

"It—you know—the dirty deed, or whatever you kids call it these days."

"We were waiting until we married," Sloan said, "and we never did."

Profound relief washed over Wendy. "So, let me see if I understand all this. Two hundred or so years ago, the two of you met at FSU, fell in love, got engaged and then separated because Daddykins here went to war. Then you both got married, to different people and we came along. Twenty years later *we* meet, fall in love and bring the two of you back together. Not even Ripley's gonna believe this."

"Brad," Abigale said, "do you remember last year when Elcon purchased a small company in Redondo Beach? I was at the office day and night for more than a week working on the deal. Well, this is the man who hit the home run with his presentation and sold us on the compelling arguments for buying them out, which I must say has proven to be a great move."

"Sure, I hit a home run, but I didn't make the team," Sloan said. "Elcon didn't have need of my services. I talked myself right out of a job."

"Breaks of the game," Abigale said. "Hey, you made out okay."

"Thanks for putting in a good word for me." His bitterness resurfaced.

"Don't make that mistake, big guy. I thought they made the right call putting you out to pasture, and I supported their decision. There's nothing personal in that, so don't take it the wrong way. I can tell you this much, I would not have been happy if you were sitting in the office next to mine and that was where it was headed. I might have ended up working for you."

"Thanks for clearing that up." Sloan stood and paced their small dining cubicle unsure of how he felt. Perhaps it was justice coming full circle—the women in his life were good at that.

"Look Sloan, if it's any conciliation, in my view, the score between us is now even."

They enjoyed brunch with champagne then strolled through the marina looking at boats and talking about sailing. Their walk ended at the *Akubra* where Sloan invited everyone on board to look around.

"Sure looks like fun," Abigale quipped. "Can you teach me?"

"I doubt it. You might not be able to handle the closeness."

"Won't bother me as long as you understand I'm not spending the night with you on this tub and we don't necessarily have to be friends. If I like sailing, I just might buy a boat of my own. Do they come in a larger size?"

"They come as big as egos."

"What's the first thing I need to do?"

"Making friends with the captain is always a good idea."

"You would say so, but you can forget that. You're not out of my doghouse . . . not by a long shot."

"So much for having evened the score. At least we've made a start."

"Tell me, Sloan, is it customary to paint graffiti on the walls of sailboats?"

"Actually, yes, it is. If the angry ex-wife breaks into the sailor's cabin and writes lewd messages on the bulkheads, it can bring good luck to the voyage. I have had such good luck since those messages were painted there. So you see, I can't bring myself to paint over it."

"When's my first lesson?"

"How about next Sunday at eleven," Sloan said. "You kids can come too. We can make a real outing of it."

Abigale arrived at the marina having first stopped at the ship store to pick up the latest in deck shoes and a foul-weather jacket suitable for an arctic expedition. Her ensemble was topped off by a sea bag embroidered with dolphins. Sloan was pleased that she had put so much thought into preparing for the occasion, but felt bad that he had not provided better guidance in the shopping spree.

"You look great." He reached out to her. "Take my hand and I'll help you aboard."

"I can manage, thank you."

Sloan ignored her rejection of his help and grabbed her around the waist to lift her over the lifeline. "I have a surprise for you," Sloan said, as he stepped aside to reveal Jake standing in the cockpit. "Remember this guy?"

"Jake, you old whore," she screamed as she rushed into his arms. "What 'n hell are you doing here?"

"Heard there was a class reunion with free booze," Jake said.

"That's all it would take to get *your* attention," she said.

"I'm the cabin boy and deck hand on the good ship *Akubra.* This here's my better half, Edie. She's the galley slave. We met in kraut land when I was over there saving the country from rack and ruin."

"I've known them a while and he's right," Sloan said. "She *is* the better half."

"Hi, everybody!" Abigale shouted. "This is my first time at sea on such a small boat."

Jake took Abby by the hand and parked her in the cockpit where she would be out of the way but able to observe as they maneuvered the boat out of its slip and into open water. Edie remained below where she brewed coffee and served it on deck. Wendy helped where she was needed, or wanted to exhibit her prowess as a skilled sailor to Brad who quietly studied every move the experienced sailors made.

Once the sloop was under sail, Jake stayed busy trimming the sails to achieve the maximum speed and the best angle of attack. "Hey, Brad, interested in learning the finer points of managing a ship under sail?"

"Sure, Jake. As you can see I'm a greenhorn rookie."

From time to time, Edie popped up from the galley to offer food or coffee to the crew, but she quickly returned to the safety of the galley.

Abigale snuggled next to Sloan and braced her feet against the leeward combing, unsure just how far the sturdy ship would lean before it capsized. She remained steadfast in her determination not to be the first to complain or show concern. She knew Sloan to be risk averse—at least most of the time. If that character trait had always governed his life, they might have been together all these years. She thought about Brad Senior. Their life together had been so rewarding, so much fun. If she had been with Sloan all those years Wendy and Brad might be siblings and in love with different people. She thought back to a time when she and Sloan were dating. It seemed so long ago. If there was to be anything between them now it would be based on the present and the future and not the history they shared.

The *Akubra* scooped her bow in a swell and doused the deck with a fine spray.

"Are you sure we have to go this fast and lean over so far?"

"Sure. Otherwise, what would be the point?" Sloan said.

"Oh." She tightened her grip on his arm.

"Heeled," he said.

"Heeled?"

"We're heeled over, not *leaning over.*"

"You sure this is completely safe?"

"Trust me."

"Yeah, like that has worked out so well."

"What say we turn over a new leaf?" Sloan said.

She considered his suggestion.

"I see you got rid of the graffiti. Will that affect our luck in some peculiar way?"

"According to legend, you have to leave the writing on the bulkhead in order to have good luck, but covering it up with a coat of paint is allowed."

"So, finally, we have the best of all worlds, huh, Sloan? Your past is covered over with clean white paint?"

"A fresh start." He smiled longingly and turned up one corner of his eyebrow.

They settled back and made small talk as if they were getting acquainted for the first time.

"Can you believe how our kids found each other?" Sloan said.

"Yeah, we took our eyes off them for a minute and look what happened."

"All we can do now is sit back and let them screw it up." Sloan said.

"You could give them pointers," Abigale said.

"Maybe it's best they listen to you. My track record stinks."

They sat side-by-side in the cockpit as if they were wrapped in a shroud of serenity like a warm down comforter on a cold winter's night. It seemed that only minutes had passed and they were off the coast of Laguna Beach.

Sloan found shallow water and dropped the anchor in hard sand. The *Akubra* swung around into the wind and leveled out. The warm rays of the February sun brought the temptation to strip down and go for a swim.

"Last one in is a landlubber," Abigale shouted. Jake donned a mask and snorkel and went off the stern. Abigale, in a borrowed a mask and swim fins, joined him.

The swim provided Abigale an opportunity to display a great looking two-piece swimsuit and a trim figure not unlike the twenty-year-old Sloan had remembered.

"Abigale, do you recall that day at the beach?"

"We made lots of trips to St. George," Abigale said.

"I always remember the first time. You wore a suit something like the one you're wearing today."

"Yeah? Well, this is the newer model, with support in all the right places."

"Don't see that you need all that much help."

"I'm a little rusty with my snorkeling. Wanna come give me some pointers?"

"Why don't you go on down. Jake's already in. He's the master skin diver."

"Right, I best go with Jake. You'd probably let me drown."

Sloan watched as she kicked her feet making splashing sounds as she tried to master the frog feet. She made one circle around the boat and returned to the fantail.

"Sloan!" she shouted. "Get down here and give me a lift up before I turn to a popsicle."

With one clean jerk, he had her standing face-to-face with him on the stern. He couldn't resist putting his arms around her. He tilted her head back and kissed her. She didn't object but treated it thoughtfully as if she was recalling that first time. She took his hands and held them in front of her and looked up into his face. She smiled tenderly then gently pushed him away.

"Not ready to get chummy just yet," she said. "Quick, hand me a towel before I freeze solid." Her lips were blue.

Sloan grabbed the nearest towel, flung it over her shoulders and began to pat her dry.

She pushed him away. "I can manage."

Edie came up from the galley with sandwiches, cold beer and soft drinks.

Sloan hoisted the anchor and made ready to set the sails on a northwesterly tack along the coastline.

"Jake, can you teach me all you know about hoisting that mainsail?"

"Sure, Little Sister, but maybe you want to learn from—"

"You're probably better at it. Besides, he never likes to get his hands dirty. Do you, Sloan, honey?"

"In that case, follow Uncle Jake," Sloan said.

Under Jake's instruction, Abigale winched the main into place. She felt the thrill of the wind pulling them forward.

"Come on, crew. We need better sail shape," Sloan instructed from the cockpit. With Jake's help, she adjusted the out-haul and the mainsail quieted down.

"See, all you have to do is listen," Jake said.

The *Akubra* sliced silently through the calm seas. The prevailing afternoon breeze allowed them to sail home well off the wind, making the ride more enjoyable for the novice sailors. They could hear the wind whisper as it passed over the sails. Edie retreated to her vantage in the salon to prepare snacks for their arrival back at the marina. The February sun sank to the horizon. A dusk-born chill blanketed the sloop.

"I think I'll join Edie down below," Abigale said, "The swim was invigorating, but it left me chilled to the bone. You don't mind, do you, Captain?"

Abigale found Edie in the salon, hovering over a steaming cup of tea.

"I need something besides cold beer to fortify me against that chill," Abigale said.

The two women sat on the cushioned benches and wrapped themselves in beach towels. Abigale prepared herself for the interrogation that she was sure would come.

"Have you known Sloan for long?" Edie started right in.

"Well, let me see now, in all about twenty years, give or take. We met at FSU."

"So, you've known Jake that long as well?"

"Oh sure, we were good friends. At least for a while. But Edie, you must already know all this history, so why are you asking?"

"I want to hear your side of the story and compare it with what I've heard. Well, mostly from Regina. Jake never talks much about those times. He never talks much about himself at all. I have to find out everything on my own."

"When I knew Jake, he was so carefree, always looking for his next conquest. Probably not what you wanted to hear about your hubby, but it's just that he was commitment-phobic in those days."

"Were you and Sloan close in those days?"

"Close? You could say so. We were planning on getting married."

"Engaged?"

Abigale nodded.

"I'd say that's close! What happened, if I'm not being too nosey?"

"He shipped over to Spain, and for a few months he wrote or called every day. Then nothing."

"Guess that gave you cause to wonder. What happened next?" Edie asked.

"I went to Spain to find out what had happened to him. Imagine my surprise when I found him playing house with one of the locals, who I presume was Wendy's mom."

Edie nodded.

"I'd been dating Brad's father before I met Sloan, so he and I picked up where we left off and married right after graduation. We moved to Anaheim where Brad Junior was born that next year."

"You and Brad . . . happily married?"

"Deliriously. We soon forgot about Sloan and Spain and all that misery."

"And never looked back?"

Abigale felt her face flush. "No . . . never."

"But you're here, and where's your husband?"

"Brad Senior died, when Junior was ten."

"That must have been rough. What did you do then?"

"Enrolled at UCLA, earned my MBA and went to work."

"Wonder why he did that?" Edie said, holding her mug of tea in both hands. "You know, married Regina when he was already engaged to you."

"The usual suspects. She was pregnant and he promised his father he wouldn't get a girl in trouble and not help her."

"Do you believe that?" Edie said, turning again to a serious note.

"I want to. Never gave me any reason to doubt him."

"You guys getting back together?"

"Please, Edie. Cut me some slack. I just found out a week ago he was divorced."

"So, you weren't a party to the breakup?"

"I should say not! We were reintroduced by our kids just last week. Wendy arranged a brunch so we could all meet. Poor kid didn't have a clue."

Edie set her mug in the galley sink. "You should know that Regina and I are close. We play tennis several times a week, and before the divorce we did lots of stuff as a family. My girls and Wendy practically grew up together."

"I hope we can be friends," Abigale said.

"Then you weren't offended by my questions?" Edie said.

"Of course not. How'd I do?"

"You passed." Edie smiled.

"Good." Abigale set her mug down in the sink along with Edie's. "Now, if you'll excuse me, I'm going topside and snuggle up to the captain. Maybe I can get an extra ration of rum. There just might be a little spark left in the old boy. Thanks for the tea and the talk."

"Here, take this blanket," Edie said. "He won't have one and it'll get damn chilly before we get back in."

Sloan put the *Akubra* in irons while they watched the sunset. The clouds to the south and west yielded brilliant hues of red, orange, pink and finally gray. Sloan slid his arm around Abigale, grabbed her blanket and led her to the bow. Jake found a bottle of wine and offered everyone a plastic cup.

"Sorry, no MD," Sloan said. "Besides, life is too short to drink anything but the best."

"My tastes have changed over the years too," Abigale said.

Sloan studied her in the rays of the setting sun caught in her wavy brown hair. It seemed to him that almost no time had passed since that evening on the beach when he came recklessly close to consummating their love for one another.

"Thought you were a sunrise man, huh, Sloan?"

"Guess that's changed too. He pointed to the medallion draped around her neck. "I see you're still wearing the ruby sea glass."

She cradled it in the palm of her hand. "Guess I'm used to it."

"Remember that evening at the airport?" Sloan said.

"Yeah. So . . . what about it?"

"I'm a sentimental old fool, that's all. Just pleased to see you hung on to it."

"Tried to ditch it, but it just wouldn't go away. After that trip to Spain, I threw it in the ocean, but the chain caught on my sleeve. I could be wrong about this Sloan, but it seems to bring me luck. Not always good, mind you, but luck of some kind."

"I've had some of both kinds as well. Mostly good. Can't complain."

"I saw what you cashed in when we acquired you. So . . ."

She pushed him away to examine his face in the fading twilight. "You know, old man, you really haven't changed all that much. Some gray around the edges and that little paunch you're growing is kind of cute."

"Not much smarter either. Still just fumbling through life, trying to make sense of it."

"Me too." She leaned back against the arm he had draped around her shoulders. "It doesn't seem so long ago that we were walking the beach where you found this piece of broken glass."

"Who knows?" Sloan said. "It might still have a little magic left in it."

LV

Abigale and Sloan began the reconstruction of their relationship. This time it was founded on principles different from before. In those early days, they had very few life experiences upon which to base their feelings. Now they were both in their forties and looking forward to marriage for their children and, eventually, grandchildren.

Sloan wondered if they could start over, considering their shaky history. During their college days, they had never slept together except for those times in the front seat of his old truck. Once on a long bike ride, they had come across a small roadside motel with a charming room and a cozy fireplace. They slept fully clothed to avoid any chance they would break their vow of chastity. Anything was fair game as long as hands stayed outside clothes. This time around, intimacy made perfect sense, but they were in no hurry.

Abigale was becoming a skilled sailor and the *Akubra* gave them access to places not available to most couples. Catalina afforded five or six hours of sailing to the island. Once there, they had their choice of places to explore. Avalon was an excellent location to spend a night or a long weekend.

If there was a hindrance to moving their relationship along, it was the demands on Abigale's time. Sloan's only obligation was to act as a marketing consultant to Elcon, a title that was turning out to be just that. His one-year contract expired; going forward, he was on a daily arrangement. Abigale had a steady job that required her presence at the office at least five days a week, and there were times when she was expected to travel with her boss.

On Tuesday, Sloan collected Abigale for lunch. "Got any plans for the weekend?" he asked. He was always careful not to take her for granted.

"Need to finish that knitting project and wash my hair. Other than that, sure. What's on your miniscule, military mind?"

"What say we rinse off the *Akubra* and sail her over to the island for a couple of days? I can get us a room in Avalon and we can walk the streets and gorge ourselves on swordfish and sand dabs."

"I have a better idea. It might cost a little more, but you can afford it."

Arms crossed, he leaned against the frame of her office door. "Let's hear it."

"What would you say to a long weekend in Apalachicola?"

"Apalach? You're talking a long haul from L.A. Can you get some time off?"

"It's all arranged. The flights are reserved and with your bonus miles we can get there and back on peanuts. All you have to do is get us to the airport and buy me dinner every night. We can walk the beach and kick up some more sea glass for our collection." One thing had not changed. The words *no* and *can't*, were not in Abigale's vocabulary.

They flew to Tallahassee, rented a car and drove to Apalachicola where they checked into a local bed and breakfast. By late afternoon, they were on St. George Island, scouring the beach for sea glass. They had just enough daylight for a short walk before Old Sol sizzled and sank into the Gulf. Sloan took Abigale by the hand and led her down to the water's edge to observe a glorious array of colors. It seemed hours before the sun disappeared into the bay. "How 'bout some shrimp and a few beers for old time sake?" Sloan said.

"Great! But I had hoped for oysters."

"Thought they were too—"

"A lot has changed in twenty years."

He laced his fingers through hers, "And some things never will."

LVI

Sunday afternoon, the clan gathered at Sloan's condo. Wendy and Brad had driven over from school on Friday evening to spend the weekend and do some sailing. Abigale had stopped by after work on Friday and never left. Sloan was on the patio preparing to grill steak and lobster, while Abigale was in the kitchen whipping up one of her favorite marinades for the grilled vegetables and roasted potatoes. Wendy was in the kitchen, too, tearing up lettuce for a Caesar salad.

Sloan glanced up from the grill. "So, Brad, how's school treating you?"

"If you mean . . . am I making a four point?"

"Not letting daughter Wendy show you up, are you?"

"She's tough when it comes to acing a test. Engineering is just harder than public relations."

"You would be right about that," Sloan said holding a hand over the coals to test their readiness.

"Dad," Brad said. "While I have your attention, there's something I want to talk to you about."

"Hand me that plate of steaks so I can work them over with some olive oil and pepper before Abby gets out here with that marinade."

"But I thought you liked Mom's marinades."

"Oh, they're okay, but a little olive oil does the trick for me."

Sloan had grown fond of Brad and was honored when he called him Dad. The two men found their beers and made their way onto the dock for some privacy.

"So, what's up? No, let me guess. You took a job in Iraq and you want me to tell Wendy that right after graduation you are out of here for a couple of years."

"Nope, I turned down that job in Iraq, but here's the real deal. I want your permission to ask Wendy to get married."

"I bet you already have."

"Have what, Sir?"

"Asked her."

"Sure, we've talked about it, but—"

"And, what'd she say?"

"That I had to get your . . . uh, you know . . . permission."

"You love her?"

Brad turned a deep red. "Sure, more than—hell, Dad, you know that."

"When did *you* know?" Sloan asked.

Brad glanced up from his deck chair. "Know, Sir?" His blush deepened.

"Yeah, when did you know you loved her?"

Brad rubbed the back of his neck. "Uh, well, almost, you know, that first day we met in psych class last year. I saw her come in the auditorium and made damn sure I sat beside her. She felt it too. It was, well . . . it's hard to put into words." Brad spoke with a nervous quiver.

"Happened when your eyes met?"

"Guess so. You could say that. Never really thought much about it."

"You know, Brad, this is not my decision alone. I can't give you permission to get married."

"Sloan, are you trying to bust my hump?"

"Hell no, it's just that your mother should have a say in this. She's the one who will have to babysit the grandkids. Me, I'm thinking of taking up golf, so I won't have much time for that kind of stuff. Abby?" he called through the sliding door. "Think you better get out here."

Abigale showed up on the patio with her marinade ready for Sloan's steaks.

"Hey, Abby, listen to this. The kids have something they want to talk with us about. A crazy scheme. Brad says they want to get married."

Wendy slipped through the door and onto the patio.

"Married?" Abigale said. She saw that Sloan was having some fun with Brad. "Not so sure about—marriage can be a slippery slope. You sure as hell don't want to take Sloan's advice on the subject."

"Okay, sure, I made a mess of things but Brad here says he's in love. You think we can believe him?"

"What do you think?" Abigale said. She stared at her son, her face stern. "You aren't going to bail on her and run off to Russia or Germany with no forwarding address?" She forced a straight face.

Wendy scolded Sloan, "This was supposed to be a serious family discussion and you turned it into a free for all."

"Mom, come on now. You know we love each other."

"Well Wendy, what do you say? Do you love my son enough to put up with all his crap for the rest of your life? I have for twenty years and believe me, he has plenty of it."

"Yes, Mom. I'm crazy about the big galoot."

Sloan stared at Brad. "So, you want permission to marry my daughter?" He turned to Abigale and then back to Wendy. He raised his wine glass. Everyone followed his lead. "Then, by darn, you have it. I'll even foot the bill, provided I get to pick the honeymoon location. We'll send you someplace in the West Indies. He looked at Brad for approval."

"Antigua or Aruba would be perfect, Dad. Or somewhere in the Lesser Antilles."

"Okay, Son. You pick it."

"There's just one more thing, Father dear." When Wendy called him Father she wanted something important. She took a deep breath and Sloan knew she was about to throw the first monkey wrench into the wedding plan.

"I want Mom to be part of the wedding, and that means you two have to bury the hatchet—so to speak."

Sloan took a deep breath and nodded. "I'll arrange a summit."

He could not expect Wendy to embark on her life with Brad without both her parents. Regina was entitled to be a part of the wedding, and she should assume her rightful place as mother of the bride, mother-in-law and, eventually, grandparent.

Regina agreed to meet Sloan at a small café on the peninsula just down the hill from Abernathy Manor. In light of her penchant for public displays of anger, this very public place seemed like the ideal choice.

Outdoor settings had been the tradition for their meetings over the years. A table in a garden or on a patio was private, compared to a booth or table in a bar or dining room. He could have invited her aboard the boat, but her last experience on the *Akubra* might still be fresh on her mind, even though it had been almost four years since that fateful day when she had fallen from the *Akubra* into everlasting riches and local notoriety as the woman who narrowly escaped the clutches of her murderous husband.

Regina and Sloan had dined at this particular restaurant on numerous occasions over the years, so he was recognized and greeted by the hostess.

He settled back with a glass of red wine and waited for Regina. He remembered the time they met at that little café in Madrid when she told him of the imminent arrival of their daughter. Now, twenty-two years later, they were meeting to discuss Wendy's wedding.

The waiter showed Regina to the table. Sloan stood and kissed her on the cheek.

"You're looking great. Have a seat."

"Not you. You're looking old and tired. Sure you're getting enough sleep?"

"You kidding? Me? No, I feel great. Never better."

"Oh, before I forget. Congratulations on dumping that piece of shit company of yours."

"It did go rather well, but that's ancient history. It's been over two years now."

"Damn it, can you believe how stupid I was, leaving all that money on the table?"

"Must've broken your heart, but you're not hurting. You did a good job of fleecing me, you and that bitch of a lawyer. Where did you ever dig her up?"

"I learned quick when it comes to hiring a lawyer you go for a shark or a crocodile. Not a wimp like that guy you hired. Hell, Honey, you taught me that a long time ago. I expected a better fight out of you."

"The wimp thought he had done a good job when I didn't land in jail. You had the upper hand with all that murder and rape stuff."

"Hey, Hon, that's all water under the dam. I'm glad to know someone as rich as you, so I can borrow when I run low." She smiled demurely. Her black eyes danced in the soft light. "So, what you been doing with yourself? Can't believe it's been that long since I've seen you," she said. "God, it's been great, but not long enough. Order me a drink, will you, Hon? Martini, dry. Now, what is it you wanted to talk about?"

"You may've heard, the kids want to get married."

"Of course, I've heard. Wendy and I are like this." She held up crossed fingers and then shrugged. "Well, I hope it turns out better for them."

"That's where we come in," Sloan said. "They'll need our help to make it work."

"I don't give a damn about Abigale or that son of hers. They can both go straight to hell for all I care."

"I can understand you feeling that way, but please don't stand in the way of Wendy's happiness."

"I hope that bitch Abigale burns in hell, husband-stealing whore."

Sloan felt a flush of anger and resentment, but he managed to remain focused.

The waiter brought Regina a dry martini and another Scotch for Sloan. Sloan studied the back of the waiter's black jacket as he walked away.

"Why would you think she stole me from you?" Sloan said softly. He forced a congenial tone to his voice.

"Don't be coy with me, you miserable bastard. Everyone knows you dumped me for her. It's the talk all over town."

"The talk is all wrong. She's an innocent bystander in all this. She has better grounds for hard feelings against me than you do. After all, if it weren't for our fling all those years ago, her life—hell, all our lives—might've been different."

"Without a doubt, that's for damn sure. Who can say how *her* life would've been? It might've been the same. She could have ended up with that football guy in spite of what we did. He may have been—what you say, her soul mate."

"We'll never know, will we?" Sloan knew that he loved Abigale then and still had strong feelings for her now.

"You'd have me believe she was not your reason for wanting a divorce?"

"I didn't leave you to be with Abigale, if that's what you mean. I didn't even know for sure where she was. I knew she lived in southern California, but that was all."

Regina pensively sampled her drink.

"I'm asking you, do this for Wendy. The kids are the ones who matter now. They're entitled to an extended family, one that's not always on the war path. Our time has passed. From now on, our lives will be all about being there for them. For the sake of the kids, you and I need to bury the hatchet."

"I would like to bury the hatchet, okay . . . in your head." She gestured with her hand across his head.

Sloan leaned toward her. "Just joking, right?"

She smiled and chuckled quietly.

"Happiness is all about finding true love, and I think they have," Sloan said.

"No such thing as true love," she groused, "only passion. And when that's gone . . ." She waved her hand dismissively. "You still think I was just some Spanish whore who wanted to marry a Yank and come to America? Isn't that right, Sloan?"

"Never thought you were a—"

"Hell, Sloan. I could've come to America on my own anytime I wanted, with no help from you or anybody. Truth is, Sloan baby, my feelings for you grew over the years."

"And mine for you. We had some great times, some good years. It just wasn't the same as . . . hard to explain."

"As your feelings for Abigale?"

"Still don't know how I feel about her. It might have gone different for you and me, but there was that thing with you and Gibbs."

"One night! That's all it was. Just my luck it's the one night you come home. Aren't I allowed one mistake?" It wasn't at all what you thought. Only talk. We were talking. He may have wanted kissing, but no—"

"We made lots of mistakes," Sloan said. "I paid dearly for mine. It's a wonder we made it as long as we did. Let's forgive and forget and move on with what is left of our lives."

"So, you want me to put it all behind me and be a good mother-in-law, is that it?"

"That's the idea."

"I'll try, but don't be surprised if I show up at the wedding with el hacha en la head."

A chill ran through Sloan. He wondered if she had it in her to wreak havoc on the wedding. Surely she was kidding.

Regina forced a smile. Venting some of her bitter feelings and turning them into a joke, seemed to dissipate the anger and resentment she had been harboring. Silence fell over the pair as they thoughtfully dressed their salads then nibbled like two rabbits in a field of clover.

She had longed for a showdown with Sloan. She had wanted to beat him, to hurt him, but she never thought she would destroy him. For three years, she had reveled in her victory, but harboring hatred for Sloan no longer brought her joy. If she was to continue a healthy relationship with her daughter, she would have to accept and embrace Brad and Abigale as family. A truly bitter pill.

Regina pushed her half-eaten salad away. "Can you forgive me for all the bad things?"

He forced a smile. "Like what?"

"The graffiti in your boat . . . Gibbs?"

"The graffiti? I'm still working on that. And the whole thing with Gibbs wasn't entirely your fault. If I'd been a better husband, you wouldn't have been tempted to find love with someone else."

"And taking you to the cleaners in divorce court? Can you forgive that? Truth is, Sloan, you had it coming." She tapped him on the arm with her index finger and smiled.

"You may have gotten more than your share," Sloan said, "but I have no complaints. Vortec sold. All's well that ends well."

She rolled her eyes. "I can't get over how you sold that worthless company of yours. Hard to believe you got someone to pay you all that money for it."

"Yeah, pretty amazing how I managed to pull that off and I still have the *Akubra.*" He made a slight bow from the waist. "Gracious of you to let me keep her."

The waiter bused their half-eaten salads and brought Regina a fresh martini.

"I'll be there for the wedding. Already have the date marked on my calendar. I want to invite some friends from the club and different places. I'm lunching with Wendy tomorrow. She and I will work on all the plans. All you have to do is write some big checks—and I do mean big. We'll do the rest."

LVII

Jake called Sloan from Napa Valley where he was attending a weekend management conclave. "Got something to celebrate," he said. "Can you get us a table at that spot where we went on your birthday?"

"Feeling ritzy, are you?" Sloan replied. "I'll take care of everything except the bill."

"Tonight is on me. Can you pick Edie up on your way?"

Sloan reserved a table for four at a five-star restaurant perched high on a bluff overlooking the ocean. He chose a table by the window with a view of the Pacific.

Sloan and the ladies arrived early, found their table and ordered a bottle of Chateau Neuf Du Pape from well above the middle of the list. What the heck, he would stick Jake with the bill since he was the one with the good news. They enjoyed their first glass while watching the sun sink into the Pacific. Saturday evening traffic from Napa could be horrific, so they expected Jake to arrive, at the earliest, by eight.

Around nine, the maître d' came to their table. "Mr. Abernathy, you have a phone call. You can take it in the private booth in the lobby."

Sloan made his way out of the dining room into the lobby and found the phone booth. "Hello, Abernathy here."

"Mr. Abernathy? I'm Officer Johnson with the California Highway Patrol."

"So, what's up? Did you arrest my daughter for speeding again?"

There was a momentary silence at the other end of the line. "Do you know Jake Morgan? Is he an acquaintance of yours?"

"My closest friend—unless he's in jail. Then no, never heard of him." The wine was doing the talking. More silence. "Is something wrong?"

"I'm calling from the scene of an accident on the 101 about ten miles north of your present location. It involved a truck and an SUV driven by Mr. Morgan."

"Accident?"

"I regret to tell you that Mr. Morgan was fatally injured in the crash."

Sloan's knees buckled. He slumped to the floor of the phone booth, the cord stretched tight.

"What? What did you—can you repeat—"

"An eighteen-wheeler forced Mr. Morgan's SUV into the guardrail in the center of the freeway."

"How'd you find me?"

"Your name and number were in his wallet as an emergency contact. We called your home and spoke with your daughter. She told us where you were."

"No mistake? You're sure it's him? Stolen . . . his car and wallet could've been—"

"Sorry, Mr. Abernathy. Everything checks out."

"Tell me what to do."

"Body's being transported to the morgue at L.A. Central, the coroner's office. Someone needs to go there and identify his body. Once that's done, you can have him transferred to a mortuary of your choosing. Will you inform his family?"

"His wife's here with me. We were planning dinner together. Said he had something to celebrate."

Sloan was still sitting on the floor of the phone booth. A man standing in the lobby pointed and laughed as though he thought Sloan was drunk and couldn't stand on his own. Sloan managed to get to his feet and swing the bi-fold door open putting him face-to-face with his heckler. Sloan gave him a shove that sent the loud-mouth flying over a sofa and landing on his head. Two waiters saw the commotion and rushed to set the inebriated patron upright. Sloan walked away. He had more to face than dealing with this jerk.

Edie was halfway through her second glass of wine and in a jovial mood. "Don't tell me. Let me guess. He's running late."

Sloan stood, his fists clenched and his jaw set. He did not know how to prepare Edie for this news. "Jake won't be here."

"What's up? The old man have a puncture?" Sloan didn't answer. She took a sip and smiled at him over the rim of her glass. "Not running off with his secretary or anything like that?" She finally saw the expression on Sloan's face.

"Edie, there's been an accident." He leaned on the table and tried to look into her eyes.

"A fender-bender? He's okay, though, right?"

"He didn't survive . . . Edie, he's gone." His words were like a swig of vinegar.

Her hands trembled. Red wine sloshed out of her glass, over her dress and onto the white linen tablecloth. Sloan was Jake's oldest and dearest friend. He would not lie or play such a terrible prank.

She turned to Abigale as if it were somehow her fault. "What do I do now?" she asked as she turned her gaze back to Sloan.

He saw shock, fear and uncertainty in her face.

Abigale shook her head and tried to speak, but her words would not come.

"I thought this might happen someday," Edie finally said, "but nothing has prepared me for this moment. It must not be true. At any minute he'll walk through that door. I know he will."

"We have to go to where he is being taken and identify him," Sloan said. He watched the color drain from her face. "Edie," Sloan said, "take a deep breath."

Abigale touched her back in a feeble attempt to comfort her.

"It might not be him. It could be someone else—not Jake."

"No, Edie, they're sure. They just want us to confirm it, a mere formality. We have to go to the morgue." Sloan choked on the word. It was too cold, too clinical. Hospital sounded better. Sloan hired a cab to take them to the coroner's office—the hospital—the morgue.

LVIII

Six days had passed since a freak wave hit the southern coast of California. The very next day, they had begun a search-and-rescue mission along the coast. Several boats had been reported missing: three sport-fishing vessels, ranging in size from nineteen to thirty-seven feet; five sailboats from twenty-four feet to a large, vintage wooden schooner just over sixty feet in length. All were missing and presumed lost. They were also on the lookout for seven men and two women who were last seen on surfboards. It was unlikely, after almost a week that they would be found.

Mornings aboard the Coast Guard Cutter *Acushnet* were serene. Captain Meriwether paced the bridge taking in the salt air and nursing a steaming mug of coffee as he puffed on his morning pipe.

Since early Monday morning they had steered a search pattern, due north for one hour and then due east for an hour, all the while scanning the horizon for signs of wreckage that might sustain life or provide some clue as to the demise of one of those missing ships.

Captain Meriwether's orders came from the bridge, "Throttle back half. Steer starboard ninety..All ahead full."

"Hey, Captain Meriwether," came a voice from the port bow. "I spotted a small life raft," Meriwether inspected the small craft through his binoculars.

"What do you make of it?"

"Well, Captain, it's a lifeboat marked as being off the *Akubra.*"

"Good hunting there, seaman. That just happens to be one of the vessels we're looking for. The *Akubra.* . .that's one of the vessels on our list. Check her out, seaman. There just might be someone still aboard."

"Ahoy, the raft. Anybody there?" the seaman shouted through his bullhorn.

Wake up, Johnny. There's folks here wantin' ta help ya.

"Go away, Daddy. Don't need no help. Leave me—"

That's crazy talk, Johnny. You need help in the worst way. Now, make some kinda racket or yell out. Wave to 'em. Do something! Damn you.

The seaman ran along the starboard rail hoping to get a good look at what or who was inside. "Don't appear to be no one in there, Captain. Least ways not alive."

"Just the same, let's put a line on 'er. Might be something to help the family put it all to rest, knowing we found the raft and it was empty."

"Aye, Captain."

"Hey, there's someone in here," the young seaman shouted. "Looks to be a goner though."

"Bring him up on deck and check his vitals," Meriwether shouted.

"Come on, Daddy. Make 'em leave me . . . like it here . . . peaceful . . . got my gardens. See all them beautiful flowers? I grew 'em all."

Outta my hands now, Johnny. Like it or not, you're getting rescued.

"By damn, Captain, he's got a pulse and man does he stink. Must be all that rotting blood and piss in the bottom of his boat."

"Go below and get the oxygen and locate the medic."

"Aye, Captain."

"All hands on deck," Meriwether shouted from behind his bullhorn.

When Sloan woke up, he found himself in a small cabin just off the main deck. He tried to sit up but swooned and fell back.

"What day is it?" he asked the medic who was fussing over some stitches in Sloan's head.

"Saturday, round fourteen hundred. We fished you out early yesterday morning. You was out cold and couldn't have stunk worse if you was dead."

"Where am I?"

"This here's the *Acushnet*, a Coast Guard Cutter, and you're riding first class in what passes for the infirmary. I'm your medic in residence, at your service, Sir."

The young ensign stuck his head through the portal and shouted to the captain, "He's awake, Sir."

Meriwether entered the infirmary and stuck his hand out for Sloan to shake. "Welcome aboard. Glad you could join us. We come damn close to feedin' you to the fish."

"So happy you decided against it," Sloan smiled. "But tell me, Captain, where're we headed?"

"San Diego, fast as we can get there."

"Why? What's in San Diego?"

"Closest port and they know us there. Hope you don't mind. I Went through your stuff and found your ID. Retired Army Captain, eh?"

"Cut any ice with the Navy?"

"Coast Guard, if you don't mind. . .depends on what you're after."

"My daughter's getting married tonight—six o'clock. Promised her I'd be there."

"Man, you're havin' a run of luck. This tub's one of the oldest and slowest in the fleet. She makes about twelve knots in following seas and balls to the wall. Wedding's most likely cancelled. Word is that LA is still in shock from that tsunami."

"You don't know my daughter. She's damned headstrong. Chopper? What about it? Can you get me a chopper? I can pay for it."

"Chopper would get you there, but there ain't no landing pad on this old bucket, and choppers are in short supply what with that tsunami and all. Best I can do is have one meet us in Dago. Mind, you wanting a chopper to get to a wedding would put us pretty far down the list."

"They could drop a sling and hoist me up."

"Forget it, Cowboy. By the time they located a chopper in the area and got it here, we'd be in Dago."

"Okay, so what time will we tie up?"

"Should make it by sixteen hundred, or there about."

"That would give me two hours. I could just make it. Is there some place I can clean up? Take a shower and shave my jaw?"

"Think you can stand up that long? You left a lot of blood in that raft of yours.

"I can manage."

"I'll get you some clothes. Sorry I don't have no weddin' tux." The portly captain laughed aloud and slapped his gut. "How 'bout a Navy-issue jumpsuit instead?"

"A jumpsuit will do. Need to contact my family."

"Give me the info," Meriwether said. "I'll get word to them. My medic had to shave your head to get at that gash. He does the hair for the crew, and I can tell you, he would a flunked out of barber school. You have a gross of stitches up there, so you might want a keep a hat on." Sloan felt the top of his head and winced.

"I'd hate fur the bride to faint at the sight of you."

Sloan jotted Abby's contact information on a pad for the captain.

"Most of the com's down in LA County. Has been since Sunday. It might take some time to reach this here lady of yours. If I do, I'll tell her you're okay and on your way to the wedding. Shower's right across the hall. Help yourself."

The lumbering cutter slowed to a stop and backed into the dock. The crew hung the dock lines and dropped the gangway.

As Sloan prepared to disembark, he paused to salute the colors and Captain Meriwether who waved from the bridge. "No luck on the chopper," he yelled. "Best bet's a taxi. Good luck!"

Sloan snapped off a final salute to his rescue team and turned to the fantail for one last look at his raft. He imagined he could see two familiar figures waving to him. One of the men saluted with his left hand. The older man waved and smiled.

Sloan staggered down the gangway and onto the dock. Six days of confinement in that raft, his cracked skull and the loss of blood had taken their toll. He spotted a bench on the dock and collapsed, his head spinning.

"Need a lift, sailor?" A voice seemed to come from right out of the blazing afternoon sun.

He looked up and into the eyes of a lady in a flight suit. She rested her wrist on the steering wheel of a golf cart. Her head blocked the sun giving the appearance that she had a halo.

"Can you get me to the nearest taxi stand?"

"Sure, sailor. Climb in."

Sloan got to his feet. His head spun. He grabbed hold of the cart to steady himself.

"Where you headed?"

"UCLA. Daughter's getting married."

"Married? I'll be damned! What time?"

"1800 hours."

His world spun.

"And you think a taxi will get you there in time?"

"Got a better idea?" He looked up at her again blinded by the afternoon sun. He blacked out and fell flat on the boardwalk. She grabbed him under the arms, helped him to his feet and plopped him down on the park bench.

"You're a bit wobbly, Sailor. If I didn't know better—look, I have a car and it so happens I need to make a run to LA."

"Then you could drive me?"

"It'd be my pleasure, Captain."

"I'll pay you."

"Climb in here beside me, we can talk about it on the way." She extended her strong right arm to steady him. "First, we need to get to my car and jettison this friggin' golf cart."

She sped through the underground parking garage until she arrived at a silver Corvette. She backed the Vette out and parked the golf cart in its place.

"Get in," she ordered Sloan. "Don't pull another fainting spell, now hear?"

"I'm feeling much better, thanks. Nice Vette."

"Helps me burn up the adrenalin when I'm not in the air."

"So, you're a jet jockey."

"Was. For the past year, they've kept me behind a desk."

"That's tough. Name's Abernathy, Captain Sloan Abernathy, U.S. Army retired." He stuck out his hand and she shook it.

"Jane Baldwin, Captain Jane Baldwin, U.S. Navy. So, Captain Abernathy, how'd you manage to come ashore at the San Diego Naval Base?"

"Long story."

"We have ninety minutes."

"In ninety minutes, I can give you the long, fully embellished yarn. But, Jane, if you make it faster, I'll give you the Reader's Digest version and a big tip."

"With some luck, I can shave a few minutes off, but luck doesn't seem to be with you today."

"Actually, I lead a charmed life."

"Charmed? That sounds like a good place to start."

"Last week, I was sailing off Catalina Island when I was overtaken by this huge wall of water. It swamped my boat, so I had to scuttle her and climb into my life raft. Somewhere along the way, I took a hard lick on the head that left me with this gash and one terrific headache." He removed his Navy-issue cap to reveal his freshly shaven and crudely stitched head. "Must've bled for days."

"If I have this straight, you were single-handing your sailboat around Catalina and took the tsunami head on?"

"To me, it was a thirty-foot wall of water. That was last Sunday. Friday, they fished me out of the drink and onto the *Acushnet.*"

"Slowest friggin' boat in the fleet. Some charmed life you lead."

"Hey, I'm alive, ain't I?"

"What was it like being lost at sea?"

"I don't remember much after the third day, and what I do remember is pretty hazy. I woke up this morning aboard the *Acushnet* and realized my daughter was getting married today. I'm supposed to give her away. The guys on the cutter fixed my head, loaned me a razor, and these fancy duds."

"You *are* one damn lucky guy, just to be here. You might want to have that head looked at. I've seen some battle wounds in my day, and that gash on your head would put most of them to shame. What did you eat all that time?"

"Shark."

"Bullshit! No really, how did you manage not to starve?"

Sloan reached in his vest pocket and came out with a bloody shark's tooth and handed it to Jane.

"Holy crap! How big was that sucker?"

"Big enough. How long 'till we get there?"

"If the roads are open, we should *make it to the church on time.*"

She examined the tooth. "What'd he do, jump in the boat and bite you on the head?" She laughed out loud.

"The head wound is most likely from the boom. I shot the shark with a flare gun." Sloan said with a matter-of-fact shrug. "How long you been in the Navy?"

"Joined right out of college. It was a great ride until just last year when they took me off flight status."

"Were you a bad girl?"

She shook a finger at Sloan. "Didn't get thrown in the brig, if that's what you're thinking." She squeezed the steering wheel and sighed deeply. "It was politics, pure and simple. I was in the astronaut program and didn't get to take the ride. They wouldn't send me back on combat duty after investing all that dough on my training. Afraid of how it would look if I ditched in the Adriatic or the desert. To hell with them. I'm thinking I'll bag the Navy and do something on the outside."

"Like what?"

"Flight school. I'll start my own flight school if I can raise some cash for seed money."

"What kinda money we talking?"

"Enough for a trainer and some hanger space, probably just north of three hundred. I can live off my retirement until the school starts to pay, but I'll have to scrape to get my hands on that kind of money. Not much good at illicit acts." Her smile eradicated her tough exterior.

"Always wanted to learn. For the last seven years, I've been sailing with my daughter and my best friend. He was killed in a wreck just the other day . . . she's getting married . . . the boat sank so . . . guess I'm just about done sailing. You done any sailing?"

"One of the ways I get a rush is crewing on racing sloops, usually twenty meters and up."

"You trumped me there. I cruise to the island and along the south coast. Love to get a rail in the water when I can."

"You born with a silver spoon or did you actually buy that sailboat you left out there in the trench?"

"I'm an electrical engineer by training. Did a stint in the Army and fifteen years with a high tech company in LA. Bought that tub with my own dough."

"So, you're fixed."

"Did the market crash last week?"

"Not that I heard. Just about everything else did, but nothing was certain after that tsunami hit. I think they suspended trading for the entire week."

"Then, I'm probably okay."

"LA County's at a standstill. Your daughter's wedding might be off."

"They promised to have it with or without me. They're determined. Fell for each other the first time they met. Amazing, huh?"

"And what about you, Captain? With a daughter getting married there must be a missus around someplace."

"Ex. Regina. 'Bout four years ago now."

"Whose idea was that?"

"Mine. Wendy was in college and I wanted to move on."

"So, you were married but you weren't committed, is that it?"

"Guess so. Found my true love, right enough. Just never got around to marrying her. Instead, I married this woman in Spain."

"Let me guess," Jane said, her eyes on the road and swerving to avoid debris. "She was in a family way." She pulled the visor down to block the late afternoon sun.

"You wouldn't happen to have a mobile phone that works?"

"Sure, help yourself, but power's still out to most of the towers."

"I'll try my lady friend, Abigale. I got her a new phone, the latest model. It might still be working."

Abigale's mobile service directed his call to a customer advisory. The operator explained in a recording that the service would be returned in one week's time. He tried her home number. It rang repeatedly but no one answered.

"I'll try the ex. She doesn't have a cell phone, but the house phone might be working. She hates anything to do with communications since my company made millions building com equipment."

Jane wheeled her silver Vette through the wrought iron gates that guarded the expansive UCLA campus. She followed signs to the Faculty Center and skidded to a stop in front of the walkway that led to the campus chapel.

"Here we are, Sailor. Hope we're in time." She handed Sloan her business card then held out her hand. "If you want to get together for some flying lessons, or whatever, give me a call."

"Thanks for the ride." He held her hand in his. "I owe you, big time." He could not help but notice her strong hands, adept at steering a jet off the back of a carrier, a Corvette over an interstate at high speed, or the space shuttle in orbit around the earth.

"Not much of a crowd for a wedding," she said, letting go of his hand. The campus was deserted. "Could've been rescheduled. I'll hang here for a few to make sure it's happening," she said, draping her wrist over the wheel.

"Bet they're all inside, waiting for me to make a grand entrance." He hobbled up the stairs and swung open the chapel doors. The large chapel stood dark, vacant, and foreboding. A notice was taped to the door.

'Abernathy / Hager wedding has been rescheduled for 7:00 PM at the home of the bride's mother. Reception to follow, in the garden.'

He turned and hobbled back into the street. "Change of venue," he shouted. He grabbed his head and winced. "They're having the wedding at my house. Well, before the divorce it was my—" His knees began to buckle under his weight.

"I get the picture," Jane said.

"Can you take me to where I can hire a taxi?"

"And miss the ending of this soap? No way, Cowboy. How do I get to Regina's?"

"Get back on the 405 and head south about thirty miles."

Jane sped back onto the 405 and accelerated the silver Vette to eighty.

"This Regina, she's your daughter's mom, but you say you never loved her? How can you be so sure?"

"Of what?"

"That she wasn't your intended mate."

Traffic was light and most of the debris had been cleared from the roadways, so Jane pushed her Vette up to ninety.

"Because I was engaged to my soul mate. Regina ended up pregnant and I married her instead. Abby married an egomaniac football player named Brad and they had a son. Brad died leaving her to raise Brad Junior alone."

"So, now . . . the two of you are back together?"

"Hard to say. All I know for sure is Brad Junior and my daughter are getting married." Sloan marveled that Jane could drive at breakneck speed and carry on an intelligent conversation.

"Let me see if I'm following this. You and Abigale reunite through your kids?"

"They'd been dating for a year without knowing how close they came to being siblings."

"You sure they—"

"Jane, don't go there. We waited like you're supposed to."

"So, you were engaged to Abigale, but never slept with her. Then you met Regina and slept with *her* the same night and ended up married to her for twenty years?"

"So, what's your point?"

"You may never know who the right one is. I happen to think love at first sight is a real and powerful emotion, not always a rational one, but it can be strong enough to overpower us, to compel us to take great risks. Consider the case of Abigail and Brad's father. When you dumped her, she may have gone a little crazy. Everyone close to her probably thought she was rebounding and maybe she was, but she took a chance. Something you weren't willing to do."

"You practice psychiatry in your spare time?" Sloan was bewildered at the insight Jane was showing.

"Masters in Psychology from Stanford. Been a hobby of mine ever since."

"Take the next exit and follow the surface street around and head west."

Sloan fell silent as he tried to absorb what she was saying. How was it she could make more sense of his life in an hour than he had in twenty years?

"Take that next left and park anywhere you can find a place. The party's at 5225. See it? There on the right."

Jane steered her Vette into a vacant spot on the curb some thirty yards from Regina's house.

"Here you are, Sailor. Looks like quite a crowd."

"May as well come in and join the party. You must be curious as all hell by now."

"Would it be okay? I won't be out of place in a jumpsuit?"

"You'll match the father of the bride. Everyone will want to meet the lady who got me to the church on time."

Jane climbed out of her silver machine and put her arm through Sloan's. "Don't want the father of the bride to land flat on his face," she said. Together they made their way to the door.

Sloan rang the doorbell. The beautiful thick oak door swung open and they were greeted by Arbela who rushed to Sloan and threw her arms around his neck.

"Ah, Señor Sloan! I think I see a ghost!"

"Not quite, Arbela. Say hello to Jane, my—uh—driver."

She pushed him away and quickly surveyed him from head to foot. "God, you look awful. Worse than ghost."

"Comes from spending a week in a lifeboat. Have they started?"

"We wait for you. Everyone by pool drinking your booze. We get call from Coast Guard man. He say you come, but not know when."

Arbela turned and ran through the long hallway leading to the patio and the pool, screaming at the top of her voice, "Señor Abernathy aquí- aquí!"

Sloan and Jane followed close behind her.

Abigale rushed into his arms. "Damn you, Sloan. We thought you were —"

"Sorry to disappoint you. Where's Wendy?"

"Getting dressed. Arbela, please run and tell Wendy that her Daddykins is here."

A crowd of well-wishers smothered Sloan, touching him to confirm that he was there in the flesh.

Jane stood quietly by, observing the excitement but not taking part.

Abigale squeezed Sloan's arm. "Who's your friend?"

"My driver. Found me wandering around the San Diego shipyard and brought me here."

Abigale extended her hand to Jane. "Can you stay?"

"For a while, if that's okay."

"Help yourself to a drink and some food. Soon as the bride is ready, we'll get started."

Sloan was overcome by a sense of order that was returning to his life. He thanked God for helping him to survive. Sloan was unsure who or what had acted to help him through six days at sea with little food and no water. His memory of the week was already beginning to fade like a bad dream. He reached in his jacket pocket to confirm that he still had Gibbs' tooth as proof that he had fought the huge animal and lived to tell about it.

Sloan broke away from the crowd and ran to the cabana where Regina and Wendy were making final preparations for their wedding march. He gave Regina a quick hug then grabbed their daughter in a long embrace. Wendy put her arms around his neck. "Father, you made it just in time."

"What happened to Daddykins?"

"For children," she said.

Wendy and Regina walked to the rhythm of the wedding march until they reached the makeshift altar. Sloan followed close behind. Brad stood next to the reverend. Catalina Island was visible on the horizon behind the altar that Sloan later learned had been constructed by his son-in-law. Sloan's blue gray jumpsuit stood in stark contrast to other members of the wedding party. Most were sporting tuxes and formal gowns. One young man wore shorts and sandals, a testament to all he had lost in the storm.

The minister instructed the congregation to remain standing and bow their heads in prayer.

The audience was seated and he continued with the ritual. "Dearly beloved, we are gathered here today in the sight of God to join this man and this woman in holy matrimony. Now, who gives this woman to be married to this man?"

"I do," Regina said.

"And I do," Sloan said.

Vows were exchanged, the couple kissed and he pronounced them man and wife. The service ended with a benediction. All quite normal.

Sloan was surprised by how quick and easy it was for these young people to join their lives for an eternity.

The bridesmaids were summarily heaved into the pool in their ball gowns.

Bryson pulled Sloan aside. "So, Sloan, you gave up on trying to out-sail me in that old barge and chopped a hole in her bilge." Bryson threw his arm around Sloan's neck and they hugged like college buddies.

"It was the only way I could get a new boat," Sloan said. "And by the way, you old whore, thanks for getting my guys home safe."

"Glad to do it, old man. So, what's next for you in the toy department?" Sloan struggled out from under Bryson's heavy arm and scanned the area for the nearest chair.

"I'll think of something. If I get another boat, you can rest assured it will be bigger and faster than that piece of shit you call a sloop. Maybe it's time to kick it up a notch." Sloan spotted a comfortable chair just before felt another fainting spell coming on.

"Yeah, like what? You're not thinkin' stink pot are you, Old Sport?"

"Yeah, or I just might get me an airplane." Sloan said, reflecting on the past week. "I just might have my fill of sailing."

Wendy and Brad changed into their traveling clothes and ran for a limo waiting to take them to LAX and their flight to

Denver. The couple had opted for a mountain resort in the Rockies.

Sloan fished in his wallet for one of his three credit cards and placed it in Brad's hand.

"Most of your expenses are already covered. For anything else you need or want, just use this. Never mind that it's water-logged, it should still work."

Jane stood alone at the front door with an empty champagne glass. Sloan poured a full glass and walked out to join her.

"Well, Jane, you rescued me from that park bench, drove me here in time to celebrate the happiest day of my life. How can I thank you?"

Jane put her arm around Sloan's neck and whispered. "You can call me the next time you feel like getting high." She pointed her half-full glass of champagne to the sky, turned and disappeared into the gray, foggy evening. He heard the purr of the V-8 as it pulled away from the curb and ripped out of the neighborhood.

Except for a few hardcore drinkers still hovering over the poolside bar, most of the guests had gone. Those remaining were determined to relieve him of his last bottle of champagne.

Sloan found a comfortable reclining deck chair on the veranda next to the pool where he stretched out and lit a cigar, something he rarely did except on special occasions. Being alive at Wendy's wedding qualified.

Regina pulled a chair up next to his. "From the looks of that gash, someone finally buried the hatchet."

"No hatchet. . . ran headlong into the boom on the *Akubra,* or at least that's what I think happened."

"Don't know if I've ever seen you so happy, Regina said. You weren't this happy when *we* got married. Well, I have some news that just might make you even happier."

"That's not possible," he said.

"At least let me try—"

"Take your best shot."

"Next week, I'm going home . . . to Madrid. There's a man there. He wants me to come to Spain and spend time with him."

"Gibbs? Tell me it's not G—"

"Oh, come on, Sloan darling. Give it up. John never meant anything to me. The one thing you were never able to figure out was what was really going on between me and the Colonel."

"I know the sound of two people making love when I hear it."

"No, Sloan, you really don't have a clue? It's time you heard the truth."

"So, you're going to set me straight? Just what *was* going on?"

"Sure you can handle it?"

"Like I handle everything that life throws at me. I'm sure it won't top six days at sea in a rubber raft."

"Don't be so sure." Regina stretched her beautiful slender, well-tanned body out on the recliner next to Sloan.

"For once, Regina, how about the truth?"

"Okay, Sloan. If you want the truth, you get the truth. My relationship with John was strictly business. He was my boss. I worked for him, same as you."

Sloan tried to reply, but the right words were not forthcoming. A few tumblers rotated in his mind and clicked into place while others would not mesh.

He sat up and swung his feet between the two lounge chairs.

Regina lurched, thinking he was about to strike her, but he just put his elbows on his knees and looked at her in amazement.

She shrugged and continued, "Your government hired women to fraternize with new officers. We were supposed to spend time with them and report on any peculiar behavior."

"A whore? You were a government-issue whore.

"I wasn't expected to be intimate, just a good companion and a good listener. I wasn't expected to go to bed with you or any of the men I entertained. Who knew you would turn out to be a toro salvaje? When you got me pregnant, I asked Gibbs what I should do. He told me if I wanted to marry you, it was okay with him, but he would no longer have need of my services. He offered to arrange for an abortion at an Army hospital. I told him you wouldn't marry me because you were crazy about some girl back in the states and you were engaged to marry her. He said that he had ways of taking care of girlfriends. You know Gibbs. He loved to screw with other people's lives."

"The letters—now it all makes sense," Sloan said. "Gibbs knew he could interrupt my communications with Abigale, and he did so by confiscating all our letters. He thought I already knew. . .that I had figured it out, about him and us."

"He assumed I told you," Regina said.

"So, it *is* Gibbs you are going to see?"

"Relax, Sloan. John's happily married . . . to the Army and his beautiful wife. He has no interest in me, then or now."

"But, you do admit having an affair with him?"

"We had our moments, long before you came into the picture, but not that night when you caught us. We were talking and laughing only. Believe me, when he saw you in the mess hall the next day, it scared the cacca out of him."

"Should've shot you both when I had the chance."

"And what of our daughter? With both of us gone, you in jail and me in the ground, who would have raised our little girl?"

"She *is* mine, isn't she?" Sloan had wanted to ask that question for years, but even now he was afraid of the answer.

"Of course, she's your daughter. Wendy is *our* love child. Just not from that first night as you always thought. That baby I lost right after we were married. I knew if you found out, you would never forgive me for screwing up your life with Abigale. When you came back from China, I made sure we got it right, if you know what I mean."

"Son of a bitch," Sloan said. "Jake was right all along. I should've let you drown that day you fell off the *Akubra*."

"Fell? I didn't fall you hijo de puta. You pushed me."

"You know I didn't —"

"You don't still believe I jumped or fell, do you? No, you pushed me, sure as I'm sitting here. My lawyers had a field day with that little incident and it cost you plenty, huh, dearest?" She rolled up on one elbow and smiled wickedly.

"Regina, for once tell me the truth."

"Who knows for sure what truth is?" She sighed. "For me being with anyone else will be a compromise. I will go to Spain and spend time with this man, not out of love, but need. Who wants to be alone? Life is meant to be lived as a couple."

"Si," he said. His curiosity would not let the matter drop. "Who is this man if it's not Gibbs?"

"God, Sloan, sometimes I wonder about you. Don't you remember the Captain? He introduced us that night in Madrid. He was best man at our wedding."

"Jameson? You have something going with my old sailing buddy, Jameson?"

"He never touched me, honest Sloan. He heard on the grapevine that we were split. Only then did he contact me. He retired a few years back and bought a little vineyard north of Madrid. He thinks we can go there and make wine together. He doesn't know jack about farming and wants me to teach him."

Silence fell over the pair.

"My darling, Sloan," she finally said. "I have loved you from the first time we met. Until that night at my apartment, I had not been with a man, not the way we were. You were a raging bull in the sack. As a kid, I had been in the vineyard with my boyfriends, but you were my first real love, my first real lover. I would have risked everything to be with you. So, remember this Sloan darling. If you're ever alone and want to start over, call me and I'll come running . . . that is, unless I've found someone else who loves me and treats me good, in which case, you're screwed." Regina rose and sauntered into the house without looking back.

The band finished their last set and packed their gear. The few remaining guests expressed their best wishes and headed for the freeway. The hangers-on, mostly Brad's fraternity brothers, huddled in front of the bar.

Sloan took Abigale by the hand and together they walked down the back lawn to look at the ocean.

They stood together, arm in arm, looking out over the vast Pacific.

"Any hope of finding the *Akubra*?"

"No, I watched her sink out of sight on her way to the bottom of the trench."

"Will you get another boat?"

"I don't know. Maybe I'll get an airplane."

"Sure, just what a man your age needs. Were you thinking a Learjet or perhaps a vintage P-51?"

"Both good ideas," he said. "You lose your necklace? The ruby sea glass. . . noticed you weren't wearing it."

"No, not lost . . . gave it away." She smiled expectantly.

"Gave it—but Abby, I gave you that necklace. You've had it for over twenty years."

"I decided it had guided me this far. Through its magic, it brought you back to me. It'll guide them on *their* journey . . . their life together."

"You mean?"

"She was wearing it during the ceremony—something old, something new—that piece of glass is older than America. At long last, we're a family—of sorts. Not in the way I wanted or expected but I find it hard to believe it has been that many years since we met at that sorority mixer."

"You know, Abigale, now that we have our kids' wedding behind us and they're off to start out on their own, we can think about us, you and me. What say we do something along those lines?"

"Lines. . .what lines?"

"You know. Maybe it's time we joined *our* souls in holy matrimony."

She seemed to turn the idea over in her mind. "In the past week, while you were bobbing around in the ocean with Jake, I've had time to think about my life and *our* future. It came easy when there was a chance we might not have a future. I've had six days of not knowing if you were dead or alive, and I must tell you, the odds were not in your favor. I have to be truthful. I'm not ready to make a commitment to you or anyone—not just now."

"I know it was tough on you. The kid's wedding, losing Jake and having me bob around in the ocean for a week. Must've been surreal, and needless to say, it took its toll on me too. You need some time to decompress, to get back on top of things. I get that. When you do, you'll be ready to tackle life again."

"Let's not sugarcoat this Sloan. Having you lost at sea was a freaking nightmare for all of us and that includes Regina. The first day or two, we were full of hope. By the fourth day, we began to accept the inevitable. We talked of postponing the wedding, but Wendy knew it was not what you would have wanted and it would mean we had given you up for dead. It was only because of her faith in you that we kept moving forward. Just an hour before the Coast Guard called, she said to me that she knew you would make it. Where she got her faith, I'll never know. I had long since given you up."

Sloan spoke in a whisper, "It's been great watching those two youngsters charge off into the unknown. It made me wonder what our lives would've been had we made it to the altar all those years ago." He turned her toward him. "I'm ready to take the plunge when you say the word."

"Sloan, Honey, you must understand. I had a good life with Brad. We were happy. Had it not been for some mysterious little blood clot that took him from me, we would still be together and no amount of persuasion from you would have ever changed that."

"I always figured you were rebounding."

"So did my parents, and so did I, for that matter. Then I realized how much I cared for him. It made me wonder if it was him I was destined to be with, assuming there's anything to that one true love crap . . . you seem to think so."

"I've always wanted to be with you," Sloan said, "ever since that first night. Now you're telling me that you aren't sure . . . makes me feel like a country dog in the city. . . Daddy used to say."

"Too much has happened." Abigale stared out over the horizon. "I need time to think, to make sense of it all. Brad Junior is thinking about law school and I want to help him get into Harvard. We are in a great place, you and me. This is no time to be making mistakes and screwing it up. Could be I'm being selfish, but I want to be sure all my needs are met. Call me selfish, but I want to be my own person, not absorbed into someone else's life. You've achieved self-actualization. I still need a paycheck to keep me going, and I need to feel I'm worth something. . . making a contribution. You spent a week on the Pacific to say farewell to Jake. You proved that you don't need me or anyone. You have always said it was about wealth and anonymity and you achieved both. You no longer need me, Regina, Wendy or anyone, for that matter."

Abigale pecked Sloan on the lips, downed her last sip of champagne and turned to walk back in the direction of the house. She sauntered up the street and disappeared into the shadows. He raised his glass to the setting sun and pondered all that had transpired.

If I find another ruby sea glass I'll never let her get away.

About the Author

R. Juan Harris spent three years in the army and thirty-seven years in software industry performing roles ranging from computer programmer to company president. Now he resides in a quaint fishing village in northwest Florida where he whiles away his days crafting stories.

Acknowledgments

Short of reading like an acceptance speech for an Academy Award, I want to thank everyone who has touched this body of work on my behalf: The Red Shirt Writers critique group that included Richard Perreault, Andrea Lewinter and Debbie Stephens; the Bay Scribblers critique group that included Dawn Radford, Debbie Hooper, Pat Bates, Sue Cronkite, Cass Allen and Nancy Petrucka.

Thank you, Pat Horn, Randy Mims and Jane Mathis. Your review of the final draft helped in your own special ways. Thank you!

Now to Adrian Fogelin, a published author, coach and teacher in her own right, edited The Ruby Sea Glass no less than four times. Without her influence this body of work would never have converged. Thank you Adrian!

My good friend John Baldwin read and critiqued an earlier draft and Gina Edwards contributed as a line editor. Thank you both.

And finally, without the encouragement and council of my darling Jane Callaham Harris, you the reading public might never have experienced the trials and tribulations of Sloan and Abigale. Thank you, Jane!

36738519R00231

Made in the USA
Charleston, SC
12 December 2014